PROCREATIVE IMPERATIVE

Despite his advancing age, Damnasus showed no signs of slowing down, neither during the day nor during the night. A worldly man for a bishop, he threw parties that delighted otherwise human satyrs and sybarites. Being a tremendous taleteller Jordan Q Tethys easily wangled invitations to a few of them.

The bishop's interests were so wide ranging he neglected some of the littler things, like paying attention to individual humanity, his more sheepish flock as well as his considerable collection of concubines. He being such a busy bee bishop, the night Damnasus led the rabble that seized the cave-temple on Vatican Hill dedicated to Mitravaruna, Tethys seized on his absence to do some seizing of his own.

Of course, no matter how willing she was, should he be caught bagging the bishop's best babe he might not be given the opportunity to seize anyone else ever again. Still, that was the truth of the matter. And, being a professional storyteller, he always told the truth, at least as far as he knew it.

Beer-sodden as he was tonight, Xmas Eve as Xuthrodites had it, he also hoped theirs was a mutually pleasurable experience. It wasn't, well, his procreative imperative was such that, come morning, he was confident their next go-round would be.

Chance frowned but Fortune favoured. He was in the privy when Papa Damn returned to his hideaway. Even more fortuitously he was as quick with the quill as he'd just been in the sack. Someday, he didn't doubt, he'd find out if Damnasus had a son or a daughter named *'Gardenias'*. Or whatever Jordan's equivalent was in Latin.

Tethys spoke the commonly understood tongue of Sedon Speak; pre-Babel Babble, as he often put it. The *'Q'* stood for *'Quill'*.

FEELING THEOCIDAL

A *PHANTACEA* Mythos Print Publication

James H McPherson, Publisher

74689 Kitsilano RPO

2768 West Broadway

Vancouver BC V6K 4P4

Canada

www.phantacea.com

Cover illustration, interior design and typography by Verne Andru

Library and Archives Canada Cataloguing in Publication

McPherson, Jim, 1951-
      Feeling theocidal: thrygragon - 4376 year of the dome / Jim
McPherson.

Bk. 1 in the Thrice cursed godly glories trilogy.
ISBN 978-0-9781342-0 (book 1)

      I. Title.
PS8625.P535F44 2008   C813'.6   C2008-904183-6

Additional print publications featuring

Jim McPherson's

PHANTACEA Mythos

including:

- *PHANTACEA* One to Six
  (various artists)

- Forever & 40 Days – The Genesis of *PHANTACEA*
  (artwork by Ian Fry)

are available for ordering through:

www.phantacea.com

Order today by:

- money order

- certified cheque

FEELING THEOCIDAL
– Thrygragon - 4376 Year of the Dome –

Jim McPherson

A *PHANTACEA* Mythos Print Publication published by James H McPherson

ISBN 978-0-9781342-0-4

First Published 2008

PRE-THEO:

THE CRUCIFIXION OF TERRIBLE TETHYS
****

"Arise, Gorgon 'Q for Quisling' Tethys," intoned the Mithrant praetor.
========

When the chained, and badly beaten, deposed governor had done so, the adjudicator began reading off his personally prepared script. "You freely admit to committing crimes of mass murder, including parricide, uxoricide, filicide and effective fratricide; this last with respect to your underlings within the Mithrant Brotherhood, who were attempting to take you into lawful custody.

"You also admit to secreting about yourself, undeclared, a number of Utopian eyeorbs, what they sometimes refer to as prison pods. Compounding your crimes in this regard, you used one of them to capture and hold onto the Master Deva intending to invest you into the sixth rung of our brotherhood's seven steps to exaltation, that of the Heliodromus."

He paused to allow the crowd's murmurings of mostly outrage die down. "Your name shall assuredly survive within the annals of infamy for you are guilty on all counts, Gorgon *'Q for Quisling'* Tethys," he pronounced once they'd done so. "Your punishment remains the only issue left to determine." To this the resultant murmurings were largely of concordance.

Even so, as if in misplaced sympathy, they quickly muted. Everyone in attendance at the town hall-cum-courtroom that late autumn day in the Year of the Dome 4376 knew no one could attain the brotherhood's final rung, that of the Father, Pater or Pope, until he turned 60 at the minimum. Yet the accomplished, but by his own actions disgraced, once exceedingly popular champion of Mithrant military might had qualified for ascent to the level of Heliodromus, or sun-runner, at the almost unheard age of 45.

That he aspired to become the Mithrants' Taurus, the military brotherhood's overall commander, was just as well known. That the Mithrants already had a *'boss bull'*, that he, Taurus Chrysaor Attis, was a deviant who kept coming back to life, and that he'd been doing so for almost as long as their third generational devil-gods had achieved individual solidity, was now believed by most to have contributed to Tethys's tragic meltdown.

With such soaring ambitions, many further speculated he'd lost his mind because he couldn't envisage waiting another 15 years before he got his shot at advertised apotheosis. Others, though, among them the presiding praetor and the devil possessing him, didn't believe he had lost it at all. They figured that, having concealed his irrational – make that maniacal – monotheistic fervour so successfully for so long, he'd just got caught out 15 years early.

To back up their suspicions they noted that only Thrygragos Varuna Mithras could confer the papacy. As importantly, Mithras invariably made a point of bestowing the Mithrants' highest accolade in person. He'd done so for approaching 4400 years – at least he had done so in here for approaching 4400 years – and wasn't about to change that any time soon. In other words Tethys's ultimate target had to have been the Great God of Justice, Light and Truth himself.

The praetor, and the devil within him, doubted a single Utopian eyeorb could have the capacity to imprison a Great God for any length of time. Since Mithras inspired approximately infinitely more adoration than the lowly devil ever would, they further doubted even the dozen eyeorbs Tethys had about him when he was apprehended could combine to do the trick.

Nonetheless, the brotherhood and, indeed, the entire Upper Head were undeniably deeply in debt to the child who first spotted an eyeorb in her father's kitbag and reported its existence to her just as courageous mother. Had they not acted as they'd done, no one could predict how many of their Mithradite devil-gods the governor – once ensconced as a Heliodromus, possibly on Apple Isle, at the very heart of the brotherhood's hierarchy – might have lured into his presence and subsequently entrapped before anyone realized what he was doing.

Their noble deeds cost them their lives but begrudge them not their eternal rewards. Their soul selves were undoubtedly already up north in the Elysian Fields, basking in the radiance of proximity to the Moloch Sedon – Grand Elysium being where the All-Father of Devazurkind held court when he, arguably the Devil Himself, deigned spend any time whatsoever on his Headworld instead of just encompassing it.

Their bodies, along with the minds or consciousness that went with them, would be rejoining their souls directly.

========

"Neither monotheism nor madness are punishable in our ages old system of impartiality," the praetor carried on, at last without any interruption. "But even a solitary murder, let alone more than a dozen of them, is abhorrent to any right-thinking person. Your actions require unambiguous condemnation and commensurate punishment.

"That said, I find simple shunning an unsuitable sentence. Similarly, banishment and other commonplace penalties such as either temporary or permanent confinement at the brotherhood's expense, conscription, demotion and/or forced reenlistment as a frontline skirmisher strike me as ludicrous. After all, short of Taurus, you'd already achieved the highest rank you possibly could within our public services.

"I need hardly remind anyone here that the Great God of Truth, Justice and Light, he and every one of his multitudes of progeny proscribe both enslavement and capital punishment. So too do his brother Great Gods: Thrygragos Lazareme, the Lackland Libertine, he of the occipital and easternmost Head, and Bodiless Byron, the Unmoving One, he of Greater Godbad; they and theirs. Decreeing an immediate, no matter how justifiable, cessation of your life is therefore beyond the jurisdiction of this proceeding.

"I could command you work toward compensation but you are also, by almost any standard, the aggrieved party. Besides, on my instructions, the brotherhood has already confiscated your property and redistributed it amongst your wife's family, the Korant Sisterhood, of which she ranked at their fifth rung, and the brotherhood itself.

"To be frank, as rich as you were, in terms of the measurements we regularly use in order to assess restitution after such mercifully infrequent incidents, you have already overpaid by a considerable margin." Again he paused, but only to catch his breath. Those in the crowded courtroom waited both patiently and silently. They sensed something extraordinary lurking on the threshold of the praetor's verbiage.

"Although enquiries have been made, through trusted intermediaries, exile to one of the dwindling number of Utopian Weirdoms does not seem an option. Your crimes are so horrendous even your presumed patron, the notoriously monotheistic, as well as anti-devic, Master Helena Somata, she of the relatively nearby Weirdom of Kanin City, refuses to grant you sanctuary.

"Furthermore, despite what you may believe – and from the looks of you, may wrongly suspect I ordered – no matter how unconscionable your deeds were I am not one for castrating, crippling and/or blinding, then releasing someone onto the streets bowl in hand. In my view that would be a kindness you don't deserve.

"Upon due deliberation, I find myself left with no other choice in this matter."

========

For all intents and purposes said matter began and ended on Midsummer Day 4376 Year of the Dome. The devil attending that glorious noon's investiture – glorious in terms of the weather; inglorious in nearly every other respect – had a name. Rather, he had a name given to him by bygone Illuminaries of Weir close to a thousand years earlier, shortly after they began returning from the Outer Earth en masse.

That name was Djinn Domitian – Djinn because he was a jinni or sky magician; Domitian because he enjoyed being dominated, hence why his fellow, third generational devils were calling him the Masochist long prior to he and they starting to become solid individuals circa 2000 YD.

Human, humanoid or otherwise sentient heliodromuses were also considered sky magicians. Except, in their case that was because they could summon devil-gods such as Domitian. Moreover, provided the devil chose to respond, heliodromuses were entitled to speak to him or her without fear of condescension or disparagement.

By contrast, Domitian not only could fly – every devil could fly if they wanted to – he could fly beyond the sky. He could fly into Cathonia, the zone or dome of devic, more specifically Sedonic, energy that had been separating the Inner from the Outer Earth since the Great Flood or Genesea of the Dome's consequential Year Zero.

Although not a particularly highborn Mithradite, Domitian was his father's favourite as well as most reliable messenger or angel. Quite correctly, therefore, everyone who knew anything about him considered him Mithras's Heliodromus. Correspondingly Domitian took it upon himself to first vet, then to invest Mithrant heliodromuses in the same way the Great God his father personally did potential Mithrant popes.

When it came to Mithras, Domitian was loyal as a dog. Slurp-sloppily for him, he also proved dumber than most dogs. Ordinarily he would have possessed, then thoroughly gleaned or mind-reamed, any potential candidates for such an illustrious position. As subsequent events made clear, he'd skipped the vetting bit. Perhaps, knowing the truth of Tethys's half-parentage, he reckoned proper procedure redundant.

This particular Tethys – there were hundreds, probably more like thousands of families in Marutia, Sedon's Cheek Lands, who had Tethys for a surname – was a Sedson. Although he'd often heard Mithras rage on about Sed-sons who'd gone bad beyond the Dome, in the now more than 4300 years of their existence Domitian had never heard of one beneath it who'd done so.

Also in his defence, other than those who didn't worship anyone, virtually no one within the bounds of Cathonia worshipped aught but Domitian, his fellow maybe 300 remaining Master Devas or devil-gods, their three, second generational fathers and their lone grandfather, the Moloch Sedon.

The major exceptions to that statement were their multiple millennia-old, pre-Earth pursuers and seemingly inexhaustible tormentors: the Hate-Sedon Utopians of Weir and their Trinondev Warriors Elite. Invariably mortal, but long-lived – barring injuries or illnesses, even the mixed bloods or hybrids lived healthily deep into their second or third centuries – they were of course, like fallen angel devils, extraterrestrial in origin.

To this day, if perhaps not for very much longer, that made them technologically far, far, advanced compared to any of the planet's indigenous populations. However, they generally stuck to their own Weirdoms, which meant they didn't play much of a role in Headworld affairs.

Besides, the majority of the purebloods living up north in the primary and still foremost Weirdom – that of Cabalarkon, Sedon's Devic Eye-Land – were inbred imbeciles too self-centred to be religious. If it weren't for their automatons and indentured underclass there'd likely be no such thing as purebloods or a Warrior Elite anymore.

In further fairness to Domitian, the devil possessing the praetor, one of the strangest, pudding-proof-unworldly traits Utopians had was that their males were black-as-midnight in a starless sky, whereas their invariably statuesque females were white-as-daylight on a salt flat. The only trace of blackness the Tethys bastard had about him was, as events evinced, confined to his heart.

Tally this up with all the other particulars they knew about *'Quiz'*, the devil within him justified to his shell, the adjudicator without him. He was a Sed-son; he was a respected Persian or earth magician who'd been judged suitable for advancement; he was a heavily decorated Leo before that; and he was a Mithrant general who'd served with distinction in countless battles and outright wars throughout the Upper Head.

No, all things considered Domitian could be forgiven for never even suspecting Gorgon Q Tethys was a closet Trinondev as well as fanatical monotheist.

========

On the Outer Earth, where enactments celebrating a variety of Mithraic and near-Mithraic mysteries had been practised for almost as long as they had been in here, most formal investitures were conducted indoors or else in caves or covered grottos. That wasn't necessarily the case beneath the Cathonic Dome. Indeed, initiations for Persian or earth magician candidates, most of who were destined for a provincial governorship or its equivalent, were the only ones that absolutely had to be conducted underground.

Likewise, if oppositely, only those rites involving potential heliodromuses had to take place in the open air. Of course there were many who regarded the entire Hidden Continent of Sedon's Head as being sort of underground anyhow – or undersea, as would more likely be the case if ever the Dome collapsed.

After all, it did constitute an effective, if slightly porous, dimensional barrier between the two sides of the Whole Earth. Nonetheless, unless you chanced upon a functional Tholos Ghost House, or something similar, and tried to get beyond it, for the vast majority of the sentient beings that dwelt on, in, under or over the Hidden Headworld, open air here was identical to open air there.

Although mountaintops were preferable, mountaintops, even hilltops of any decent height, were in short supply within the vast, formerly mostly undersea plains of Marutia, Sedon's Cheek. As the joke went, the mighty Moloch above us all had a mighty smooth complexion. In the absence of a mountaintop, let alone a respectable hill, the ceremony took place atop a manmade mound overlooking the parade ground within the main Mithrant encampment outside the provincial capital.

As the still reigning governor, Gorgon Tethys and his retinue, including his wife of nearly 30 years, his parents and her Korant of a mother, his three sons, four daughters and their attendants, were the last, but one, to arrive for the Midsummer Day's pomposity. All were resplendent in their gold, emerald and crimson attire. All eagerly abided in assured anticipation of Gorgon's elevation to sky magician.

A prestigious promotion was certain to follow. In all likelihood it would initially be an appointment to engineering overseer of canal and roadwork in multiple provinces. After that, perhaps within a few short years, he'd be made consul to the Taurus or beyond him, chief representative of a highborn Mithradite Master Deva. Whatever lay ahead it would soon be bye-bye backwater governorship, hello Ap Isle.

High above them came the sound of a fanfare trumpet, whereupon the one missing ingredient appeared, as if out nowhere, strutting on the air itself. The tawny furred, lion-headed, four-winged devil was tooting on his own horn, his Tvasitar talisman or Brainrock power focus; part of what made him, and kept him, a solid individual.

Djinn Domitian wasn't alone. All those with him were doing a ditto. Except they, not being devils, had to flap their wings in order to fly as they blew. They were, to a one, yazata Angelycs, Domitian's cannibalistic, yet nevertheless devoted adherents.

Like so many of the Head's diverse dozens of mostly sentient life-forms, Angelycs were products of Old Eden's long pre-Genesea, pre-Sedonshem landing, and even pre-Golden Age of Humanity experimentations into the so-called God-country of creative science. The majority of them dwelt far to the north of Marutia in the Mystic Mountains, Sedon's Crown. Yet, because their unstinting devotion increased his already considerable devic prowess, Domitian rarely went anywhere without a few nearby.

He alit. They stayed aloft. Tethys's youngest, a pretty, blonde haired 6-year old sporting pigtails to go along with her newest and sassiest outfit, tugged on her mother's dress. "Now, mommy?" she asked.

"Let me do it, darling," responded her mother. She accusingly eyeballed her husband and childhood sweetheart before that. "What game are you playing at, Quiz?" she demanded as she rummaged about in her handbag.

Gorgon earned the name Quisling because, from almost the moment he learned to speak, he was forever quizzing his elders. Over 40 years later that hadn't changed overly much. Evidently he had no idea what she was on about. On this, the biggest day of his life since he became a Persian five years earlier, he was in the process of rebounding at her the same question when she produced an odd-looking object.

Domitian gawked, horrified, recognizing what it was instantly. Tethys did ditto, gawped, apprehending that, whatever it was he'd been playing at, this game of his was suddenly over. The eyeorb cracked open; a solitary eyeball extruded out of it on prehensile tendrils. It focused on the devil.

Not every devil had a third eye in the middle of his forehead. Still, other than the occasional Cyclops, multi-eyed peacock or the Byronic, APM All-Eyes, most did. Domitian's third eye bulged. Then it tore out of his skull and slurped into the eyeorb. His spirit being self came next; his subtle matter, daemonic body immediately thereafter.

Quick to react, Tethys grabbed the devil's power focus before it followed suit. So shocked was she by everything transpiring, his wife dropped the eyeorb, filled-up eyeball already retracting.

"Godless heathen," Tethys shouted at not just her. Swooping low, he snagged the now shut eyeorb as if on first bounce, whereupon he tore the bag out of his wife's grip, dumped the prison pod into it and flattened her with an elbow to the jaw.

"Godless devil-worshippers," he began screaming over and over again as he set to amassed murdering.

========

Anyone with a modicum of sentience, let alone intelligence, could wield a devil's Tvasitar talisman. That's what made them so valuable. Power foci were also mutable. As if he'd practised it for years, Tethys willed Domitian's into a shaft-like approximation of a Trinondev's tapered eye-stave.

With more of a yank than a thought, he pulled out a second eyeorb and rammed it atop the transformed trumpet's thicker end. It didn't open – eyeorbs only opened when they were taking in devils or their azura offspring – but what it did do was far more visually interesting as well as, in its own way, effective.

Like the latter day Roman legionnaires currently dominating traditional territories of Thrygragos Varuna Mithras on the Outer Earth, the Mithrant Brotherhood had long used a golden eagle as one of its primary totems. Having spent all except the first five years of his life subject to brotherhood discipline, that he chose to manifest a thunderbird as his wholly self-encasing gargoyle might have been expected.

In retrospect, that he could take off and fly like one might have been as well. Trinondevs, the elite warriors of Weir, could, so why couldn't he? However, probably no one could have anticipated the scythe-like blade he similarly manifested out of its oversized, ovular tip. His Korant in-law was his first victim – she'd made the mistake of trying to help her daughter stand up again – but more than a dozen others fell just as swiftly.

Screeching imprecations he scythed down anyone who came too close to him. As soon as there was naught on the mound save he – a blood-splattered, anthropomorphic bird of prey, standing overtop of occasionally still-twitching corpses of his family and those of his invited guests who hadn't fled – arrows loosed from onrushing legionnaire archers rendered him akin to a pincushion in serious need of plucking.

Although arrows couldn't pierce all the way through his thunderbird exoskeleton, that must have been when he finally regained a scrap of sanity and took off, Domitian's faithful, but dumb as they come, Angelycs in pursuit. As for why he cut off his wife and youngest daughter's heads – and attempted, too hurriedly to be successful, to do a dot-ditto to all his victims – there was a perfectly logical explanation.

"He must have thought we were devil-possessed," concluded his wife.

Reclamation specialists brought in from the far north had skilfully reattached her head to her neck such that she could testify at the inquiry and subsequent trial, which convened shortly after the autumnal equinox. She was hardly the only one that Valhallan seamstresses, skin weavers and bone technicians pieced back together for the same or similar purposes.

Within a few days of the mound massacre, the bodies of those proven salvageable were occupied by devazurs: devils in the case of his wife and their youngest daughter; Sangazur spirit beings in the case of the rest of his family and friends. A few of the fallen legionnaires and most of Domitian's Angelycs, who didn't so much fall as were dropped as they tried to prevent his getaway, benefited from identical restoration.

With their bodies came their minds, if not their spirits per se, and with their minds came memories of their lives. They couldn't have testified, let alone testified truthfully, otherwise. Devils and their azura offspring could make anyone except pureblood Utopians, whom they couldn't possess, talk true. They also couldn't lie any more than they could disobey their fathers or senior-born siblings. And, thanks to them, neither could those they possessed, not even ambulant carcasses.

"Silly daddy," agreed his reanimated youngest, head in hands. "Unless it was dilly-saddy, tra-la tra tee-hee," she added with a typical giggle. "We weren't even there in the square."

The girl's head was in her hands due to the fact the devil child – unless she was a demon child – who occupied her wasn't as accomplished when it came to possession as her adult-sized brood sister, unless she was her devic mother. The former had named herself Tralalorn after the ridiculous, fay-saying rhymes she was always inventing, whilst truly ancient Illuminaries had named the latter Pyrame Silverstar.

Pyrame's possessive technique was irreproachable, but Trala just couldn't get it right. In seeking to reanimate the dead girl she'd unintentionally whooshed the cadaver's newly sewn-on head off her neck like a cork. Pyrame was there so she picked it up and handed it back to her. However, proclaiming herself much better at ventriloquism, an evidently embarrassed Tralalorn wouldn't countenance any attempt to reattach it.

The praetor presiding at both the inquiry and trial demurred. He couldn't stand Trala's actual head – scarlet skin, two-toned pink and red hair, cute but pointy little horns and nastily sharp-looking fangs – sticking out of the corpse's neck while, at the same time, the Tethys girl's deadhead, lips moving, appeared to speak.

He found it so distracting that, after she had a tantrum and refused his request to let a different devil or a symbiotic Sangazur take her place, he ruled she couldn't give any more evidence on behalf of the Tethyses' dead daughter. There wasn't much point anyhow. When it came to Tethys, his motivation was no more an issue than his guilt.

How to get rid of him was the question.

========

He, a thunderbird gargoyle, fled the encampment with one full prison pod and eleven empty ones in his wife's satchel. The pursuing Angelycs were his only immediate problem, but what could manufacture a killing blade could also project them. Feathers flew much more so than the Angelycs did. In short order he was alone in the sky.

He had no real escape plan, though; certainly no safe place he could get to today. He'd count himself charmed if he got much beyond the encampment. Eyeorbs leached off thought waves. That meant they worked best in crowded areas and cities, packed military bases being ideal.

Needs be he'd have to come to ground soon. He realized that. What he really needed, though, was a psychopomp. A legendary, mono-horned, talarial-winged, raven-headed riding deer would be ideal. A non-daemonic griffon, a Valkyrie's swan, a Pegasus like Attis rode, or some suchlike mount capable of traversing the Weird, the dark grey, universal substance of between-space, would do just as fine.

Mono-horned ravendeer were extinct and none of the other psychos he knew about grew on trees; at least they didn't grow on any tree he knew hereabouts, so there wasn't much hope of finding one. That meant he'd have to steal a horse or a donkey and use whatever high-tech magic – as far as he'd ever seen or heard there was no such a thing as non-tech magic – was left in the eyeorbs in order to cloak his looks in the equivalent of a faerie glamour, a witch-seeming, a second skin or a serpent splendour.

Kanin City was a long way north. It'd take at least a week to get there from here on horseback, but at least he'd shucked the Angelycs. Then he had it. Devils didn't just will themselves from place to place through the Weird. They employed their power foci to cut themselves through it to wherever they desired beneath the Dome. And what did he have in hand, currently masquerading as a Utopian eye-stave?

A devic power foci of course! If only he could get it to work properly. He wouldn't want to cut himself into one of the cyclopean city's megalithic walls, would he? That would be an entirely different kind of stone than the ongoing one he was currently experiencing. It'd definitely be more crush than rush.

It was a tremendous idea, one worthy of a sun-runner. It was also very nearly the last one he had as a free man.

========

By Sedonic decree Master Devas were not allowed to kill. If they did, so went the Devil's rationale, they might deprive themselves or their fellow devils of the invigorating adulation they needed to survive, as other than spirit beings, and deserved, for all the good works they did on behalf of their devotees. They did, they'd also deprive the Moloch Sedon of his procedurally generous, funnelled-up share of it. Which would never do.

That was why the silver, star-shaped object did not kill him the same as a ninja's throwing star would have, had it been thrown by even a neophyte Samarandin assassin from Sedon's Tongue. It did not slice him in twain like a meteoric silver star falling from the sky would have, were such a thing possible, which it might be, theoretically anyhow.

What passed through him, what brought him to ground, was no ordinary, silvery star shape. It was also different than any ordinary devil. He almost instantly regained his feet, though not his thunderbird over-coating, which required too much mental effort to maintain given who was solidifying before him. That he was a Sed-son, and therefore by definition a deviant, had nothing to do with his rapid recovery. He was just in great condition for a 30-year-old, let alone someone in his mid forties.

The devil finished materializing. Wearing, or at least appearing to wear, a silver shawl and a similarly satiny, ankle-length sheathe dress, she was bodily beautiful. That she intentionally left her breasts uncovered had nothing to do with a desire to show them off. She co-ruled the devic third of Crete during the devic goddesses' 500-year Middle Sea matriarchate on the Outer Earth and that was how Etocretan women of the time disported themselves.

There was nothing human or even devilish about her cranially, however. Skull-wise she'd describe herself as triangularly pyramidal. In terms more precise, her head was akin to a rock-hewn tetrahedron. Out of each side of its three stony top-slabs a solitary eye glared. And that was it – just a single, glowering eyeball: no hair, no ears, no eyebrows, no noses and no mouths.

She nonetheless spoke and he nonetheless heard her. "You've blown it big time this time, big boy."

"Been a while, mom."

"Half-mom, Gorgon. You just mutilated your other half-mom."

"She was a devil worshipper. Fact of the matter is she worshipped you."

"I don't have worshippers. Your half-father Sedon is all I need now and have needed ever. We are the Perpetual Presences."

"And as a Sed-son I help maintain the Cathonic Zone. You've told me that many times before. Didn't realize you were at the investiture."

"I wasn't, almost but not quite yet. We were delayed. Tralalorn was pouting as per usual. She wanted to ride her chimera here, but Stynx's got indigestion. Chimeras with indigestion are unwelcome interlopers at celebratory gatherings, especially gatherings amongst highly flammable mortals.

"Not only that, Stynx has three heads and the necks to go with them, which can be a slightly off-putting sight when you're not from Apple Isle. By the time we got there you were trying to escape. When did you become a monotheist?"

"Tell you what, I'll answer you if you first answer me why my prison pods aren't sucking you in even as you're non-mouthing-off not five yards away from me. The one my late wife pulled out of her bag got Domitian next thing to automatically. And don't tell me they're duds. They can't all be duds."

"Around me they can. I made them, didn't I. Made the first ones, truth told, many multiple multi-millennia ago on New Weirworld. Rather, truth told better, the Female Entity made the first ones, the templates for the rest of them. But I humanize her when she's around. She likes being human; likes fucking her Herr Hel Helios. And not just him either, I can attest. She wouldn't make anything that could harm me, would she?"

"You'll have to kill me first, half-mom, because I'm not going back voluntarily. And devils don't kill or I'd be dead already."

"Monotheists, we'd kill. No use to us, are they – aren't you? You, though, I won't kill, not right away anyhow. Come to mommy, youngster."

What she could and did do was possess him. Plus, even though the devic smithy, their Prometheus, never made her one, she was really very good when it came to using other devils' Tvasitar talismans.

========

Happily for Djinn Domitian, the devil's few surviving Angelyc-followers still in the area managed to release him. They did so within moments of Pyrame Silverstar capturing Gorgon Tethys – and their return to the murder mound, as one – by getting their hands on the prison pod containing him, then exercising faith-fomented willpower on it. Pyrame also gave Domitian back his power focus. As a deserved tribute to her overall wonderfulness, her non-Sedonic lover Chrysaor Attis had gifted her with plenty of others over the more than 2500 years of their relationship.

That night, as a thank you, the Masochist played a raunchy dance number taught to him by Helios called Sophos the Wise more than that same more than 2500 years earlier. He did so, to the usual very loud and genuinely enthusiastic approbation, by tooting his fanfare trumpet out of his back end.

Talented fellow, for a devil, that Djinn Domitian!

========

Also happily, for not just the mortal chimera, Trala's Stynx had only barfed, not burped, in excitement moments after Domitian concluded his exhibition of nethermost chops. Unhappily for one immortal in particular she'd barfed, three heads concurrently, all over the devil child and her pretty, tailor-made, green, gold and crimson party dress. Thus provoked Trala promptly burst, ear-splittingly loudly, into such a temper Pyrame had to repeatedly threaten to take her home to Apple Isle before she shut up.

After multiple millennia of life, most of the last five – along with Pyrame uniquely for Master Devas – as a solid individual, shouldn't she have grown up? Not if she didn't have to, which she didn't, that answered that. Even if it wasn't necessarily by name, brats everywhere worshipped her and Tralalorn hated to disappoint her fans.

Ostentatiously her crocodile tears were, howsoever briefly, protozoan crocodiles creeping down her cheeks until she swallowed them anew.

========

"Since releasing you as you are is out of the question; since death remains solely the preserve of the individual, with respect to the individual alone, and that of the mighty Eye-Mouth above us all, what ordeal would you have me decree? Should I deem it sufficiently challenging, such that only an act of Sedon could cause you to survive, I shall grant it.

"Speak, Gorgon *'Q for Quisling'* Tethys!"

"Let me die as he died."

The praetor and the devil within him congratulated each other internally. They'd anticipated precisely that request. Externally it was all either of them could do to suppress a solitarily smug smile. "Let you die as you believe he died, you mean."

"Have it your own way, praetor."

He did. They both did. Not that he was ever without it but the devil was glad he brought his horn. Tethys entering the afterlife was the perfect opportunity for him to practise a lament he'd also learned from the Male Entity millennia earlier.

Heliosophos called it taps for some reason.

========

The crowd parted to let them pass.
Devils they had to be. Devils they were; everyone agreed.

========

Virtually none of those on or within sight of the highest prominence here or in any neighbouring territory, what everyone already referred to as Murder Mound, had ever witnessed a crucifixion, or any other kind of execution, before. Many of them had seen the two devil-gods before, however. They, along with Domitian and some other, never identified and imperfectly remembered, devils had been frequenting the area ever since they first popped out of the Weird months ago now, on the summer solstice.

Even if you wanted to, which you probably didn't, it was hard to forget a 3-eyed, brazenly beautiful, devilish woman with starkly silver hair to match her shawl and sheathe dress. Wet dreams, for men and women alike, were made of her. It was far harder to forget her devic brood sister, unless the Hidden Headworld's third perpetual presence was Pyrame's demonic daughter by the Moloch Sedon, as many believed. She was the stuff of nightmares.

So over-the-top fearsome were they, the devil child and 3-headed Stynx, whom she was riding, had become instant legends in the staid townships and grain-growing farming communities of the lower- to mid-Cheek Lands. No longer occupying the dead Tethys girl, whose body as promised the Angelycs had transported uneaten to the Elysian Fields, Tralalorn had seemingly acquired a fancy new outfit just for the occasion.

A frilly pinkish or mauve smock underlay an embroidered, variously reddish tunic. With brownish stockings and riding boots to match, perhaps in deference to the cooler weather she offset it with a sleeveless, brocade jacket the colour of thick, rich wine. Although their clothing seemed more suitable to a ballroom than a Golgotha, whatever else you say about devils you had to admit they had style.

Humiliatingly naked, scourged raw as well as bashed about worse, the nevertheless ever-quizzical Gorgon 'Q for Quisling' Tethys looked down upon them from his perch on the cross. "Come to gloat?"

"Aren't you supposed to say something more desperate, like: 'Oh, mother, why hast thou forsaken me?'"

"Fuck you, Whore."

"My, my, such language," scolded Pyrame Silverstar. As Tethys must have known, many devils called her Sedon's Whore when she wasn't within earshot – not that devils needed ears to hear any more than they needed howsoever many or few eyes to see, noses to smell or mouths to speak.

"And in front of the little one too: Bad Gorgon, beastly Gorgon. But, to answer your question: Not me, I'm more the mourning sort."

"Not me either, wee-the-pee daddy. Met my pet yet? I call her Stynx on account of she stinks almost as much you do, boohoo. She's cleaner the wiener, though the hoe."

"I'd rather meet your maker, Lorna. Then I could kill him!"

"You wish," said Pyrame.

"Can't I devolve him, mommy?"

"Into what? He's already an ignoramus."

"Mean, mommy. He's too small to be a hippopotamus."

Tethys didn't so much choose that moment to give up his ghost as the ghost chose that moment to usurp his being. Pyrame could have predicted it. As far as devils were concerned, when dealing with monotheistic maniacs mockery is often the best medicine. Besides, the praetor didn't have three eyes; he wasn't carrying a fanfare trumpet; and where else would the Masochist be except inside a scourged then crucified man?

Tethys physically inflated; his head not so much ballooning as becoming akin to a billowing boulder. His lower legs and feet extended, easily reaching Murder Mound's ground, upon which the legionnaires had raised the wooden cross, him on it. Nails hammered through his now expanding wrists popped out. Backup cords tore free as his arms thickened, outstretching the crossbeam.

With a flex of his suddenly muscular shoulders he snapped the beam in two. "You want to be worshipped as a god," he bellowed for the benefit of those already quaking beneath him. "You act like a god, not a simpering toady of some celestial Blob!"

Pyrame and her maybe demon-daughter exchanged glances. Out of the nowhere that was the everywhere between-space Tralalorn produced her white dwarf meteorite: a head- or ball-shaped mass of feces-reeking, faeriedust-spitting, endlessly self-kneading material. Shape shifters were often called face dancers but her White Dwarf seemingly went from one contorted, doughy face to another as it roiled into and out of itself.

"You should have said fool, mommy," she chastised Pyrame.

"So you could say?"

"Toadstool, dummy."

The enormous ignoramus had three eyes now. Tawny fur was replacing flayed skin. A leonine head and four sets of wings, the smaller pair's tips pointing up, the larger pair downward, like a regular angel's, would soon follow, Pyrame felt sure. They did. So too did his fanfare trumpet. A deafening blast later yazata Angelycs fluttered up from the panicky congregation, most of who were nonetheless too cat-curious to flee.

"Don't you dare!" she shouted, realizing what the jinni was doing.

"Why not, priestess?" Djinn Domitian blared back, raising Tethys's corpse out of his bulk and up to the yazata Angelycs like the sacrifice they took the former to be. "Waste not, want not, that's my motto. Besides, he's dead already."

The Angelycs took hold of the proffered carcass's arms, head and legs, two or three per appendage. Dead or only nearly dead – devils may not kill but their adherents did, prolifically, more often than not in the names of their devil-gods – they proceeded to rip him apart as if a humanoid, New Year's Eve cracker or party treat.

"Gruesome gruel!" exclaimed Tralalorn, a confirmed vegetarian.

"Good thing you wore red, Trala," said Pyrame, as the now definitely late Gorgon Q Tethys's blood and guts rained overtop the two of them.

========

Between-space one devil, unless it was the Devil, never imperfectly remembered – due to the fact he was never remembered period, not unless he fully manifested himself, and was perfectly forgotten the moment he vanished – pocketed his Tvasitar talisman, a panpipe. He didn't smile in satisfaction of a movement well played.

The fiend never stopped smiling!

****

THEO 1:

THE WEIRDOM OF KANIN CITY
========

Helena Somata contemplated the night's sky.

She knew the names of most of the stars. The dimmer ones, those that filtered through Cathonia, the Cathonic Zone or Dome, she knew from her decades living beyond it, in Rome and swaths of both its eastern and western empire. The brighter ones didn't exist out there but, having been born and having lived most of her life in here, on the Hidden Continent of Sedon's Head, she often wondered if the Outer Earth's stars were the same as the Inner Earth's stars.

Were they cathonitized devils?

========

Two Masters, three High Illuminaries and 40 years earlier, Helena was living in an Anthean Shelter – an Anthill, as the joke went. As part of the process of attaining the level of an Ant Nightingale, the title bestowed on tiptop witches within the Antediluvian Sisterhood of Flowery Anthea, she was instructing Ant Astartes as they progressed through the second seven-year period of their training.

To qualify for Astarte-training you first had to have a daughter, one who was going through the first seven-year period of Ant-training even as you, her mother, went through your second. Having had Constance, Helena was past that. Having only had a solitary boy, whom she named Christian after her mother's thus far strictly Outer Earth faith, Constance had never qualified for her second seven-year period of training. As events transpired, she never would.

The Anthill was mostly between-space, within the Forever Forest of Wildwyck, in the southernmost area of the Head's Occipital Region, just north of the Gypsium Wall, Sedon's Hairband. Most of 2,000 miles eastward, Hamilcar Suryad ruled the Weirdom of Kanin City as its Master. Constance was married to Egbert Grudal, Kanin's then High Illuminary, Master Hamilcar's heir-apparent and, as shortly came to pass, successor.

Hesper Suryad, Hamilcar's wife, an Ant Nightingale borderline better skilled than her at the time, contacted Helena via witch-stone — their sisterhood called its witch-stones Anthean Agates — with news that Constance's Christian had recently just up and vanished. Apparently Constance was heartbroken at the loss. She wanted to see her mom. Could Helena come visit?

Sure she could. And did, via agates, which also functioned as stepping stones through the Weird: the dark-grey matter of between-space and of much more than that, of all there was, of Samsara, of mundaneness itself. She arrived to discover the Weirdom besieged by Mithrant legionnaires under the leadership of their Taurus, Chrysaor Attis.

Reputedly the Attis was an immortal deviant, the possessive half-son of a Master Deva, Kore-Eris, aka Strife or Discord — as well as Marut Kanin, after whom Marutia, Sedon's Cheek, was named — and her Great God father, Thrygragos Varuna Mithras himself. While there were many deviants, only the Attis was immortal. Rather, since he kept going away and coming back, younger and a whole lot stronger than he had been, only he seemed to be immortal.

Ant Nightingales and Illuminaries of Weir had a theory about that. They speculated the Attis was one man — the Universal Soldier — with a thus far endless number of successions dating back some 2300 years plus.

To be specific, his hypothetical first birth occurred within a century of Master Devas gaining individual solidity, something their subsequent azuras never could attain. In other words, an Attis was killed, usually in battle or by assassination; another Attis would appear soon thereafter to take his place. As Helena proved, it was no theory.

She walked out of the Weird onto one of Hesper's agates. She thereby found herself in the huge assembly hall within Kanin City's incessantly added-onto Masters Palace. Veils drawn, perhaps as many as 50 turbaned, indigo-robed, Trinondev Warriors of Weir surrounded the Master's throne.

The eyeorbs atop their eye-staves were open. Off them what amounted to Kanin's house guard manifested their individual or family gargoyles, which they could harden and project at will. That should make them an unstoppable force. Yet therein he sprawled, Hamilcar Suryad, dead, pierced through with dozens of hilt-less blades that were already dissipating between-space. And there stood his assassin, none other than her grandson, Christian born Grudal.

Like male Utopians everywhere he had black skin. Unlike the male Trinondevs there he dressed in the gold-trimmed, emerald and crimson uniform of a topflight officer in the Mithrant military. Given his youth he couldn't be an officer. Given he'd lived in Kanin City for most of his 20 odd years, he shouldn't belong to the Mithrant military anyhow. Mithrants venerated devils, Thrygragos Varuna Mithras foremost, whereas proper Utopians, even hybrids like Kanin's Utopians, existed to annihilate devils. Christian had been properly raised. His parents saw to that.

Helena was struck by more than just Christian's outfit. His cobalt-coloured cloak, spiked helm, sheathed sword, the javelin he held and, indeed, his entire being shone with the telltale glow of Brainrock-Gypsium. That indicated he possessed devic talismans, or power foci, aplenty. Even though he only had two eyes, it further suggested he was possessed. If so then the Trinondevs' prison pods weren't functioning the way they should.

Constance, his mother, her daughter, was in tears. She had wrapped herself around the legs of her husband Egbert. As the High Illuminary only the dead Master ranked higher amongst Weir's Trinondev Warriors Elite. Constance, Helena instantly perceived, was begging Egbert not to have his Trinondevs execute Christian.

For his part, Christian was laughing. "Good to see you again, granny," he chortled, spotting her stepping off Hesper's agate. "Will you please try to talk some sense into these imbecilic hardheads?"

========

That was then. This was now.

========

Like most Utopian women, Helena was white as daylight. Of course, it being less than a week before the Winter Solstice – which those who lived beneath the Dome had as occurring on the 25th of Tantalar – there wasn't much daylight these days. Accordingly, she was wearing a fur-fringed, hooded cloak made of bleached wool overtop a beige gown, with warm leggings and heavy boots underneath it.

Today was her 128th birthday. Arguably due to the ability of Utopians to use very nearly the fullness of their intellectual capacity, that was already approaching three times the life expectancy of the indigenous, genetically compatible humanoids in this day and age. It nonetheless wasn't much by the standards of her people.

Utopians arrived on the then Whole Earth roughly 700 years after their eternal enemies, the three generations of devakind. Purebloods aged slowly. They could lead healthy and productive lives that extended well into their third or fourth centuries. She wasn't a pureblood. There weren't any purebloods left in the Weirdom of Kanin City. The vast majority lived some 1500 miles farther to the north and west in the postdiluvian Weirdom of Cabalarkon, Sedon's Devic Eye-Land.

There hadn't been any purebloods down here, and in the few remaining other Weirdoms on the Headworld, for an extremely long period. That was why devils could possess hybrids like her. Then again she was also an Anthean Witch. The agatine eyes she wore ensorcelled her against devic possession. Or so she believed.

She'd been possessed for a time, more than a hundred years ago, by the devil her Illuminary ancestors named Pyrame Silverstar. That was beyond the Dome, though, where witchcraft wasn't overly effective.

Son George – Georgie, as she called him – had promised her an unforgettable party later on tonight. He'd been coy as to what would be so unforgettable about it but she didn't doubt there'd be abundant drinking and dancing. She never drank and didn't dance much herself, not anymore, but Georgie was like father, like son, in that regard. He loved his beer, his terpsichorean frivolity, his sirens singing and his tale-tellers either reciting or improvising stories of romance and daring-to-do. Most of all he loved to accompany all of the above on his wooden recorder.

He swore he'd heeded her desires and ditched Bad Rhad, as she referred to him. She was happy about that. Rhad struck Helena as a godless sybarite and, even if the Hidden Headworld's gods were mostly fallen angel devils from one of three tribes, she had no use for godless sybarites.

Georgie had taken up with the ever-smiling panpipe-player ostensibly from Apple Isle, Sedon's Human Eye-Isle, after Mithrant legionnaires began setting up camp in the nearby Gregarian Fields, Sedon's Mole, less than a month back. Were it not for one thing, Helena would have thought him a devil; a Master Deva, to use another Illuminary-coined term.

True, Bad Rhad had only two eyes. Third eyes were easily subsumed, though. True as well, Trinondev Warriors of Weir, even apprentice Trinondevs like her son, could suck third generational devils and their azura offspring, who didn't start coming into existence until about 2500 years earlier, wholly into the removable eyeorbs they placed atop their eye-staves. That was why their eyeorbs were also known as prison pods.

Masters of the various Weirdoms, of which only Kanin City was altogether antediluvian, had eye-staves too. She didn't think Rhad was a devil because she'd tried to take him out. Nothing happened. And her ability to concentrate on the task at hand was unrivalled. Plus, her eye-stave, her Master's Mace, was the oldest in the world. It was so old, pre-Earth old in fact, it generated its own eyeorbs.

She'd go to her party, eventually. She'd listen, outwardly appreciatively, to whatever group of musicians, taletellers, singers and dancers her last surviving son had hired for it. She might deign to tap her feet. She might smile more than she ordinarily did. She'd eat heartily and converse as cheerfully as she could manage. First, though, it was tomb-time.

One hundred and twenty eight years of life, she reflected: two husbands, the first of whom, coming up to a hundred years ago on the Outer Earth, had divorced her; the other of whom, Georgie's father, who'd always been a wanderer, simply hadn't bothered to return home, 15 years ago now; and three offspring. Of the latter, only Georgie remained.

Of her lone daughter and lone grandchild on this side of the Dome, only their bodies in their Tantaluses, filled as they were with supposedly life-preserving Cathonic Fluid, lingered. However, unlike thousands of her similarly ensconced ancestors, albeit mostly up north in Cabalarkon, Constance and Christian would never revive, not even briefly, no matter how much of her own blood she dripped into their transparent sarcophagi.

They were dead when she immersed them and, if she had her way, dead they'd stay.

========

Forty years past Helena didn't have time to open her mouth. Heedless of his wife's pleas, son-in-law Egbert ordered their son, her grandson, slain on the spot. His Trinondevs grimly set to the task. Their gargoyles, some of which were based on life-forms never imagined, let alone seen, on either side of the Whole Earth, began co-agulating around them as if stone armour. Christian laughed the more. Before they could mentally muster and thereupon project their psychical weaponry, via their eye-staves, he transformed in front of their eyes.

Almost instantaneously he went from the black skin of a typical Utopian male to the golden-brown skin of the Attis. As he did so, he physically grew, bulking up, until he was a near giant perhaps six and half feet tall and almost as broad as he was wide. Just in case anyone there didn't apprehend who he was in reality, as if out of no-where – what was actually the everywhere of Samsara – he finished adorning himself with the rest of the Attis's distinctive regalia.

Predominantly, though hardly exclusively, that consisted of the Thrygragos and Trigregos Talismans. In terms of the power foci dedicated to the three Great Gods, they were already visible: Thrygragos Lazareme's impenetrable, shape-shifting, cur-rently cerulean Cloak of Many Colours; the face-dancing Mask of Thrygragos By-ron, which he kept as a spiked helmet; and the equally changeable Cross of Thrygra-gos Mithras, which he retained in the form of a javelin.

In terms of those dedicated to the three, long pre-Earth lost, Great Goddesses, the curved sword, called a harpe or falchion, sheathed at his waist had to be the body of Demeter. Presumably he'd ejected its instantly regenerating blades between-space in order to slay Master Hamilcar. Now, the soul or shield-mirror of Devaura appeared strapped to his right arm. At the same time, the mind or crown of Sapiendev appeared around the brow of his helm.

A seventh power focus, the kibisis or bottomless bag of none other than Flow-ery Anthea herself – the inspiration for similar objects carried by many witches, Hele-na amongst them – materialized slung over his right shoulder. In it, she'd heard, he held dozens if not hundreds of other devic power foci.

That the satchel, shield and sword were within easy, cross-chest reach of his left hand was proof positive of the thoroughness of Christian's transfiguration. He'd been right-handed. The Attis was a leftie, the same as his reputed non-devic half-fa-ther, the Male Entity.

The Trinondevs' psychical armaments erupted. The deviant must have already cut himself elsewhere between-space because their many substantial, as well as percep-tible, castings had no effect on the ghost of himself Attis left behind. As it altogether vanished he announced, for all there to hear: "Oh well, I can wait."

He did. So did the Mithrant legionnaires he led as their Taurus. The siege last-ed another hundred days.

Circumstances ascribable to this then latest succession of the Attis – who, hav-ing power foci aplenty, didn't need witch-stones or even a psychopomp to traverse the Weird – contrived to shorten Hesper Suryad's time as Egbert Grudal's High Illuminary and designated successor to a couple of months. Similar circumstances conspired to limit Constance's time in the same position to weeks. Hardly coincidentally, what amounted to Egbert's interregnum lasted precisely a hundred days. Helena Somata had been Kanin's Master ever since.

All she had to do to reach its Mastery was abolish that Attis. To do that all she had to do was sacrifice one Gypsium-fuelled, onetime space-faring cosmicar, him in it, along with its pilot. Said pilot, her claims to the contrary, wasn't Egbert's automatic replacement as Kanin's Master. That was also how Helena verified one Attis succeeded the previous Attis.

She still had the internally burnt-out husk of the cosmicar, a good percentage of its pilot's body, and the retrievable bits and pieces of the Attis who'd been her grandson, Christian Grudal; hence the tomb-time. What she didn't have was the Attis's regalia, shredded as it had been. Taurus Chrysaor Attis had that, no longer shredded. She knew because he had all of it when she tossed him unceremoniously out of the Weirdom a couple of months ago.

He should never have expressed a desire to put Hinny the Hippy to sleep. Georgie loved his pet psycho.

========

Forty years ago, as today, Mithrant legions controlled much of Sedon's Upper Head, an area comparable in size to the Roman Empire. Geographically speaking, the Upper Head might actually have been larger than the combined territories ruled by Helena's then still living firstborn: Constantine, so-called the Great.

The parallels between the two empires didn't stop there. The most obvious comparison was that, for the most part, Mithrant and Roman legionnaires worshipped the same Great God, Thrygragos Varuna Mithras. The obvious difference was Mithras lived in here and, due to the Dome as well as the Devil's intransigence when it came to maintaining it, couldn't get out there anymore.

Another similarity was, given their limited manpower and easily imitated military equipment; both empires had expanded about as far as they could. Another difference was there were no Weirdoms on the Outer Earth. That explained why Attis and his Mithrants were after Kanin City's originally extraterrestrial weaponry. There was nothing new about that of course. They'd been after it for close to two millennia, probably longer.

However, ostensibly because they needed it themselves, if only to prevent their Weirdoms being overpowered by Mithrants using their own weaponry against them, Masters refused to share their technology. Like Hamilcar Suryad and, indeed, like their hundreds of predecessors, Egbert Grudal was no different. Constance was, though. She loved her son, even if he had become the latest Attis, much more than she loved her husband. So she let him in on the real reason Masters didn't share their hardware.

Only Utopians, with their evolved capacity to use close to the fullness of their mental might, could get the damn stuff to work. Regrettably, unabated inbreeding was increasingly causing Utopians to lose that capability. Furthermore, their materiel worked best in combination with Trinondev eye-staves. Think of them as the functional equivalent of devic power foci, daughter informed son under flags of truce, and you wouldn't be far wrong.

Another thing to be said, in general terms, about the city-state's leftover extra-terrestrial equipment was no one, not an Illuminary, nor even the most intellectually able pureblood living up north in Cabalarkon, knew how to reproduce it anymore. The Attis got hold of Kanin's ordnance, he found a way to use it and he exhausted it, he could never manufacture it anew.

No matter. He wanted it. If he had to hire Trinondevs as mercenaries in order to exploit advantages their equipment would give him over territories he hadn't as yet brought under the lawful rule of the Mithrant Brotherhood, then so be it. What was the problem? Ah, but that was the kicker, wasn't it? Mithrants were devil-worshippers and Utopians were as genetically incapable of allying themselves with devil-worshippers as devils themselves were of lying, breaking their oaths or disobeying their fathers. Give it up and go away.

The Attis refused. There were no more flags of truce under which Christian's mother could come visit him. In unison, as if a concretion of faceless gargoyles on invisible appendages, Kanin City's cyclopean walls began, day by day, to creep ever outwards. Attis responded by uprooting his legionnaires' camps farther and farther away from the city-state. Once the walls reached their limitations of creepiness, he had his legionnaires use their own technology, their catapults and suchlike, to lob over top them whatever was at hand.

The land provided. Hills excavated and rocks flung, the forests shrank. He was impressed with the Trinondevs' resistance. Their psychical barriers covered the sky at the same time they defied his miners. He alone could cut himself through the Weird into Kanin City. He did. The Weird was hardly the only thing he could and did cut through.

He started by killing the old Trinondev who'd been training Christian in the multifarious uses of eye-staves before he became the latest Attis. A week or so later he came through and killed an Illuminary, then someone else the next week. A couple of months into the siege he came through and confronted the Nightingale, Hesper Suryad, Egbert's replacement as High Illuminary and his designated successor.

Employing the coercive qualities of the Crimson Corona – aka the Mind of Sapiendev – tête-à-tête, he had her open Kanin's Solidium-shielded vaults, the one place in the entire Weirdom he couldn't get to via between-space. He thereupon made off with all the full prison pods stashed inside it.

The next time he came through he killed her. In a feeble, placatory gesture, Christian's father succumbed to the wishes of Kanin's populace and replaced Hesper with Christian's mother as High Illuminary. Master Egbert, presumably after consultation with his wife, thereupon did something superficially even stupider.

He authorized his Trinondevs to take out a half dozen of their more functional cosmicars – which Constance claimed only they could fly – and launch an aerial assault on the Mithrant legion besieging Kanin City. Such aggression, while hardly unheard of for a Master of Weir acting in defence of his realm, played right into the Attis's hands.

Again employing the coercive qualities of the Crimson Corona, this time long distance, Attis compelled the pilot of the lead cosmicar to turn it on vessels piloted by his fellow Trinondevs. The ploy very nearly backfired. Simultaneously deprived of his free will, yet nonetheless somehow able to pinpoint the Attis's whereabouts, the Trinondev crashed the cosmicar rather than turn it.

Attis reacted in time to avoid the impact. Dozens of his besieging Mithrant legionnaires were not so fortunate. Neither was the Trinondev pilot, who turned out to be none other than Christian's father, Egbert Grudal. His rage unbounded, Attis exacted compensation in very much the same unkind manner.

A whirlwind of death, he slashed between-space, single-handedly taking on the Warriors of Weir piloting and manning the remaining cosmicars. In this he acted precisely as a devil would. Except, since devils themselves were only allowed to use their power foci to kill equals, of whom there were next to none, he didn't respond through intermediaries. He did it personally, as only an Attis could.

Fallen angel devils considered Attis about their only equal. Consequently, had he gone up against especially higher born members of any of the three tribes, they'd have retaliated, likely beaten him back and maybe even killed him, again, without fear of their grandfather cathonitizing or ill-starring them. As it was, as psychically strong as they were, the Trinondevs didn't stand a chance against him.

In the normal course of events, at least in the multi-millennial tradition of Kanin City's Weirdom, Christian's mother Constance, as its High Illuminary, would have succeeded Egbert as its Master. It was certainly in that capacity she came to him a few days later. She flew the Master's replacement-cosmicar to his campsite by herself. Plus, she carried the Master's Mace, the oldest eye-stave in the world.

To show his own good faith, he greeted her in the bath, naked as the day she bore him. As Constance would have known, however, him greeting her naked was less a risk on his part than a ruse. He could materialize the Thrygragos and Trigregos Talismans about himself with a mere thought. Similarly, on the obverse side of the coin, the membership of not every sisterhood loved life as much as that of the Antediluvian Sisterhood of Flowery Anthea.

Killer witches such as those belonging to the Hellion Sisterhood – which might have been founded during the pre-patriarchal era of Eden, itself destroyed more than 1500 years prior to the establishment of the Anthean Sisterhood just before the Great Flood of Genesis – could have come off her witch-stones between-space. Doing suchlike, they could then have attempted to assassinate him, albeit with not quite a thought.

None of that happened. Negotiations ensued.

Constance would allow Trinondev Warriors of Weir to pilot and man cosmicars on his behalf only if they volunteered to do so of their own free will. To get around their conditioning, Attis agreed to employ them solely against the strongholds of devils, not against the small number of freeholds that had thrown off the yoke of devic dominance. Furthermore, in that respect anyhow, the only Warriors of Weir she'd permit to volunteer had to have had their psyches, their mindsets, via their eye-staves, pre-attuned to specific cosmicars.

They wouldn't attack Kanin because, should they dare to even consider it, their superior minds were just as attuned to shut down, meaning their assigned cosmicar would immediately cease to function, crash and burn. In return he'd have to lift the siege, withdraw his legionnaires at least as far as Sedon's Mole and agree that, for a change, it would be his Mithrants who paid tribute to her Utopians, not the other way around.

"That's precisely the sense I was trying to talk Master Hamilcar into months ago. What's changed – Helena Augusta's influence?"

"I banished my mother, sent her back to her Anthill above the Gypsium Wall; no choice offered, none asked, just done. I'm Kanin's Master now. Shall we go?"

No fool he, Attis read her, Christian Grudal's own mother, using the Crimson Corona. She firmly believed she was the Master of Weir. She'd certainly gone through all the ceremonies and rituals every previous Master had in the roughly 4,000 years since Utopians took over Kanin City. Most importantly she held the Master's Mace.

Although nonetheless personally satisfied as to her authenticity, he fully appreciated the talents of an Ant Nightingale such as his grandmother. He compelled her to do exactly as he required. Then, fool he, Attis did as bade and got into the cosmicar with her. Together they flew back toward Kanin, she in thraldom and he in anticipation of a triumphant welcoming.

He got what he wanted; what the Mithrants had long wanted: the Weirdom's Utopian technology. True, via the Master's Mace the real Master's mental might activated just a sampling of it from afar, but he took the full brunt of it. He got killed. All the power foci in the world couldn't prevent him being shredded by particle beams built into the insides of the cosmicar. So did his mother, even more so with respect to the shredding. Desperation had consequences.

Constance Somata-Grudal was indeed Kanin's Master, in her mind. Her mind, and every other part of her, was intentionally misinformed. The Master's Mace had already practically, if not exactly handily, passed to her mother, Helena Somata, Helena Augusta. It had done so, at the moment of Master Egbert's death, by the unspoken yet irrefutably psychical sanction of the Utopian populace. It proved hardier, more salvageable, than their bodies did. It wasn't shredded whatsoever.

Forty years later Helena still held it. And with it she held onto the Weirdom's Mastery. Her daughter's death, her grandson's death, well, mother always knows best.

========

That same 40 odd years later …

========

You can't preserve life once you're dead. There's nothing to preserve besides your corpse. Unless, that is, you or someone else, a Valkyrie or a Rakshas demon perhaps, had first turned you into an Ambulatory Dead Thing. Which, amazingly to many, wasn't such a dead tricky thing to do, provided you had the wherewithal.

Only Master Devas and their azuras, Sangazurs and Nergalazurs most notoriously, could reanimate Dead Things. Since that made them the handiwork of their pre-Earth enemies, Utopians minced zombies on sight. They'd been doing so for the same nearly 5,000 years they'd been just as planet-trapped as devils. Why shouldn't they? Old habits were much harder to kill than Dead Things.

Furthermore, so long as their willpower was strong enough, Trinondevs could suck azuras into prison pods as easily as they could their devic progenitors. That being the case, and even though they could suck a dozen or more azuras into a single pod – in contrast to no more than one devil per eyeorb – they rarely bothered with them. Other than motivationally, in all senses of the word, azuras were as harmless as they were essentially useless. Warriors of Weir reserved their best efforts for capturing and holding onto devils and their talismans.

Unfortunately their successes were limited to realms where devils didn't dominate and, on the Head, such places were few and far between. As for the Moloch Sedon or a Great God, Helena could dream, couldn't she? Yes. And sometimes dreams did come true, didn't they? For some, not for her, she morosely mused.

Lost in reverie, unattended but unafraid, supremely confident in her abilities within her own Weirdom, Master Helena strolled through the megalithic city's firestone-lit, cobbled streets until she reached her destination. Unlocking the garden gate, she entered the high-walled enclosure. Shutting the gate behind her, she sensed somebody about to join her.

Suddenly realizing what, if not who, that was, her breath shortened, her heartbeat quickened and her eyeballs boggled in eagerness.

========

Maybe there always is a first time after all. Happy birthday to me!
****

THEO 2:

THRYGRAGOS VARUNA MITHRAS

========

Jordan Q Tethys appraised the Mithraeum's ceiling.

========.

Mithraea were Cave Temples ostensibly dedicated to an exceedingly ancient Asiatic deity still most commonly known as Mithras. Although his worship, under that name or variations thereof, predated the Ages of Pisces, Aries and possibly even Taurus, two and a half centuries earlier the manifestly insane, Syrian-born emperor Heliogabalus began to refer to Mithras as Sol Invictus, the Invincible Sun. As such the Roman soldiery, predominantly, continued to worship him. However, from what he'd been witnessing during his travels throughout the Empire, that likely wouldn't be the case much longer.

Tethys knew the ceiling was supposed to represent the night's sky, but it was crudely done. He'd seen better ones in the nearby port of Ostia as well as elsewhere within the Celestial City. He nonetheless felt obligated to finish sketching it before the crazed mob of monotheistic zealots he'd seen massing below Vatican Hill arrived to destroy it.

Damn Rome's Spanish-born bishop anyhow. Damasus should have been called *'Damnasus'*. That's certainly the name he'd give him once he returned home and told his tales.

========.

Thrygragos Varuna Mithras regarded the interior dome of the beehive-like Tholos.

========.

Indentured yazata Angelycs built the Whole Earth's original Mithraeum for him late in the first century of the Dome. They'd done so atop the antediluvian, multi-stepped mastaba that surmounted Theopolis Hill on Apple Isle, Sedon's Human Eye-Isle. Mithras had taken over the then flat-topped mastaba, renamed it the Mithradium, and made it his home, as well as the centre of his worship, shortly after the Flood.

For payment they naturally wanted to consume him. Angelycs were like that. To satisfy them he contrived the doctrine of transubstantiation and fed them bread and wine, alongside what subsequently became a frequently repeated, ritualistic feast of bull braised in its own blood. The bull in particular seemed to fit the bill. After all it was the Age of Taurus.

Tall, emaciated and hunched over, Mithras had a long, grey beard and wore a filthy robe that looked no more capable of withstanding a proper washing than he did himself. He resembled a Father Time figure whose annual reign was about to run out. It wasn't. Tantalar was only the second month of the Mithradic Ternary, the tenth month of the Sedonic year.

He glanced at the oversized hourglass standing to one side of his torch-lit sanctuary at the pinnacle of the Tholos. A Tvasitar talisman, it was a gift, a token of filial devotion, from Chrysaor Attis, his ever-enduring deviant offspring. The Attis, rightly fabled as the Universal Soldier, acquired it as a consequence of combat against one of Mithras's still surviving, hundred-plus, devic daughters. A Lesser Apocalyptic, Desiccated Drought made the same mistake so many others had over the centuries. Rather than funnel her worship quota through him, she preferred to send it directly to Father Sedon. Crime reaps punishment in the lands of Mithras.

He'd set its sands running at midnight, the start of the Mithranalia: the Upper Head's weeklong celebration of his brilliance and the equivalent of Imperial Rome's Saturnalia, which the Romans named after one of his myriad other identities. They'd run out at its conclusion, Mithramas, his feast day, the customary date for the Winter Solstice. Due to the fact his Outer Earth devotees were abandoning him in hitherto unprecedented numbers, he'd already deemed it differently this year. And if Thrygragon went badly, many multiple millennia more than a year's time might run out on him.

Most of the blame for this sorry state of affairs lay with that traitorous Sed-son, the Roman Emperor Constantine, who was decades dead out there, and his meddlesome mother, Helena Augusta, a hybrid Utopian who was still sadly alive and the Master of the Weirdom of Kanin City in here. At least she was as of this minute. She headed his Doomsday Book for payback after Thrygragon. Utopian Weirdoms were blights on the landscape.

With an effortless wave he vanished the beehive's cupola. Now he regarded what the Dual Entities – who insisted they'd randomly time-tumbled to the Whole Earth's far future at least as often as they'd appeared in its now distant past – called the Milky Way. Its shimmering luminescence, faint and diffuse, filtered through the intermediate gauze of the Sedon Sphere. Having been through much of it during the multiple millennia he was on or part of the Sedonshem, Mithras reckoned it would have been better named the Bloody Way.

They'd lost, more so than left behind, literally millions of third generational Master Devas as the Sedonshem wound its way from the second Weirworld to the then Whole Earth. Sure, they were little more than pulses of spiritual evanescence, but they were invaluable. A high percentage of them, congealed together, kept his two brothers and him, as well as their usually female bunkmates, solid individuals throughout most of that nearly interminable journey.

Indeed, they'd lost so many that by the time the Sedonshem landed atop Kanin City, 669 years before the Genesea, he and his brothers were almost as insubstantial as all but a couple of their remaining offspring, including their preferred bunkmates, stayed until around 2500 years ago. Even the Devil Sedon looked to have suffered from an enforced diet. When it came to devic nourishment, possession beat starlight any day of the aeons, while adulation, duly offered, was positively fattening.

Today, to borrow a word he picked up from the ever baffling, even ineffable Male Entity – Heliosophos or Helios called Sophos the Wise – when Mithras occupied him most of those same 2500 years ago, the Great God felt anorexic. He wondered, despairingly more so than whimsically, if anyone would notice him if he turned sideways.

Remedying his pathetically deteriorating condition was the main motivation for Thrygragon: as in gone, gone, gone his Thrygragos Brothers.

========

Mithras smirked.

========

Typically circular, upwardly tapered and domed Tholoi, of which there were dozens of variants up and down Theopolis Hill, always reminded him of boiled eggs sticking out of the ground – or a stone, cup-like container in the case of his Mithradium. And that in turn reminded him of the strangest story the deviant Legendarian, whom Mithras regularly consulted with respect to current events on the Outer Earth, recounted of his nativity.

Crack! Sky-Father Varuna's spermatic lightning hit the Mother Earth virgin's ovum in the form of a raised, navel-like boulder or omphalos – an egg hardboiled to the point of petrifaction – and, voila, he was born. Ha! Certain misconceived Outer Earth mythologies aside, as well as his occasionally cripplingly severe and sometimes regrettably long-lasting schizophrenic episodes, he and Varuna weren't separate beings. Varuna was just his first name.

The Legendarian, who claimed to have copied the entire library of Alexandria with his devic half-father's power focus, had even learned a term for the event: *'petra genetrix'*. Not only that, he'd come back with a date for it: Year of the Dome 3800, or thereabouts. Ha again! As if! To cite just one example of how nonsensical the notion of him being born a mortal, only to go on to become humanity's saviour, he gave Hammurabi his famous code of laws, minus the state-sanctioned executions, when the Babylonians revered him as the Sun God Shamash.

And that was something like 1600 years before he was supposed to have been born.

========

At his request, the Legendarian once in awhile regaled him with the utter strangeness of the egg-myth of Mithras. The Earth virgin, who had to have been derived from Mediterranean Athena and others of her by then long familiar ilk, had a name: Anahita or Aban. Just as his had done in earlier creeds naming him as Varuna, Mithras, or both, as the binomial god Mitravaruna or Varunamithra, her adherents venerated her as a fertility deity. How that jibed with her being retroactively declared a virgin mother, well, divinity had its dividends.

Perhaps as perversely as his own spermatic lightning impregnating her with himself, a different version of his nativity had Anahita conceiving him via the preserved seed of Zarathustra. Since Zarathustra, or Zoroaster, had died, at the minimum, in the vicinity of 400 years previously, Mithras reckoned that accomplishment almost as impressive as a fertility goddess regaining her maidenhead in order to oblige him with an unsullied birth.

Circa 3800 was hardly the first time Zarathustra helped him out. During his lifetime the Iranian- or Persian-born prophet revealed the existence of a monotheistic deity he called Ahura Mazda. And, allowing for the garbled gibberish spoken by those living beyond the Dome, didn't that sound much like Varunamithra? It had to the Legendarian and it did to Mithras. Not surprisingly either: Zarathustra's post-Magian patron was the Persian Emperor Darius, a succession of his deviant half-son, the Attis.

'Petra genetrix', or a moderately more normal nativity achieved, on what was in here the 25th of Tantalar, the mortal Mithras lived a normal life until he had an epiphany of sorts in his 28th year. From that day forth he preached of the unparalleled majesty of Ahura Mazda day in, day out. In the process he attracted at least a dozen apostles, hundreds of disciples and thousands of suitably slavish supporters. In order to secure both their devotion and their salvation, he also performed obligatory miracles. He made the lame walk, the blind see and the deaf hear. He healed the sick and raised the dead, he himself amongst them.

This Mithras, in all probability a make-believe character, one who sounded more akin to the Egyptian Osiris than to any other Mithras 30-Beers told him about, did his storybook best to appear man-as-god-walking-amongst-men for 36 more years. Finally, some 64 years after his birth, from a rock, or a re-enlivened tadpole, he ascended into heaven, where he either rejoined or replaced Sky-Father Varuna.

The Great God would have reckoned the entire fiction laugh-out-loud ludicrous except that, again according to the Legendarian, the forces of monotheism propagated virtually the same preposterous confabulation today, beyond the Dome. Their nominees for the world's saviour had different names of course, Christ and Mani being two of the more recent. Still, as Heliosophos, the Male Entity, might have said, in that disturbing future-speak of his, Mithras should have demanded royalties.

What he was getting instead, as Helios might also have said were he still around, or around again, was his just desserts. Which, contrariwise, was perfectly fine with Mithras so long as his Thrygragos Brothers were left nibbling on his table scraps.

========

As the legendary 30-Year Man was fond of remarking, Mithras's name translated as *'friend'* in a startling number of languages spoken beyond the Dome. Since always irresponsible Lazaremists – not his, as an enforced rule, generally dutiful Mithradites – possessed his birthparents when he was conceived, it was a minor paradox the deviant came as close as the Great God did to having an actual friend. Then again the Legendarian would happily tell his tales to anyone who plied him with beer, plenty of beer, which was how he earned his 30-Beers nickname.

30-Beers had stacks of knacks, to quote him. He being essentially a Lazaremist, not too many of them were admirable. Mithras being Mithras, the Great God of Justice, Truth and Light – more, of civilization itself – found his history as an unrepentant oath-breaker by far the most reprehensible.

Arguably his ability to keep coming back consciously was the most extraordinary thing about him, but his thirst for beer had to qualify as the most legendary. It was very nearly as unquenchable as his approaching monomaniacal quest for information, particularly about the putatively original Unnameable.

In that regard he'd pieced together a supportable chronicle of, as he put it, the comestible near-debacle of 725 Pre-Dome. That was the year the Sedonshem landed on the Moon. Mithras remained inside it, as part of it, when, as a precautionary measure, their father deposited Thrygragos Lazareme on the planet's surface. Along with a good-sized scouting party made up of Master Devas from all three tribes, his task was to check out the lay of the land, as it were.

In many respects it was providential Sedon chose prudence over recklessness. As Lazareme soon reported, they'd quickly come across exceptionally long-lived editions of the Dual Entities not so much laying on the land as ruling it – and, Heliosophos being a resolute anarchist, not so much that either.

Although Helios and his somehow humanized Mnemosyne Machine were going by the names of Alorus Ptah and Trishtar Thrae, the Outer Earth's Book of Byblos remembered them as Adam and Eve. Because of that, certain superstitious fools believed to this day – and to Mithras's mind defiant of logic – that Adam-Ptah constituted the Male Entity's first lifetime.

It fell to Thrygragos Lazareme, in effect the Legendarian's half-grandfather on both sides of the bed, to find a way to kill Helios. In order to do so, that Great God allied himself with the time-tumblers' sworn enemies of the era. These were the soulless chthonic creatures generically referred to as daemons – demons without the letter 'a' being one of their least tolerable subclasses. The Entities had captured and imprisoned their undying aristocracy within Andy the Androsphinx hundreds of years earlier.

In an effort to garner the unsavoury shape-shifters' support, he allowed far too many of those participating in his scouting party, including the 30-Year deviant's devic half-parents, to fuse with a contingent of the dull-witted but extremely dangerous – not to mention, as it turned out, plainly duplicitous – tricksters. The resultant conglomeration of earthborn and skyborn saboteurs launched an assault on the Androsphinx as one, as the Unnameable.

Unfortunately Andy gained his name because Lazareme and those on his expedition had also learned by then of the existence of a Gynosphinx, whom they in their ignorance came to call Ginny. The Dual Entities must have been starving them unto voraciousness because one demon-devil-combined Unnameable quickly became dinner for two nameable sphinxes, hence the Legendarian's characterization of events in 725 PD as a comestible near-debacle.

When in his cups, which he often was – even his own devic children referred to him as the Libertine – Thrygragos Lazareme would laugh sardonically that he was flabbergasted to hear Sedon and those with him on the Moon, his two brothers especially, hadn't heard Andy and Ginny belching.

As far as Mithras was concerned, in 20/20/20 hindsight, the fact that it was so obviously a trap invalidated the supposition Ptah's was Helios's first lifetime. By his own admission Helios didn't know anything about devils in his first lifetime. So how could he have laid a trap for them? Then again, also by his own admission, Helios didn't know when, or as whom, he spent his first lifetime.

Nonetheless, and howsoever begrudgingly, he had to give his firstborn brother credit because, before 725's solar year ended, Lazareme and his firstborn daughter, Harmony as she was now known, conspired to poison Helios. And, as everyone knew even way back then, when Helios dies he goes back into the time stream taking Machine-Memory with him, her as the innards of Trans-Time Trigon.

Still, it wasn't until decades later, in 669 PD, that the Devil Sedon dared leave the Moon and bring his Sedonshem to ground atop Kanin City, whereupon it pulverized everyone and everything underneath it.

As luck would have it, over 5,000 years later, his ongoing connection to the Prison Beach's She-Sphinx would grant Mithras a decisive advantage over his two brothers come a week from today. Oh, he'd provide them both with the option of not immediately meeting their maker, their Father Sedon, eye-to-eye as it were, as stars in the night's sky, but he hoped the Lackland Libertine in particular would prove too arrogant to take him up on his offer.

As for his most hated brother's firstborn daughter, the Unity of Unrequited Desire as he thought of the Harmony Unity, death voided marriage contracts and his ewe for Aries, Marut Kanin, as Illuminaries first had her, unaccountably disappeared over 300 years ago. As a result Mithras considered himself a widower. Just as Divine Coueranna, in her shells, had been his Boss Cow during Taurus, Harmony might consent to become his fishwife for Pisces.

If she didn't, he'd likely take her anyhow, regardless of her wishes, but indubitably for her own good. He'd take her in the middle of the Mole, the Gregarian Fields, in the freezing cold of midwinter, if needs be. That was what his and the Attis's Mithrant Brotherhood did. They called it the spoils of war.

And what, by definition, was the potential Theomachy to come except war among the gods?

========

All third generational devils were born triplets.

========

His torchbearers, equinoctial Spring and equinoctial Autumn – whom Illuminaries named Tammuz and Osiraq, but whom the Legendarian said the iconography of Cave Mithraism had as Cautes and Cautopates – were no different. Sedon cathonitized their triplet, Midsummer, also male, because on one of his solstice feast days, nearly 2,000 years ago, he got so blazing drunk he inadvertently triggered a volcano on the Outer Earth island of Strongyne that claimed thousands of its mostly female inhabitants.

The torches they'd left in his Mithraeum aerie were burning down. Thinking about Datong Harmonia, as bygone Illuminaries had unimaginatively named Lazareme's Harmony Unity, made him feverous. Just because he could, Mithras ignited one hand. Next he tore off his arm and replaced one of the dwindling torches with it. Growing that arm back he then did the same with the other arm.

Mithras enjoyed playing parlour games. He also felt himself in an atypically upbeat mood. Anticipating Thrygragon cheered him immeasurably. He might soon find himself tempted to put on a much younger seeming and go down into nearby Corona City, the oldest still-populated metropolis on either side of the Dome, whereupon he'd seek some action. Then again she rarely came anywhere near here. So, since any action he did get undoubtedly wouldn't be with Harmony, why bother budging?

His mood nose-diving again, like an Edenite vimana or a Trinondev cosmicar about to crash and burn, the Milky Way still made him think Bloody Way instead. Even so, once you counted their dozens of remaining, third generational offspring, and the thousands of azura and non-azura possessed fighters they'd bring with them, it could be that the Gregarian Fields, Sedon's Mole, would run much bloodier come Mithramas.

It definitely would if his two Great God brothers did not at last accept longstanding reality and embrace him as their superior in everyday practical terms. They would, though. They had to, he fretted. If they wanted their tribes restored and their adherents breathing after their submission, they'd have no choice in the matter.

Only he could cause the She-Sphinx, All of Incain, to release those she held, those the Attis imprisoned within her, because only he had the requisite authority over All's mistress, the female of the two adult Perpetual Presences.

========

In his view, subordination – what some called henotheism, namely a state of affairs in which there are many gods but only one prevails as the King or God of Gods – was small price for his brothers to pay for his forbearance and intercession on their behalf with All of Incain. He, the deservedly declared Sire of Civilization on both sides of the Dome, had nonetheless experienced it many times over the millennia on the Outer Earth, where neither of them was ever venerated under any name.

During Vedic times, for one, his binomial alter ego, Varuna or Uranus, as some Middle Sea westerners had him, came to be considered the ultimate ruler and judge; the one who sets the parameters within which everybody could thrive, warrants and ensures contracts, forgives and punishes sin. For two, circa a thousand years ago, that curious fellow Zarathustra – he of the potent, not to mention swimmingly preserved spermatozoa – acknowledged him, Mithras, by name, as the *'Judger of Souls'*.

That Zarathustra also spoke of him as his God's divine representative on earth made no never-mind to Mithras. As much as it looked and sounded like Varunamithra, Ahura Mazda meant Lord Wisdom in Zarathustra's native tongue. He was therefore more of a concept than a unique entity. Since Mazda's emblem, a winged ring or sun-disc, was as close as he came to having one of his own, Mithras got his reverence second-hand.

Zarathustra additionally had him – had Ahura Mazda, make that – in eternal conflict with Angra Mainyu, aka Ahriman or Aryanman. That did somewhat bother Mithras. Only a madman could oppose wisdom manifest and madmen were self-destructive, not eternal. In the Great God's considered, as well as considerable, judgement there was no such thing as evil. There were just right and wrong decisions made.

Mithras once asked the Legendarian why a prophet would invent an insane antagonist. To give his priests something to rail on about, the deviant glibly ventured. Priests had to eat too. Mithras almost cut off his beer supply for that spume of simplicity. One of the names under which he received devotion in sensibly syncretic faiths was Olympian Apollo, and 30-Beers' response didn't satisfy his Apollonian requirement for a rational explanation.

All right, so the Dual Entities, the Male and Female Principals, were the first to name him Varuna Mithras, many multiple millennia ago pre-Earth. All right, so they were often portrayed as overseeing his activities, Helios as the Sun and Mnemosyne as the Moon. All right as well, so self-sanctioned ministers and hierophants purporting to do to his will had their more artistically inclined acolytes repeatedly depict him, surrounded by the 12 Signs of the Zodiac, slaying Taurus the Bull and thereby moving the heavens.

So what if the Romans of the present day showed him looking like his simultaneously mortal, yet thus far effectively immortal half-son, Chrysaor Attis? So what if the Persians of the not-so-distant past, for devils, had Ahriman-Aryanman-Mainyu, instead of either Mithras or Attis, as a bull-slayer? So what if the Etocretans, 50 human generations or more before Zarathustra, had a supposed son of Olympian Zeus, also a judger of the dead, one Rhadamanthys by name, as another bull-slayer, unless it was just as a bull-rider?

It only verged on sacrilegious to think that, if Rhadamanthys-Ahriman-Mainyu did exist, he had to be Father Sedon. Should the callous, frequently out-and-out cruel, near-omnipotent, mighty Eye-Mouth in the sky agree to lower the Dome – or to chew just a teensy hole in it, such that Mithras could get outside again on a regular basis – there'd be no need for Thrygragon. Neither would Outer Earthlings need to invent imaginary deities, perfect or imperfect. They could shake hands with him, Thrygragos Varuna Mithras, the All Gracious Guarantor of Covenants.

Inexplicably fearing for his own survival, Sedon would never deign to do something so eminently reasonable. Consequently Mithras didn't know how much longer he would last. He did know henotheism, for devil-gods anyways, was preferable to monotheism. Anyone who thought differently had to be as nuts as Zarathustra's fantasy foe.

And henotheism was what he, ever so magnanimously, was offering his brothers. They didn't submit, didn't subordinate themselves to him, then they and not he would be responsible for their demise. They'd be the authors of their own 'theocide', to coin a word.

========

One of the tricks to monotheism, the Legendarian explained to him, was to downgrade gods to angels or saints. For example, with respect to Mithras, one creed nowadays revered him as St Michael, an archangel, whereas a basilica dedicated to a proselytizing martyr by the telling name of St Saturnin had recently been built over a Mithraeum somewhere in Gaul. Overall though, that same creed demonized devils as fallen angels. Which was fair enough, in a way, since devakind did indeed come from the stars, the heavens, if not precisely Heaven.

That in mind Mithras returned his attention to the Sedon Sphere.

He expected to spot a falling star and, sure enough, one star was twinkling almost as luminously as Star Sedon, the Moon's after dark competitor for intensity above the Hidden Headworld. Did that indicate it was falling? Not precisely. His masochist, his angelic courier and most reliable Heliodromus, Djinn Domitian as Illuminaries had him, was merely returning from his Mithras-mandated, mailman mission to the Moloch.

The Great God of Civil Sensibility hoped the mighty Eye-Mouth in the sky hadn't chomped on him too severely. Messengers weren't supposed to enjoy themselves until after they returned with their responses.

========

The prophet Zarathustra's precursors, the fire-worshipping Magians, believed they could summon demons if they knew their names. And maybe they could.

For his part, Mithras didn't accord otherwise inexplicable magic any credence. Bygone Illuminaries of Weir did. Except they hoped to subsequently summon their devic enemies — whereupon they'd forthwith slurp them into their prison pods — by assigning them names.

They were disappointed. But that didn't prevent them naming devils, and the first they thus named was Pyrame Silverstar.

========

Illuminaries derived Pyrame's surname from the fact that, even though she was ever earthbound, they fancied her a shining light compared to that of Sedon, who was a dark star during the day. As for her first name, Mithras himself could attest she was hot-tempered, as well as hot-bodied and seemingly always hot-to-trot, to use another of Helios's favourite phrases from the future.

However, even though words beginning with 'pyr' or 'pyro' generally denoted heat or something to do with heat, Pyrame actually came from pyramid. It was an appropriate root in that, when he was on the Inner Earth, Pyrame attended Sedon in the Grand Elysium pyramid wherein he lived and held court.

Furthermore, the Legendarian was one who hypothesized that denizens of the Outer Earth built their copycat structures in order to attract Sedon and Pyrame to their locales and thereby earn special treatment. It certainly fit with the prevailing belief beyond the Dome that Sedon was Satan and that he dwelt in hellfire.

Devils tended to address each other by attributes or distinctive features rather than names. For instance, they'd been addressing his commonest go-between as the Masochist ever since he, Mithras, used him to spice his transubstantiation dodge in the First Century YD. Devils regularly addressed Pyrame as the Pauper Priestess because she had neither a power focus to call her own nor a realm to make her home.

As for devotees, she served Father Sedon, not herself. As a result she didn't need any devotees. She had Sedon and that was more than enough. She had him because she alone could successfully occupy the mortal women he, occupying mortal men, impregnated in order to produce his necessarily male and invariably mortal sedons, small case, three or four times a human generation on either side of the Dome.

Master Helena's Emperor Constantine being an egregious exception, Sed-sons seldom amounted to much. Yet the deviants' existence somehow or other allowed the devils' All-Father, as well as the daemons' antediluvian-acknowledged king, to preserve the integrity of Cathonia. By this means sedons therefore helped keep the Inner Earth separated from the Outer Earth.

Wise men, witches, devils and Illuminaries of Weir alike speculated it had to do with retaining a mystical bond between heaven and earth. Still, no one could be entirely sure how or why Sed-sons were so essential. Rather, if Sed-mom or Sed-dad, or both, were sure, they weren't confiding said sureness to anyone else, not even to Mithras, Sedon's indisputable favourite.

Third generational devils were the offspring of the Six Great Gods and Goddesses. The Pauper was one of his, at one time, innumerable multitude of devic children by the traitorous Trigregos Sisters. Spirit Beings the lot of them, barely 250, half of them female, got as far as Sedon's eventual Headworld, thus living through the Genesea.

With very few exceptions, Illuminaries of Weir never got around to naming any of those lost in the Flood or earlier, for whatever reason. That included the entirety of his third-born brood of three. However, because of the virtually unique circumstances not so much of her survival as her revival, as it were, they named Pyrame Silverstar over 3,000 years before they got around to naming any other Master Deva.

So, yes, a number of others did indeed survive the same way she did. But, no, they, inside their shells, did not do so because they were on any of the myriad islands and islets comprising the then Archipelago of Pacifica when Sedon raised the Cathonic Zone all around it out of his own essence. They survived because they were there inside of All, Incain's already self-declared invincible She-Sphinx.

Like them a member of Lazareme's ill-fated scouting party back in 725 PD, Pyrame was one of the Master Devas that fused with chthonic daemons to form the Unnameable. After All and her just as moderately semi-sentient male counterpart ate the conglomerate creature, the Dual Entities one way or another immobilized the two sphinxes: Andy the Androsphinx on the Giza plateau in what was even then called Egypt and All – who, being more self-conscious than Andy, disliked being referred to as Ginny the Gynosphinx – on the then island of Incain.

There, shortly after the Genesea subsided beyond the Dome, approaching 4½ millennia ago, Pyrame's Sedonshem-lover, Dark Sedon himself, managed to break her loose. And that fact was what made her virtually unique. What made her absolutely unique was the additional fact that they'd been Sed-mom and Sed-dad ever since. Which was something else that was okay with Mithras.

Thanks to the Legendarian's investigations, he now knew how, always assuming they were the ones who did it, the Dual Entities immobilized both sphinxes. He also knew the Unnameable's actual name, not that it held any real power either. Its head, though, that was a different matter.

He knew where that was as well: in the Attis's bottomless bag!

========

Although, by their very nature, devils were as incapable of disobeying their fathers as he was of disobeying his father, Mithras didn't order his offspring about like his two brothers did theirs. Why should he? He'd made a literal religion for himself as the Great God of Truth, Light and Justice.

As the guarantor of contracts, his word was his bond. So, admittedly with Attis and his Mithrant legionnaires poised as an omnipresent backup, he negotiated with them instead. He could order them about, though. And, if only to forestall him commanding her to do precisely as he pleased, Pyrame was by and large accommodating.

He'd never have to send the Attis after her either – not to force her compliance, nor to enforce their agreements – and it wasn't because her position as the Sed-sons' only possible Sed-mom made her untouchable. When she wasn't in here or out there being conceptive Sed-mom, Pyrame and Attis were lovers. They had been, for him succession after succession, for many hundreds of years.

Mithras approved of their relationship. No one covered his or her angles better than he did. That was why he sent his Heliodromus upstairs. He didn't want his father-who-art-the-heavens angry with him if he decided to abolish his two Thrygragos brothers a week hence.

========

The tiny twinkle brightened, bloated. Ergo, the Masochist was slowly returning from his rendezvous with the mighty Eye-Mouth in the sky.

How should he greet him, in what semblance? More to the point, what semblance did the Moloch Sedon prefer to adopt these days? Was he still going with the veneer of a near-naked, red-skinned – not red-furred – satyr? Probably.

True, as if to make himself appear less oafish and more fearsome, he usually sported stubby horns, filed-sharp teeth, a forked goatee and tongue, a braided ponytail and a spade-bladed tail. But did he have to carry a pitchfork with him, like a labarum or a sceptre, whenever he held court in his Grand Elysium pyramid?

Couldn't he come up with something more creative? Did he really not want to disillusion his admirers – his vilifiers more like – that badly? In short, even though they hadn't been seen in hundreds of years, did he really not want to let down the Dual Entities by appearing as other than their conventional visualization of their everlasting antagonist, their Satan, their Devil Incarnate?

Probably not answered that. As much as anything even vaguely hircine offend-
ed Mithras – merely contemplating Tralalorn and her goatish chimera, something he
strove never to do, made him gag involuntarily – Sedon delighted in the look. HaSha-
tan the Peacock Angel, wasn't that the latest name the Legendarian said some otherwise
forgettable Middle Eastern sect referred to Sedon on the Outer Earth these days?

Unlike the Female Entity, who could remember everything, hence her given
name Mnemosyne, which meant memory, he had no great memory for names. But it
could be. At any rate, he'd soon find out if his father persisted in the guise of a hay-
loft bumpkin.

The Masochist – who, with a fanfare trumpet for a power focus, doubled as his
herald as well as his chief sun-runner – had a non-forked tongue with which to speak
and three eyes with which to see. Hopefully Sedon spat them out, still in his head,
when he spat him out of Cathonia.

========

Mithras learned Zarathustra's concept of dualism pitted Ahura Mazda against
Angra Mainyu long before the Legendarian came into being during the first third of
the Dome's 41st Century. Since then, 30-Beers regularly used his insouciant charm to
gull Incain's She-Sphinx into tongue-tugging him to her moribund male equivalent
in Egypt. As a result the taleteller had acquired a degree of expertise on various wor-
ship-robbing, monotheistic movements proliferating beyond the Dome.

For years now he'd been returning more and more convinced that the vividly
explicit distinction their proponents drew between a hypothetically single God and
a nearly equal Satan, with their corresponding afterlife rewards for lifestyle performance in either a paradisiacal Heaven or a polar-oppositely horrendous Hell, was what
was making them so successful.

Irony of ironing boards, as he put it, the Legendarian therefore blamed the
debilitation befalling him, Mithras the Inner Earth's Great God of Justice, Light and
Truth, as well as the avowed advocate of freewill, on Mithras the Outer Earth's dot-
ditto, its acclaimed lawgiver, guarantor of contracts, righter of wrongs and champion
of a civil society.

Devils did not believe in a hereafter, unless they were already experiencing theirs
here on the Head. Devils were all about the here and now. Yet, by defining what amounted to good and evil in terms of demonstrable crime and remedial consequences, he'd
unwittingly driven himself to the precipice he was teetering on today.

Immortality was habit forming. He had to chance the results of trying to over-
arch his brothers as the Head's primary deity. Ends justified the means. Absolute rul-
ers not just on both sides of this world, but everywhere he'd ever been throughout the
heavens, complied with that dictum as the lone unbreakable law.

After Thrygragon devic adulation would have to channel through him before it
reached his father. Once it did, once he attained the hitherto unprecedented position
as its final filter, then, and only then, would he at last begin gleaning a slight commis-
sion. Only in that way would he be able secure his here, for now and forevermore.

Needs be the Moloch Sedon would remain the nominal God of devil-gods. Mithras couldn't do anything about that. A Hidden Continent howsoever momentarily

bobbing up in the middle of the North Pacific Ocean, as the Dual Entities referred to the region, would as likely sink as remain above water. And he hated swimming.

At least he couldn't do anything about it yet. Not that he particularly wanted to either. Just as there would have been no Sedonshem to transport them safely out of the second Weir System – after Heliosophos had his Mnemosyne Machine ignite the first Weir Star, thus rendering it the sudden supernova that, in the briefest of instants, finished off conceivably billions of Master Devas, their host-shells with them – there would be no Sedon Sphere above and about them without his father around to compose it.

Sedon looked after them. He always had and for that his descendants were unendingly, as well as genetically, grateful.

Due diligence done, more than three centuries of listening to corresponding generations of the Legendarian tell his tales, he'd convinced himself he could withstand everything his brothers could potentially throw at him. Of course just as Thrygragon could mean gone bye-bye, endgame bye-bye, for them, cooperation could mean much more than them going down a rung or two compared to him.

A return to the stars inevitably awaited them. But not the stars in the Head's night's sky, the Sedon Sphere, alongside its namesake, though Bodiless Byron would be right at home up there. He wasn't called the Unmoving One for zilch times zip. The stars beyond it, the real stars, from whence they came, the bloody Milky Way and galaxies much farther away than it, the cosmos itself, those were the stars that beckoned.

Things would be different this time, however. Mithras was all in favour of monotheism. So long as he was the Mono Theo!

========

His Heliodromus materialized out of the Weird, alighting beside Drought's Attis-donated hourglass. Seeing the condition he was in, Mithras couldn't decide whether he should laugh or cry. Before he expectorated him from Cathonia, the mighty Moloch had ground Djinn Domitian up so thoroughly he must have replenished his stock of toothpicks for a year with clumps of the Masochist's affected, angelic feathers.

Suddenly Mithras lost his option to either laugh or cry. He also lost his supper. He buckled over, spewing out his innards.

Damn Trala! What was she doing riding her cursed, three-headed, lactose-reeking chimera anywhere near Theopolis Hill anyhow?

========

Standard wisdom had her as Pyrame's third, simultaneously born, immediate sister, the one besides Desiccated Drought. Standard wisdom also had her as naming herself, perhaps in a pique, but definitely after the nonsensical rhymes she was always inventing, not long after Pyrame acquired her name.

There was no denying Tralalorn constantly addressed him as daddy. Then again she addressed almost everyone, devil and non-devil alike, as either daddy or mommy. There were many other, far more abnormal things about her, though. Perhaps the most incongruous of them was she had a power focus, called the White Dwarf, most of two millennia before the Anvil Artificer crafted for himself his very first talisman: an anvil.

Indeed, Trala had so many disquieting qualities Mithras never could accept her as his daughter. He reckoned her Sed-mom and Sed-dad's firstborn, their only immortal thus far born on the Whole Earth. To his mind irrefutably, that made her less a delinquent devil than a complete cacodemon, an evil genius who just happened to be a vegetarian. He justifiably referred to her as Sedon's Demon Child.

Her shells, if shells they were, were invariably young girls. Worse, they always looked the same. 30-Beers described her as a mini Miss Moloch. He was right too, though he did hazard the penalty of sacrilege – commonly punished by the Devil discharging a thunderbolt electrifying the spinal cord – when he did so. As if in an effort to avert charges of blasphemy, the recurring deviant was always quick to add that, alas, unlike him, Sedon had the requisite might to remain resolutely male.

Worst of all, the Demon Child's shells never aged. If she did cast splendours about them, as her apologists insisted, did she consume them utterly, as a flame did wood, paper or papyrus? In which case, the moment she burnt out the first one, shouldn't Sedon have instantly ill-starred or cathonitized her? The answer had to be yes.

Mind you, to be fair to his father, only Pyrame and Tralalorn, if she was the second, third generational devil to become mindfully embodied, were autonomous individuals prior to the eruption of Sedon's Peak circa 2000 YD. He therefore may not yet have realized he could cathonitize anyone besides Mithras and his two brothers, whom Sedon, highly significantly, had never designated Perpetual Presences. Still, what about the nearly 2500 years since then?

Alternatively, if her body was not a shell, if it was her own and if she wasn't Mithras's daughter, might that make her the first, fourth generational devil? Could devic spirit beings be born with non-daemonic, subtle matter bodies of their own? If so, as a few optimists who probably should have known better speculated, did that make the Demon Child the repository of Master Devas who never made it to Pacifica prior to Sedon covering, draining and terra-forming it into his Headworld?

The only person who would dare to answer these questions was the little horror herself. Except, her answer usually went something like: 'Tra-la tra-gee, your brain's a pea!' Whereupon she'd point her faces and, sometimes, feces flashing White Dwarf power focus at you and it'd be just that. You didn't want to sneeze or your peabrain would be in your handkerchief and you'd be stuffing it back up your nose reflexively, if not exactly smartly.

After Father Sedon and definite daughter Pyrame, Trala constituted the Head's third, albeit never an adult, Perpetual Presence. You trifled with her, absolute aberration that she was, the mighty Moloch above would strike you down with finality as much as he would with a jolt of lightning.

Even though soulless daemons more like persisted than subsisted, the invaluable, long ago proven irreplaceable Korant Sisterhood in effect adopted her millennia earlier, when their devic goddess, Divine Coueranna as Illuminaries named her, was still his primary bedmate. Consequently she ordinarily dwelt right here on Apple Isle, Sedon's Human Eye-Isle.

Happily for him – to use a euphemism he often did when he found himself inadvertently thinking about her – the miserable little horror 'abided' in the vicinity of Mt Maenalus, Kore's Volcano. And it lay on the southern side of the island, a decent distance, by foot or by hoof, from his Mithradium of an eggcup.

Since, for the better part of 2500 years, mere proximity to her ever re-engendered chain of chimeras invariably made him vomit, her staying much nearer Mt Maenalus than Theopolis Hill amounted to a multiple centuries' pre-agreed-upon condition of her continuing residency on Ap Isle. She knew that. Yet, he couldn't help observing, between heaves, that throwing up his last meal and an increasing pile of its prandial predecessors was precisely what he was doing.

Freewill or no freewill, devil-gods couldn't disobey their fathers. Ergo, didn't that make proof in the proverbial puke-pudding her not being his daughter?

========

There were seven rungs up the ladder in the modern Roman version of his self-promulgated rites from close to the Dome's Year Zero, what the empire's soldiery also referred to as Cave Mithraism. The Pope, Pater or Father – Mithras's stand-in, of whom there could be as many as he wanted there to be – was the top rung, the Seventh. The Heliodromus or sun-runner was just below it, the Sixth. In descending order the rest were Persian, Leo, Miles, Bridegroom and Raven.

One reason Domitian assumed the vague likeness of a yazata Angelyc on a semi-permanent basis was because Mithras spiced their first feast upon completion of this Mithraeum, atop his Mithradium, with essence of Masochist. A second reason was the fact that, in not just Persian Mithraism, angels were considered messengers of the gods. A most important third reason for his chosen semblance was that even lowborn Mithradites flourished once they'd acquired sentient worshippers. And, no matter how lowbrow they were, Angelycs would do as well as any.

He appeared angelic in that he had four feathery wings. A single set of two sprouted out of each shoulder blade. One wing on each side pointed upwards; the other, the bigger one, pointed downwards. That he was additionally 'leontocephaline', that was due primarily to a suggestion made by the Legendarian, incarnations earlier.

The recurring deviant, at Mithras's request, had visited any number of Mithraeum Cave Temples on the Outer Earth. He'd come back recommending Domitian start sporting a lion's head because Mithras's heralds were often depicted as having one. It was this 'leontocephalous' the Great God focused on once he finished adding his lunch and breakfast to his supper on the beehive's floor.

His Heliodromus perched over him; the lion-headed face regarded him worriedly. His breath stank almost as foully as Trala's now passed, goatish chimera always did. There was something else about him as well. The mouthpiece of his power focus, his fanfare trumpet, was sticking out of his mouth tube foremost. Did that mean its bell-piece was sticking out of his ass?

The Devil Sedon had masticated the Masochist big time this time. It was pure wonderment it hadn't resulted in the trumpeter's endgame. Yet, his angel's condition … Tralalorn riding so close to his Mithradium despite his oft-expressed desire – he dare not order Sedon's Demon Child to do anything she didn't want to do – that she stay in the Mt Maenalus core of Apple Eye-Isle … Did he really need to ask? He did anyhow.

"You've a message for me from my father, jinni?"

The angel grinned from ear to ear, whereupon his lower jaw dropped off, broken mouthpiece with it. He nevertheless continued trying to speak. His upper jaw thereupon fell off, tongue detaching from throat with it. Mithras promptly picked up both jaws, extracted the trumpet's mouthpiece and clipped them together. Tongue betwixt them, he rendered them leonine dentures, at which point they bit him.

This was not going well.

========

He shuddered hearing the faith-fanaticized throng thunder through the cave temple's external seal, screaming imprecations in their zealotry as they did so.

========

No question of it, he wouldn't have anywhere near enough time to literally draw to a close his rendition of Vatican Hill's ceiling. Already they were smashing their way through the Mithraeum's seven outer chambers toward him, he in its dead-end sanctorum, its Holy of Holies. By the time they were done, there wouldn't be enough left of it to warrant a return visit.

Damn that Damnasus to purple perdition anyhow – or to whatever shade his monotonous God coloured this Hell of his this week!

He wasn't a spiteful man, even if he was a deviant. His preferred payment was beer, cold if possible, a warm bed, shared or alone, and good fellowship. But he always made sure he got paid. Besides, his procreative imperative was twitching and he knew just the lovely lady who could satisfy its itch.

Jordan Q Tethys flipped back a few sheets of his splotch-pad, signed then dotted its pre-prepared drawing and made his getaway.

Leave the future for the future – and the Dual Entities. For him the present was what little was left of his daily allotment of a maximum thirty beers.

========

'Amen' either of them might have added; should either of them still be around.

****

THEO 3:

THE UNITY OF PANHARMONIUM

========

Year of the Dome 4376

The three-eyed entity solidifying in front of her was definitely a devil. Unjustifiably immortal, the corruptive seductress manifested herself between her and the irreparably damaged cosmicar perched on a plinth in the garden's hub. Inside that selfsame cosmicar, so many decades ago, Helena Somata had long distance sliced and diced her daughter and grandson telekinetically, as only a genuine, consensus-empowered Master could.

Initially a snare she'd effectively rendered an instant meat grinder, it served as their tomb as well as a reminder of their unforgivable disloyalty to the Utopia of Weir.

========

Helena materialized her pre-Earth eye-stave, her Master's Mace, off one of the witch-stones she wore as jewellery. She mentally activated the eyeorb atop it, causing it to open. Nothing happened this time either. Maybe her eye-stave manufactured duds. Maybe Bad Rhad was a Master Deva after all.

"That's not nice, Hel," the devil said. "Especially not after I came all this way to wish you the top of the season."

"Harmonia!"

The absolutely gorgeous, butterscotch-skinned devil didn't bother to nod. It was more an exclamation than a question anyhow. This was a known entity: a first-born, Thrygragos Lazareme's Unity of Harmony or Balance. They'd met many times in the past – albeit on neutral ground, not in her very own Weirdom – so Helena recognized her right away.

Antique Illuminaries had the Unity, one of three, as Datong Harmonia. Although Datong, meaning '*Great Harmony*', came from the Outer Earth Chinese, they reputedly did so in memory, pun probably intended, of the legendary daughter of Love and War, an obscure Mediterranean myth inspired by the Dual Entities in their second lifetime together, circa 2,000 years ago.

As if to offset her soft, finely featured face and long, dark, richly crinkly hair, she seemed covered neck to toe in glowingly golden chain mail underlain with a tanned, ankle-length chemise. Her broken chains, the bracelet-like manacles they extended from off her wrists, her scales-of-justice earrings and neck-torc, even her slippers, appeared to be fabricated out of the miraculous Godstuff her younger brother in Lazareme, Tvasitar Smithmonger as Illuminaries had him, used to make devils their talismans.

Alternatively called both Gypsium and Brainrock, many hypothesized it was all that remained of the primordial Godhead, from whence exploded the current cosmos. More pertinently, reputedly she was the first devil, other than him of course, for whom the Anvil Artificer, as devils had him, crafted a power focus – her neck-torc – that wasn't intended for a Great God or a Great Goddess.

That and that alone might explain how Harmonia could avoid instant imprisonment. Surely no devil had willpower stronger than the 40-years' Master of the Weirdom of Kanin City. Unless … "You're taking an awful risk coming here. I guess that means you aren't all here, doesn't it? You're wayfaring in the Wild Weird."

The devil, being a devil, could appear to be anything. She could also appear to be anywhere beneath the Dome. "Am I? If you say so then I must be. You are Kanin's Master."

Harmonia was smiling. Reputedly Helen of Troy, after whom Helena Somata may have been named, had a smile that launched a thousand ships, most of which sank. The Unity had a smile that could launch thousands more. Rephrase that, Helena mentally retracted, almost ashamed to have thought it in the first place. It was a load of figurative night soil; the sort of stinky sewer spillage son Georgie's poetical pals might spout.

Being a devil meant Harmonia had the potential to literally sink and raise ships just by smiling. Given their near-omnipotence within an environment of fervent, if not necessarily fanatical followers, it was a very good thing their grandfather, the Moloch Sedon, the solitary first generational devil – Satan, the Devil Himself, Helena believed – didn't allow devils to kill.

When they did – wilfully or just accidentally – he ill-starred or cathonitized them straightaway, thus rendering them stars in the night's sky, Cathonia, the Dome. Which was one reason it was also known as the Sedon Sphere; another being the entirety of Cathonia was composed of Sedon's essence. Since the debacle that was the Great Flood or Genesea of Genesis, cathonitization was as close as devils ever came to dying.

"Oh, I wouldn't think that if I were you," countered the devil.

"You're reading me."

"Could be I am. Could be I were you; as in I'm in you."

"Impossible."

"Oh, right. You're an Ant Nightingale. You're wearing agatine eyes. They protect you against devic possession. No matter. Top of the season anyhow."

"Thanks – and today's my birthday as well; not that you'd care. Or come anywhere near Kanin if you didn't want something more tangible than an expression of gratitude. You and I may never be on the same side but we've enough in common to join forces once in awhile. How dare you tempt me on my own turf? I should abolish you for foolhardiness alone. It'd serve you right."

"Didn't you just try?"

"Half-heartedly. There's another way to eliminate devils?"

"More than a few, as it happens. Cutting off their head's one, but then you have to dispose of it properly or they'll just screw it back on. But by far the most effective is to deprive them of worship. Which is also to say of worshippers. Which is the other reason I'm here."

Harmonia now looked so solid that the overhead firestone, on its obelisk, cast her shadow. Although, the Master supposed, that could be as much of a sending as the illusion of her physical presence.

"Congratulations, Helena. The absurd monotheism you and your pathetic pals propagate is working; at least it is beyond the Dome. Mithras is becoming so desperate for true believers he's challenging his two brothers for theirs. The Attis hasn't handpicked, then brought together, over in the Mole, two legions of his most reliable veterans for a hootenanny."

"A what?"

"A jamboree, a frolicsome spree replete with food, music, fun, and games."

"Like a birthday party."

"Just so. In fact he's intending to celebrate it on Mithramas, the upcoming Winter Solstice, his feast day. His Angelyc messengers delivered the invitations and both Thrygragos Byron and my own Lazareme-lazy Thrygragos of a devic daddy have agreed to attend it."

"With all your extant cousins and siblings in tow?"

"Along with the equivalent of two legions more for the gore of our own score," she fay-said in response. "It has the makings of rushing through a bonfire into a bloodbath."

Earthborn – and largely still Earth-loyal – faeries were far more inclined to bend knees, those that had them, to Lazaremists than they were to either Byronics or Mithradites, members of the other two devic tribes. Partially as repayment for the troublesome wights' modest attentions, though not for their sometimes highly immodest displays of affections; partially because they found it entertaining; Lazaremists like Harmonia tended to be prattle-prone to fay-saying.

"That doesn't sound very devic to me. Aren't you afraid that your odious grandfather will ill-star the lapdog lot of you?" Fay-saying was infectious.

"And leave the Headworld godless? Or, worse, leave it ripe for your preposterous brand of righteousness? Not a chance! As far as Sedon's concerned we devils are more than welcome to go at each other, as far as we're concerned as well. Victory over one leaves more adherents for the rest, elementary arithmetic that. The Attis has made a nearly 2500-year career out of sticking Master Devas, from all three tribes, into All of Incain on behalf of his devic daddy, Thrygragos Mithras."

"Now you're talking to the converted. Good for him, I say. If he weren't such a cold-blooded killer I'd kiss him on both cheeks for it. Actually, now that I think about it, there might be bits of both sets of his cheeks, top and bottom, floating around in there. Lend me your chains. I'll use them for a sieve. Want to watch?"

Unlike Trinondev eye-staves, anyone with any intelligence, anyone at all – you didn't even have to be flesh and blood – could use a Tvasitar Talisman. Save for one minor problem that arguably made them the most valuable objects on the entire Inner Earth, perhaps in the entire cosmos.

That problem? Other than devazurs and the occasional deviant, predominantly but not exclusively the Attis, they bit the hand that held them. Plus, they generally did so fatally, albeit only eventually. Much better for mortals to acquire then sell them to someone a whole lot richer and stupider.

Harmonia all but ignored the taunt. "Very funny, Master. As for our supporters, them going at each other in our names sums up the history of the Head, doesn't it? At least it has done pretty much since the time we devils started to mindfully gain individual solidity circa 2000 YD. But for far too long we've been stuck in a morass of uneventful stagnation; an unhealthy standoff, to put it another way."

"You look fairly healthy to me; make that unfairly healthy."

"I'm popular. I may not be as popular as my father but I'm way more popular than my two immediate brothers are outside their spheres of influence. That's because their worshippers worship me at the same time they worship either Order or Chaos."

"Because you keep them apart."

"Hey, it's preferable to watching television."

"To what?"

"To something I picked up from the Female Entity, like hootenanny and jamboree. I humanized her once, a long time ago. The Dual Entities are time-tumblers. Around and around they go in no particular order. They've been in the future as well as the past. Television's a machine, a kind of view screen with external inputs like the revelatory fumes coming out of Sister Metis's cauldron. You've a version of it on your cosmicars."

"So we do," Helena twigged. "Come to think of it, so do I. And so do you and most other devils. Only we call it far-sight."

"Your eyeorbs are ever-so-useful, aren't they?"

"That they are. Why risk a full-blown confrontation with the Mithradites? Under the yoke of Attis and his military forces they've been controlling the Upper Head for hundreds upon hundreds of years. And, from what I understand, they're finally making inroads into Lazaremist territories. Hasn't Dandset Typhon established an autonomous Mithradite region over in Wildwyck, an area that previously belonged to your Lord Order exclusively?"

"Autonomous is the key word, Master, though I prefer protectorate. There are plenty of de facto devic protectorates on the Head. The most recent, Geld Neargon's Androgynia, west of the Aural Sea, comes immediately to mind. So do such long-standing domains as Satanwyck, Mythland and Lathakra. None of them pay tribute to Attis and his Mithrant legionnaires. Indeed, the Thanatoids claim they direct their devotion straight to Sedon himself; that Mithras doesn't figure in their personal prayers whatsoever."

"They're firstborn, Harmonia, like you. Maybe they don't have to."

"Ask yourself this, Master: Why should they be the only ones? Why should there only be a few inviolable protectorates?"

"I'd rather ask you why you're really here?"

"Come on, Hel. You're the Master of Kanin City. You're its High Illuminary. You're an Ant Nightingale. Surely you can answer that yourself."

"Mockery gets you nowhere, Unity. Indulge me or I'll see how I do whole-heartedly."

"Got me quaking in my golden slippers now."

"Go away."

Harmonia ignored that as well. "Here's a juicy little chunk of dirt you might want to add to your Illuminaries' sump of whaledreck on devils. Consider it my birthday present. Attis and his legionnaires have never been strong enough to make much of a dent in our territories. The fact is Moorset and Androgynia operate under Order's auspices. So in that respect he's actually denting into their territories, not the other way around.

"Mithras is insatiable, though. For many hundreds of years he's been relying on his Outer Earth adherents to give him a leg up on his brothers, who don't have any adherents of their own beyond the Dome. Now that he's losing them at such an alarming rate, well, he's got to replace them somehow. And he's hoping to replace them in here, at our expense.

"Consequently he's finally decided to use his Great Godly prerogative to summon all his outstanding offspring to his side. He reckons their sheer numbers will tip the day's balance in his favour. His overconfidence is such that, in his conceit, he's already named it Thrygragon, as in gone, gone, gone his Thrygragos Brothers. We intend to ensure it becomes gone, gone, gone him alone. And you can assist us."

"You're right. I knew that was it. You want our extraterrestrial weaponry, the same as the Attis and his Mithrants have for centuries. Why should we favour one devic tribe over the other, even if it is two tribes against the other, as it seems to be this time? We'd rather see you slaughter each other, taking as many of your devotees with you as you can. The only way I'd authorize a foray against any of you is if it was the Moloch Sedon over there in the Mole."

"Because nearly 4400 years of being trapped beneath the Dome have left you Utopians so decrepit you've lost the wherewithal to repair, let alone recreate, anything you lose or wreck. And that includes your flying machines and their built-in munitions. You'll only have the one shot and, if you take it, you want to employ it against he who is above us all.

"You are clear to me, Master. You're as transparent as those Tantaluses in there containing the remnants of your daughter and grandson."

How did she know that, Helena had to wonder? Then she wondered if she had to wonder it because the Unity was indeed inside her making her wonder what she wanted her to wonder. Firstborns were almost as wonderfully powerful as their three fathers and solitary grandfather. Sometimes Helena wondered if the three surviving, firstborn females were already incarnations of the Trigregos Sisters.

"Yet that is precisely how you can assist us. For you see, assuming granddaddy isn't out already, visiting his Daddy Cabby up in Cabalarkon or holding court across the Zone of the Sleepers from it in Grand Elysium, he'll have to come out, come out over there, in the Gregarian Fields, if he wants Mithras to survive.

"Which he may or may not want but, hey, say he does, one word from him, to either of his two other sons, and they'll have to obey him. One word to any of us, from our fathers, and we'd have to obey them. That word is *'stop'*."

Master Helena knew where the Harmony Unity was going now. She liked it so much she as good as repeated it. "Sedon will have to come out of the sky in order to rescue Mithras. You want us to take him down when he shows up in the Mole because you're genetically incapable of disobeying your parents."

"Bang on the war drum, Hel!" The Lazaremist grinned even more vivaciously. "Except – listen to me, Master, this is important – as you've just alluded, only our solitary grandfather and fathers are left. Our mothers were abandoned on the Second Weirworld. You tear him to shreds, like you did them in there, and take what's left of him into your eyeorbs, your destiny is fulfilled. The Dome will collapse, one way or another the planet will be whole again, and you can go back to the stars. So can we."

"Unless you decide to reassert your polytheistic hegemony over the Whole Earth."

"Some of us may attempt to do just that, myself included. In the name of love, peace and harmony, it goes without saying. Paganism is good for the soul, especially when you can shake hands with your gods. Which is sort of funny considering Mithras claims to have invented handshakes. We take him out. You take out Sedon. Thrygragon Done becomes Panharmonium Won. Interested?"

"The devil is in the details, Harmonia."

"Then call me *'details'*, Helena."

She did. They spoke some more, this chilly, frosty night in mid Tantalar 4376. Helena Somata was stunned at the audacity of their plans, of the plans made by devils, many of them women, from all three tribes, evidently under the Unity's tutelage. Quite frankly she found it difficult to accept Mithras had left himself so vulnerable. She couldn't comprehend why he'd let something like that transpire.

"Because we've egged him on by appealing to his ego, the very thing versions of his mystery cult assert his upper level initiates have eliminated. Mithras fancies himself a rooster, a cock of the block. He believes he has accounted for every eventuality but so do we. We can counter anything he concocts."

"Not to mention turning him into an omelette."

"More like a scrambled ego." Harmonia finished detailing how they intended to make him stand still and take his reward for millennia of manipulative malfeasance, as she fay-said. It was Helena's turn to smile. It would work. "Of course it will. Unless Sedon comes to his rescue Mithras can't survive."

"Don't tell me you can read him as well."

"More like we know who's been reading to him."

"In bed, no doubt. I knew there had to be a hen involved. Celestial God Above Us All, Harmonia, you're so fucking shameless." Everyone who knew anything about the three Unities of Lazareme knew how she kept her two fellow, firstborn brothers mollified. She slept with them. Chaos or Order – Abaddon or Yajur, as Illuminaries named them – grew jealous of her sharing her lovemaking with one or the other, she slept with their mutual father and he'd order either/or to back off.

"Unless you're a closet Korant," the Unity retorted, fay-saying yet again, "Monogamy's for monotheists and mongooses, Master. You jump to your conclusions, you leave me to jump on my own chosen partners."

The Moloch Sedon first, you next, Helena silently resolved. Out loud she said: "So now you've accounted for every eventuality. Very well. You provide the Brainrock; I provide the far-sight, via our eyeorbs, the cosmicars and the Trinondevs to man them. You do, we'll roll out a bloody red carpet for the Devil the moment he pops up, or down, to save his favourite."

"Consider it done."

"So who has been reading to Mithras anyhow?"

"Who else? Your hen-pecked husband."

========

The assassin rumbled out of the Weird.
At least Helena presumed she was an assassin.

========

That she was a young Saur Tsarina was manifest. Her being an anthropomorphic stegosaur gave that away. Worse yet, she was a Sari Witch, had to be. Otherwise she couldn't have come off one of the witch-stones Helena habitually kept about her person even though Masters of Weir in their own Weirdom were, approximately, infinitely more powerful than any Ant Nightingale.

Worst of all, Stegs were always hungry. Plus, they were omnivorous.

Although reptilian, anthropomorphic Saurs did not have a dinosaur's size. Rarely more than 10-feet tall and maybe three or 400 pounds, they were nevertheless mammoth for a vaguely humanoid species. Stegs were still Stegs, though. The Sari Witch had double rows of cartilaginous plates or extruding disks running up and down her backbone. They culminated in a bulky, formidable tail tipped with what looked to be iron pitons but were presumably exceedingly sharp shards of bone.

She didn't wear much in the way of clothing. What did drape her seemed little more than strategically placed rags that might once have been an actual sari. There was no mistaking her gender. Feminine anthropomorphism required breasts, proportionately huge in her case.

As became instantly obvious, Helena was wrong about her motivations. The Steg hadn't come out of the Weird to assassinate her, not immediately anyhow. The young Saur Tsarina went straight for Harmonia. She might not have wanted to kill her. It could be she only intended to rip off her neck-torc and keep it for herself.

Harmonia looked momentarily shocked to see something that massive, that evidently ferocious, with all those teeth, barrelling at her as if from out of nowhere. Then she looked to be not there herself. The Steg thereupon somersaulted head over heels, head over tail as well, like a grotesque, improbable acrobat, only to come up nicely on her feet or hooves or paws. Master Helena was marvelling at her coordination when the Steg rounded on her, a third eye glaring in her forehead.

That had to mean the Unity was finally all there, albeit entirely inside the Saur Tsarina. Helena renewed her concentration on her Master's Mace – Trinondev eye-staves amounted to the Utopian equivalent of a devil's power focus. The eyeorb slotted atop it opened, a disembodied eyeball stretched out of it on prehensile filaments.

The third eye in the Steg's forehead bulged, whereupon it tore out of the Sari Witch and into the Master's prison pod. The orb promptly detonated, hurtling Helena onto her backside. Despite the dampness of the garden's ground, the Master was more muddled than muddied. She glanced up in time to witness the Steg being hoisted into the air, Brainrock manacles clamped onto her legs, arms, tail and neck.

Datong Harmonia reappeared, far more gargantuan than the Steg. The manacles extended from the ends of her chains. Showing off, the Unity briefly played puppeteer, the Tsarina her puppet. Helena's Mace was the oldest eye-stave in the world. It manufactured its own eyeorbs. A new orb replaced the one that blew apart, the Unity proving too much for it to contain.

In either disgust or boredom, Harmonia jerked the Steg bodily at Kanin's Master. Then she released her. Helena's instant gargoyle of the moment, an outrageously puffed-up grizzly, intervened between them, cushioning the Steg's fall and preventing her from crushing the Master beneath her. Harmonia enlarged herself the more. Now towering high above the walls of the garden, she beamed with the radiance of a golden moon.

"You better send hundreds of Trinondevs against Sedon, should he chance to pop by come Mithramas. Then you better pray they've stronger wills than you seem to have. Otherwise he'll flatten your Weirdom and every Utopian half-breed inside it. It wouldn't be the first time he did that either."

"Devils can't kill," Helena, unbowed, challenged right back at her.

"Wrong, Master. Sedon only forbids us killing potential adherents. We can, do, and will kill equals and never-believers. You Utopians qualify in the latter category. Bear that in mind instead of an overstuffed teddy bear. Besides, who's going to cathonitize grandfather? He is Cathonia!" That said Harmonia disappeared apparently for real this time.

"Classically unimaginative, devilish pomposity," Helena muttered to herself analytically, as if to preserve her dignity.

The unbound, at least outwardly dispossessed Steg proved as resilient as she was fit and coordinated. "Wow," she exclaimed, seemingly genuinely, as she helped Helena to her feet. "I had no idea devils could do that sort of thing. I especially had no idea they could do that sort of thing in a Weirdom."

"They can't," said the Master, chafing under the criticism. "My last husband, before he went away, used to say devils sacrificed creativity for immortality. But that was no common devil. That was a firstborn and there's nothing common about first-borns. Illuminaries believe their subtle matter bodies still contain the residue of Master Devas."

"As opposed to azuras," understood the Saurian. Master Devas were third generational; azuras were fourth generational. Thus far, nearly 2500 years after they started having azura offspring by each other, only Master Devas demonstrated the ability to reanimate de-brained, daemonic bodies and thereby render themselves solid, completely self-aware individuals.

"Her name's Datong Harmonia, by the way. She's a Lazaremist, the Unity of Balance as well as what she terms Panharmonium. What crazed you to go after her: bloodlust, misplaced loyalty, hunger, greed? Saurians are devil-worshippers. You should have known better."

"Just because we worship Mithradites, that doesn't make us as thick as our skulls. I went at her because I thought you were in trouble."

Helena felt abashed, embarrassed she'd initially thought the Steg might have been an assassin or after the Unity's power focus, no matter how valuable it was. "Well, thanks for trying anyhow. Me, I'd recommend you stay away from devils in the future. So, what are you doing here? Kanin City doesn't see many Saurs. More to the point, who are you?"

"You were late for your party. Georgie knew I was a witch so he sent me to fetch you. As for who I am, well, my first name's Saudi but Georgie made me promise not to tell you my last name. Your party's not a surprise but he's a band of surprises in store for you."

Despite the chunky, too-few digits and razor-sharp, too-long claws, her forepaws resembled humanoid hands. She dropped a glitz – as the Sari Sisterhood called their witch-stones, their glittery bits – at her feet. "Shall we go? Grab a paw. We'll have ourselves a fabulous entrance."

"Thank you, Saudi, but I'm perfectly capable of making my own way there. Besides, I prefer my entrances dignified. For me it's tomb-time first anyhow. Care to see what I did to my only daughter and her son 40-odd years ago?"

"Do I look like a seamstress?"

========

Tears shed, tomb-time terminated, Helena Somata accompanied Saudi the Steg Sari to her birthday party in the ever-expanding Masters Palace. There, amidst the trappings and cyclopean stonework of the huge hall, she ate heartily. She shuffled her feet appreciatively to the music Georgie's collective provided. She smiled and conversed cheerfully with the band members' mothers – albeit with the exception of Saudi's late mom, whom the Steg admitted she'd eaten, as was traditional amongst Saurs Tsars and Saur Tsarinas alike.

Content as she outwardly seemed, Kanin's Master of Weir nevertheless couldn't keep her eyes off the young man strumming on a lyre. More dark than light, he could pass for Georgie's visibly skinnier twin brother. Having noticed her interest in the lyrist, an amply proportioned Marutian woman with skin blacker than either of the lookalikes walked up to her.

Whereupon she announced, proudly and loudly, so she could be heard over the din the musicians were making: "That's my boy."

"And that's mine," Helena responded, indicating Georgie, who was gleefully tooting on his recorder when he wasn't quaffing from a mug of ale.

"Looks like he enjoys his suds."

"Like father, like son."

"Mine too. Everyone calls him Yeast. Chances are that's mine as well."

"The beer?"

"The beer. In that respect I'm like daughter, like mother, and like father, going back ten generations at least. We Pilsners have been brew masters for Mithrant legionnaires for so long they don't dare call a war unless we've first set up a booze-tent behind their encampment. You should try some. All the recipes we use were originally Utopian."

"As were you, and your ancestors, from the looks of you and your Yeast. Mixed-blood Utopians generally go either black or white the longer they stay away from a Weirdom."

"Unless they go striped. I'm Hopi by the way, of the Family Pilsner in case you missed that."

"I'm Helena, of the Family Somata. We keep our maiden names if not our maidenheads." She was trying to be clever. She wasn't succeeding.

"I know who you are, Master. When I was just a wee one, a mere babe sucking on my ma's nips, my parents set up their booze-tent a lot closer to Kanin City than mine is now, out in the Mole. Sadly, we had the opportunity to experience your vimanas in action firsthand."

"They're actually called cosmicars, Hopi. Vimanas were Edenite, prior to Humanity's Golden Age. Mind you, there are a lot of reasons why not just my Illuminaries think Edenites descended from wayward Utopians. The similarity between their flying vessels and ours, the fuel both use, is only one of them. Sadly, action firsthand – how old are you?"

"A little over 40. We Pilsners are so faraway from the teat of our extraterrestrial bloodline we haven't lived in a Weirdom for hundreds of years."

"Sadly, action firsthand?"

"Yes. Not to fret, Master. I've forgiven you. My daddy may have fried 40 years ago, when your predecessor – unless it was already you – decided to let loose your vimanas, or whatever you call them, and put our backyard tent-city to the torch, but I got yours instead. And he keeps coming back to me."

"You got my daddy?"

"Your old man."

"My father was slain by the Attis. A fine reward it was, too, after he spent all those years training him to become a Trinondev."

"Training your grandson, don't you mean?"

"All right, call it training my grandson if you prefer. I'm sorry about your father but what's it got to do with mine?"

"Not keeping up on your colloquialisms, are you? What's common parlance outside Kanin's obviously uncommon inside it. Take a good look around, Master. My Garden is blacker than most of the non-Utopian men here. But the troupe your proper Utopian boy's gathered to help celebrate your birthday – don't you think there's something more than familiar about them besides their love for my suds? Familiar as in familial?"

Georgie chose that moment to call a break. He approached Hopi and his mother hand in hand with a young Northerner, one of the troupe's fiddlers as well as featured singers. From the looks of her, the beauty – and she was beautiful, if scrawny, silvery blonde non-Utopians could count as beauties behind Kanin's walls – was still in her late teens. That made her about the same age as Hopi's Yeast, whom the brew master had also called Garden for some reason.

Spotting what, more so than who, was behind them, one mother snapped another mother an anxious glance. "By daddy and old man, Master," Hopi replied to Helena's unspoken query, "I mean your hubby. And mine! And hers!"

The 'her' in question, Helena had realized, was a Valkyrie. The shapely, even muscular, nicely preserved and therefore only vaguely older-looking woman following Georgie and the teenager had to be the latter's mother. Swan Maidens, minus a maid's claim to maidenhood, could still ride swan-psychopomps when they went to work.

Valkyries were choosers of the slain. They hailed from Valhalla, Hell's Halls, a Mithradite territory in the Head's north, within or just below the Mystic Mountain Range, Sedon's Crown. Helena didn't need an introduction. She didn't care what her given name happened to be. The Valkyrie's surname didn't matter either. Seeing her, the Master of Weir knew right away whom they, jointly, would shortly choose to slay.

Holy Matrimony, even on Sedon's Head, the Domain of All Devils, was a sacrament inviolable. And didn't Thrygragos Varuna Mithras, albeit through the Attis and his legionnaires, guarantee marital contracts? Might it be time to backtrack on the commitment she'd made to the Harmony Unity? Might be!

The Moloch Sedon could only cathonitize Master Devas, not Masters of Weir.

========

Year 725 Pre-Dome

In all the galaxies, in all the solar systems, and on all the worlds they'd encountered the Male Entity over the perhaps 200 millennia since devils such as he and the rest of the devic scouting party he led came into existence, Thrygragos Lazareme had never seen him as an impossibly mobile, if not altogether impossibly huge, granite atrocity with a lion's body. Yet that was what was galumphing at him over the sand dunes: a gigantic he-lion seemingly made of rock with the head of Heliosophos.

Luckily, if only because immortality did not ensure inedibility, Lazareme was stand-ing invisible between-space.

========

It had been just under a year since his father, their grandfather, deposited them on the planet's surface. Highly significantly he'd quickly learned its natives gave it a name: Earth. Amazingly, though hardly propitiously, the Dual Entities used the same name for their patently non-mythical birth world. Frustratingly, Lazareme had al-so discovered members of its globally present, always human, so-called *'rainbow class'* were impossible to possess.

While they constituted nowhere near a majority, their seven living patriarchs, who seemed to come from seven distinct human races, their invariably, dazzlingly at-tractive women and their similarly multiracial descendants didn't amount to a privileged few either. Furthermore, these ex-Edenites, as they still thought of themselves, were so technologically advanced they must have had considerable contact, in the howsoever-distant past, with space-faring Utopians from the First or Second Weir System.

Banes on planes – their generational ships, which were designed by the Mne-mosyne Machine after she split off from First Weir's Mother Machine during Helios's third lifetime – these Utopians somehow or other managed to track devils everywhere they went. Worse, once they found them, they with their ships-generated eye-staves, they plagued them even more successfully than the Dual Entities usually did.

The all but ubiquitous golden apples Earth's rainbow class ate didn't just render them impossible to possess. The fantastic fruit bestowed upon them phenomenally long lives compared to the planet's far more numerous primitives. Of these last, al-though sentient, if not always humanoid, from what Thrygragos Lazareme had gleaned none of them could digest the damn stuff. Still, their mere existence gave him hope. An anarchist at heart, he specialized in fomenting rebellions.

Of course, assuming it was the same world, none of this meant the time-tumblers were currently in residence. Nonetheless, Father Sedon wanted to be sure they weren't before he brought the Sedonshem downstairs from the planet's solitary moon for good. Which was bound to be bad for many of its inhabitants, since the best possible good for devils required them extending their unholy hegemony over everyone else.

Sure enough, they were; at least an improbably mobile, blocky and potentially belligerent behemoth bearing Helios's head was down here.

========

"Look," indicated the witch standing beside him between-space.

His firstborn daughter possessed her, an avowed, apparently self-determined-ly non-rainbow woman. At that time, as per most things devic courtesy of the Dual Entities, only he, Sedon himself, and his two, second generational brothers, Thrygra-gos Byron and Thrygragos Varuna Mithras, had personal names. His daughter went by the name of whomever she occupied. At present she controlled the intriguingly, Mother Earth worshipping *'naturalist'* calling herself Hecate.

He obliged her, them, the Hecate two-thing, and was stunned by what he be-held. Thumping straight at the male monstrosity was an almost equally enormous she-lion. Proportionately only slightly smaller than her male counterpart, the stone lioness had the face of the Female Entity, Miracle Memory, effectively chiselled onto her equivalent of a head. Not so bizarrely, given who was occupying her, the witch beside him sported much the same visage, albeit with a third eye.

They collided; the ground visibly shook, though neither he nor Hecate felt it in the Weird. Their courtship, if you could call it that, now that was weird: rough and tumble, bites and bellows, altogether reminiscent of real lions except pebbles not fur flew.

"Those are the sphinxes?"

"There are dozens of different kinds of sphinxes, dad. Those are Andy and Ginny, exactly as I told you. Rather, they're exactly as Hecate told you. Ready?"

"They're Mandroids. They have to be. I recognize the type and so should you, child."

"I do. They're constructs made mostly out of Stopstone, Brainrock's counterforce, mixed in with Brainrock itself. Weir's original Mother Machine manufactured them to house the spirits of psychically adept Utopians whose flesh and blood bodies were beyond reclamation. It was their answer to immortality."

"So you'll recall what she did once she realized we devils were out and about."

"She animated bestial bags of them with synthetic intelligences and set them loose to eat us. Which they did a very good job of doing."

"That's only because so many of your idiotic, later-born cousins and siblings thought to acquire physical bodies after supplanting Utopian intelligences."

"They did."

"Some did, sure, but most didn't. It was a classic ploy, a sucker punch until then without precedence. Talk about idiocy, even inbred imbeciles aren't that stupid. Mandroids are machines, girl. No matter what animates them, psychic soul-selves, dead Utopian adepts, devic or artificial intelligences, once she figured her Mandroids had most of us, Weir's ever-calculating Mother Machine shut them down. In effect she hardened ours, immobilized within hers, forevermore."

"And, from what you've also told me, you being Hecate, the sphinxes have already done a dick-dildo to your daemonic aristocracy."

"Andy did. And he didn't precisely do a dick-dildo, dad, or a dot-ditto for that matter. Earthborn daemons are bodies with minds but without souls. He devoured them bodily, physically, literally, absolutely."

"So you say."

"Hecate does as well. Devic oaths are inviolate."

"Sometimes, methinks, thou protests much too much."

"Hecate doesn't need to think. I have her, body, mind and soul."

"At the risk of repeating myself ..."

"Fay-faerie-fair enough, father. Listen to me. Ginny's a recent concretion, a matter of decades or a few centuries, no more. The Dual Entities have been around for over 700 years in this incarnation of theirs. He calls himself Alorus Ptah whilst she goes by Trishtar Thrae. Whatever names they're using, for those two longevity always begets lunacy."

"As well as psychic acuity?"

"You're not getting cold feet, are you? I shouldn't have to remind you Grandfather Sedon obliterated the main Mother Machine in Helios's third lifetime. And you're his firstborn, as I am yours. Besides, I thought we'd agreed to go for it."

"We did. And I'm as horny as you are. But ... Mandroids?"

"Hey, it's the shit that spatters. One little turd, so long as it's the right one, and we'll have Anti-Patriarch Cain's muck-mama back again. Trust me on this."

He did, shut his eyes and thought of Father Sedon as he transferred his consciousness into lion-sphinx-him just as she did a ditto, albeit first out of Hecate and then into lioness-sphinx-her.

========

Coitus climaxing furiously, Andy and Ginny, the Androsphinx and the Gynosphinx, went galumphing off, as close to paw in paw as was paw-possible. They left in their wake something of a sandstorm. Lazareme had got off, and got out, in time to see them go. He hadn't been eaten. Well, that was something. Ginny paused, dropped a load. Trailing behind them, beside him, the witch with him pooper-scooped it up.

"It's the wrong one, the king not the queen." Hecate growled, in her own snarl. His firstborn already back inside her, she bared a breast anyhow; let the little shit suckle. "He'll have to do."

"My daughter?"

"I'll keep her. You want her back; it may cost you your entire expeditionary team. Then again it may not."

"Hey," Mother Nature's manure-man, momentarily detaching its lips from Hecate's left nipple, demanded to know: **"Where was I?"**

"In heaven, honey," Hecate responded.

Thus Thrygragos Lazareme helped re-whelp Daemonicus.

========

Year of the Dome 4376

"Daydreaming, dad?"

"Still looks like night to me, Harmony."

"Night-dreaming, dad?"

"Put that way, I guess so."

"In my High Seat?"

"Seems so."

"Of us?"

"Of Andy and Ginny, yes."

"No wonder you're hard as a rock. Mind if I join you?"

"Why else am I here?"

"To hear how things went with Master Helena?"

"Besides that."

Horniness was only one reason third generational Master Devas, along with their three second generational fathers, were thought of as devil-gods on, in, above or below not just Sedon's Head.

****

THEO 4:

PANPIPES PLAYING PERTURBATION
========

Bilge bucketfuls of theological dogmatists had played or were playing prominent roles in Imperial Rome during the tumultuous latter half of the 44th Century of the Dome. Among the more noteworthy, Jordan Q Tethys included such perhaps understandably ignorant but, as far as he was concerned, unworthily respected demagogues like Eusebius, Jerome and Augustine, the anti-popes Felix and Ursinus, retroactive pope Liberius and his thus far official successor as Bishop of Rome, Damasus himself.

He listed Unitarian Arianism, Trinitarian Christianity, Gnosticism, Manicheism, Cave Mithraism, Pelagianism, and seemingly innumerable varieties of polytheistic paganism as just a few of the conflicting creeds stirring the chamber pot within the empire and its environs. Victory for European, Near Eastern and circum Middle Sea monotheism nonetheless looked to him a foregone conclusion late in this Year of the Dome 4376.

The Moloch Sedon raised Cathonia, the Cathonic Dome or Zone, out of his own essence, hence also the Sedon Sphere, in order to separate the Inner from the Outer Earth. 4376 YD therefore marked four thousand, three hundred and seventy-six years since the onset of the Genesea, the Great Flood of Genesis.

========

Outside Rome, in 4312 YD, Constantine Caesar had a portentous vision shortly before the Battle of Milvian Bridge. Despite being outnumbered four-to-one, his forces emerged from the cataclysmic clash triumphant. Some said that was because he was a superior general. However, his reputedly British-born mother Helen was among those who claimed her God granted him both his vision and subsequent triumph.

Facts or fables aside, Constantine definitely went on to establish the pre-eminence of the Church of Rome. For that reason, even though he didn't accept Church-sanctioned baptism until lying on his deathbed a quarter century after Milvian Bridge, many monotheists were already referring to him as *'the Great'*.

In that respect the Mithraist who set off the irreversible decline of Roman Mithraism was hardly the first. From what Tethys learned during his investigations on behalf of the Great God Mithras himself, Persian Mithraism began its ascent amongst Outer Earth militarists under Darius the Great, whereas it was the Macedonian, Alexander the Great, whose soldiers brought it west, into Europe and thence to Rome under the great Octavian, Caesar Augustus.

Bishop Damasus reached adulthood during Constantine's reign. Now a hale seventy, or thereabouts, he'd acquired quite a few claims to fame if not precisely greatness of his own.

For one, as near as Tethys could make out he was the first to usurp the Mithraic high priest's title of Pater Patrum, Papa or Pope for himself as well as, after revising history, for his predecessors and those to follow him. For two, he replaced Greek with Latin as the principal liturgical language of the still-struggling Church. For three, by emphasizing the Roman legacy of the martyrs Peter and Paul – who, and if only because of his birthplace in Tarsus, might himself have been an initiate in Mithraic mysteries – he declared the Celestial City the Apostolic See

Despite his advancing age, Damnasus – as Tethys labelled as well as libelled him – showed no signs of slowing down, neither during the day nor during the night. A worldly man for a bishop, he threw parties that delighted otherwise human satyrs and sybarites. Being a tremendous taleteller Tethys easily wangled invitations to a few.

It was at one of them he first heard the epithet some of his critics, monotheistic, polytheistic, henotheistic and atheistic alike, used to defame him: *'the ladies' eartickler'*. As he soon found out, ears were no more everything Damnasus tickled than his tongue was everything he employed when it came to the ladies; when it came to in or on them either.

Opportunely for Tethys, his interests were so wide ranging he neglected some of the littler things, like paying attention to individual humanity, his more sheepish flock as well as his considerable collection of concubines. He being such a busy bee bishop, the night Damnasus led the rabble that seized the cave-temple on Vatican Hill dedicated to Mitravaruna, Tethys seized on his absence to do some seizing of his own.

Actually, he'd protest, the word *'seizing'* carried with it too much in the way of stigma – as opposed to the stigmata so many zealots of a masochistic persuasion inflicted upon themselves in Rome – to precisely reflect what he in particular had been up to this past week. *'Wooing then doing'* was a far more appropriate phrase. He'd say and she'd agree, if she dared, their coupling was entirely voluntary.

Of course, should he be caught bagging the bishop's best babe, he might not be given the option to protest anything. Still, that was the truth of the matter. And being a professional storyteller he always told the truth, at least as far as he knew it. Beer-sodden as he was tonight, Xmas Eve as Xuthrodites had it, he also hoped it was a mutually pleasurable experience. It wasn't, well, come morning he was confident their next go-round would be.

Chance frowned but Fortune favoured. He was in the privy when Papa Damn returned to his hideaway, one of many, unexpectedly. Even more fortuitously he was as quick with the quill as he'd just been in the sack. Someday, he didn't doubt, he'd find out if Damasus had a son or a daughter named 'Gardenias'. Or whatever Jordan's equivalent was in Latin.

Tethys spoke the commonly understood tongue of Sedon Speak; pre-Babel Babble, as he often put it. The 'Q' stood for 'Quill'.

========

Taurus Chrysaor Attis rode a Pegasus-psychopomp between-space.

========

It was Mithramas morning; the very day his half-father decreed would go down in history as Thrygragon. On his back-winged horse, he materialized out of the Weird, the dark-grey Universal Substance of Samsara, of all there was, on the Prison Beach of Incain. All there visibly was its She-Sphinx, the self-proclaimed All Invincible.

Unlike her empty and consequently millennia-moribund male counterpart on the Outer Earth's Giza Plateau, the Gynosphinx had back-wings of her own. Also unlike the Androsphinx, she didn't have a man's face. Instead, she had that of a woman: that of the Female, not the Male Entity. Besides her protrusive, humanoid breasts, her modicum of intelligence, her vocal chords and her ability to more manufacture than mother many a monstrous Mandroid, yet another thing that differentiated the two enormous, not exactly stone-carved sphinxes was All had a third eye.

As he dismounted, it blinked. Attis's on and off lover for well over 2,000 years' worth of successions flickered out of it; made herself whole before him.

This perpetual presence was as myrionymous as he was, had perhaps even more names than he did. Privately, the Hidden Headworld's devic gods referred to her as Sedon's Whore. Utopian Illuminaries of Weir, who were born and bred to hate devils, began calling her Pyrame Silverstar long before they started giving names to the rest of her fellow, third generational Master Devas. Provided she didn't go tetrahedral-headed on him, Pyrame was fine with Attis.

A shape-shifter, like so many of the Head's uncanny populace, she presented herself deliberately enticingly. Darkish-skinned, as bodily beautiful as always, her Etocretan or Egyptian style sheathe dress left her splendid breasts bared. Her long, silvery hair glistened in the early morning light. When they were together she usually kept her third eye suppressed. Today, though, she let it glimmer in the centre of her forehead.

Devic eyefire could burn anything, but it was also coercive. If he balked at All's terms, she may have been planning to unleash it at him. He had no intention of balking. She said: "It'll still cost you two cohorts."

He feigned outrage: "A thousand of my best legionnaires! That will decimate my army."

"The She-Sphinx is as good at figures as you are, Chrysaor. Ten for one, that is the price she demands to release those you request."

"What'll I do with their bodies?"

"Don't be daft. Devils don't kill and neither does All. She requires only the azuras within them, not their lives."

"Azuras motivate many of my men. Rob them of their azuras and they might rebel. They rebel; the rest of my men might turn on them. It's our father's enemies we need be slaughtering, not our brothers-in-arms."

"If that's the case then you've raised a sorry excuse for an army."

"Two legions I've raised and brought with me to Sedon's Mole, 10 thousand men, almost all veterans. The Great Gods Byron and Lazareme can call on at least that many each. They lack our discipline and armaments, true, but they are no less loyal to their deities than my Mithrants are to our father."

Devils rarely acknowledged deviants as their siblings or cousins but Pyrame indulged him with merely a gentle reminder of that: "Your half-father."

"As you please."

"And as you don't," she dug somewhat deeper. "Admit it, lover, your army losing a thousand of its azuras isn't what troubles you. It's what you'll have to lose in order for father's Hundred to regain the fullness of their abilities."

All of Incain gurgled. Then she burped. Then she spat out Jordan Tethys.

========

Awe, reverential fear, dread mingled with veneration: comparatively commonplace stuff on a hidden continent that virtually everyone who dwelt on, in, above or below it knew was a hidden continent. Nonetheless, after a while there was something of the ho-hum about seeing an immortal god or goddess walking amongst you.

A Pegasus-psychopomp bearing a familiar, head-to-toe-armoured rider in front of an unfamiliar, for most, and apparently oppositely unarmed passenger flying out of the blue, even if was the grey of between-space? Yawn-inducing that. Seeing a gigantic, winged sphinx emerging behind Peg? That was so unusual it qualified as awe-inspiring.

How could something that size fly? And was she really made of stone?

========

Situated to the southeast of Sedon's Human Eye-Isle, roughly equidistant between it and Sedon's Ear, native Marutians called the Gregarian Fields the Mole of Sedon's Cheek. Hoop-shaped, hence the Mole bit, with a diameter of perhaps 200 miles at its widest, as part of the pre-Flood archipelago of Pacifica it had once been an island unto itself.

Evidently it had also been a sacred site because, rising everywhere you went in the Fields, you found barrows or burial mounds. All settled onto one of these man-made hillocks on the outskirts of the main Mithrant encampment. Fortunately, presumably intentionally as well, it was deserted.

On Peg, as he'd named his Pegasus in a moment void of inspiration, Attis circled above the nesting She-Sphinx for a dizzying minute or two. As he had since they emerged from the Weird, Tethys hung onto his belt for dear life. The Taurus guided Peg to ground and helped him down. They exchanged fare-thee-wells, promising to reconnect come sundown to pop some pills, as not just they referred to knocking back pilsner beers.

Tethys didn't have to recommend a place either. Attis knew where he'd be and, come what may, didn't expect him to wait until he got there. They both knew he'd be up to a minimum of 20 by then.

Peg flapped off, carrying the Taurus toward the Praetorium, his general headquarters in the midst of the Mithrants' characteristically organized, quadrangular camp. It wouldn't be the Attis's anymore, though. Tethys had spotted Thrygragos Varuna Mithras's Tholos-style tent, the Great God's pathetic excuse for a pavilion, from the air. It didn't have to look pathetic but Mithras was big on appearances and he'd been going through some serious downtime of late.

What was it he said the Male Entity diagnosed him as suffering from a couple of millennia ago? "Bipolar disorder," came an answer out of the air. Pyrame followed her vocalized assertion physically. Last night's frost and modest sprinkling of snow may or may not melt so she'd put on a woollen cloak. It had been almost as cold in Rome so he already wore something similar.

"Technically father's a manic-depressive. Me, I prefer to think of him as suffering from omnipotent anxiety. Althean witch-healers like your fauna friend, Pusan Wanderlust, treat it with drugs as uncomplicated as the element Lithium. While there's no reason the same thing or something like it wouldn't work on a Great God, Mithras enjoys wallowing in a psychosomatic mire too much to take anything."

"Were you in me or in All?" he asked her familiarly. Relatively speaking, though never in the Biblical sense, they'd known each other since not long after he'd first said hello to daylight and it didn't slap him in the face or on the rump.

"All. She's as thick as the Stoprock or Brainstone bricks that look to compose her. She'd have got lost without me."

"You're not going to go over and kiss your devil daddy's feet?"

"Not until my juniors make sure they're clean; between the toes, too. It's going to be quite the day. I hope you've brought extra splotch pads."

"Don't need them, do I? Got my devil daddy's Tvasitar Talisman, don't I?"

He tapped the faux-feather stuck into his Liberty Cap, which he'd drawn to himself, along with the rest of his clothing, despite having to leave Rome in a bishop-pricked hurry hours ago now. He hadn't left it behind because it was the cephalic symbol of free men across the Roman Empire. He had drawn it to himself because it was a convenient place to store his quill.

"And it makes its own," he added, rubbing the scar tissue in the centre of his forehead. It always itched when he was around devils. Pyrame didn't take offence.

"You don't approve of Thrygragon, do you?"

"Why bother asking? You're a mind-reader."

"Just making conversation."

"Got a half-grandfather, on both sides of the bed, who might be a Great God gone after this afternoon. What about you?"

"I'm Sedon's Whore, Jordy. For me there's only one devil and it's the Devil."

"Inflection noted. Would you tell me if the Dual Entities are back?"

"In other words, would I tell you if I'm humanizing the Mnemosyne Machine?"

"Doesn't she always single you out?"

"Do I look like Harmonia?"

"No, but you are a devil. You can look like anyone you damn well please."

"So can you."

"Only if I draw myself to look like someone else. You're not going to tell me, are you?"

"Only because I don't know. You think Helios has hold of Mithras again?"

"Quit telling me what I think, Pyrame. Mania means madness in my dictionary and I reckon Thrygragon is the act of a madman, not a Great God of Civil Society who's renowned for thinking sensibly. Odds are two to one your uncles and their highborn offspring are going to make molecular mincemeat out of Mr Myth in the Mole this afternoon. Yet you don't seem to care."

"Couldn't it be I can't care?"

"So they are back. Except she has you instead of you having her."

"The Mnemosyne Machine made All, right. But Mnemosyne, the Etocretan Moon Goddess, mothered the muses, also right. I can't recall their names but you'd probably agree that two or three of them were famously fabulous singers." Tethys couldn't recollect their names either. He was pretty sure there were nine of them, though, and that all were fabulously famous singers. What was she getting at?

"As we chat, ever-so-pleasantly, Taurus Attis is ordering his lieutenants to decimate their ranks, one for 10. Within a matter of minutes a thousand legionnaires are going to surround this mound. All's going to take out their azuras, releasing devils she's been holding for sometimes hundreds of years, sometimes for as many as a couple of thousand years. You know how she's going to pull it off?"

Ah, that was it. "I can hear her humming already, Pyrame."

"Then hear All sing and judge for yourself if I've Memory either way."

"You're going back inside her?"

"Brainstone may be the stuff of Samsara, Jordy, a concretion of Brainrock and Stopstone. But it imparts zilch in terms of brain function. All's a glorified Mandroid. That makes her about as bright as the new moon. She couldn't possibly remember the refrain by herself. Draw yourself up a chair, cousin. Sit back and enjoy the concert, so long as you can stand it."

"Sit it, don't you mean?"

"Always punning, aren't you?"

"And fay-saying future-speak. I'm a wordsmith just come from a home in Rome. I glean from Harmonia and thee, Pyrame."

========

They carried on amiably. He admired her quip-wittedness. She left him as soon as Attis's selected legionnaires started gathering en masse. Moments later the She-Sphinx puffed out her cheeks, expanding her chest even more disturbingly. The show about to begin, he drew himself to a decent sightline a couple of barrow mounds away before he drew himself a chair to sit in.

Splotch pad in lap, faux-feathery Brainrock quill with its transcendental Gypsium ink poised, he sought to do more than just enjoy the concert. Pyrame's inference aside, if not her inflection, he was no devil. He earned his livelihood.

All's song began melodiously enough, but it quickly degenerated into a caterwaul. In a way that wasn't surprising. Bodily, but for the size, wings, humanoid face and female features lower down, the She-Sphinx did resemble a cat, a lioness. Then, having been in fairyland futilely questing for any trace of his ever wayward, but by now presumably irretrievably lost, devic half-father, Rumour of Lazareme, her song began to sound scarily familiar.

While there were an appalling amount of fairylands in, on, above or below not just the Hidden Continent of Sedon's Head, All wasn't caterwauling. She was yowling like a banshee. To fay-say, which he was woefully wont to do; it was a tune that tolled tomb. The question was for whom? For a Great God, for two, for all three of them, or for the thousands of soldiers who would spray out their arteries and drain their veins as palpitating pawns in their power play?

There'd be scads of scarlet sketches made today, he felt sure. It'd be thirsty work.

========

Tethys knew he was much more than any run-of-the-mill taleteller. Sooth said, which he always strived to do, he fancied himself more than the Headworld's unofficial historian. He was raconteur. He was reporter. He was recorder. He sketched whenever and wherever he watched his-story, or her-story, unfold. Or collapse, as history might do today. Oh for the glory days, eh? When men were men, women were women, and life was long because apples were golden.

All was doing her exhalation-inhalation routine over there, squalling as if there was no tomorrow, which there may not be. As much as the She-Sphinx could be enjoying a satisfying meal, her doing so didn't provide him a visual feast. Although he knew what she was up to, the devils coming out of her were as invisible as the 10-times azuras going into her. Graphic artistry required vision but, with or without a musical score, it also required visibility.

Oh, he'd take liberties. He always did. He was mostly a Lazaremist. Clearly it was past time for his initial guzzles of clarity. Beer for him was the incredible thinking fluid. In order to facilitate the process of deciding how best to creatively show her taking azuras in and sending devils out, he had to first slake his thirst. Inspiration for depiction would ensue.

Even though he'd ridden to the Mole behind the Mithrants' Taurus, travelling between-space always left him feeling parched. Then again the mere act of breathing dehydrated Tethys. No one on the Head produced a finer pilsner than his wife and nor should they. After all, which was moderately humorous considering how he got tongue-tugged from one side of the Dome to the other; Pilsner was Hopi's maiden name.

Her booze-tent was somewhere out there in the vast, pell-mell sprawl of hangers-on peddling their wares, hardly all of which were liquid, beyond the legions' almost as massive but precisely laid-out encampment. To get to it he didn't have to ask directions or even walk.

He was also better off than psycho-riders such as the Attis, who actually had to have a sort of psychic rapport with their psychopomps – hence, at least in part, the mnemonic, psyche-prompt. They first had to envisage, with their mind's eye, geographical highlights of where they wanted to go. Only then could their beasts transport them to it between-space. Tethys getting himself to Hopi's booze-tent was as effortless as drawing himself there.

Long ago her ancestors began to design their booze-tents in the form of a beer barrel or keg. With their round shapes and domed roofs they bore a striking resemblance to the beehive temples so prevalent up and down Theopolis Hill over on Apple Isle, Sedon's Human Eye-Isle on a map of the Hidden Headworld.

Although it had been many a moon since he'd seen her and their children, he didn't think she'd have altered it much. He splotched a drawing of it out of his quill onto his sketchpad and, sure enough, the background began filling in right away. A squiggled signature and a dot later, he materialized outside it.

========
What fresh hell was that tethered to the hitching rail?
========

First look said Mandroid. Second look said, no, altogether alive that hell. Possession wasn't what animated the undeniable oddity. Third look said dumb as they come. It wasn't a faerie perversion. Plus, it was too docile to be daemon or demon, agathodaemon or cacodemon: the former being more indifferent than benevolent whilst the latter was a man-eater. That must make it a domesticated animal, but what kind?

Size-wise, albeit only from a distance, it might pass for a stumpy but thickset deer, mule, jackass, or dwarf donkey. Except, how do you account for the furry-looking, tightly matted, black feathers and crow's head? And what's with the wings: dinky ones on either side of its four upper hooves or fetlocks and stunted ones sprouting out of its shoulders like that of an immature or diseased Pegasus or hippogriff?

There was nothing else for it. He plucked quill from cap yet again, splotched out his splotch pad and set to sketching.

Something nagged at him and it had nothing to do with wondering whether the hotchpotch beastie was a nag. The music coming from Hopi's booze-tent wasn't helping him concentrate. The sound of someone playing panpipes made the scar tissue in the centre of his forehead itch even more than it did when he was in the vicinity of devils. While, having just come from witnessing All at work, he knew the Mole was positively cancerous with Mithradites, this was far worse.

As if to go with the spooky sounding panpipes and the almighty itchiness he was already experiencing, blood blockages banging brain-boggling bongos picked up the tempo. Itching unbearable, headache throbbing up a thrombosis, panic rooted, frightening him almost heart attack apoplectic. Dread means dead. He detested the dance macabre.

Abruptly, with Tethys verging on plunging the nib of devilish daddy's talisman through his numbskull, thus instantly quill-killing him, the pernicious piping died down without him dying. Talk about wish fulfillment – an attribute of his devic half-mother, Titanic Metis – he could think straight again. Blessed relief, even he couldn't draw silence.

Many folks found the sound of panpipes as soothingly agreeable as he found it irritating to the precipice of suicidal. He couldn't recall them making him quite so unaccountably fearful and almightily itchy before but, lamely rationalizing his thankfully non-piss-pant reaction to what he'd just endured, perhaps that's because they also made him forgetful.

Taxonomically the cud-creature had to be related to a ravendeer, the very specie Sedon charged Mithras, via the Attis, to extirpate unto extinction after the Fall of Lucifer some 2,000 years earlier. Pyrame mentioning she didn't look anything like Harmony should have triggered the mnemonic he needed to twig his recognition of its heritage.

Which was also kind of funny. He was a regular laugh riot today, wasn't he?

========

He had never come across either of the Dual Entities, the Male and Female Principals, as some accounted them. However, everyone knew that, whenever a devil humanized Machine-Memory, she could pass for a two-eyed ringer of the female Unity, minus the chain fetishes.

In defiance of their Grandfather Sedon, and probably their Father Lazareme as well, her brood brother, the drunkard of the two, Unholy Abaddon, kept a herd of ravendeer in the Cattail Peninsula's Whiplash Range. Chaos did that sort of thing just because he was Chaos.

Those same two millennia ago, in what could have been his first lifetime – but, from what Tethys understood, could have as easily been his second lifetime – the Male Entity nearly disposed of the Moloch Sedon. From all reports he did so without even knowing Sedon existed, let alone that he'd helped create him. Which was why it could have been either his first or second lifetimes. According to their self-promulgated chronology, they didn't consciously encounter devils until his third lifetime.

Whichever lifetime it was, the Male Entity spent most of it as Cadmus Agenorid, the supposedly Phoenician-born prince who became the King-Founder of Grecian Thebes. After surviving heroic adventures that rivalled anything the Attis, under any name, lived through almost as often as he didn't, he took to wife a demigoddess by the name of Harmonia.

Ostensibly the daughter of War and Peace, this Harmonia was in truth none other than the Unity of Balance herself. Contrary to the once popular Theban, as well as the related Cretan cycle of myths regarding the pair, she didn't give up her divinity in order to marry him. Rather, because he was aging and therefore dying, whereas she wasn't, she somehow gifted him a form of immortality, an apotheosis of sorts. Thus in effect exalted or ascended, King Cadmus assumed the name he'd gone by ever since: Heliosophos, Helios called Sophos the Wise.

Until then always harmoniously inclined, she brought him beneath the Dome to attend a get-together sponsored by Thrygragos Varuna Mithras in his capacity as peacemaker. As remained so today, it was nominally his Age. Except again, it turned out Mithras was in one of his longest lasting, memory robbing funks at the time.

It therefore wasn't Mithras Harmony took Helios to meet; to meet again, rather, since, five centuries earlier, during his seventh lifetime, the time-tumbler and Mithras were literally inseparable. It was a highborn Mithradite masquerading as his father.

Well after the fact, much later-on Illuminaries named him Domdaniel. Devils of the era referred to him by his attribute, which was pride. For the better part of those same five centuries, Pride had reigned as Satanwyck's first Prime Sinistral. That made him the Sedon-designated, earthbound ruler of earthborn daemons: demons and faeries both. That therefore made him Sedon's viceroy.

Realizing immediately not so much who Helios-Cadmus was as whom he'd become – Heliosophos, one of Sedon's co-creators come his fifth lifetime – Sinistral Pride promptly possessed him, whereupon he ever-so-appropriately assumed the appellation of Lucifer the Light Bringer. Not content playing second fiddle to Sedon, at least among demons, the Luciferian joint-being attempted to effect a reordering of the Head's status quo as drastic as that which Mithras was planning to mastermind today.

It was a highly significant episode, one that had approaching apocalyptic ramifications on both sides of the Dome. They entailed an equally convoluted sequence of events. The taleteller had read, then stashed, a number of tee-tee tails recounting various aspects of what Sedon ended up judging, rightly or wrongly, a mass-murderous, albeit alcohol-fuelled, catastrophe.

Mithras's Midsummer may never have seen Mithras's Pride dimly shining down on the Hidden Headworld before he too was upstairs doing a ditto. And that's where they both remained: ill-starred, mass murderers stuck within the Mithradic quadrant of the night's sky. Indeed, they shone so close to each other they could probably converse without psychically shouting.

Tethys pulled off his Liberty Cap and fingered the ridges on some of the tee-tee tails he had glued to his scalp with their own ichors. Nope, he couldn't lay a hand on any of them there. He did recall a couple of suggestive titles for the epical affair, though. Since the mainstays of Lucifer's uprising were soulless heaps of shape-shifting, Mother Earth-faithful, chthonic creatures supportive of the *'bigger is better'* theory of intimidation, perhaps the most common was Gigantomachy.

However, because of the manner by which it literally ended so badly for Pride, not all that long after he got hold of Helios, another term for it was the Fall of Lucifer. Given the way the mishmash critter, chewing its cud, kept looking at him so dejectedly, that struck him as the most suitable for this moment and this place.

Mithras was mindfully elsewhere. Attis had been an early casualty of the Gigantomachy thus far without succession. Due to the ability of the Luciferian army to traverse the Weird as if foxes into a henhouse with an open door policy, the other Great Gods, Unmoving Byron and Lackland Lazareme, were sorely pressed. It consequently fell to the Moloch Sedon to descend to the rescue.

He being every daemon's acknowledged lord and master since Ragnarok, which occurred a couple of hundred years pre-Dome, what other choice did he have? He had to come downstairs to deal with his arrogantly deluded, seconded subjects' revolt. It was precisely what Lucifer was waiting for – in fact he, Helios and Pride simultaneously, was waiting for him right here in the Mole.

As soon as Dark Sedon showed up corporeally incarnadine, quadruple-tined pitchfork in hand, the joint-being led the charge of a demonic cavalry against him every which way there could be, given Samsara's universal substantiality. Uniformly, as well as ubiquitously, their mounts consisted of raven-headed psychopomps with talarial wings and scintillant mono-horns that could ill-star or cathonitize devils.

That they could cathonitize devils was a reality. It was also a redundancy. The mighty Moloch already was Cathonia. Sedon nevertheless seemingly gone for the duration, the raven-buck the two-in-one Lucifer rode reared victoriously. It thereby bucked him off, hence the Fall of Lucifer.

Harry the Horsy Harrier, that's what Lucifer nicknamed him. Hairy the Cacodemon Impaler would have been more apropos. The disloyal steed drove his unicorn-like horn into their combined chest. Helios died, whereupon he either randomly tumbled into the space-time continuum for the first time or went back into it for the second time.

Unless he somehow got away between-space, that is. Which he might have, albeit not for long since Harmonia claimed to have killed that Hel-him and Sedon didn't cathonitize her for it. Whatever the case, at the moment of his death, Harmonia, then on the Outer Earth island of Strongyne, would have instantaneously lost his Memory.

She would have also lost her sanity, howsoever momentarily in terms of devic longevity. And she did. Nihilism personified as Nemesis, a solitary Female Fury, for a while she challenged Divine Coueranna, Myrionymous Kore, Mithras's jilted ex from the zodiacal Age of Taurus, for the dubious honorific of maddest of the man-hating mad goddesses.

Sinistral Pride joined Dark Sedon up top, a deliberately kept luminescence-suppressed star in the night's sky to this day – better make that to last night or tonight. Once Thrygragos Varuna Mithras regained his subliminal equilibrium and Chrysaor Attis succeeded himself, the first task Sedon set them both was to hunt mono-horned ravendeer to extinction.

Chaos, whom Tethys found far more companionable than Lord Yajur, as Illuminaries named the Unity of Order, claimed he wasn't being contrary just because he kept a herd of non-mono-horned ravendeer in the Cattail. He hunted them still, didn't he?

========

The one time Tethys met the Moloch Sedon, in his Grand Elysium pyramid, the Entities' Satan admitted he'd been chortling about Pride's fate next to non-stop since his fall. As Sedon himself stated, he was the only one who ever won a Sedonplay.

Tethys might not like it but he couldn't contest it.

========

Disquiet returned.

The critter made him nervous. Was it a phobic phantasm given flesh? What if it was? Creatures of nightmare didn't just make an intangible home in his head. They proliferated tangibly throughout the Hidden Headworld. Besides, it was tied up and didn't have a horn. So that couldn't be all of it. Unlike the tee-tee tails stuck to his scalp, he couldn't put a finger on what the rest of it was, though.

Maybe, minus a panpipe, with the lead instrumentation having been taken up by someone tooting on a recorder or wooden flute, the music still emitting from Hopi's booze-tent continued to affect him adversely. Maybe the ghastly banshee wail the She-Sphinx had been screeching upset him yet.

As long or as often as he lived he'd never comprehend soldiers. Sure, from the moment the first pointed stick was invented anyone with any sense sharpened one for his or herself. But what made fighters sure they had a soul capable of transmigration anyhow? Whatever happened to the notion of just saying no? What if they called a war and nobody came? Besides, getting killed hurt like hell in Kore's dogcart.

For most of 700 years, ever since Alexander of Macedonia conquered Persia, the exclusively male armies in and around the Middle Sea prayed to the Great God Mithras. While, as he'd just verified firsthand, that was no longer the case beyond the Dome, on the Inner Earth well in excess of half its organized soldiery still did. Indeed, something like half its sentient population, hardly all of who were human, let alone males or soldiers, did too.

As for whether the Head's Mithras and the various Outer Earth deities of the same or similar names were identical, Tethys never committed one way or the other. Religion and reason rarely walked hand-in-hand and, over the years, he'd learned the hard way to avoid suchlike controversies.

He didn't approve of Thrygragon. He told the Great God that many times face to face, in no uncertain terms and to no discernible effect. That hadn't prevented them from howsoever hypothetically discussing it in detail, and at length, over and over again. He and Mithras were pals, drinking buddies, even though he'd never seen the Great God consume anything stronger than honeyed water. Mead it wasn't.

They'd whiled away many mainly pleasant hours, he quaffing his daily 30-beer allotment of Mithras's barely passable suds, atop his Mithradium, Theopolis Hill's uppermost Tholos and the Whole Earth's indisputably original Mithraeum. The last time they parted company he'd left it as he entered it, as Mithras's friend. So that couldn't be what was gnawing at him.

Sketch done, he slurped his splotch pad back into the nib of his feathery quill. He did so mostly mentally, just as the Attis would do any of his trophy power foci into his kibisis or bottomless bag, itself arguably a devic talisman. After returning his quill to its Liberty Cap resting place, he mussed his hair reflectively. More like his tee-tee tail hair-plugs, he scoffed to himself self-deprecatingly, since he didn't have much hair left of his own.

It not being a thinking cap he put it back on, hauling its extremities down as tightly over his ears as they'd go without tearing. It was cold up here in the Mole, much colder than Rome, he decided. Not being otherwise psychic, he nonetheless gave Hopi's tent more than just a cursory once-over visually.

Whoa! Was that it, what was making him so anxious? Not his hair, Tholoi, and not the one atop Mithras's Mithradium either!

What was he thinking on his way here from the Prison Beach between-space? Crete, that was it. Hopi's tent reminded him of a Tholos and Crete, more so than any other place except maybe Anatolia, in its then contemporaneous, but just as long gone centuries of Hittite dominance, was speckled with Tholoi.

Seeing Pyrame and Attis reunited reminded him they hadn't always been together. They especially hadn't been together as lovers on Crete circa 2000 YD, which was about when the Attis was born for the first and, in a manner of speaking, only time. That was also among the last times Silver Star Pyrame admitted living together with Dark Star Sedon as if they were contractually bound to fidelity as husband and wife.

Minutiae fascinated Mithras almost as much as his blackouts frustrated Tethys. Fine, the Great God couldn't aid his inquiries into the Unnameable because he was still on the Moon in 725 PD. But, nowhere near so fine, the blanks in his memory rendered him next-to-useless when it came to filling in the worrying gaps so many of Tethys's telltale tee-tee tails had with respect to tales that tactilely seemed to be about Mithras.

The 500 years of the mad goddesses' Middle Sea matriarchate, and the 500 years of Etocretan ethno-history paralleling it, was one of the most curious. It coincided with Mithras's longest lasting, demonstrable bout of bipolar dysfunction. Could bi-polarity be contagious? Could she have actually been living with Mithras? And, if so, how could he have forgotten it?

Tethys loved women. He loved women even when he was a woman. Harmo-ny requited desire for a select few; Pyrame did too, when she was one of two halves. They were interested in him; he had a coin with the head of either/or on either side. They agreed to requite his desire for or/either whichever side flipped up; he'd die and go to heaven. No further requisition required!

What else? Presage it! Sedon's commonest guise – the mighty Eye-Mouth in the sky preferred to appear as a satyr-sort when he was down here rubbing substantial shoulders with the unwashed and non-shiny. What instrument did satyrs play? Pan-pipes answered that. Most devils enjoyed his company. One devil definitely didn't, the only devil that could get away with killing because no one else had the where-withal to punish him.

Of course Sedon didn't just look or play like a satyr. He imbibed like one too. So, was the Devil himself down here, piping up a fear fraught sonic storm for com-plimentary samples of his wife's pills? Was Friend Fortune – Lady Luck being anoth-er of that highborn Lazaremist's most common appellations – favouring him with a last ditch way out, as she had last night? Was Friend Mithras presenting him some sort of presentiment?

He did a goose and had a gander skywards. It was impossible to tell. Sedon was a dark star during the day. Tethys couldn't deny the warning signals were there, though. Or could he? Be Apollonian, not Dionysian, Mithras always advised him. Try thinking rationally, he rephrased said freely afforded advice for his own better comprehension.

No one was playing panpipes anymore. Someone was playing a recorder. Maybe that's what he'd been hearing all along. Maybe Hopi had their eldest with her. She'd insisted on naming him, a boy who must be in his late teens or early twenties by now, Garden rather than Jordan because a Jordan was a chamber pot in Marutia. Everyone else called him Yeast. He strummed a lyre, but he attracted musicians wherever he roamed. Tethys being a lifelong recorder, maybe someone honking on its homonym had served to over-stimulate his little grey alarm cells.

Bugger premonitions to perdition! They were pedestrian, predatory to positivism and, purely to provide a proper perspective, preposterous. Worst of all, they were predictable. His devic half-mother was Titanic Metis, Wisdom of Lazareme. Metis didn't claim prescience, a faculty for divining advanced knowledge, but she'd taught him to go with his gut.

Right now his gut told him he was so skittish because he was going through withdrawal symptoms and needed to take his medicine. Tethys prayed, though not to the mighty Eye-Mouth possibly no longer entirely in the sky, that if he was down here and that had been him in there, the Devil left some pills for him to pop.

The immediate prospect of beer number one calmed him down immeasurably.

========

Jordan 'Quill' Tethys flipped the booze-tent's flap open, stepped inside it and stopped stone cold motionless. It wasn't that cold in the Mole. Nor was it because someone was pointing the Unnameable's severed head at him. No one did; no one could. It was in Attis's kibisis. It wasn't because Sedon was there either, if he ever had been.

He recognized plenty of others, though. Tholos might mean beehive, but he'd just entered a hornets' nest.

****

THEO 5:

THE VAM ENTITY

========

"Daydreaming, dad?"

*Thrygragos Everyman opened his three no doubt bloodshot eyes wearily. He regard-
ed his firstborn daughter blearily. She regarded him, what, warily? Or was that just how
he saw her, drearily? The girl could be such a scold.*

*It felt as icy cold as the northernmost taper of Tantal Thanatos's Lathakra, Sedon's
Horn, always did. Except it was the Gregarian Fields, Sedon's Mole, on Midwinter Day,
the day of the solstice. That much he could recall. Who in this frozen hell had he and Abe
been popping pills with last night anyhow?*

She was right, though. The sun was awfully bright, emphasis on awful.

"So it seems."

========

Thrygragos Varuna Mithras, Light of the World, Sun of Righteousness, Sol Invictus, was a god as old as the Vedic Aditya, as ancient as Sumer; older in fact, much
older, pre-Earth old. No longer a beaming sky-king with the face of the sun, the hair
of its rays and the horns of the crescent moon, he'd fallen so far from the zenith of
his majesty he'd convinced himself he'd reached its nadir. Unless it was into his grave,
which would be an embarrassing and probably impossible feat for an immortal, he
couldn't go any lower.

Depressingly saturnine – in the sense of being grave or morose, rather than vi-
brantly Saturnian, in the sense of being carefree, at the pinnacle of his powers – he was

pale, ashen. His brows furrowed. He wore the threadbare black robes of a perpetual penitent. His beard, once as pristine as sunshine, was shaggy, unkempt, dusted with age and as grey as the Weird itself. Everything about him said leaden.

Today, Mithramas, his feast day, he was heavy with the burden of time instead of buoyant with the assurance of timelessness. He sat in the gloom, on an ordinary wooden chair, with only an ordinary stick candle, on an ordinary wooden table, to light a relatively large but otherwise ordinary canvas tent. He was the Great God of Ordinariness, if not exactly of futility.

A glass and a pitcher of fresh spring water were the only other things on the table in front of him. No one else was there. Then someone else was: "Father?"

Mithras raised his head. The speaker entering his tent unbidden was a near giant, six and a half feet tall and almost as broad as he was wide. Not an inch of his skin was visible. Metal-plated gauntlets, ones with raised knobs on their knuckles and topsides, covered his hands. A fearsome war mask hid his face. From the top of his head to the tip of his toes, a hooded, multi-coloured cloak obscured the rest of his body.

The cloak was cinched around his waist by a belt that seemed to be constructed from human vertebrae. From his right shoulder hung a satchel or single-pouched saddlebag that held much more than would seem outwardly possible. Strapped to his right side a scabbard contained the standard sabre of a legionnaire officer. It had a P-shaped grip and an X-shaped guard.

The mask was hinged onto a Hellene helmet reminiscent of an ancient gorgoneion. Fringed by long spikes and plumed with the garuda-like feathers of a female sphinx, it protected his entire head. In addition to a pair of boggle-eyes and a protrusive tongue, the mask featured two long horns like those of a bull and the gruesome caricature of a boar-demon's head complete with up-turned tusks.

Looped around his neck was a circlet inlaid with glowing rubies or fully red bloodstones from which depended a blazingly golden sun-shape embossed with a lion's head. Strapped to his right arm was a shield burnished to a mirror's sheen. In his left hand he held a slender yet solid, metallic javelin pointed at either end.

His hooded garment had so many colours to it the fabric itself might have been fashioned out of stars forged in the night's sky. The Great God didn't need his devic eye to know that, underneath it, his remarkable child was wearing a tunic made from the hide of an enchanted elephant or some such near-impervious beast, a front and back plastron, greaves and talarial winged sandals.

His every shred of clothing, every ornament and armament he had, shimmered with Brainrock. They were devic talismans won in single combat, the spoils of glorious battle against undying foes. To Attis, his legions' Taurus or Boss Bull for more than half his latest succession, victory and defeat were meaningless concepts. Dead or alive, he would survive: He, Chrysaor, the *'Golden Sword'*, the Universal Soldier.

Mithras said nothing.

========

Realizing belatedly the gravity of the mistake he'd just made Attis vanished his regalia. Regardless of whether there were negotiations to attend, even a universal soldier dared not enter the presence of the Great God of truth, light, justice, covenants, civil society, freewill, and so much more, accoutered as he had.

Barefaced, clad only in a plain cotton tunic and ordinary sandals, with a red, Phrygian cap on his head, Attis snapped to attention. He stood silently, unwavering, respectfully – he hoped – maintaining eye contact with the Great God. A distance across the tent, he at his ordinary table, Mithras still did not speak. Nor did he avert his eyes, either in disinterest or in disdain. Did the third one just spark? What was wrong now?

Attis's skin glistened golden-brown. There was nothing he could do about that. It was no illusion. He wasn't a witch or a wizard. But neither should there be any surprise about it. A hero's skin should always gleam such. Icons he'd seen of champions such as Adonis, Perseus, Bellerophon, Achilles and Romulus; of non-Constantine Greats such as Darius and Alexander; indeed, of Mithras himself: Didn't they all have golden-brown skin? They did!

So did renditions of statuary, mosaics and paintings depicting them, as prepared either in here, from his sketches, or on the Outer Earth by that recurring deviant, the Legendarian, whose artistic abilities were among the most legendary things about him. And as they should as well: Attis had been all of them, and many more besides them, in their day.

He tried again: "Apologies, sire. I came in haste from Incain and did not think to change before rushing in to bring you my good news."

Nothing! He doffed his cap. Still nothing! Stifling a sigh he went down on one knee and lowered his head. Focussing on the tent's canvas flooring, he began counting off the seconds. His devic father wouldn't make him go for the full face and belly abasement routine, would he?

He'd reached thirty, half a minute, before Mithras deigned to speak. "Arise, my son."

Attis did so, smartly coming to attention again. However, he resisted the impulse to hail Mithras with the empty-handed, single-outstretched-arm salute his legionnaires accorded him as their Taurus. His half-father would realize he'd only vanished his regalia, that he could rematerialize it instantly, and that therefore he was still in his presence armed and armoured.

It was too late to pray his latest succession had been born at least in part with the blood or skin of a daemonic salamander. How hot would the eyefire blaze?

========

It was coming back to him, painfully.

========

He, Thrygragos Lazareme, the Lackland Libertine, and Harmony's fellow triplet, Unholy Abaddon, the Unity of Chaos, had really tied one on last night. Harmony might have as well, though not Lord Yajur, as Illuminaries had named Order after his vajra thunderbolts. Yajur was simply too orderly to let himself get disorderly.

In two-eyed human forms they'd gone to this big, barrel-shaped booze-tent beyond the Mithrants' military camp. Harmony had set it up, so he and his Unities weren't the only devils there. Musicians played raucous dance tunes competently well. They popped kegs of pilsner beer like pill bottles and downed them like it was good for them.

Fun, frivolity and frolicsome fellowship abounded on the eve of Thrygragon. Son drank father under the table. Lazareme felt what he was lying on. It was the table. He wondered if Abe had bothered to pay for it or just up and took it, him on it, to the encampment of Chaos's Cattail Irregulars, where Harmony had just awakened him.

She helped him off the table. He groaned as he straightened up, creakily. His head hurt. So did his back. As Thrygragos Everyman, sentient invertebrates perceived him as not having a backbone. But he did and it still troubled him in the morning. Fortunately, for most of his existence, and all of hers, he could call on a divine chiropractor.

"Mind telling me what you were daydreaming about?" she asked him as she worked on de-kinking his spinal column. Harmony handy-dandily manipulated her Gypsium chain-ends as if she had a hundred heated fingertips. A most welcome sensation of loosening release washed over him.

"Something to do with that Hecate-Hellion, the one who held onto you after Ginny pooped out Daemonicus that first year we were down here."

"After All pooped out Daemonicus," the Unity, who had a spectacular memory, corrected him. "The She-Sphinx has always called herself All, as in the all-invincible. Only no one knew that until grandfather sprang the Pauper out of her a few years after he raised the Dome and she told us. Ginny's just what everyone called her back then on account of she's a Gynosphinx."

Ministrations done, she held up the downy overcoat Abe Chaos must have draped over him as a blanket prior to going wherever he went to pass out. A typically mixed-message token of filial affection, it was made from the black feathers of a ravendeer. The Moloch Sedon did not approve of ravendeers. The Great God not so much of freewill as unbridled self-indulgence wore it with corresponding pleasure. Even immortals had irresolvable issues with their parents.

As per usual marvelling at her restorative touch, he slipped into it easily. "Whatever you say," he said. Then he added, gratefully as well as graciously: "Thanks. If anyone gives better back massages than you do, she has to be an octopus with pillows for suckers. Mortals don't know what they're missing."

"Some do."

He eyed her quizzically. She did have more of a glow on than was usual even for her. For some, he supposed, the morning after the night before wasn't cause for consternation. "Whatever you say again. I'm hungry."

"Bangers and beans are coming up, dad. I took the liberty of ordering them already. Her name was Hecate, by the way, though she was a Hellion. You killed her. She didn't think devils could kill but that's how you got me out of her."

"How you came out of her, don't you mean? She died in my arms, as I recall, with her eyes wide open. Except she died with three eyes wide open. Then her body spontaneously combusted and she went up in smoke."

"Talk about a hot date, eh?" Harmony smiled, thus melting away the last of his morning chills. Methandra Thanatos – Mithras's Virgin and that Great God's other remaining, non-cathonitized firstborn – may have had Heat as her attribute, but Harmony's smile could probably reduce an army of King Cold's ambulatory icemen to instantaneous puddles.

"The Hellion had to be part daemon. That's how she managed to hold onto you for so long. But the smoke was all you, wasn't it? I can't imagine ever seeing a prettier spirit being. Then again, since spirits are usually invisible, maybe I daydreamed that too."

"You've been dreaming a lot about Andy and Ginny lately," she said as Chaos's attendants brought them their brunch. "It's the Unnameable, isn't it? You're worried about its head. I told you it's all been arranged. From what the Silverclouds were saying last night, even Bodiless Byron agrees. Panharmonium dawned with Mithramas."

"Something besides that, I think, though I'm so fucked-up I'm not sure what."

"I can empathize. I fucked up last night too. Only I'm not sure who."

========

"Either relax, Attis, or go out and pay your respects to a latrine."

Was that a reprieve, a chance to re-enter naked? Eyefire might have been preferable to sarcasm. At least his half-father hadn't bid him sit. There was no other chair in the tent and he hated to think what Mithras would say if he ended up squatting on the floor.

He relaxed, stood at ease. "I'm fine, father."

========

"You have brought them?"

"Ten thousand men, sire; most of them veterans of the largest and mightiest army in the history of the Whole Earth."

"Not your paltry legions, boy. My devils?"

"As many as I could muster."

"Explain."

"I cannot bring the stars down from the night's sky. That is Great-Grandfather Sedon's domain."

"This is no time for humour. I'm well aware of that. The others? Did Incain's Gynosphinx yield the prisoners I designated?"

"At a cost of a thousand of my finest fighters: Ten for every one of your devic children the Mandroid agreed to release. She followed me to the Mole through the Weird. Even as we speak she's collecting their azuras, the fullness of their effectiveness. She's making a hellacious racket doing it too."

"So that's what that is. I thought someone was screwing my angel with a pine tree."

Attis allowed himself a slight smile. Earthy humour was prized on both sides of the Whole Earth. Plus, Mithras's Masochist was a notoriously noisy dingdong even when he wasn't trumpeting fanfares. "All insists she needs that much replacement energy in order to continue to function as she has for millennia. It was the best the Pauper could do."

"All 10 thousand would have been small price to pay."

"As you say, sire."

"And the rest, those below the Sedon Sphere?"

"Of those you asked for, all but two."

"You mean Cold and my overheated Virgin refused! I am to go up against my brothers and their firstborn without my own?"

"I did not say that, Lord Father. They are here, responsive to your request for their aid, although Lathakra's Fire Kings and Mythland's Intuit hunters are bivouacked separately from my legionnaires. Apparently they don't like each other much either, so my stewards had to camp them apart from one another as well.

"The same holds true for the Prime Sinistral's agathodaemons and cacodemons, Dandset Typhon's Rajputs and Ophidians, the Saurs of the Floodlands, the Lizarados of the Lake Lands and the Glorious Dead of Valhalla. Your transsexual's guy-gals and gal-guys turned up too but, in keeping with Geld Neargon's policy of neutrality, they'll only scout, cook, run messages and supply medical attention as the need arises.

"No matter how loyal they are to you, many of your devic offspring are as incompetent as your brothers are when it comes to drilling into their forces who's their real enemy."

"Superficial irrelevancies. Which two refused?"

"The two who are my eternal enemies. And they did not refuse. I refused to go to them, not even to ask for help on your behalf. They are beneath your contempt, sire. They are traitors to your blood. I am all you need, all you have needed for over 2,000 years. I act as your fists. My legions are our strong, uncompromising arms."

"You continue to underestimate the magnitude of what I plan. What use are mere mortals against gods?"

"You know my opinion on what we are about to embark upon today. Have I not conquered two-thirds of the Head for you? Could I not conquer Lazareme's Cattail and Occipital regions as well as Byron's southern realms given time? As I have always said, provoking this confrontation between you and your brothers, your gods against their gods, is ill-advised."

"How dare you speak to me in such a way! I have explained in depth why we must strike now. Panhumanist Xuthrodites, their monotheistic dupes and supporters of the Celestial Sphere, with its impossibly everlasting afterlife in a *'better'* place for the suppliant, are robbing me of my adherents on the Outer Earth. Without them I weaken by the moment.

"As strong as you and your legions are, you cannot conquer hearts and minds. You can kill and you can take but what I require must be given freely. You cannot force genuine devotion; only token lip service and usually then only with a whip in your hand."

"I am familiar with the funnel-up flow of devic worship, sire. Illuminaries did not name my woman Pyrame just because she, in her shells, lays in pyramids with great-grandfather, he in his shells, when he requires her to conceive more of his mortal Sed-sons."

"More humour?"

"A feeble attempt at it, I grant you. I merely meant mortals, with or without azuras inside them, worship devils. Devils worship you and your two brothers while you three in turn worship the mighty Moloch in the sky. It is a pyramid effect, with Sedon at its apex, that's all I'm suggesting."

"Joking of such matters approaches blasphemy. Your pyramid effect is my reality. It is staring at you. I am a shade of my former glory. Vast numbers must venerate me freely. Yet vast numbers on the Outer Earth are being lost on a daily basis."

"I am not denying that. But why does it necessarily follow that those who worship the sons and daughters of Byron and Lazareme will switch their allegiance to you and yours the moment you vanquish them? What if All-Father Sedon gets wind of your plans and intervenes on their behalf? Worse, what if they vanquish you? Or what if those worshippers left after you're done with their deities succumb to the lure of monotheism like your followers beyond the Dome are doing? The analogy of eggs in a basket strikes me as apropos."

"Bah! The only reason Outer Earth mortals are diving headfirst into the muck of Pure Faith is they lack ocular reminders of our magnificence. Yet, with the exception of your shared whore, the non-deviant likes of me and mine can't make it outside as easily as we once could."

"You can't make it outside at all – because All would eat even you."

"Yet more humour?"

"A play on words, that's all. The eating habits of the twin sphinxes are as the Legendarian says: They're writ in Brainstone."

"I can make cracks too, son, but only Father Sedon can make one in the Dome. And, despite my entreaties, he refuses to open even a little one for fear it'll result in a leak leading to the inundation of his precious Headworld. After the fiasco of the so-called Crimson Conspiracy, what, three and a half centuries ago, I can't say I blame him either. Still, that leaves me with only one way to restore even a modest measure of my previous primacy."

"Henotheism: with you acknowledged as the top god standing at the tip of the biggest pyramid beneath Star Sedon. I've been known to drink with the Legendarian too, father."

"Only I drink water or juice."

"Mixed with royal jelly."

"Meaning I'm drunk with power. At least he has the gumption to come right out and say it. Crete, Egypt, the Hittites, Persia, Macedonia, and most recently Rome, I have trusted your vision, not my own, to sustain me for far too long. If anything I am drunk with defiance. I cannot force Sedon to crack, let alone lower Cathonia. But I can make him dependent on me for the veneration he requires to retain it."

"Forgive me, father. Yours are admirable words for an admirable sentiment, but they reek of desperation."

"Perhaps they do, Attis. But they don't reek of defeatism or complacency. I can no longer afford to give you time to piecemeal-conquer the rest of the Head. We do it today, my immortals alongside your mortals, and to do that I need all of my children at my side."

"Then you should have ordered Divine Coueranna and Cruel Plathon to your side yourself. I can neither forget nor forgive them for what they put me through during the mad goddesses' depraved matriarchate beyond the Dome.

"The agonies I endured over those five centuries, the number of times I died on your behalf, the number of times I struggled back from the grave in order to re-espouse your societal suzerainty, your vision of wisdom, science, uncompromising fairness and the rule of law; the nearly 2,000 years I have continued your battle since then – with little or no assistance from you, I might add. No, going to them would be too much like reopening old wounds."

"And your whore wouldn't appreciate that, would she?"

"That's unfair, father. Pyrame is Sedon's Whore. She's my lover."

"No more unfair than you blaming me for what Kore-Concord and the Bull did to you, over and over again, succession after succession, after I tossed her out in favour of her brood sister, your half-mother. What was I going to do: make you illegitimate?

"Besides, I thought one was the other. How could I not? Blame the Dual Entities if you have to blame anyone."

========

"During the day," Thrygragos Lazareme read off the cut-off tee-tee tail he'd found in the pocket of the ravendeer-overcoat he still wore even though a combination of wintry sun, food in the belly and Harmony's back massage, not to mention her smile, had warmed him Great Godly greatly, "Father Sun loved Mother Earth but, come the night, he loved Mother Moon. Unless you count sunlight as life-engendering as well as life-maintaining, both relationships were platonic."

"Which beats 'Plathonic'," the Unity of Balance quipped.

========

"It wasn't him, was it?" her father asked.

"I think I'd remember if I'd bagged the Bull of Mithras last night, dad."

"Good. I mean, you can and of course do bag whomever you please. But, you know, as much as I enjoy bangers and beans I'd hate it if the sausage I just ate once belonged to someone I knew. It'd put me off my appetite and, considering the undignified grandstanding you've assigned for me to perform today, I'm already put off enough."

"My days as Nemesis are two millennia worth of long gone. What's the rest of it say?"

In terms of recalling how they'd independently fucked-up as a result of last night's debauch, Lazareme was thus far doing better than Harmony. That Abe Chaos drank him under the table he subsequently transported though the Weird, with him on top of it, was the easy bit. They were sitting across from each other, the remnants of the brunch they'd just polished off between them on the very same tabletop.

"Father Sun was hot for some real action so he set up a proxy body down below. Call him Helios. Mother Earth responded first. Call her proxy body Primeval Lilith.

They had a proxy son. Call him Cain. Not to be outdone Mother Moon sent a proxy body of her own downstairs. That'd be Trishtar Thrae. A few months later Helios had himself a second son. Call him Abel.

"You'll have heard how Cain slew Abel and how Father Sun wouldn't let Mother Moon tit-for-tat slay Mother Earth's proxy daughter's poxy son. You might not have heard that Mother Moon was so pissed she built the Androsphinx to eat her rival's Lily, however. She did. You can still see it, too. It's in Egypt."

"Allowing for your poxy paraphrasing, that's as true as the sky is blue," Harmony confirmed, fay-saying cheerfully. "Pyrame, Attis and Jordy come out of the between-space doorway between its legs whenever they traverse Cathonia. Oh, no!"

"Who was it – Savage Storm?"

"With Gravity right there? Even I'm not that brazen."

Illuminaries of yore as well as lore named the Silverclouds, the last of Byron's firstborn set of three, Rufous Rudra and Umashakti after a pair of Vedic deities whose attributes came closest to matching their own. Devils had no problem with Silvercloud because their self-generated vimanas, or vehicles, were silver clouds. They additionally called Savage Storm the Beast of Byron because non-daemonic were-things native to the Unmoving One's mountainous lands in the Lower Head acclaimed him their devil-god.

Even though Thrygragos Byron himself, being all head and no body, resembled the moon, devils also referred to Gravity as Byron's Moon because she physically waxed and waned with it. As well as being immediate siblings, they considered themselves married and, indeed, were mostly faithful to each other.

Since their most passionate adherents invoked the spirits of devil-gods in fertility rituals and marriage ceremonies, fidelity was fairly commonplace amongst devazurkind. "No, it was one of the musicians, the panpipe player, I think." Lazaremists tended to be the exception that proved the general rule of monogamy.

"Funny, I don't remember any panpipe player there. You sure you didn't go off with the fauna? Pusan Wanderlust's a female satyr."

"I wasn't that drunk. Neither was she. Besides, Pusan was all over Order."

"Oh, no!" Lazareme suddenly echoed her.

"What is it?"

"I've just remembered where I got the tee-tee tail."

"Where?"

"Off of whom, put better. I guess we've both got a weakness for musicians."

"Not the fiddler with the high soprano? She's just a kid."

"No, the witch-drummer you said you tossed around in Kanin City last week. I started dancing with her after you left."

"You were dancing with a Steg?"

"Hey, she had nice knockers, for a saurian."

"Drummers would have nice knockers. I'm surprised she didn't eat you."

"She may have mentioned something along those lines."

========

"Kore did have me castrated, father," Taurus Chrysaor Attis protested, more vehemently than intelligently. Had All of Incain already released Sinistral Wrath? Could be – he was fast losing patience with Mithras's apparent indifference to his presence.

"Then she had me crucified, on whatever tree was handy, or on one of those wooden crosses not just the Romans are so fond of these days. And she did do it over and over again, succession after succession, for hundreds of years after I killed Helios for his seventh time."

========

The Pauper Priestess and the Masochist reported the non-Roman crucifixion to which he was referring to Mithras a couple of months ago. Because it involved a couple of high-level Mithrants Attis knew personally, he too learned of the mini-scandal it caused from the same sources.

One of them, a Mithrant praetor, indulged a whimsy of the other, an admittedly homicidal, hence thoroughly disgraced earth-magician and former governor of a minor and mostly forgettable province a week's ride south of here. Rather than sending the latter to the frontlines as an arrow-magnet or first-to-die skirmisher, which he should have for such heinous crimes, the former apparently cited precedent and instead sentenced him to punishment by ordeal.

The logic behind the sentence dictated that, should he survive it, it had to be due to an act of Sedon. Should he deservedly die by it, well, technically it didn't constitute a state-sanctioned execution. Capital punishment being proscribed in every devil-dominant domain in the Upper Head, the praetor no doubt figured he was being clever.

However, as demonstrated by the Crimson Conspiracy – which, granted, occurred on the Outer Earth – surviving a crucifixion didn't necessarily mean it had to be an act of Sedon. The praetor should have realized that before he decreed it. Fortunately Domitian intervened and fed the monotheistic mass murderer to his Angelyc adherents, some of whom the killer had counted as if coup among his victims.

The truly disturbing aspect of whole affair was that the perpetrator of all this misery was a Sed-son, an offspring of the mighty Moloch and his Whore. Regardless of whatever vileness they perpetrated, both Sedon and Pyrame tended to be overly protective of their half-sons. Consequently, it was a wonderment the yazata cannibals hadn't suffered from terminal indigestion.

That they hadn't suggested to Attis they currently had a superfluity of Sed-sons mystically holding up the Sed-Sphere.

========

His half-father should never have insulted Pyrame Silverstar. He'd challenged Master Devas for less and Mithras had no Tvasitar talisman to defend himself with; that due to the fact he'd given his away to Attis shortly after his birth most of two and a half millennia ago. He did have eyefire, however, and that should be all he'd need to make Attis regret his outburst.

Nonetheless, Mithras continued to seemingly pay hardly any attention to what he was saying or referencing. His apparent apathy was so exasperating it struck him it might even be deliberately provocative. Fathers had killed sons before, and vice versa. He'd killed Helios and Helios had killed him. If the flames came, and he didn't re-materialize his regalia in time, it would be the first time Mithras had killed him. Who could say if he'd stay dead if that happened?

Intelligence counselled prudence. Anger, though, rarely begot a rational reaction. Quite the contrary, anger almost always begot rashness. "I may have wreaked varying degrees of revenge by ruining the Bull nearly as often as he ruined me but, never forget, I couldn't have got Helios out of you without the Pauper's help. She deserves much more than your scorn. It smacks of jealousy."

That taunt finally proved one too many for his father to endure in silence. "First desperation, now jealousy: Are you done lecturing me yet? The Whore provided you with the wherewithal to get Helios out of me because she wanted his Mnemosyne out of your birthmother and back into the time stream along with their Trans-Time Trigon. She resented the Female's influence on Incain's Sphinx and that's the truth of that."

"Be that as it may, father, it is equally correct to say that the moment they were gone Kore-Coueranna dubbed my half-mother Kore-Eris, Strife or Discord, even though she was the bellicose one."

"I haven't forgotten that either. And, for all I know, Concord was responsible for Discord's disappearance most of 400 years ago. But there's nothing new about spousal reprisal. It's as old as this hill. Besides, we're not here to discuss the better part of 2500 years worth of no matter how bitter history there is between you and my bull. We're talking about my present predicament and what we're going to do about it."

"Then it's as unfair as you accusing me of defeatism. I am conquering the Head. Yes, it's only bit-by-bit, but I am conquering it. Yet now you're telling me you prefer to rely on your multifarious immortal children instead of your lone mortal son; that despite the fact I keep coming back to fight for you anew. It is beyond bearing."

"It is the only way."

"What is? To rely on those who rebelled from your authority, those I punished on your behalf, battered mercilessly in single combat, imprisoned on Incain, and whose power foci I confiscated? To rely on them instead of me!

"Time and time again I challenged Kore of the Many Names and humiliated her pet monstrosity, he of the many forms. I defeated my own Death, Death as the Byronic Vanthysces, and Death as Yama Nergal, King Harvest. I could defeat Death as Thanatos, King Cold, or Death as the other male Nergalid, Gravedigger, should you so require. I'd win the world, the universe, the cosmos, for you, my father. Do not renounce me."

"Yet, in my hour of utmost peril, you could not swallow your misdirected sense of self-importance and honour a simple request to call the Corn Queen and her blasted bull from their Hell. You have failed me, child. I cannot abide that. Reveal your talismans. Then take them off and pile them there on the floor. Without them my hundred devils will be even more useless than your thousand men without their azuras."

Attis's annoyance was by now so uncontrollable he did the first but not the second. Once again he stood before the Great God visibly armed and armoured. "Are you commanding me, father? I, your one truly dependable child! If so then why didn't you command the other two to be here?"

"Do as I say, boy. Strip! At my pleasure, I may send word for you to return and reclaim those that aren't already claimed by my Hundred. But you shall obey me now!"

"I refuse."

"As you will. That is your right as a free man. Leave me!"

========

"Dancing with a Steg," Harmony marvelled anew.

========

"No wonder you buggered up your back. I really do hope you didn't follow through on her, um, mentioning along your line. The damage she could inflict, I'm shuddering so hard I'm surprised my chains aren't clanking."

"No reason they should be, Harm." Recognizable by his Tvasitar Talisman — a tri-tined trident — Unholy Abaddon, the Unity of Chaos, stepped out of the blue that was the dark-grey universality of Samsara, the Weird, of all there was between-space. "So long as you take the proper precautions, it's safe enough. Saur Tsars have to be compatible with Saur Tsarinas. Otherwise there wouldn't be any little Saur stars. Got a beer, dad?"

"Hair of the dog that bit you, eh, Abe?" Glad for the interruption, the Great God their father surreptitiously pocketed the tee-tee tail he'd been reading to Harmony. He'd glanced ahead and didn't like the look of where it was leading.

"More like its scales." Abe Chaos wasn't quite himself yet. Unless his regular self was a stegosaur, which it wasn't. "Odour got the hair."

Lord Order — Lord Yajur, as Illuminaries' had him — must have taken that as his cue to make an appearance. He did. He'd gone goatish.

========

Obediently Chrysaor Attis left his devic half-father alone. Rather, he thought he left him alone. He no more had than they'd been alone together.

"He knows, brother," *chuckled the ever-unremembered newcomer.*

========

Mithras didn't realize someone else was there until he spoke. Even then it took him a surprisingly long time to figure out who had spoken. Finally realization, and with it profound shock, hit him. "You!"

"Come now, brother. You can do better than that."

"Rhadamanthys?"

"Only after I was done as King Sodom and then only after you mistook me for Father Sedon and caused the Male Entity to attempt to assassinate me by asteroid. And, even then, only if I am to call you incompetent, which you are, but that would be impertinent.

"Or would you prefer Zeus? That was you, wasn't it? One of you! The Great God reduced to infancy, the one the Etocretans' human king, who was always designated Minos, sheltered in a mountaintop cave while the Female Entity's perverse goddesses sought to extirpate you forevermore."

"You're making that up."

"Am I? Remarkably, some Outer Earthlings do recall me as Judge Druj, that's true. And in what passes for their catechism 'Druj' does mean 'the Lie'. But, when it comes to you, I'm not making up anything."

"Be silent! I no more had the Demon Child devolve Uranus after I emasculated him than I caused the Dual Entities to attempt to assassinate Father Sedon. I did not even get hold of him until well after they dropped Trans-Time Trigon atop your twin cities. You try my patience. Leave my sight."

"An order? How fitting, how foolhardy! Shall I call you Marduk? Shamash? Ahura Mazda? Ormazd? Spenta Mainyu? Assur?"

"Ahriman!"

"Let's not be so formal."

"Smiler, then."

"Much better. While there are tremendous advantages to never being remembered unless I let myself be seen, only to be forgotten the moment I depart, it does gall me to be so slowly recognized. It's as if I don't exist."

========

Mithras didn't blurt. Yet he'd just blurted out great gouts of nonsensical verbiage that had a no matter how faraway clang of accuracy to it. What was it about this Smiling Fiend anyway? Could Lie inspire Truth? Who was he in actuality? And why was he here, on this day of all days? More to the immediate point, how could he hope to remember he even existed?

The Great God dug his fingernails into the tabletop and twisted them deliberately hurtfully. Pain was a mnemonic.

========

The Devil Sedon had one name. So did Unmoving Byron and Everyman's Lazareme. But, despite efforts his followers made over the millennia to combine them into a binomial, Mitravaruna or Varunamithra, he always had two.

When he was feeling generous, the mighty Moloch who was both his father and his practical mother complimented Mithras with words to the effect he had two names because he was simply too powerful to be just one god. Indeed, as the Legendarian often complained, there were so many holes in his collection of personal recollections he could well have been a lot more than two distinct deities simultaneously.

The male of the two putative Cosmic Principals – Adam-Kadmon, according to some current Cabalists the Legendarian also told him about – had loosely labelled him schizophrenic. Helios had even joked that the term *'splitting headache'* was coined for guys, even if they were gods, like him.

To that, and to Helios's further assertion that he suffered from a mental illness more correctly categorized as bipolar disorder in his future-speak, Mithras countered that he was better branded the bi-solar disabler of disorder. Helios thought that was kind of comical but, then again, he enjoyed word games as much or more than any fay.

Plenty of creeds the Eurasian world over allegedly had Mithras as being but one-third of an imaginary triad. At least one of the many legends the Legendarian brought back from the Outer Earth concerning him conceptualized this consequential VAM Entity as the Male Trinity, the first true Thrygragos.

In unsettling hindsight Mithras recalled he'd been thinking about Ahriman – if not Smiler per se – a week ago, while he was waiting for his Heliodromus to return from the Sedon Sphere with his father's acknowledgement of his perceived need to go ahead with Thrygragon. Had this witless asshole been there not quite invisible? Had he spotted him out of one corner of any eye? Had he somehow sensed his pestilential presence?

The VAM Entity, he could recall that legend. By its reckoning Mithras was the sun of day whereas Varuna was the moon and stars of night. As for Ahriman, he was the darkness of a starless, moonless night, of a total solar or lunar eclipse, of beneath the ground where plants root, minerals are found, and the dead are buried.

Today was the first time in a very long time he recalled there might actually be an existent 'A' between the 'V' and the 'M' of his names. The Prophet Zarathustra may have been mostly wrong about him, but he may have had an inkling of something right about Ahriman – if the word 'right' didn't make that an oxymoron.

Mithras prided himself on his attention to detail. He'd peppered the Legendarian with queries about Zarathustra's manifestly self-destructive counterbalance to his Wise Lord, Ahura Mazda. What were some of the epithets under which he'd denounced this Smiling Fiend? Angra Mainyu, the Emir of Evil, was one, a risible one. There was no such thing as evil. The Prince of Pain was another. But that referred to pain in a metaphysical sense, not as a physical pain in the proverbial butt.

Judge Druj, the demonic Duke of Deception, the Lord Protector of Liars – more, the living epitome of the Lie: that was the best one. Third eye or no third eye, Smiler had just referred to it, so he was as good as admitting he couldn't be a devil. True devils were as incapable of lying as they were of violating their sworn oaths or disobeying their fathers.

The Great God allowed himself a glimmer of optimism Father Sedon would count the fiend his equal. Then again, if he couldn't remember Smiler existed unless he was standing right in front of him, then chances were the Moloch couldn't either. Sedon was many things, but he was neither omnipresent nor omnipercipient.

So what would it matter if he just killed him outright, right here and right now? If nothing else it'd provide practice for this afternoon's potential Theomachy, should Byron and Lazareme not deign to subordinate themselves as he anticipated they would. While Sedon hadn't precisely acquiesced to Thrygragon, he hadn't expressly forbidden him killing them, had he?

Rationally as always, the Great God forbore meditated murder for the nonce. Instead, Mithras reassessed his ever-mocking, ever-unwelcome visitor dispassionately.

Smiler was dressed in a black robe with deep pockets. A flat-topped, mitre-like headpiece with its cowls tied under his chin concealed his hair; assuming he had any, which he didn't seem to, not even in his nostrils. He did have a thin face, high cheekbones, narrow lips, a prominent nose, and laugh-lines around his mouth and all three of his eyes – the top one no doubt being illusionary, a result of demonic shape-shifting or maybe even an implant.

His unadorned, spindly fingers were too long by at least a knuckle each. There also seemed, on second then third glance, a few too many of them, which made him as polydactyl as he was pestilential. Other than his face and hands, no other part of his pinkish, nearly red skin was visible.

His sash – which, as a prince of pain, probably doubled as a scourge – radiated with Brainrock intensity. A shrunken, skinless skull dangled from a slender chain strung around his neck. The necklace, not the skull, had to have been made of the same miraculous Godstuff devils additionally knew to call Gypsium, the same as they knew Mithras was Mithras, Byron was Byron, Lazareme was Lazareme and Sedon was Sedon.

As he'd just advised Attis, you could blame that on the Dual Entities. They'd somehow learned to call them by those very names in their earliest lifetime, before they began randomly tumbling through the time-space continuum whenever the male of the otherwise impossibly inseparable pair was killed. Which provoked another thought: Could Smiler be Heliosophos repossessed and come back to torment him?

He doubted it. Helios might have overstretched himself when he opted for the Sophos the Wise add-on, but he was neither stupid nor particularly cocky. What with Sedon decreeing he be killed on sight, he wouldn't dare to brashly walk in on him like this. He especially wouldn't walk in on him disguised as an obvious demon. With the exception of Tralalorn, if she was a demon and not a devil, Sedon had never proscribed their killing either.

On the other hand, Mithras's most hated Thrygragos of a brother, the Lackland Libertine, was as brainless as he was full of himself. Confident Mithras couldn't harm him, he might do it as a lark. He'd be wrong about that of course and, upon reflection, even a fiddlehead like Lazareme would have to realize he'd be wrong about it.

Mindful of the stakes intrinsic to Thrygragon, however, he might be tempted to send someone to attempt to assassinate him. Had Smiler just hinted as much? Regardless, his brother in Sedon wouldn't try to do it himself. An unmitigated coward, he was addicted to the pleasures of the flesh and fiercely preservative of the immunities godhood granted him to indulge himself, without fear of consequences.

Accordingly, if indeed Lazareme were that terrified of being knocked down a rung or two on the pyramidal steps-up of devic devotion, he'd have assigned either Abaddon or Yajur to do the dire deed. Unless he sent Unrequited Desire, re-embodied as Nemesis, as Nihilism Incarnate, that is.

The Great God of reasonableness didn't think that too likely. Harmony was the love them and leave them alive sort. As much as her despondent, onetime lovers might long for a return engagement, they rarely committed suicide. Rather than bitterness, better memories and wetter dreams were her usual legacy. In any event, none of the Unities, nor any other devil for that matter, would come at him masquerading as this smiling fiend. For one thing, how would they remember what he looked like?

No, he was exactly as he presented himself. He was Doubt, his personal adversary and private demon.

========

"To me you have never existed, Smiler. At your presumptuous best, you are the last remaining triplet from my initial laying with the Trigregos Sisters. You have never served me. Have you come to offer obeisance, just as your siblings shall shortly? If so, you'd best dig yourself a deeper pit in the dirt than I'll require any of them do."

"You're such a droll troll, brother. I am no more your son than you are a Thry-gragos. You are a pretender to Sedon's throne; a pretender the mighty Eye-Mouth in the sky allows sit in it solely because he too is a pretender. He wishes to seem the All-Father of devazurkind not just so he can lord over his sons and daughters. He does so, as they too believe, in order to lord over his actual brothers, Bodiless By-ron and Lackland Lazareme.

"Look sincerely into yourself. Recognize the veracity of my words. You do not order your so-called children around like genuine Great Gods do theirs. It isn't due to conformity to any higher principles of free will as you purport, though. You do not order them around because you cannot. You are not their father any more than I am your son.

"We are the firstborn of Thrygragos Sedon: greatest of the Great Gods, to be sure, but a Great God only. And you, friend, are simply a Master Deva."

Apollonian enthusiast that he was, Mithras finally flashed himself a sensible thought and a codicil: Not witless, witling – whittling! Fingernails became claws, the better to bore into wooden tabletop.

"Wait! We're both liars. I have you now. You're the latest excretion of that earth-born and earthbound lump of chthonic crud known as Daemonicus in pre-Flood times. As grandiose as your true name may sound, you've never travelled the stars, never walked in the far off planetary system of Weir, of either Weir.

"Were I not otherwise preoccupied I would flick that false eyeball out of your forehead and prove it to you and all who would bear witness. Shall I do that, Smiler? Shall I dispel this tent, reveal you to the amassed armies of the Head, then demon-strate the truth of my words, not yours? Yes, perhaps I shall do just that."

"It would do you no good. For the time being I choose to keep myself con-cealed. If I do not wish to be seen, I cannot be seen. Even you, eye of the son, eye of the moon, cannot perceive me. I am darkness. I am your third eye blinded. By day's end I will reunite you with our other brother, whose skinless skull hangs from my neck." With his too many, overlong fingers the polydactyl poltroon tapped the skull he was referring to for emphasis.

"Which one is he, by the way? Which one are you: Mithras the sun of the dawn and the day or Varuna of the reflective moon and the stars? No matter. Soon both of you shall be side by side again. There's no need to thank me. The pleasure will be entirely mine!"

The Smiling Fiend produced a panpipe out of the usual nowhere that was the everywhere of the Universal Substance. Tooting a lament, he left Brother Mithras au-dibly muttering inanities to himself.

Thrygragon had begun highly harmoniously and, for Smiler, it was progress-ing more and more fortuitously. Maybe, when the time came, he should declare the Winter Solstice his feast day. No, better make it Solstice Eve. It was the longest night of the year after all.

========

The Great God caught himself talking to himself out loud. Vaguely he wondered if he'd really descended that far. And what's with the bleeding fingertips?

He looked down. For some reason he'd scraped a letter 'D' into the tabletop he was leaning on so disconsolately with his elbows. Why would he do that? Why would he render it at an angle of 90 degrees clockwise? Why did he scratch it with pronounced horns and grinning so gleefully, like the bottom half of a Hellene gorgoneion minus the fangs and extruding tongue?

Thrygragos Varuna Mithras smiled, briefly.

========

Capric as he appeared, Lord Yajur did not hold a panpipe. He held his own power focus, a long sword with an ever-regenerating vajra thunderbolt for its blade. Thrygragos Lazareme braced himself. Backbones should never be used as lightning rods.

The moon was already out, albeit only in a manner of speaking. It wasn't the real moon any more than it was Helios's Milady Mnemosyne. It was Thrygragos Byron. The incomparably beautiful – to just about everyone – Unity of Balance plopped the last chunk of beef sausage into her mouth.

It was time to make Mithramas Mithras-less.

****

THEO 6:

HARD BODIES

========

The recorder player ceased tooting the second Jordan 'Quill' Tethys walked into the booze-tent beyond the Mithrant legionnaires' main campsite.
In the hush that followed he rapidly performed a mental inventory.

========

For a facility Cheek-side of a huge, howsoever-temporary military encampment very few present wore uniforms. Indeed, most of those there, hardly all of whom were human, wore clothing typical of Marutian tradespersons on a cold morning in late Tantalar: tunics or shirts, pants or leggings, leather boots or thick-soled sandals, and overcoats or sweaters.

A good percentage of them were women. Of them, an even more disproportionate number looked to be in their late thirties or early to mid forties. That indicated most of those there were service suppliers, though likely not prostitutes. Of course, what with the strong possibility of a devastating battle much farther out in the Mole come this afternoon, there wouldn't be many soldiers or officers around at this time of day anyhow. Had it been otherwise, well, that would have been curious.

The only one he'd been expecting to see when he entered the booze-tent was its proprietor, the barkeep. Hopi née Pilsner didn't let him down. It was the company she kept that did. He recognized most of the older women in particular right away. That he did wasn't so much curious as exceedingly perturbing.

Hopi was a stout, black-skinned woman he'd married mostly because she was an excellent brew master. Over the years they had four children who survived infancy, a girl and three boys. She'd probably left the youngest three west of here, on her family's farm, under the doting care of her no doubt still hale and hardy mother and stepfather.

Their talented eldest – Garden to his mother, Yeast to him – was not only present he seemed to have taken up the recorder. The lad must be past 20 by now or close to it. Oddly, he looked somewhat older than that. He was also much plumper than he'd been the last time he saw him three or four years ago.

Tethys himself had reddish hair and fair skin, prone to burning. So, in that respect at least, Yeast and his siblings were far more like mom than like him. In every other respect, though, he was a regular chip off the old paternal blockhead. Partying heartily, while swilling Hopi's pilsners, likely accounted for his unexpected maturation and expanded waistline. Nonetheless, Tethys was surprised to see him favouring a totally different instrument.

Adults, men only moderately less so than women, got as teary-eyed as post-pubescent girls did when Yeast strummed on a lyre while ardently intoning romantic verses, much of which he'd either composed himself or stolen from his father. Plucking was always preferable to blowing. You can't tongue and mouth melodies instrumentally at the same time you're emoting poetry passionately.

Additionally, it being well before noon, it was a mite disappointing to see him awake and making music rather than in bed making love. He should be out sowing his wild barley. Every Tethys, male or female, inherited a procreative imperative. One only had to look around the canvas enclosure to appreciate just how successful he'd been at attending to his obligations. He wasn't so much polygamous as he was polyamorous.

He'd married the slender, snow-white Swan Maiden for her fragile beauty. Needless to say she didn't stay a maiden for long. Neither did she stay a fragile beauty. The Valkyrie – Volsanga Nibelung was her name – was another who'd packed on the poundage. Except, having not seen her in well over a decade, hers looked to be pounds of pulchritude. To his two jaded eyeballs she remained a stunner.

Her weight gain wouldn't much matter to her job security. Unless you had to be a maiden to ride them – which you didn't – psycho-swans could care approximately zilch about bulk. Why would they? Heft tipped next to no scales between-space. Like girth, witches could never conjure shelters off their witch-stones if it did. Neither could Attis store the talismans he wasn't sporting perceptibly in his kibisis.

Valkyries had no qualms about killing folks. While admittedly they usually stuck to those who were already mortally wounded, they did it for a living. His main problem with Volsanga wasn't her occupation. It was she was a Hecate-Hellion, a member of a sisterhood so old it didn't just predate the Great Flood of Genesis. It predated the Golden Age of Humankind.

Hellions venerated Mother Earth and, as such, tended to be anti-devil. As a tale-teller, the aphorism 'each to his own' amounted to a cornerstone of his craft. And, to be fair, that didn't necessarily mean they were anti-deviant. He'd never told Volsanga he was a deviant because Hellions specialized in the usage of soul sinks. As a very specific kind of deviant, the last thing he wanted was to have his soul sunk.

Was that their son? Handsome bloke. From the looks of him he was still in his mid to late teens. That'd make him their youngest, Gordon or Glee, the one who came after their daughter, Ute, whom he'd tentatively identified as the fiddler. Since she'd be about the same age as Yeast, Tethys was happy to see she gave the impression of being really, really healthy.

An excess of beer can adversely affect one's capacity to perform adequately sexually. Regrettably, if perhaps not quite so undesirably, it also tends to addle both the short term and long term functions of one's cranial competency. At one time or another he must have known the names of nearly everyone there, but that wasn't the case anymore. It especially wasn't the case when it came to the children's names.

Of the mothers there, the circumstances of their brief relationship caused Durga's to spring to mind right away. A Rajput princess who'd seduced him, not the other way around, he'd married her because they got caught. Like others were of olives, her kingly father was fond of nuts before dinner and Tethys wanted to keep his attached. From skin colour alone, the lone possible fruit of their loins had to be the apparently thoroughly hung over fellow with the multi-stringed lute.

Not all of these hornets were human but all of them were sentient beings. The Lizarado lady, what was her name? He'd been going through an experimental period of drawing himself into second skins of different species and, even for him, there was always a first time. That might account for the evidently motherless young Steg there as well. Sometimes he simply couldn't resist a challenge.

The Ophidian? That hadn't been a first time. Ophidians delighted in sexual variations. Plus, they had such interesting appendages. Second skins had their drawbacks, though. He could match exterior forms, including functional genitalia, but not natural immunities. This one was part scorpion, which was why he left her.

As for the terpsichoreans and sirens, he'd needed them. He could beat, bow, blow, pluck, pound or squeeze almost any musical instrument there was, but he couldn't dance to save his life and didn't dare sing for his supper for much the same reason. The noise he emitted when he tried was best described as noisome. His voice stank. He did his wooing with words spoken.

He was a poet and he knew it.

========

Hopi ended the awkward silence. "Ah, Jordy, come on in, pop a pill. Curiously enough we were just talking about you."

"Then perhaps I should leave you to it." Sometimes poetry failed him.

The recorder player spoke next. It was only then that Tethys realized why he looked older and fatter than Yeast should. He also realized he was in even worse trouble than he'd initially figured. It wasn't so much that he couldn't immediately think of any other black-skinned son he might have had besides Hopi's three. It was more what the young man said.

"Dad? Mom and I were sure you were dead."

========

Perched on a purported burial mound Mole-side of his legions' military camp, All of Incain continued to squawk away like a murder of crows that somehow apprehended they were about to be mass-murdered. From the vantage of a similar barrow quite a distance away, in the heart of the Praetorium, Chrysaor Attis distractedly scrutinized the show, or lack thereof, that the Gynosphinx was putting on.

========

He'd never disobeyed his half-father so seemingly irredeemably before. Then again he couldn't recall the Great God ever ordering him to do anything so blatantly stupid before. Why couldn't he, the embodiment of level-headedness, grasp that his refusal to doff his regalia, to surrender everything he'd won in single combat on Mithras's behalf over the course of multiple centuries, wasn't just about him, the Attis? Was the Great God that depressed? Was Mithras feeling that theocidal?

As justifiable as resentment was in Attis's mind, the entire episode felt wrong, like they'd both been manipulated. Yet it also felt inordinately invigorating. He could hardly wait to find out whom Mithras would send against him. It'd have to be a highborn. Only a highborn would dare to take him on and, again thanks mostly to him, the Attis, there weren't too many Mithradite highborn left loose.

The man who'd out-wrestled Death, a variety of them, including his own, again and again, could think of only two still extant Mithradites who might prove worthy opponents. Not at all coincidentally both were Devil Deaths he hadn't gone up against in the past primarily due to the fact Mithras had never implied he should do so.

Because his power focus was a spade, Master Devas, as well as their three fathers, called the younger of the two both Planter and Gravedigger. A fourth-born whose fellow triplets were Domdaniel Pride and Cruel Plathon, he commonly manifested himself as black-skinned as a full-blooded male Utopian or Outer Earth, sub-Saharan African. For various reasons, bygone Illuminaries named him Zuvem Nergalis.

Devils called the eldest, a firstborn no less, King Cold. Tantal Thanatos to Illuminaries, reputedly he actually fought fairly, if ferociously and thus far always victoriously. Doubly or trebly ironically given the Thanatoid's deathly aspect, his chilling attribute and his invariable masculinity, his power focus was a two-headed war-axe or twibil known as a Labrys.

On Crete, the southernmost landform in Europe, during the man-hating mad goddesses' depraved matriarchate of roughly 2000 to 2500 Years of the Dome; a Labrys came to symbolize a woman's internal reproductive system. A lot of the reason for that was the presence on nearby Strongyne, the Isle of Strong Women, of his immediate sister and nowadays-constant companion, Heat to her brother's Cold.

Illuminaries named the female Thanatoid Methandra after Mediterranean Athena. Devils referred to her as Mithras's Virgin despite the fact a persistent and oddly self-aware spirit being by the name of Klannit, arguably the Whole Earth's first and only known, pre-Genesea-born devazur, considered Tantal and Methandra to be her parents.

Between them, Gravedigger and King Cold likely had as many or more patrilineally loyal azuras than Mithras did. That meant they could ordinarily call upon tens of thousands of fanatical followers. Ordinarily wasn't down here in the Mole, though. It was up there, in their vast, northwestern holdings: the Nergalid's Elysian

Fields, where it seldom rained, and the Thanatoid's Lathakra, where the temperature rarely rose above freezing.

As formidable, even invincible, as they may be in their homelands, Attis figured he could handle them this far south. For one thing they only had a single power focus each whereas he had more than a hundred; considerably more than a hundred once you counted the power foci he'd confiscated from Byronics and Lazaremists. At least his half-father, borderline sensibly, hadn't had him negotiate with All, via Pyrame, for their release. His cousins remained bargaining chips.

Contemplation achieved calming. He was the Universal Soldier, the Golden Sword, yet he was also the Mithrants' Taurus. No matter how agitated they became, military leaders could never allow themselves to succumb to emotionalism. Confidence was a good thing but there was no excuse for overconfidence. It could and too often had proven fatal to not just him.

Like his Thrygragos of a father claimed he had for Thrygragon, Attis felt obliged to mull over every alternative. Might Father Mithras be setting him up to take a fall, as he had Sinistral Pride closing in on twice a millennium previously? Or might he be setting up the last two Mithradite Devil Deaths he hadn't outwrestled in order for him to take them down?

Attis steeled himself for either/or. Sooth said he wasn't overly concerned. Included in his collection of devic power foci were the only six that made any real difference. The Six Sacred Objects, as he thought of the Thrygragos and Trigregos Talismans, served him, not anyone else. Moreover, at the risk of irrationally ascribing to them the slightest smattering of sentience, they seemed to take a perverse pleasure in helping him take out devils.

They could and would see him through anything. They always did, eventually.

========

The boggle eyes of his bloated boar's head mask granted him far-sight. Activating psychically this aspect of his arsenal of abilities, he zoomed in on the diminishing crowd of legionnaires surrounding the hillock upon which the She-Sphinx made her roost. There were a lot less left than he'd initially reckoned. To judge by that yardstick, she was maybe three-quarters to four-fifths done exchanging their azuras for Mithras's Hundred.

Although, even with far-sight, it was difficult to tell from where he stood, outside his devic half-father's pavilion, matters seemed to be proceeding without incident. He should be proud of his men's discipline. Either that or he should be proud of the disciplinarians he'd had his lieutenants send along to guarantee they filed back into camp rather than flee into the Mole and thence to the immense, onetime undersea plains of Marutia. This afternoon's death toll would be high enough without him having to add deserters to the carnage.

He wasn't happy about the overhead onlookers, however. The enormous vultures – rather, their riders – better be careful. The Vultyrie, as the grotesquely oversized buzzards were collectively known, carried the Sangazur-animated Glorious Dead of Valhalla. All's ghastly squalling must have attracted them as if moths to a flame. He hoped the She-Sphinx didn't get greedy. He had plans for them.

While there were plenty of other flying beasts of burden amongst the nominally Mithradite armies gathered throughout the Gregarian Fields – including more than a few of Peg's fellow Pegasus-psychopomps and the psycho-swans of the Valkyries themselves – his living legionnaires understandably refused to ride most of them. That meant the Valhallans, having for the most part been Mithrant warriors when they were alive, came the closest he had to a reliable air force.

As far as Attis was concerned, Sangs were a boon better than a boom on any battlefield. So long as the corpses they motivated weren't dismembered, crisped or pulped irretrievably, they could fight on indefinitely. Plus, since Sangs invariably had Mithradite parents, any soldier, once slain, then reanimated, would carry on the fight on his side, regardless of whose side they'd been fighting on previously.

In a way it was downright disheartening there were so few of them.

========

Something splattered in front of him not 20 feet down slope. Now what? Pterosaur shit, unless it was dragon lizard shit. That answered that.

They were chasing each other, high above him, ages old enemies from Sedon's Sweat Glands just north of here, in the Flood and Lake Lands respectively. There were dozens of them: Saurians on the backs of the former; Lizarados on the backs of the wyverns, who were more gliders than flyers and couldn't breathe fire even if you'd fed them exclusively on chilli peppers for a year. So where were the Prime Sinistral of Satanwyck's winged demons? They probably fed on them both.

Ah, here they come; didn't want to be left out, he supposed. He could have predicted it. In fact he had as good as predicted it only a few minutes ago when he complained to his father that far too many Mithradites couldn't distinguish who their real enemies were. He was a prophet and he'd just proved it.

At least the Valhallans had enough sense to start dispersing. Although the zombie-like, so-called Inglorious Dead, as animated primarily by Nergal Vetala's azuras, were little more than bricks-thick, walking appetites incapable of functioning during even the briefest of cloudbursts, being dead on the Head no more necessarily meant imbecilic than it did immobile.

Then he heard voices coming from Mithras's tent. A devil must have come through between-space the moment he left his father alone. He couldn't place the second voice but there was somehow something at once vaguely familiar as well as distressingly sinister about it.

Why did All have to wail so much like a fucking banshee anyways?

========

"Please assure your mom I'm very much alive, son," Jordan Tethys said, hoping to stay that way for the foreseeable future.

"Oh, I will," the recorder player promised. "Want to come with me and tell her yourself? I've a psycho right outside."

"That thing's yours?"

========

"Don't call Hinny a thing, dad. She's got good hearing and it might hurt her feelings."

"It's a she?"

"With feelings."

"And good hearing, I got that. What the hell is it? Sorry, what the hell is she?"

"Mom calls her a hindy-pomp but I call her Hinny the Hippy. Hippy's short for hippo, which means horse, but Hinny's just for hinny. You know, like a jackass."

"And calling her a jackass won't hurt her feelings?"

"It's what she looks like from a distance. She won't mind."

"Jackasses don't have feathers for fur, a minimum of ten wings and a crow's head, son; not even from a distance. Besides, if she's a she, shouldn't you call her a Jill-ass?"

That brought smiles and more than a few good-natured chuckles from his sons and daughters in particular. It wasn't just the younger members of those collected in the booze-tent who responded in kith and kind either. One of his favourite sayings was *'laughter's the finest dope'* and maybe it was. He certainly wasn't a dead dope yet. He might even get a free beer or two before it was quill-quickly time.

Besides, to the best of his recollection, none of the mother hens here and, by extension, none of their undeniably very good-looking batch of chicks knew he was a deviant. Then the Valkyrie opened her mouth and he instantly commenced to reconsider the advisability of that confidence.

"Best go tend to your Jill-ass, Georgie," she said to the recorder player, as if he was one of her own. The name didn't twig any jolts of recognition. He probably had as many sons named George or Georgie as he had Gordons, Gordies, Jordans or Jordies.

"You two, too," she added, instructing Glee and Ute, who were her own.

"Come on, mom," Ute objected. "Today's going to be my first time out. I can take it."

Both declarations boded poorly. Mother hens – even if they were mother swans – were notorious for wanting to shield their young from unpleasant sights, especially ones they were about to inflict on much more than just their children's sensitivities. As for a swan maiden about to embark on her maiden voyage, yet eager to hang around for just a few more moments, that smacked of a desire to watch a pro in action.

Beer had been the death of him before. So had jealous lovers. This one looked to have the makings of both. Romance and reason were two other things that rarely walked hand-in-hand. Often life was good; rarely was it fair.

The stingers these mostly humanoid hornets had were daggers.

========

As colourless, as virtually invisible, as their non-deviant offspring by themselves were, Attis could sense the hundred Master Devas the She-Sphinx was blinking out, as she blinked in his men's azuras, gathering around him. If it was possible for spirit beings to slaver they were slavering. He'd anticipated it of course.

He, not Mithras, had what they wanted after All, capitalized.

========

Pyrame Silverstar had unnecessarily forewarned him of it on Incain. His half-father had in essence echoed her a few minutes ago. Other than their capacity to coerce, next to irresistibly, the lesser beings they possessed, without their talismans or power foci devils were little better than their own azuras. They could hardly wait for him to discard their Tvasitar-trinkets, whereupon they would pounce on them like dogs to bones, or jackals to cart-kill, and become solid individuals again.

Theirs could be a long wait. He, the Mithrants' Taurus in this succession, as he had been for closing in on countless previous successions, was no lesser being. Indeed, so long as he had the Godly Glories of the Thrygragos Brothers and Trigregos Sisters on or about himself, he couldn't be possessed.

Nor was he a complete fool; that despite the rites of Hilaria, which his Mithrants conducted every spring on Sedon's Human Eye-Isle and in which he often participated as their chosen Attis, albeit only on the night before Fool's Day, when they sacrificed his surrogate. Seeking revenge, retribution and/or the perceived reversal of humiliations suffered in centuries past; as soon as they had hard bodies again one or another of them was bound to attack him.

If he had to die once more today, perhaps never to succeed himself again, better it be fully armed and at the hands of his half-father's enemies, Byronics or Lazaremists, instead of his treacherous Mithradite siblings, aunts and uncles.

========

The Gynosphinx finished her inhalation-exhalation routine. Mercifully at last shutting up, she spread her wings and sprang into the air. Flapping them now, she effortlessly kept right on going. Attis had to admit that seeing All soar inspired awe. For the winged demons, pterosaurs and wyverns that'd been pestering her, she also must have made for a truly terrifying sight.

Even though Pyrame claimed she didn't kill, the She-Sphinx wasn't averse to nipping at the flying beasties as she scattered them. Of course she might be doing it at Pyrame's urging, but he didn't think so. All may be a Mandroid, and hence mostly a machine, but she was capable of independent thought. She probably didn't appreciate them shitting on her any more than he had they on him.

He saw them coming the moment she vanished between-space, presumably to return to Incain. Forget All, forget awe, no sight could be more galling!

========

He'd have to chance it. He reached for his Liberty Cap. Too late! Someone snatched it off his head, faux-feathery quill in it. Cap and quill hovered there, in mid-air. A form began to harden out of the air. Devils could do that, so could dire wraiths. But this was neither.

"Sylvia?"

"I'm Aerial, asshole," the sylph fay-said. "Sylvia's the deadly dryad. Have a seat."

Obligingly a vacant chair scampered up to him on its four legs.

========

Sylphs were faeries with transformative talents. So were dryads. The former were air sprites, hence her hardening herself out of the air itself. The latter were wood wights, hence the scampering chair. He felt disinclined to sit. He felt inclined to flee. He couldn't do it. His feet were rooted to the straw-tossed floor. That'd be a Plantagenet slipping between its slats. The next question wasn't so much which one as what kind.

She produced a thorn, scratched him with it. He felt faint, sat down on Sylvia. "Long time, no see, Barbara," he muttered as the fast-acting toxin took effect.

She kept growing. Plant people could do that sort of thing. So could dryads, though they tended to be oaken. Soon she had a flowery face, a winsome body, humanoid limbs to go with it, and a lovely fragrance. "Actually I'm Jardin, your daughter. Mama Barbara is in the vase. And before you ask, that's water she's sucking up. Mom stewed in her own juices last night. So did a few of us. You missed quite the bash, dad." Barb's fay-folks were vintners.

"Isn't war wonderful?" said the Rajput princess. Durga would say that. Even on the Outer Earth Rajputs belonged to a warrior caste – castes being Lord Yajur's method of keeping order without actually having to give orders, which Lazaremists disdained doing. "Otherwise we never would have had the opportunity to get together like this."

"We've different hair and skin colours, dad," said her son, the lutanist he'd identified as one of the worst sufferers of last night's after-effects. Tethys avoided hangovers. He approved of lutes, however. He turned his quill into a lute almost as often as he turned it into a lyre. "Some of us are even from different species. But we all look sort of alike. I'm Ravi, as in rave, by the way, and, no, we've never met. You abandoned mom and me before I was born."

"Funny," Tethys observed, eying his cap and quill. Aerial held them as if a snake in a nest. She wasn't far wrong. There was still a chance. "You don't look at all like a grapevine, Ravi, or an Ophidian or a Steg."

"I don't look like a chair either."

The chair in reference developed arms, the better to hug him tightly. She didn't let go, pinning his hands to his lap. Someone had done his or her research. "I'm Wooden," the chair introduced herself, "As in Wooden Tethys. But you can call me Woody, everyone else does. I hear you've been a very knotty boy."

"You're barking up the wrong tree on that, Woody," he protested, lamely.

Usually trees didn't grow so fast. Then again trees, even oak trees, usually weren't dryads. "And my bark's every bit as bitter as my bite," she fay-said. "I'm Sylvia, in case you haven't figured that out yet. Saudi tells us you're a deviant, in all senses of the word."

"My mother was a Sari witch," volunteered the Steg. Although her name sounded only vaguely similar to Jordy, Saudi did sound like something a dinosaur might be named.

"We're like mother, like daughter, in that respect. But she had better eyes than you had control. She saw your maracas glint when she told you she was pregnant. You buggered off later on that same day. Mom spent years looking for you but, hey, she was looking for a Steg, wasn't she?" Saurians mostly played percussive instruments. It was more convenient to turn his quill into maracas than a set of backbone marimbas.

"Not so very long ago, just before a pterosaur tried to make her its supper – and only half succeeded before I stomped it into my pet psycho – we were both on Ap Isle. We told the Korants' Boss Cow about your maracas and she figured out who you were, her son." Ah, Tethys thought but didn't say, that explained that then. It was this incarnation's mother who terminated his last incarnation's expected 30 years of longevity somewhat prematurely.

"My mother's a witch, too," Georgie volunteered. Like Glee and Ute, the black-skinned recorder player seemed reluctant to heed Volsanga's directive and exit the booze-tent forthwith. Normally Tethys approved of non-compliance. Except when it came to obeying their father – his half-grandfather, on both sides of the bed – Laza-remists were the rebellious sort.

Wait a mini-minute! Did he say witch? Oh, no! Georgie's mom had to be Hele-na Somata. Although the long-lived, slow-to-age, non-pureblood Utopian was born in here, she first ventured outside more than a century ago. Pyrame Silverstar promptly got hold of her and, one in the other, they had perhaps the most successful Sed-son ever, none other than the now long dead, but obviously then in-the-future Roman Emperor, Constantine the posthumously-declared Great.

The cumulative effect of what must be close to 15 years' worth of beer consumption since he'd abandoned them, plus the easily forgotten fact that Constantine was no blacker than Helena or him, explained his failure to recognize Georgie right away.

Either the Outer Earth's air had a bleaching effect on boys born of part-Utopi-ans out there or Helena had imbedded a self-adjusting, glamour-casting Anthean Ag-ate in one of Constantine's teeth. Knowing how much difficulty witches had func-tioning to the fullness of their abilities out there, Tethys reckoned the latter less like-ly than the former.

"A tiptop witch, an Ant Nightingale," Georgie added, thereby confirming his dreadful epiphany. "Once she saw the lot of us together, she asked a bunch of ques-tions and figured out who you were. It sounds to me that, next to the Attis himself, you're about the most famous deviant still around."

"Still around certainly sounds good to me." No matter how much beer he con-sumed, Tethys excelled at keeping track of his 30-year life-allotments. Bodily he was only 50. He had to have a couple of years left, didn't he?

"I'd have said infamous," did say Volsanga, who was a witch too.

"Your big brother Jordan still alive, son?" he asked Glee, hoping to mollify Vol-sanga by showing some degree of interest in their family.

"His name's Jotan, dad. Or should I call you granddad. Jot's wife's due today."

"You do know what a wife is, don't you, dad?" contributed Ute, whose voice and looks seemed the only pleasant things about her. She probably wasn't a Hellion, yet, but attitudinally she struck him as more of a chip off the maternal blockhead than off the paternal one.

"Haven't you figured it out yet, Ute?" said Hopi. "Jordy's an unmitigated jerk. Make that a perfidious polygamist, to fay-say some. His problem isn't what a wife is, it's what a husband's supposed to be. He couldn't spell faithful even if Aerial gave him back his quill."

"You should be thankful Master Helena's such a do it by the book type, taleteller," provided Durga. "Because, if it was up to me and a few others here, Georgie would have been right about you being dead already. You do recall my father's recipe for roasted nuts, don't you?" Tethys winced involuntarily. "Ah, I see you do. Well, so do I!"

He knew his legends; that's why folks aware of his deviancy generally referred to him as the Legendarian. Consequently he knew Durga's father, King Yama, was named after Underlord Yama Nergal. Appropriately, as the acclaimed devil-god of miners his Tvasitar Talisman was a pickaxe.

However, long before Tethys was born the first time, the Underlord hooked up with Nergal Vetala. One of Mithras's moon goddesses, Vetala was by far the most fruitful of female Master Devas; hence why her fellow, third generational devils addressed her as Fecundity.

The Nergalid thereby attained the status of a fertility god, King Harvest. As such he also became a Devil Death. Chrysaor Attis beat the, from then on, as often as not, scythe-wielding Mithradite unto Incain for withholding tribute from the Taurus's Mithrants – an unpardonable sin in the Upper Head. But some deviancies transferred from parents to offspring generation after generation.

His did, albeit only vaguely. There was no guarantee his son or daughter, or grandson or granddaughter, would become him just because he was his or her father or grandfather; or his or her mother or grandmother, for that matter. So, if King Yama was connected to King Harvest in terms of half-parentage howsoever far in the past, Durga may have inherited his penchant for grimly reaping. Mind you, maybe she just enjoyed roasted nuts.

"In other words," Aerial cautioned him, "You better play your cards right. You do, you might last long enough to see Jotan's kid." But not for much longer, Tethys appreciated.

Only devils and some deviants could cast glamours as effectively as an Ant Nightingale. He nonetheless harboured no illusions about Helena Somata or her by-the-bookishness sensibilities. During her final years on the Outer Earth, Constantine declared her Augusta. That title had not only bestowed nominal greatness upon her. It also granted her the divine right to life and death. Which, as far as Tethys was concerned, was an altogether illegitimate authority for anyone to arrogate, but one she evidently took to quite gravely, allowing for some atypical gallows humour.

Within a few years of returning inside, she became the High Illuminary as well as the Master of the Weirdom of Kanin City. Less than two decades before he sauntered into her life, she personally extinguished her only daughter and her only known grandson in here. That her grandson happened to be a succession of the Attis was as much a testament to her prowess as a consensus Master of Weir as it was to her ruthlessness.

She'd have no more qualms than she'd have anywhere near as much trouble disposing of him. Oh, she might risk offending Durga and steer clear of mutilation while he was still breathing. But there'd be a show trial and a public scourging, to be swiftly followed by a good old fashioned, Roman-style crucifixion. Then again, in deference to this fabled redeemer of hers, she might opt out of the wooden cross routine and go for the gallows instead. Hopefully he'd at least be unconscious before she had him drawn and quartered, then consigned his remains to the local pigsty.

No, he didn't have to be psychic to know what Helena had in store for him. He did need to be psychokinetic, however. And he was when it came to devic daddy's Gypsium quill.

========

There, running on the air itself above the Gregarian Fields, multi-headed Cereberant or Keres hellhounds pulled a wheeled cauldron.

Through the boggle eyes of his bloated boar's head mask, he could see Divine Coueranna standing in back of it. She looked fit to split, which, given the time of year, she would. In front of her, Brainrock bident in one massive paw and the hellhounds' reins in the other, loomed her charioteer and fallback-companion of much more than two millennia: Cruel Plathon, the Bull of Mithras.

Seeing them proved too much for Chrysaor Attis to accept. Whirling, reflexively clutching his right side as an old wound in it painfully ripped open, he re-entered the tent of the patently duplicitous devil he addressed as father.

========

"Had second thoughts, boy?"

"Whom were you talking to? I heard voices."

"Myself. What do you want?"

"You've been deceiving me all along. You commanded them to come."

"Only humans and demons are that devious," sneered Mithras. "If they come, it's of their own volition."

Removing his external spoils, Attis heaped them in the middle of the pavilion's floor. Clad only in ordinary sandals and a peasant's tunic, without any of his purloined goods and glories to cover him, he stood once again revealed as the golden-brown warrior. After dumping dozens more Tvasitar-trinkets out of his bottomless bag, he tossed it – the kibisis itself, along with howsoever many more dozens of talismans still inside it – atop the pile.

Still clutching his side, blotches of blood already staining his tunic, he flung apart the flaps of the pavilion and strode defiantly away from it. The hundred presences he'd felt surrounding him moments earlier, some already spirits gaining shapes, roiled past him into it.

He didn't care. He gave them his back. If the cowards wished to strike him down, let them do so as cowards did: from behind!

He had never felt so free in all his successions.

========

Woody had his hands pinned to his lap. Clever as that was, no amount of research into his very nearly unique deviancy could account for his innate guile. Tethys thought his quill out of Aerial's grip and into a sixth finger on his left hand. He didn't need to splotch out his sketchpad. Instead he splotched a pre-signed getaway sketch out onto his pants.

True, trees usually didn't grow so fast. They always had pointy tipped branches, though. Getting killed hurt as much as ever.

========

Children should never be allowed to witness the skewering of their father. No matter how much they might hate them; neither should most wives be present when a pointy stick suddenly extending from a humanoid oak impales their husbands. Plentiful puking and all-around voiding quickly became the odoriferous order of the moment.

"What the fuck?" cursed Sylvia, the deadly dryad, as she retracted her bloody bough.

"I'm alright, mom," said her daughter, the chair upon which the Legendarian's body was still draining. Sylvia's tree branch hadn't quite pierced all the way through Tethys's back and thereafter into their daughter's front.

"Not you, Woody," said Sylvia. "Where the fuck did his extra finger go?"

To gain a better view, Woody grew humanoid. Springing onto two feet from her consequentially awkward, knees challenging, backwards crouch, she let the remains of her father slide unceremoniously onto the tent's straw-covered, slatted floor. "What extra finger?"

Like the dryads an exception to the puke-rule, Saudi caught the reference straightaway. The sylph continued to clutch Tethys's Liberty Cap, but the now dead deviant's quill no longer stuck out of it. Tossing mothers and half-siblings aside effortlessly, the Saur Tsarina rumbled across the canvass enclosure and stopped, towering over Tethys's sprawled corpse.

Facially Saurs weren't the easiest to read but her voice betrayed equal measures of anger and frustration. "Damnation, Sylvia!" she swore, railing at the elder dryad, whose sap clearly ran as coldly as the Steg's blood did. "You promised me his quill. What's happened to it?"

"If I knew that," countered the Mother Oak, "I wouldn't have an empty acorn."

"You still will eat him, won't you?" Durga, another exception to the puke-rule, asked the Sari Witch. "Minus the nuts, I mean."

"Jotan!" sputtered Ute Tethys, between heaves. Even when they were wholly swan maidens, ravens cawed comprehensibly to Valkyries.

Volsanga née Nibelung heard it too. Responsive to her honk-like blat, her psycho-swan flew out of the Weird. Volsanga was on it and back between-space before anyone had time to react. Then something else came out of the same interspatial nowhere. It was a psycho-pterosaur, a Terror Donna.

"Sorry, Durga, no nuts," said Saudi, as her soul-self-animated psychopomp – another reason for the mnemonic, psyche-prompt – gobbled up as well as down Tethys's body in a couple of gulps. "Want her to lick the mess off the floor while she's at it, Hopi? Or should we wait until everybody's done spewing?"

========

Jotan Tethys didn't perceive Divine Coueranna in back of her flying cauldron.

As was her wont, come the Winter Solstice, appearing to be nine months pregnant, aka Myrionymous Kore looked to be herself only to her fellow devils and someone like the real Attis, albeit only because he was looking through the Mask of Byron at the time. To everyone else, Jot included, she appeared to be whom she was occupying: Meroudys now Tethys, last spring's Corn Queen for a Day, about to burst with birth.

Last spring's chosen Attis did perceive Kore's Charioteer for whom he was, standing in front of his dear wife and snapping the reins of their psycho-hellhounds. He panicked, irrationally but understandably.

========

Cruel Plathon – the fearsome, multi-horned Bull of Mithras – slavered visibly. And he had such huge teeth. He was hauling his Meroudys in from Apple Isle in order to offer up her and their newborn, or about to be born, rendered bled, to the Moloch Sedon, whom Jot had heard revelled in eating babies.

That was how Mithrants and Mithradites alike would secure Sed-sire's aid, and their corresponding success, come this afternoon's pending Theomachy. It had to be. Regardless of the fact that everyone except apostate Horrites – like the homicidal Persian he'd heard about a few months back – and other suchlike maniacal monotheists knew Master Devas and their progenitors reviled, not revelled in, blood sacrifices, Jotan felt sure of that.

Bursting away from his escort he raged off in the direction of the Praetorium, above which the glorified dogcart by now circled. Thinking him belatedly crazed by the departure of his recently All-claimed azura – which, given his baseless paranoia, he probably was – his companions tackled him. They then proceeded to hammer on him with his very own hornpipe for trying to skedaddle.

A raven saw their faith-fanaticized brutality transpire. It was no ordinary raven. Neither was it a psychopomp. While it couldn't talk, its cawing was instantly picked up and echoed by hundreds of other Hellion-trained ravens in the Mithrants' campsite and its environs. Not just Hellions comprehended squawking ravens.

========

By his own admission, 30-Beers, the legendary 30-Year Man, never quite grasped the concept of soldiering. The real Attis might therefore have predicted that the first previously azura-occupied, sentient being within the scope of All's range to rebel would be a Tethys. Not being out and out prescient, what the real Attis would never have foreseen was that the first Tethys to rebel would be the second Tethys to achieve Attis-surrogacy in comparatively recent history.

Rather, Jotan was only the second Tethys he could recall, off the top of his head, winning a Mithrant Paternalia. Then again, as prodigious as it was, his memory wasn't perfect. Besides, it only encompassed two and a half millennia worth of personal successions. A Tethys could have won the Paternalia before he came along, he supposed. But he doubted it. For one thing, what would they have called him – an Easter Bunny?

As an accomplished military strategist, Attis grounded his calculations solely on logic and logistics. Yet, as soon as he found out Jot's surname during the course of last spring's Hilaria, curiosity got the better of him. He thereupon made inquiries as to his designated surrogate's complete parentage.

As a result he probably would have been able to predict that the first person to attend him, albeit via the Weird, was his mother, Volsanga born Nibelung.

========

A glowing quill appeared on his chest. Jotan breathed anew. Only moderately spitefully, his mother re-killed him. Bye-bye Brainrock quill.

========

Swan Maidens gathered slain warriors worthy of perpetuating. What with 40 thousand and more men at arms massing in the Mole, on two if not necessarily three sides, today had the makings of a banner day for harvesting heroes. It was about time, too. Of late devils and their enforcers, primarily Attis's Mithrant legionnaires, rarely countenanced anything beyond the occasional minor skirmish in the Upper Head.

Such slim pickings made earning a living something of a groan for Valkyries. They had quotas to keep. Despite the incontestable skilfulness of Valhallan reclamation specialists, corpses didn't last forever. Besides, if he could, which he probably couldn't, Hell's Halls were too good for her despicable ex. Jordy didn't deserve to become a Valhallan, a Sangazur-reanimated member of the Glorious Dead. Her son did, if only as a member of its marching band.

She cracked something skull-like and crystalline against Jot's forehead. Mom and son were momentarily embracing. Properly prepared crystal skulls made excellent receptacles for Sangazur Spirit Beings but they also worked in reverse, as soul sinks.

"Sedon curse the Tethys-deviant to Belialma's Satanwyck," Volsanga swore out loud as soon as she realized the crystal skull she'd smashed on her unfortunate son's deadhead wasn't re-forming. "Another of the dastard's bastards must have just died."

========

It wasn't Ravi Tethys – not yet it wasn't anyhow.

========

Minutes after Volsanga flew off between-space on her psycho-swan, the severely hung-over Rajput prince's Mama Durga marshalled some of his half-brothers and sisters to help carry him out of Hopi's booze-tent. Many of the others who'd been there left at the same time. George Masterson was among them. Untying Hinny the Hippy from the tethering post, he spurred her into the Weird.

Although he wasn't following Volsanga, he was heading in the same direction. His masterly mother had charged him with keeping an eye, preferably two, on the Mithrants' Praetorium. She'd even helped conjure an invisible gargoyle about his eyestave in case he needed it. He'd just been taking a break from his duties. Mama Hel wouldn't mind. She liked Ute Tethys almost as much as he did.

It was past time he got married and settled down, they both figured. So don't do anything untoward, she'd warned him. You see anything out of the ordinary – like, say, the Devil himself baking babies over a baptismal bonfire on a pitchfork – you and

Hinny scamper straight back to Kanin City. It wasn't that Helena feared he'd end up like his wayward father just had if he didn't. She was afraid he'd end up as his father.

Unlike Georgie, being evening entertainers rather than daytime tradespersons many of those suddenly up and leaving the enclosure didn't have anything remotely pressing to get back to doing. Furthermore, the veritable stampede – the majority didn't even finish their drinks – had little to do with the fact that, to a one, they were still sick to their stomachs. Nor did it have to do with the stench they'd made while emptying them. That might never go away. Memories of it never would, that was for sure.

Lingering queasiness aside, Ravi was the only evacuee ill unto incapacitation. However, hanging around to watch a Terror Donna lap up the messes they'd deposited on the tent's slatted floor with such gusto, along with most of its straw, made no sense to approaching every man, woman or child, human or nonhuman, amongst them.

Self-preservation dictated their departures. Pterosaurs were as notoriously indiscriminate as they were insatiable.

========

Yeast Tethys, Garden to his mother, had indeed been out sowing his wild barley.

========

Diddling done for the nonce, he strolled into Hopi's 90% empty booze-tent arm-in-arm with his barley bin, as she'd referred to herself more than a few times during the multiparty, polyamorous orgy she instigated after last night's bash. She was a fauna, a female faun or satyr. She loved doing what fauns did best; namely loving. Her name was Pusan Wanderlust. If it weren't for the existence of the Attis and the Legendarian she'd be the most famous deviant still around.

Stegs had wicked, piton-spiked tails. Saudi Tethys swatted Yeast Tethys with hers big-time, endgame-time. Pusan had a Tvasitar Talisman of her own, a shepherd's pedum or crooked staff. She was also known as the Trailblazer. Trails weren't all she blazed. Saudi, on her Terror Donna, fled between-space. Both were blazing.

Sure enough, Tethys's quill began materializing atop Yeast's body. Woody went for it. Trees burnt too. Being barely 20, Woody's bark was nowhere near as fire-resistant as her mother's. Appreciating that, Sylvia dropped an acorn. It popped like an overcooked chestnut full of poof. Both dryads sank into the ground. Roots were wonderful, especially when they could lengthen as easily as they could retract.

"Could do with some assistance here," Pusan cried.

In terms of Sisterhood affiliations, she was an Althean, after the Greek word 'althainein' – meaning 'to heal' – and Amalthea, the she-goat who suckled the Classical Greeks' mythological Baby Zeus. Simultaneously siphoning nearly negligible fragments of an individual's life force from a volunteer into victims of violence or unexpected disasters, so long as there weren't too many of them, was how Alts worked their healing hoodoo.

No one was swifter to respond to Wanderlust's plea for sharing his or her howsoever-evanescent essence than the younger of the two Plantagenet vintners. Like Georgie did Ute – and vice versa – Jardin Tethys fancied Garden Tethys. It worked as well. Yeast breathed anew. So where had the quill gone this time?

========

Durga Tethys did enjoy roasted nuts, though son Ravi preferred chestnuts. Leaving him alone in the tent where his half-brothers and sisters deposited him, she went out to get him some. When she returned he wasn't there. Neither was his multi-stringed lute. The two turbaned soldiers she posted outside his tent were completely flummoxed. They hadn't seen him go anywhere.

Maybe she'd have some proper nuts roasted today after all.

****

THEO 7:

THE HEADLESS GORGON
========

Taurus Chrysaor Attis paused at the edge of the mound on top of which Thrygragos Varuna Mithras conjured his pavilion out of the Weird. Djinn Domitian awaited him. His half-father's four-winged, tattered angel jerked his lion's head significantly skyward.

The Keres-pulled, wheeled cauldron in which rode the Korants' goddess, Kore-Concord as devils generally referred to Divine Coueranna, looked to be making its final go-round overhead before coming down for a landing.

"Shall I blow them in, sir?" queried the Masochist, fanfare trumpet at the ready.

"I'd rather you blow them up."

"Of course you would, sir, but that isn't what I asked. By the way, there's a hubbub of rhubarb going on over there."

"How about I pipe them in instead?"
========

Perseus rides Taurus the Bull, slaying him. At least he does in the night's sky above the Inner and the Outer Earth. That Perseus and that Taurus were and are constellations. Reputedly the hero Perseus slew more than a few monsters in his day, most notably the gorgon Medusa. That Perseus and that Medusa were mythological characters. The reality wasn't all that much different.

In the legend of Perseus, Medusa was a mortal who had the power to petrify men just by looking at them. With winged sandals he'd borrowed from Hermes, the messenger of the gods, Perseus flew to Libya, where she lived with her immortal sisters, Stheno and Euryale. Thanks to Hades' dark helmet of invisibility he was able to sneak up on her. Catching her reflection in a mirrored shield provided by his patron, Olympian Athena, Zeus's heady daughter, he could avoid looking directly at her face, not that she could see him anyhow.

With an adamantine sickle, also given to him by Hermes, he decapitated her. Slipping her head into the magic wallet Athena lent him, he dumped her body in the Middle Sea on his way back to Greece. At that point Pegasus and Chrysaor, Medusa's until then unborn sons by Poseidon – Neptune, as the Romans had the simultaneously horse, earthquake and sea lord – popped out of her lacerated neck fully grown.

One Chrysaor of legend was born grasping a golden falchion, a thick broadsword or harpe with a slightly curved blade that was still in popular use today among Attis's legionnaires. A less sanitized version of the same myth had Chrysaor born as a golden-skinned giant whose thick blade grew out of his crotch.

In that version Perseus snapped it off Chrysaor whereupon, leaping onto Pegasus, he flew off to attend to the rest of his adventures. One of these ended with him rescuing wife-to-be Andromeda from a he-monster of the sea, the Kraken. Presumably he used the golden giant's blade on the Kraken and not on Andromeda.

Those were two versions of his-story abbreviated. In a way it was too bad the ancients didn't have an incarnation of the Legendarian around to tell them the straight goods. Then again the ancients tended to twist tales much more than the deviant ever did. Thus, while the gist of their versions weren't altogether a heap of horse hooey, the Tethys-truth of the matter was much duller.

The real Perseus was the Attis in one of his comparatively early successions. The winged boots he'd acquired from Irisiel Mercherm, as later-on Illuminaries named Lazareme's female sun-runner or Heliodromus, his Angela, with her feet still in them. Similarly he already had the magic wallet, Flowery Anthea's bottomless bag or kibisis. It was akin to the Dual Entities' Trans-Time Trigon in that it followed him from succession to succession; his transmutable, Brainrock spoils inside it.

Neither Hades, whomever he was, nor heady Athena, Mediterranean Athena or Methandra Thanatos as bygone Illuminaries had her, gave him anything except, in her case, grief. He'd had the dark helmet of invisibility, the mirrored shield and the curved blade since his first lifetime.

They were variations on the commonest forms taken by the Trigregos Talismans: the Crimson Corona, the Amateramirror and the Susasword. Which in turn were named after the lowborn devic 'cousins' who tricked Tvasitar Smithmonger into forging them in the first place some 2500 years ago: Byron's Crinsom, Lazareme's Ama-Tera and Mithras's Susal, as Illuminaries retroactively named the just as long ago cathonitized threesome.

Along with the Thrygragos Talismans, he'd left them in his half-father's pavilion. Now was the first time in all his successions he was without any of the six Great Godly Glories; the first time since Pyrame Silverstar helped him acquire them from the Weirdom of Cabalarkon in his initial existence, put more accurately.

The ancients didn't have many stories featuring Medusa's mythological sons by Poseidon. However, Tethys collected versions of the myth of Bellerophon and the chimera wherein Bellerophon was named Chrysaor. It was one of the few times he'd been correctly identified by his Entities-given name and there was no doubt Perseus's Pegasus did play a part in Attis's Bellerophon succession.

So did Chrysaor's falchion, albeit as his phallus. Bellerophon was a randy bugger.

========

Cruel Plathon was Perseus's Kraken. As resolutely male as Dark Sedon and Tantal Thanatos, somewhat uncharacteristically for him the multi-horned monstrosity was also Bellerophon-Chrysaor's arch foe the chimera, a goatish female horror.

Tralalorn, the Head's ever-girlish Perpetual Presence, forced trans-sexuality on him as an intentionally belittling form of retribution. He never should have swallowed the Demon Child's White Dwarf. It not only gave him indigestion, it gave him fiery breath. Thankfully Bellerophon exterminating the chimera ended the Bull's short-lived state of embarrassment.

Plathon wasn't the Medusa, though. She'd be in Mithras's pavilion retrieving her Tvasitar-trinket.

========

Thrygragos Varuna Mithras conjured more so than erected his tent. He'd done so on a little hump of land rising from a well-trodden, frost-flaked cattle pasture in the centre of the two Mithrant legions' main encampment. On instructions from his leontocephaline herald, Djinn Domitian, those who prepared the Praetorium to become Attis's general headquarters left the barrow mound and part of the cattle pasture surrounding it otherwise unoccupied for just such an eventuality.

The ground shook, toppling both Attis and the Masochist onto their butts. Behind them the Great God's plain, ever-so-ordinary and unprepossessing tent suddenly grew into a splendidly huge, golden Tholos, one finally worthy of a Thrygragos. Evidently Mithras was showing off. As he hauled himself onto his feet, the Masochist typically exclaimed what a delightfully entertaining experience that'd been.

The four-winged Heliodromus would, Attis thought to himself, as he got as far as his knees. On Fool's Day, Black Lazam, as part of the spring rites of Hilaria, Domitian endured the brunt of the punishment Mithrants and Korants alike inflicted on that year's surrogate Attis. While he didn't grin and bear it – the pain was real, he just absorbed most of it in lieu of his shell – he enjoyed it so much he'd been coming back for more for literally centuries.

The ground shook anew, knocking them both bums-backwards again. When the quakes finally subsided Attis looked to lion-headed Domitian and mouthed the query: "Disaster?" Headless Ramazar, the Apocalyptic of Sudden Destruction, was disproportionately fond of earthquakes. He might have just recovered his Tvasitar Talisman, a blowpipe when Attis confiscated it from him successions earlier. Of course it could be anything now.

"Unless it was Sinistral Wrath, sir," Domitian counter-proposed, not daring to even try to rise again quite yet. "He was prone to stomping his feet a lot."

Grim Thordin, as Illuminaries of Weir named Wrath, had an adze for a power focus. Usually he puffed on it as if it was a calabash pipe. Which was why devils also called him the Prince of Pollution. At least Wrath had a head and a consequential mouth with which he could smoke his accordingly altered talisman. Ramazar-Disaster didn't; hadn't had since shortly after becoming individually solid.

So how did he utilize his blowpipe? He collected severed heads, gifts from his adherents, and had them do it for him, naturally. He also collected hats, often with the heads that had them on when they were decapitated still wearing them.

Devils may not kill but they delighted in deviltry.

========

Feeling the worst was over; the Masochist helped the Attis to his feet.

"What was that you said, jinni?"

"The hubbub of a rhubarb, sir?"

"No, about piping them in?"

"I don't pipe, I blow."

"Sorry," Attis apologized. "I must have misheard you."

"You must have."

"The rhubarb then?"

"Suffering-Sapienda-you and Black-Lazam-me, we just got hammered endgame big-time with our own horn. Fortunately his mom arrived in time to stick a Sang into him, so it didn't prove precisely terminal."

"Somebody tried to kill Jotan Tethys?"

"No, some of your overenthusiastic legionnaires definitely did kill him, whereupon his mom in effect resurrected him. I'm suspicious. You know who Kore's got?"

"Last spring's Corn Queen for a Day."

"And you recognized All's squall?"

"It sounded like a banshee's wail, an anticipatory death's song, yes. From what you just told me, it's already tolled for Jotan Tethys. Only you think it's tolling me and thee as well, don't you?"

"No, I think the Pauper's tolling All for Papa Light, Truth and Justice. And I think she's doing it on Grandfather Sedon's command, as a final warning to him to back off this Thrygragon he's so desperately declared before it's too late."

"Not again!" Attis's exclamation referred to the ground raising up to slap him in the face, unless it was the other way around, as it sometimes seemed.

This, they agreed as they both stayed down this time, was definitely Wrath stomping his feet on the ground in anger. Attis could empathize. A few minutes ago he was ready to stomp Mithras into it, the ground. Might their mutual father – half-father in his case – have just denied the former Sinistral permission to go after him?

And what was with the all-new land bridge?

========

The land bridge silently tempted them to walk across it. Domitian declined. He may be a masochist, but he was also perceptive and suicidal he wasn't.

========

There was nothing natural about the bridge. It was shaped like a solitary wing, a female sphinx's wing. The Taurus did walk across it. He did so as far as the next hillock. There was nothing natural about it either. For one thing it too hadn't been there moments earlier. For another it was shaped like the shaved bald topside and backside of a sphinx's head.

Someone was waiting for him. She held the symbols of Pharaonic authority: a crooked rod and threshing flail. She sat on a boulder, a knob-like bump on All's cranium he'd never noticed the Mandroid having before. She patted it with the flail, bade him sit beside her. He hesitated. Pyrame Silverstar had gone tetrahedral-headed on him. He did so anyhow.

The She-Sphinx retracted all but her head and bump. She did something else as well. All of a sudden the hillock looked entirely natural, as if it had always been there. The fabulously female Perpetual Presence, as she proudly considered herself, was another who made a point of covering her ass. Only she sat on what she was covering its loveliness with – the Prison Beach of Incain's self-proclaimed All Invincible Gynosphinx.

"You're bleeding again," Pyrame said, without a mouth with which to say it.

"I'm not sure it ever stops."

"Baloney. I've seen them too."

Even in a peasant's simple tunic the Universal Soldier remained an imposing specimen. With his long, thick, dirty brown to reddish hair, leaf-green eyes and golden-brown skin, he would have been beautiful, an Adonis, had his heavily muscled body not been covered with scar tissue. All except one were from this succession. It, the one she was referring to, had indeed begun weeping anew.

The lancing in his side transferred with him despite his recurrence in numerous subsequent bodies. Since acquiring it that was how he demonstrated to his legionnaires he'd returned from the grave yet again. As Pyrame implied, he'd received it courtesy of Cruel Plathon, the Bull of Mithras.

He hadn't been with her then. He'd been with All-Eyes, the third-born Byronic Love Goddess whom bygone Illuminaries eventually came to name Aphropsyche Morningstar, APM for short. Neither had the Bull been a bull in that early-on succession. He'd been a wild boar and Attis had indeed been Adonis.

"So you gave in," she put to him after he settled down beside her.

For a bump on the head of a glorified mechanism it felt exactly like a boulder. Then again Mandroids were mostly composed out of Brainstone or Stoprock, a mixture of Gypsium-Brainrock and Solidium-Stopstone somehow hardened out of between-space and then animated. The Female Entity, miraculous Mnemosyne Machine that she was, really knew what she was doing when she wrought All of Incain, aka Ginny the Gynosphinx, hundreds of years' pre-Genesea.

"So I gave in. I expect you'll have to too. Sedon's Whore or not, Pyrame, flaunting those things won't make you any more popular with your siblings. Their original owners will be wanting them back."

"I doubt that," she said, nonetheless surreptitiously slipping the rod and flail into her just as glowing waistband. "Correct me if I'm wrong but didn't you take them from their original owners on the Outer Earth, whereupon you left their spirit selves out there as if ghosts to haunt wherever you left them?"

"No, you're right. I've beaten up so many devils I sometimes forget where I beat them, in both senses of word, the place and the part of their body."

"Want to borrow my cloak?"

"Actually I wouldn't mind. Sure you won't freeze?"

"I'll be getting the cold shoulder with or without it on, Chrysaor. Besides, I look good with goose-bumps."

"You'd look a whole lot better with your regular head."

"To you and Sedon, maybe. To my fellow Master Devas, never."

"It looks like we're about to find out for sure. Here they come."

========

Most devils were vain, prone to affectations, especially around each other. A head shaped like a tetrahedron was a tribute to Pyrame's imagination if nothing else. Four flat, triangular sides, the upper three of which slanted upwards to an apex, while meeting the bottom fourth identically so in each corner, certainly made her unique looking. That the only facial feature the upper three had was a solitary eyeball staring out of each of them only served to supplement her distinctiveness.

Emphasizing her matchlessness so inimitably was pure hubris. It was also unnecessary. As the lone, proven effective, conceptive half-mother of the Moloch Sedon's mortal Sed-sons, everyone who knew anything about the much more than four millennia long relationship between her and the devazurs' All-Father already acknowledged Pyrame was without peer.

It was only early winter, but pond ice and frost had been forming during the night for a couple of weeks in the Cheeks and Upper Head. There'd even been a sprinkling of snow overnight, some of which could be seen adhering to treetops in the distant woods. Ordinarily devils weren't affected by chilly weather. However, because she had no adherents of her own, Pyrame might welcome the warmth her woollen cloak provided.

She nevertheless took it off and handed it unselfishly to Attis. Gratefully he draped it around his shoulders. Golden-brown warriors may give the impression of being godlike, but they could freeze to death the same as any ordinary mortal. Besides, he was as vain as she was and, in the company they were about to be keeping, shivering betrayed weakness.

Underneath her cloak Pyrame wore the same sheer, sheath dress she'd had on earlier that morning on Incain. Immodesty aside, there it at least made a degree of sense. Being about as far south as one could go on the Hidden Headworld without having to swim, the Prison Beach was warm throughout the year. It still covered her from the ribs to the ankles, was still tied at the waist by a corded papyrus belt and was still held up by embroidered suspenders that went between her bared breasts.

She'd added some touches to it since Incain. A decorative neckband or torc now attached to its straps. Appended to it was a uraeus, an ornament fashioned into the likeness of a sacred asp or cobra. Like every Tvasitar Talisman it gleamed with the telltale luminescence of Gypsium-Godstuff.

As well as Sedon's Whore, devils called her the Pauper Priestess. Her lack of adherents was one reason for that, but there were many others. The uraeus, the rod, the flail, her waistband and most of the rest of her visible and invisible accoutrements were not her power foci. Tvasitar Smithmonger – the highborn Lazaremist devils generally addressed as the Anvil Artificer, after his primary power focus, an anvil – never crafted a talisman specifically for her because, for some reason, she had no need of one to remain a solid individual.

Pyrame had the ability to wield the power foci of her siblings in Mithras and her cousins in either Byron or Lazareme. While there was nothing special about that – anyone, not just any devil or any deviant, could do that – she took a perverse pleasure wielding the talismans of devils what fans she did have overpowered on her behalf. Attis had given her much of those she undeniably did flaunt at her request. Their talismans amounted to trophies.

Without power foci, devils were just spirit beings. Unlike azuras, they could and generally did dominate the sentient shells they were forced to possess in order to survive with their wits altogether intact. That was slight consolation for what those the Attis stuck in All of Incain had lost, though.

Brainrock talismans gave Master Devas supernatural attributes, what made them worthy of worship in the first place, yes. But, along with almost anything else, they also stored their subtle matter bodies, what allowed them independent mobility; regenerated them, too.

The mutual enmity Attis and Pyrame bore Divine Coueranna and Cruel Plathon, both of whom were higher born than she was, was what bound them initially. Sex was only a logical extension of that bond. While not compatible species in terms of being able to have each other's children in any ordinary sense, humans and devils in humanoid form were quite capable of loving and making love to each other.

Devils were also quite capable of hating humans. There wasn't much point in hating those who worshipped you, however. Attis knew himself to be an altogether different matter. Devils could and, more often than not, did hate him. As their proven equal the Moloch Sedon would never ill-star anyone for killing him.

Many had, some more that a few times, but he kept coming back. He was ever mindful that one day he might not. Not just because he was the Universal Soldier, that was why he never surrendered; why he always fought to the bitter end. He might go, but he'd never go quietly.

Unfortunately, without his regalia, the one day he went, never to recur, could be today.

========

One by one, holding or wearing their retrieved power foci, and no doubt thoroughly abashed, a hundred, newly re-solidified Master Devas slowly filed out of their father's no longer modest tent. Some were completely naked. That was their choice. Devic bodies were de-brained demons. Although none-too-bright themselves, certainly not when compared to all except the lowest born Master Devas, be-brained demons could shift shapes. What could shift shapes could easily grow clothes out of what amounted to their skin or hide or whatever.

Safely away from their father's dramatically enlarged, now superficially splendiferous pavilion, deferential reverence swiftly gave way to oddly muted euphoria. The

Great God must have impressed upon them that any real celebration of their emancipation from All of Incain, and the corresponding repatriation of their collective godhood, would have to wait until after this afternoon's inevitable triumph over their cousins in Byron and Lazareme.

Attis and Pyrame sat casually chatting together on the All-camouflaged hillock as their siblings congregated in the rapidly churned-up pasture below and off to the side of Mithras's mound and Tholos. The devils, some of whom were truly horrifying to behold, reminded them of little children, of any species, strutting and preening about in delight at having a new outfit, even if it was just an old body.

Nattering softly but nevertheless excitedly to each other, only a couple of devils glanced their way. No one came up to them, they on their rocky bump atop a hump, and perhaps that was just as well. He may be a marvellous model of martial masculinity but right this minute, in tunic and cloak, with his side dribbling gobs of goo and he without a goblet to catch any of it, the golden-brown warrior felt more like a golden-brown chump.

Always one for making a showy entrance, Plathon whipped his non-winged, yet still airborne, psychopomp-hounds above the field a couple more times in descending circles. He finally brought Kore's wheeled cauldron, and Kore-Concord herself, to a squashy landing in the midst of the re-embodied devils.

Nine months pregnant, Divine Coueranna, as bygone Utopian Illuminaries named Ap Isle's onetime primary Apple Goddess, levitated out of it. Not surprisingly she did not let her always bare feet touch the ground, just hovered a couple of inches above it as her juniors in Mithras milled about, no doubt for some begrudgingly, paying her homage.

Thus far everyone there was her junior. Even Pyrame and Plathon were below her in the Mithradite pecking order. In truth, with Phantast the Dreamweaver a star in the Sedon Sphere since the disgraceful failure of the Crimson Conspiracy – which Dream co-masterminded with Kore's almost as long gone brood sister, Strife-Marutia – only Tantal Thanatos, God-King of Lathakra, and their other immediate sibling, Mithras's Virgin, she of Mythland, were her seniors.

The Virgin was as mad, or perhaps even madder, a mad goddess than Concord was at the height of their 500-year, Middle Sea matriarchate on the Outer Earth. Illuminaries named her Methandra after another fabled virgin, Mediterranean Athena. Her attribute was Heat whereas her brood brother's attribute was Cold.

With such seemingly contradictory characteristics, it was probably to be expected they were close to inseparable. As Attis's occasional drinking buddy, Jordan Q Tethys, the legendary 30-Year Man, was prone to saying: *'Opposites attract opposites'*. They didn't attract in bed, though. Much to Tantal, Mithras and, before them both, Sedon's immense aggravation, Methandra was resolutely a virgin.

In comparison, other than the Great God their father, who was undoubtedly hunkering down in his refurbished Tholos awaiting Kore and Plathon to come pay him due obeisance, on their knees, and in all probability the two Nergalids, Tantal had more azura offspring than any other male Mithradite. By that measure alone, as

Tethys was also fond of declaring, King Cold couldn't be anywhere near as frigid as his immediate sister.

With so many fawning over Kore-Concord, hardly anyone was paying attention to Plathon, who was born in the next surviving brood below the three Apple Goddesses. He was paying attention to them, though. More specifically, unless he sensed All's presence, which was unlikely minus her wing-like land bridge, he was paying attention to him. If, wherever they were, Methandra was Heat and Tantal was Cold, then the glare the Bull had fixed upon him was a tribute to the two eldest Mithradites remaining. Attis shuddered with sweat, or vice versa.

Then someone definitely was paying attention to Plathon. She was ruby red, stark naked, voluptuous to an extreme and evidently hornier than he was cranially. She barrelled out of the Weird, bowled him out of Kore's cauldron, flung him onto his back in the field's muck, and promptly got down to some serious petting.

Kore-Concord skewed her face in disgust. Her lone lasting, immediate sister, Kore-Concupiscence, Satanwyck's reigning Prime Sinistral, was humiliating her yet again. She, Lady Lust, did it every year on Suffering Sapienda, the night before Black Lazam, when, occupying the Korant Sisterhood's Corn Queen for a Day, she lay with their hated father, he occupying the Mithrant Brotherhood's designated Attis.

The Bull had a luxuriant pelt. Prior to leaving their Hell, inside Ap Isle's only active volcano, Mt Maenalus, Concord probably had her acolytes thoroughly wash and comb it out at the same time they groomed her hellhounds. It wasn't lush anymore; that was for sure. To Attis's two eyes, even from this distance it looked positively frothy.

"Hell's Belle and the Beast, eh, lover," Pyrame said, chuckling. "I wonder if Bad Daddy Thrygragos put her up to that. Apple-Kore and the Bull should have gone straight in to see him."

Bygone Illuminaries named Sinistral Lust Belialma, after Beltis, the female form of Baal, a Semitic fertility god who, for once, wasn't him. Baal was the very same Bull with whom Lust was currently reacquainting herself in typically disrobed Belialma-fashion. Devils weren't the only ones who called her Bouncing Belle, however. Having half-bounced with her as recently as nine months ago, Attis sometimes did too.

"Looks like the Bull's gone straight into her instead."

That crack got Pyrame going. She began chuckling the more, which was disconcerting given that, unlike the Moloch Sedon, the Headworld's mighty Eye-Mouth in the sky, none of her three side-eyes did double-duty as a mouth. They did sparkle, though, once she caught her breath, not that devils needed to breathe as such.

"Illuminaries should have called her Kore-Coitus."

"She certainly seems good at mud-wrestling. Maybe Illuminaries should have stuck with Beltis. Belting Beltis has a nice ring to it."

"Especially in a boxing ring."

"Wrestling ring," Attis corrected her good-naturedly, if only for the sake of consistency.

"Inspirational, I call it."

"Whoa. Here? And now? I'm not sure I'm up to it. Besides, Jordy always says Lust beds them, but Fecundity bags them."

"He's talking about marriage. Kore-Concord's all about divorce."

In part because he wasn't dependent on having offspring in order to succeed himself, but primarily because he was always on the move and Pyrame saw to it he was well looked after sexually, Attis rarely married. Nonetheless, that got a guffaw out of him. He must have guffawed too loudly because Pyrame not only ceased chortling, she gripped his right arm so tightly he reflexively withdrew the hand he'd been using to staunch the boar-tusk-lancing as if to protect himself.

"Damnation! She's heard you. Your face might be different, but your laugh must sound the same. Whistle for your Pegasus; get yourself out of here. All and I'll handle her and find you later. Damnation doubled! It's too late. Here she comes."

"Save All until you need her, Pyrame. There's nothing to worry about. I've already seen her and the boulder we're sitting on is still the only stone around. Besides, I left Whistler's whistle inside dad's tent. Oh, and while you're at it, stop mixing up your mythologies."

"Me, mixing my mythologies? I made most of them!"

"You made up most of them, you mean, and most of them weren't written down until starting maybe a thousand years ago. Even so, you're up mixing Bellerophon with Perseus." Attis enjoyed playing word games. Fays did too. Could be the rumours about his original birthparents were true. Could be the Dual Entities weren't human or humanoid time-tumblers. Could be they were fucking faeries. Faeries were tricksters after all.

"Bellerophon was Perseus."

"Only in the sense I was both of them. But I wasn't both of them in the same succession. Close, yes, and you're right, Bellerophon's alternate name was Chrysaor. However, he no more jumped out of her neck after I, as Perseus, chopped off her head than Pegasus did. The other thing about Bellerophon is his chimera was an aspect of Mithras's Bull, not Byron's Stallion. Byron's Chimaera is my Peg's devic half-daddy, though."

"Then why did Illuminaries call him Glimmenmare?"

"Devils like you can shift shapes at will, Pyrame. Why shouldn't you be able to shift sexes as well?"

"We can," she countered. "Mithradites just have more integrity. With the exception of Geld Neargon we consider trans-sexuality an abomination almost as vile as the Unnameable."

"All the more reason Byronics would then."

========

"That's very heartening to hear," said the Medusa.
The serpents coiling out of her skull must still have good ears.

========

The first thing that struck Attis was she hadn't struck him unto stone just by looking at him. The second was that she was carrying the bottomless bag he'd discarded in their joint father's tent moments earlier.

It wasn't her power foci; at least Tvasitar Smithmonger, Anvil the Artificer, the devic Prometheus as many thought of him, claimed not to have fashioned it for her. He'd done it for a very highborn daughter of Lazareme, a Number Two born daughter of Thrygragos Everyman if someone like Jordan Tethys could be trusted: none other than Flowery Anthea herself.

Attis had never personally encountered this Anthea – aka the Mistress of Life, Lazareme's embodiment of the spring season and in whose honour the first full month of that time of year, the second in the Lazareme Ternary, was named. Devil-despising Illuminaries must have admired her, though. Why else would they have named her after the Anthea of the antediluvian Anthean Witch Sisterhood?

Her having died most of two millennia before his first birth, he'd never encountered the pre and post Golden Age Anthea either. However, he knew she was the nominal wife of Xuthros Hor, the Tenth Patriarch of Golden Age Humankind, and the very man who caused the Genesea nearly 4400 years ago. Xuthrodites, devazurkind's consistently covert, conscientiously behind-the-scenes enemies, were named after Xuthros, whom the Outer Earth's Bible had as Noah for some unaccountable reason.

Although there were many, as-yet-unconfirmed rumours of an upstart, Hellions-associated group calling themselves Horrites, as far as he knew for sure Xuthrodites weren't found within the Sedon Sphere. Beyond the Dome, where he'd encountered hundreds of them over the centuries, well, clearly that was a different matter.

Xuthrodites formed an all-male brotherhood the same as his Mithrants did. Anthean Witches, who were found beneath the Dome in relative abundance, were their equivalent of in here's far more plentiful Korant Sisterhood. Most Mithrants married Korants. When they weren't on campaigns, they lived with them monogamously, albeit with occasional, yet always explicable lapses.

The rumours began when the mass-murderous Persian from down south – the one who almost became a Mithrant Heliodromus, managed to eyeorb Domitian and, but for Pyrame Silverstar, would have successfully fled the scene of his crimes once his perfidy was revealed – provoked such a high level of consternation some months ago. Notwithstanding him, and them, the murmurings, Master Devas did indeed often refer to Xuthrodites as Horrites. They did so because it sounded reminiscent of the word whore.

Since 'whore' implied payment for services rendered and devil-gods never paid for anything – rather, with your unreservedly directed devotion, you paid them for the good works they did on your behalf – whore for them was a pejorative term. In that respect Outer Earth Ants were Xuthroditic whores.

Attis had never come across the devic Anthea because she didn't last long as a solid individual. He'd heard a few deviations – to pun à la 30-Beers – of what had become of her over the course of his successions but, other than she didn't shine out of the night's sky, no one seemed to know where she was anymore.

Korants, who demonized the self-centred, unapologetically freewheeling ways of libertarian Lazaremists and their devotees, claimed she was burning on a perpetual pyre somewhere between-space off the Forever Forest of Wildwyck, which was on the eastern, occipital side of the Hidden Headworld. He'd heard the same thing from Lazaremists and Byronics, so that may well be the case.

Fittingly, according to the Korant account of her story anyhow, the pyre was of her own firing. Flowery Anthea's self-confessed and self-punished offence was two-fold. Firstly she was unfaithful to her man, devil that he was; secondly she was unfaithful with a woman, devil that she was.

For Korants, homosexuality was criminal. How could you have children if you only had sex with the same sex? Short of adoption you couldn't; the answer was that uncomplicated. Plus, adoption only meant you could raise children, not have them save possessively, like pots and pans or, if you were well-off, jewellery. Only married couples could adopt on Apple Isle – or most anywhere else in Marutia and the rest of the Upper Head for that matter. And, by definition, only members of the opposite sex could marry.

Although they'd never gone so far as to forcibly outlaw the practice due to the fact that sometimes, when they were far from home, certain needs had to be attended to, Mithrants like Attis thought much the same thing. Indeed, staffs and distaffs generally concurred that Korants should spend most of their lives from 14 to 40 being barefoot and pregnant, preferably with replacement legionnaires.

Which, come to think of it, probably explained why Divine Coueranna always went about barefoot. Attis definitely knew why she was almost always pregnant in midwinter, rather than in springtime, which would make a smidgen more sense. Bouncing Belle was the 'love them and leave them' sort. She left pregnancies to the shells she was occupying whenever she excited anyone sufficiently to get in the family way.

Unless it was with someone she judged worthy, such as her Thrygragos of a father, King Cold or the Bull, Kore-Coitus – as Pyrame had just dubbed beguiling Belialma – wasn't one for having azuras either. Her other immediate sister, his half-mother, Kore-Discord, Strife, Marut Kanin or Marutia, had thousands of them, more than a few a year going back to before 2000 YD. Except, until her disappearance in the aftermath of the Crimson Conspiracy, circa early on in the second third of the 41st Century of the Dome, she stuck almost exclusively to Mithras.

Reputedly Kore-Concord, Divine Coueranna, hadn't had any azuras since her last batch with their mutual father just prior to Discord, humanizing the Female Entity, supplanting her in Mithras's affections. She'd been inside plenty of other sentient beings when they conceived deviant babies, though. That was why Korants considered her their Goddess of Motherhood and Childbirth, as well as most everything else.

Devic possession was healthful; so was azura possession, and not just because the Dead couldn't reanimate without devils or azuras to mobilize them. As additional proof of that, the rare devil who dared tamper with the inevitable and seek to cure an otherwise terminal illness – or remedy a wound or injury, no matter how grievous – did so by possessing the individual dying until enough azuras could be summoned to take his or her place.

Furthermore, when howsoever foolishly answering a call to save the life of more than one adherent at a time, devil-gods did so by infusing them with a superfluity of their azuras. They were hardly ubiquitous, there weren't always an abundance of azuras around and, even when there were, it didn't necessarily work. But, when it did, that was one of the major reasons devils were regarded as gods throughout most of the Hidden Continent of Sedon's Head.

On the Devauray of last spring's week of Hilaria, two days after Suffering Sapiendev, the night of the Korants' Queen for a Day's defloration, their High Priestess – who went by the honorific of Miracle Maenad – would have examined the young woman to determine if she was pregnant.

If she was, which she was, Miracle Maenad would have deemed it not only safe but also appropriate for Djinn Domitian to *'resurrect'* that year's Attis on Sedonda Sun Day. Thereupon, with much pomp and ceremony, his surrogate would, and did, marry the Corn Queen on Mithrada Moon Day.

Although the names came much later, such was the way it had been on Apple Isle since the early years of the Age of Taurus, the way it had been since perhaps even before the Flood. The no longer precisely late Jotan Tethys was last spring's Attis. Kore-Concord was occupying the Korants' Queen for a Day, whom he himself had half-impregnated. It was Apple-Kore's yearly duty to keep her safe and sound until she gave birth. She looked minutes away from yet another job well done.

He still hated her.

========

He didn't hate the Medusa. She didn't even frighten him. Even without the six Great Godly Glories, or any other devic power focus, why should she?

========

"Especially since our father has tasked me with killing Byron's Stallion," she finished saying, stopping within easy spitting distance.

Well over 2,000 years had passed since Attis, as Perseus, stuck her inside All on Incain and confiscated not just her head. Nonetheless, the Medusa remained as fearsome to behold as any gorgon. Naked except for a glowing girdle – the other thing he'd confiscated all those centuries ago – in addition to her snaky hair she had four arms, filthy fangs and perspired blood. All of that then was right but, somehow, all of her today was wrong.

"Wouldn't you rather kill me instead?" Attis put to her, without bothering to either stand or hawk at her any spare phlegm he might have congealing in his throat.

"Of course I would. And I will. It'll be my reward come this evening. So Father promises and Great Gods never lie."

With surprising speed, tetrahedral-headed Pyrame rose to his defence, leaping to her feet and inserting herself bodily between him and the gorgon's gaze. "You may have regained your head, lowborn, but surely you've lost your mind. Otherwise you would not dare violate Grandfather Sedon's dictate against killing lesser beings."

"Every Attis is fair game, Egyptian. You know that. He has earned a final death."

One of Pyrame's many epithets was indeed Egyptian. Calling her that, though, indicated just how long the Medusa had been out of action. The Pauper Priestess hadn't

lain with the Moloch Sedon in the Great Pyramid of modern-day Egypt since probably before Attis went to Libya, at her request, and disposed of the conceivably twelfth-
born gorgon in much the same way Outer Earth myths recounted.

The enticing bitch should never have tried, and temporarily succeeded, taking
Sedon away from her.

"He has given up his goods and glories. What you are talking about isn't just
tantamount to murder. It is murder." When Dark Sedon discovered she couldn't bear
sedons, small case, the same as Pyrame could and did, he tried to leave her. The Medusa thereupon smote him. Make that stupefied him – she turned him to stone.

The damnedest thing was that none of them had any idea the Dual Entities
had time-tumbled back into the devils' then present and that Miracle Memory had
hold of the Medusa instead of Pyrame or the Unity of Harmony. They knew how she
smote him, though. Both her and Harmony did. Not only that, they hadn't kept it
a secret.

"Didn't I tell you?" proclaimed the boggle-eyed, snake-haired temptress. "From
now on you may address me as Mater Matare, Mother Murder, the Apocalyptic of
Death."

Chrysaor Attis took that as a challenge. He too was on his feet in an instant.
Brushing Pyrame aside as effortlessly as he would the strands of a weeping willow, he
confronted her face to non-stonily fearsome face. "Why wait? Let's get to it. The Bull's
inspired me and there's nothing I like better than wrestling Death Devils. Or would
you rather just give me its kiss right this minute?"

Without waiting for a reply, he grabbed the mostly naked, four-armed gorgon,
pulled the hell-spawn against himself, chest to nearly as bare chest, and smacked her
full on the lips. She was so shocked she glared at him with all three of her eyes wide
open. Eyefire was next. He braced himself. While devic eyefire could burn anything
as well as it could coerce, devils were so conditioned not to kill they mostly used it to
jolt, not to toast someone unto burnt cookie crumbs.

The Medusa, whatever she'd decided to call herself, blinked instead. "You got
my message, Attis." As if to emphasize she was done with him she spat on the ground
then rounded on Pyrame. Oddly to both of them, the Pauper Priestess had gone silver-haired and humanoid-headed again, albeit still with three eyes.

"And Kore says this is for you, whore. There are lots of unclaimed talismans
inside it, but neither she nor father before her would let any of us take them as sup-
plements to our own. Has to do with something she called Panharmonium, she says,
but you'd know that."

She flipped Flowery Anthea's kibisis at her. Pyrame caught it. "Don't either of
you be here once this is over." Without another word, the Medusa spun away and
stalked off downhill – down All, as yet unbeknownst to her – in order to rejoin the
hundred-odd other, mostly re-embodied devils in the cow pasture.

Significantly neither of the Apple Goddesses, Kore-Concord or Kore-Coitus,
were with them anymore. The Bull wasn't either. They must have finally gone into Mithras's Tholos to pay overdue respects to their father. All eyeballs, three per devil, save
for a couple of mono-balled Cyclopes, were now on them alone.

"That was crazy, Chrysaor," Pyrame, finally with a mouth again; a very inviting mouth, ripped verbally into him. "If I wanted a rock for a lover I'd have taken Petra Liber, only he's been cathonitized almost as long as we devils have had power foci. You should be as hard as this boulder."

"It isn't a boulder," he reminded her in little more than a barely audible whisper. "It's All of Incain. Besides, if I should be, then so should you. Except her head wasn't glowing, her girdle was, wasn't it? And you realized that as fast as I did, if not faster."

"So? Her girdle's her power focus. It's called a cestus, by the way. But maybe you're right. Maybe she realized we're sitting on All. The Masochist did."

"She looked directly at me, Pyrame. I provoked her on purpose. But you intervened on my behalf just as readily. If she could still turn men to stone, even if she can only turn them to stone for the short term like the Cockatrice and the Basilisk, she would have turned me any number of times already. When I was Perseus, her head glowed as brightly or brighter than her girdle. Mark me, something strange is going on."

"Aren't you getting ahead of yourself?"

Attis took her meaning instantly. He hadn't as yet picked up on why she'd gone back to being silver-haired, three-eyed and humanoid-headed, though. Then he did. "A head? Of course! Whatever else he is, Father Mithras is not that far gone. And, despite what he says about losing vast quantities of his adherents on the Outer Earth, he can't be that desperate either. But you and your siblings might be.

"Gods damn you bitches to Kore's Hell! That's why they're here, Kore and the Bull. You're not going to fight the other two Great Gods. You're going to throw in with them, they and their spawn. It's the Unnameable whose head the Medusa had on when I chopped it off. And it's his head that's in the bottomless bag."

"Wrong, lover."

"No, you're lying. You have to be. You're going to turn the Unnameable loose on Mithras."

"Devils are veracious, not voracious. We can't lie any more than we'll kill lesser beings. And you just kissed the wrong bitch. Kiss the right one this time."

"Huh?" Attis was thick. Silver-haired, Silverstar was irresistible.

"The Unnameable is a she."

========

She embraced him more so than they embraced each other. The cobra uraeus animated, sprang; its fangs clamped onto Taurus Chrysaor Attis, Mithras's Universal Soldier. It bit into his golden-brown chest. He pitched forward; unconscious by the time she caught and then gently lowered him to the ground.

"Well done, Queen of Courts. I was afraid you'd resist putting down your pet worship-killer."

****

THEO 8:

THE SMILING FIEND

========

Instantly reverting to her tetrahedral-headed self, Pyrame Silverstar rotated her entire body on the fulcrum of her neck in order to 'face' the one who'd just spoken to her.

"And who might you be, friend devil?"

========

"Friend?" the fiend chortled, smiling in that perpetually amused manner he didn't so much affect as never tried to stop doing. *"How very sharp of you, my poor, pathetic priestess. As you're perfectly aware, 'mithras' means 'friend' in a surprising number of old as well as still extant Outer Earth tongues. Yet today it means 'enemy'. Funny how time twists things, isn't it, Tanith?"*

So startled was she, Pyrame almost ignited her eyefire. As it was her eyes, one on each triangular side of her upper head, bulged very nearly to the point of popping out of their sockets. Smiler looked even more delighted than usual.

"Your eyeballs betray you. You're shocked. Don't be. I know all about you; know all the names you took beyond the Dome, wherever you went, wherever you were worshipped.

"Don't like Libyan or Etocretan Tanith? Would you prefer I call you Astarte? How about Inanna, goddess of the Outer Earth's first post Genesea civilization, that of Sumer-Shinar; Astroarche, Queen of the Stars; Ishara, Ishtar or Athtar, Lady of Justice; or Ashtoreth, Goddess of Byblos? Maybe you'd prefer Ashtart, Attar-Samayin, Asherah, Attart, or Aethra. Personally, I've always had a fondness for Astraea, Queen of Courts.

"Recognize me yet?"

"You're not Sedon."

"Perhaps not, but I was Sodom to your Gomorrah. And long, long before that I was the demons' king whilst the Moloch Sedon was only the devils' king. I was Daemonicus the First and Only to your Primeval Lilith, to your Demon Queen of the Night. We are binary beings, the real Great Gods of Civilization. You and I, not a pair of time-tumbling, occasional annoyances, should be remembered as the true Dual Entities, the true Male and Female Principals."

"Except no one can remember you unless you're physically standing right in front of them, can they? It's been quite a while, Judge."

"Not as long as you might think. Nonetheless, credit given where credit is due, you're quicker than most."

"I'm to gather credit for this madness is yours, not any of my elders."

"Ah, but I am their elder. Not even Mithras is older than me. I am, however, no more entitled to credit for Mithras's madness than anyone else except him and, perhaps, Sedon himself. We two are measly opportunists. So are all the rest of we remaining, of all three tribes. I trust you have all you need."

"I have All, if that's who you mean. You're standing on her."

Unfazed, the Fiend smiled even more broadly. *"I am aware of that, pauper. I was in the Weird, unnoticed and unremembered by you, it, Attis or the jinni, who were grovelling on the ground outside my brother's Tholos when it raised the land bridge to the back of its head out of its wing.*

"Not very subtle that, the Bull and Kore must have seen you do it from the air. Was that your way of reminding them you fancy yourself running this show?"

So mesmerizing was his voice, Pyrame was about to confirm his allegations when something he'd just said gonged her mental alarum. "Brother? Oh, that's right. You claim to be the Ahriman between Varuna and Mithras, don't you? I'd forgotten."

"Of course you did. Yet I am the middle third of the VAM Entity. Dark Sedon is just my father, the greatest of the Great Gods to be sure, but only a Thrygragos. You're my forever lover, more so than either the Moloch or the Attis ever have been, and you should remember all of that by now. Are you implying you don't?"

"I remember Judge Druj, the Lord Protector of Liars. What you don't seem to remember is that All detests being referred to as a thing. Aren't you afraid she might eat you?"

"For all the monster machine's built-in capabilities, it has no more sense of my presence than anyone else looking at us does. I am allowing only you to perceive me. You have All to protect you, but only from your fellow Master Devas. It cannot protect you from me, should I choose to become disagreeable or cantankerous.

"As long ago prearranged between you and the so-called firstborn, everything you think you'll need to conclude your aspect of the deal is in that bag, is it not? Nonetheless, I can't help but notice Attis still breathes. Is that not a breach of the Panharmonium Accord you and the exquisite Unity of Balance struck with your uncles, siblings and cousins?"

"So now you're trying to convince me you are Father Sedon. Except you can't be, can you? No matter what artifice he's come up with lately, All would have immediately sensed Sedon and eaten him already. Her makers, the Dual Entities, made that her prime directive seven centuries prior to their descendant, Xuthros Hor, unleashing the Genesea."

"Eaten or exploded trying, I'm aware of that too. Father Sedon's your real target, isn't he? Brother Mithras is just the lure, the bait. You've kept Attis alive, for now, because he'd never turn on his half-father. But he would turn on his grandfather. You'll use the Unnameable's head on Mithras, but you'll unleash Attis, armed with the Godly Glories, Master Helena's Trinondevs, with their Brainrock-powered cosmicars, and finally All, with its Stoprock, on Father Sedon as soon as he shows up to rescue his favourite.

"I admire your balls, especially the balls you females have. Let me guess, the Entities brought the Trigregos Sisters back with them this time. And they've taken hold of, who else, the last three surviving firstborn daughters."

By that, she knew, the fiend was referring to Byron's Moon, Lazareme's Unity of Balance and Mithras's Virgin. Pyrame also realized that, if she could believe him, whom she dare not, Methandra Thanatos was actually a second born of Thrygragos Sedon: that he, the Duke of Deception, along with either Varuna or Mithras was Sedsire's other remaining firstborn by the three Great Goddesses.

Which in turn solved the mystery of Mithras's missing third-born brood of three. They hadn't been lost in the Great Flood of Genesis after all. That was because Mithras's third-born were actually his second-born: the three Apple Goddesses. So much for devic infallibility, she mentally noted; at least so much for it when it came to their memories, she added, howsoever futilely given who was talking at her more so than to her.

"The Mnemosyne Machine clearly has you but who does Heliosophos have? Could it be Mithras again? Might it be Lazareme? Even though it has been a very long time since I've encountered a Helios with blue skin and golden hair, they do often look alike, don't they." Smiler was hardly the only one who consistently saw Thrygragos Lazareme that way. Pyrame did too.

"You're all ever-so-clever but, unless Helios does have him, aren't you severely underestimating Mithras? Make sure of one before you take on two, that's my best advice to you."

"Fay-saying now, Judge? Let me see, does that prove you're Sedon, Daemonicus, the King of All Demons either which way, or just a smiling fiend of no consequence any other way? While you're trying to make up your mind, why don't you just go away and leave me alone? You're wasting my time."

"Oh, I'll happily leave you to attend to your dirty deeds as soon as you answer me both respectfully and unambiguously. How can you be sure you truly do have everything you'll be needing to dispose of Brother Mithras?"

"Why don't you just spit it out, Judge? The Medusa said it was full of unclaimed power foci. Are you suggesting Mithras claimed the Unnameable's head for himself?"

"I wouldn't know, would I?"

"But you'd like me to find out, wouldn't you? You'd like me to have a look inside Flowery Anthea's laughably called *'magical wallet'*. If I turn to stone, you'll keep it. If I don't, you'll concoct some other amusement for yourself. Are you the one who has Helios? You are, I'd hazard that Kore-Concord is really Kore-Discord, and that Machine-Memory has her again, because I sure as fuck don't."

"Such language! Such convolution! Such unwarranted distrust! All I'm suggesting is I wouldn't want Thrygragon to fail because you and your plucky gal-pals lack what you, in your cocksureness, are so certain you have already. Please, feel free to do as you please."

"*'Do as you please'*, hmm. Did you just give yourself away? Are you a libertarian Lazaremist, Thrygragos Everyman himself, perhaps? Please me, charlatan, alleviate my curiosity!"

"Should I recommend a lens-maker? You must need monocles on each side of your upper head. Do I look like any man's god?"

"No, you look like a prat with a panpipe."

"And you look like a caricature Egyptian standing there as you are with your breasts brazenly hanging out and turning royal purple in the cold.

"Pyrame, indeed! Other than your link through Incain's Gynosphinx to the otherwise moribund Androsphinx on the Giza Plateau, there is very little of the Egyptian about you, is there? Sumerian, Libyan, Cretan, Hittite, Canaanite, Phoenician, Babylonian, Persian, Scythian, Greek, Macedonian, even Roman or Chinese, but surely not Egyptian!

"You hate the Great Pyramid of Giza, consider it a low grade replica of the one you think you share with Thrygragos Sedon in Grand Elysium. And perhaps it is. But mostly you hate Andy the Androsphinx. Understandably, I suppose. Even though that's where you fused with my Lily, you did waste most of a millennium imprisoned inside one sphinx or the other.

"And who but who I say I am would know any of that? Deny me no longer!"

What was non-verbally undeniable was that he was finally getting to her. Nonetheless, Pyrame struggled to resist the unwelcome and, she still felt, unwarranted reawakening of her no longer just ancient memories. They had to be inaccurate, if not out and out bogus, didn't they? Had he, whomever he was, somehow implanted them in her subconscious to be triggered, painstakingly slowly, the moment he appeared before her? Was that possible?

"Your Primeval Lilith was imprisoned inside the He-Sphinx. And so were you, as Daemonicus. If you were Daemonicus and not just a turd-trickster, as I've also heard tell. That's why the Female Entity built the atrocity in the first place, to hold onto the daemons' hierarchy forevermore.

"Hundreds of years afterwards, Thrygragos Everyman and Eventual-Harmony accidentally broke you out of him. They then formed the Unnameable, with me part of it, in order to release her. I was among those trapped inside him when All and her mate ate us. But I doubt the Dual Entities realized the two Mandroid sphinxes shared the same interspatial stomach, for want of a better word. There you have it, though – something you're allergic to, namely the truth.

"That told further, the only reason All hasn't eaten you already, Judge, has nothing to do with your howsoever impressive, yet solely self-serving elusiveness. She's allergic to shit."

"Prat, shit, turd-trickster, charlatan? Demean me at your own expense, priestess, but know you this: I have naught save abiding admiration for you, for both aspects of you.

"Adoration of you predates Mithras's Virgin, Concord's Kore-Isis and Everyman's Harmony, whom Confucius preached must be cherished above all else and whom the Egyptians had as Feathery Maat even though her power focus was and still is the Chains of Justice.

"You were the burning light at the dawn of civilization beyond the Dome: Venus or Lucifer, the Daybreak Planet. And I was there holding your hand throughout your endless incarnations."

"You speak proudly of days of infamy; days that ended in defeat and mortification. Gone are Queen Gomorrah and King Sodom; gone are Lady Tanith and Lord Rhadamanthys. You are no longer the Laird of the Laughing Lands. Yet, by All-Father Sedon's grace, I remain the Perpetual Presence whilst you, whom I thought obliterated so long ago, are simply Smiler, not even Ahriman, an appellation of unspeakable dread that belongs to Sedon if it belongs to anyone.

"As always, though, you are more demon than devil, more faerie than fearful, except to yourself. Only now you've become an outcast from your own body. You're too cowardly to reveal yourself to the world, except in dribs and drabs, for fear the world, or someone on, above or within it, will finally rid itself of you.

"Besides, we don't reincarnate. We persist."

"Quibble as you must. Without us there would be no law, no reward, no punishment, no concept of responsibility and the consequences of irresponsibility. The Sedon-cursed Horrites, toadies of the Celestial Sphere, sought to assassinate us with their filthy asteroid two and a half millennia ago. Although all they succeeded in doing was destroying our twin splendours, they proclaimed it an unparalleled victory.

"It was nothing of the sort of course. But I cannot forget the role either Varuna or Mithras played in that second deadly debacle and I will never forgive whichever one is left for countenancing it. Today Brother Mithras will reap the harvest of his betrayal."

"That he will, though not because he was once two and certainly not because one or the other, or both of them simultaneously, betrayed you, their third. Never forget, Judge, no one except you recalls you even exist on a day-to-day basis. Why should we suddenly care about affronts suffered by someone who doesn't exist?

"No, Mithras shall reap the harvest of his betrayal of us, the true sons and daughters of the Thrygragos. We are about to exercise our freewill, yes, but we shall never allow you to claim credit, even complicity, for what we are about to do. We won't dispose of one false father in order to have him replaced by another, especially one who was once wholly part of the same sham god of hollow greatness."

Absently, as if a kind of mnemonic to self-counsel patience, Smiler tapped the skull depending off his neck-chain. *"Outer Earth Horrites consider themselves direct descendants of Xuthros Hor and his predecessors. To this day they refer to their leader as 'the patriarch'. If so then they are the foolish patriarchs of an even more foolish human race.*

"They have fallen so far from their pre-Flood Golden Age they now live in the darkest days of their evermore-darkening Dark Ages. In a way they're fortunate there are no more golden apples out there because what sad excuses for lives they have left are as mercifully brief as they are unrelentingly wretched.

"Horrites boast they destroyed Sedon with the Genesea. They say they destroyed me with Sodom and Gomorrah and he whose skull this was on Strongyne 500 years later. Now they seek to destroy the last of us by elevating a misguided maybe-Celestial they helped exterminate 15 hundred years after Strongyne to the status of some sort of three-in-one, yet nonetheless solitary God.

"Three-in-one, a trinity, a Thrygragos, the nerve of them! So parched are they for ideas, in order to lionize this confabulation of theirs they declare Mithramas their so-called saviour's birthday. Then they solemnize Hilaria with a passion week stolen directly from various Rites of Spring already observed throughout the whole of the globe, foremost in here that of your very own Attis's on Apple Isle. And that's just the start of their debasements.

"They think we devils are a spent force. They have thought as much for well over 300 years, ever since the abysmal failure of the Crimson Conspiracy, yet another example of Mithras's madness. Why Sedon did not cathonitize him, instead of his lackeys, I'll never comprehend."

The fiend became more animated, more insistent. His rictus grin never wavered. As if unable to control himself he grew visibly before her. Pyrame did not deign to raise her arms in token warding. This was just bluster, not even wind, although he was long-winded. She would hear him out then he would go away. Like he always did, she now remembered.

"In their secret temples on the Outer Earth, with their idiotic initiations and ridiculous pastimes, the meanings of which they've entirely forgotten, Horrites still congratulate each other on their forbearers' fictionalized triumphs over our, admittedly, sometimes unkind kind. But they are wrong; they could not be more wrong.

"Father Sedon raised the Cathonic Dome to save us from the Great Flood. You and I both survived SAG. While blowing Strongyne's heart into the sky did destroy the matriarchate so many of you devic goddesses had established out there, it was not the end of either Varuna or Mithras. That victory was mine alone.

"I was the one who vanquished one or the other after Strongyne. I will excise the other one today. His skull will adorn my chest like our brother's does. I come to

you, Tanith, Astraea, Inanna, because I am not so self-sufficiently stupid as to sup-pose that male can live without female; that female can live without male.

"Embrace the last of the Thrygragos. Embrace me. Renew our vows. I am re-lentless. I cannot be defeated. Today dies the last of my triplet brothers. Tomor-row His Grace the Disgrace, the Lord Laziest Lazareme; next Bodiless Byron; fi-nally the mighty Moloch himself will come to ground. And we shall have him. Se-don knows it as well, deep inside himself.

"You and I, my lady of the stars, you and I together shall have the stars. We shall watch the Celestials quail beneath us."

"You are insane!"

========

"I didn't say I was going to kill him, whore. All I said was he looked so easy to kill."

Shocked as if out of her reverie, Pyrame once again rotated her subtle matter, dae-monic body on the fulcrum of her neck. Instead of apparent nothingness, in terms of any-one, she faced Cruel Plathon, the multi-horned monstrosity that had plagued her treasured Attis for more centuries than they cared to remember.

========

Where did that notion suddenly come from? It reminded her of the Female En-tity: the Mnemosyne Machine. So did that thought. Mnemosyne meant memory,

For Sedon-sparked purposes primarily of denigration, Pyrame mythologized Helios's Milady Memory as the Titanic or Etocretan goddess epitomizing the moon. That thus trivialized Mnemosyne bore the Nine Muses of Middle Sea tradition by her nephew, the patriarchal god-king known as Zeus – as in *'Deus'* or God – but there was nothing of the mythic about the Female Entity.

Deemed by many the feminine of the two Cosmic Principals, she was the *'Sophia'* to Helios's *'Sophos'* – except she was much wiser and approaching infinitely more pow-erful. Of the pair, though, he had to be regarded as her superior if for no other reason than that she was mostly a machine he not so much designed as had built.

As such she did everything he told her to do. Over the multiple millennia of their coexistence he'd programmed into her the capability to do damn near everything a machine could do anywhere or at any time. Plus, when he died and tumbled back into the time stream, she did too.

But why, Pyrame silently questioned, was she thinking of Miracle Memory? They weren't back, were they? They, Attis's birthparents, the constructers of both Egypt's Androsphinx and All of Incain, the co-creators of the Moloch Sedon and, therefore, through him, of devazurkind itself? If so, were the Dual Entities the puppet masters behind today's opportunistic unmaking of Mithras soon to become reality?

"I agreed to take him down, Bull; to snuff out his life if necessary and if only for the time being. I did not agree to lay him out for you or anyone else to slaughter. Besides, I understand Father Mithras has already promised him to the Medusa. Mo-ments ago she told us she's re-christened herself Mother Murder because of that as-surance."

The highborn Mithradite was more Minotaur than bull. In truth he wasn't much of a bull at all. For one thing he was bipedal. For another he had four horns instead of two. The two growing out of his forehead looked bullish enough, but the other two were distinctly ram-like, curving forward, seemingly to cover or replace his ears.

He, the Apis of Apple-Ap-Ape-Apis Isle, had crests of bone above and below his two ordinary eyes. His third eye sprouted just about where his eyebrows would meet had he had eyebrows. His snout was a tad pushed in, flattened inwards and slightly to one side, but his jaws protruded. His teeth were breathtaking, to put it mildly. So was his breath.

Although his arms and legs appeared to be as strong as a bull, he actually had arms, definitely non-bullish that. He was very hairy, especially around the area between his waist and upper thighs, muddy as well after his romp in the muck with Bouncing Belle. Decidedly the most bullish things about him were his hooves and his power focus: a staff, rather a bident, whose twin tines were glowing horns. Deathly bullish!

"Which must gall you no end, priestess, although the Primary Apocalyptics are as thrilled to have all three of the gorgons back to help whelp their azuras as they are at having their dicks back to do it with. It'll be interesting to see what their original mates do about it all."

Antique Illuminaries named the other two, definitely lowborn gorgons after the immortal sisters of Medusa found in the Middle Sea myth of Perseus. Generally speaking Stheno appeared as a hen-headed cockatrice, whereas Euryale appeared as a reptilian basilisk. Although Attis, as Perseus, did encounter them after Pyrame, not heady Athena, sent him in pursuit of the Medusa, he did not dispose of them, for the first of a few times, in All on Incain until a much later succession.

The three male or Primary Apocalyptics made up the entirety of Mithras's Eighth. They were, to their fellow devils: War, Plague or Disease, and Disaster. Devils called their highest born as well as at one time commonest mates: Drought, Malaise and Flood. Along with Famish, the Apocalyptic of – depending on her mood – Famine, Hunger or Pestilence, the Leper's Lady and Disaster's Duchess of the Deluge constituted the three female or Secondary Apocalyptics. Those three also made up the entirety of Mithras's Tenth.

Most devils counted Drought, whom Illuminaries had as Cathune, as coming betwixt and between them. As a third of Mithras's Ninth, most agreed further, that made her Tralalorn and Pyrame's brood sister. Eventually intentionally fallow, she detested War's profligacy. Respectively Malaise and Flood were none too enamoured with Plague and Disaster themselves.

Like Drought to War, jealousy was most of the reason Flood wasn't as big on Disaster as she'd initially been. In that regard, Disaster's first disaster was literally losing his head over Flowery Anthea. That event came within a few decades of devils gaining individual power foci and, with them, the daemonic bodies that granted them solidity. He – Nakba Ramazar – had been collecting hats donated by his followers, often with the severed heads that went with them, ever since.

As for Malaise to Plague – aka Carcinogen the Leper – after living together as man and wife for so many centuries they made themselves so thoroughly sick of each

other that various forms of sickness became their specialities. They were so unbearable to be around Thrygragos Everyman coined the phrase *'familiarity breeds contempt-
ibility'* just for them. They grated on one another so much so that by the time Attis
stuck them in All they were probably glad for the break.

"Father informed us of the arrangements you made with him," Plathon put
to Pyrame. "Yet you only agreed to take Attis down if he refused to turn over his ill-
gotten Brainrock booty such that our brothers and sisters in Mithras could regain the
wholeness of their beings. He did and you took him down anyhow. Who else have
you made arrangements with, pauper?"

"Hadn't you better ask that of your mistress, Bull? She did send the Medusa
over with the Lazaremist witch's kibisis after all. Would you like to have a look inside
it? Even so soon after your most recent encounter with Lady Lust, it could be a very
hardening experience."

"Thus speaks Sedon's Whore," snorted Plathon, whose idea of humour was every bit as earthy as Pyrame's.

"Thus speaks the fabulously female Perpetual Presence. Never forget that. If
Apple-Kore ordered you to take Attis out, before whomever Father has tasked you to
slay kills you instead, then have done with your bullshit and get to the go. Rest assured, I'll fight you and everyone else any Kore might care to send over until there is
no one left to fight.

"Do you doubt me? Do any of you seriously believe Grandfather would jettison me as readily as he seems prepared to jettison his three sons? I know my part in
this Theomachy and I shall act as the need arises."

"Even if the Anvil Artificer refused to forge you a power focus," countered Plathon, "Which I believe is a compost heap of Celestial God-Garbage, you should have
asked him to make you an ear. Even the Graii have an ear. Last I looked, moments ago,
they've six of them, two apiece. I came over to kill him again, he'd be dead already."

The Graii, though Mithradite Master Devas, were the gorgons' even lower born
servants. The hags' hearing was fabled, but they shared their power foci – a single eye,
a single tooth and a single tongue – amongst themselves whenever one or another of
them wanted to see, bite or speak.

"I heard you the first time. So why did you come over? To say hello hell-spawn,
to find out why I dropped him or to find out on whose behest I dropped him? I did
it on my own, if you have to know. Shall I tell you why?"

"Please do."

"Then answer me this. Can you deny your success rate at killing Attis is zip?"

"On the contrary I am very good at killing the Attis. In fact, although I haven't
been keeping score, I do believe I have killed him more often than he has, in a manner of speaking, killed me. Then again killing the Attis hardly constitutes killing a
lesser being, does it? That's why Grandfather never deigned to cathonitize me. Killing
him is more a matter of self-defence than anything else."

"Allow me to rephrase. How many times have you gored him unto death or
brought him to Kore such that she could castrate then crucify him? How many times

has he succeeded himself? In other words, how many times has he effectively risen anew?"

"I just told you. I haven't been keeping score."

"Neither have I. The point is he does rise anew. Has it ever occurred to you that he does so because Mithras never dies?"

"Ah, I see!"

"Ah, exactly: IC as in intercourse. Although he may prove to be as immortal as you or I or any other devil you'd care to mention – once folks like you stop killing him, that is – he may equally prove just an ordinary mortal. I like Attis the way he is: young, human and virile. Without Mithras around he may not come back and I don't want to risk losing him quite yet."

"Not while he's still good for rolling in the hay, eh?"

"Or banging in the barnyard, to put it in your terms."

"Hay's fine with me; just about anywhere is fine with me. I'm with you when it comes to hoping he does prove to be an immortal. Only I have better uses for an immortal than as your non-Sedonic substitute whenever Grandfather's too busy upstairs keeping the sky from falling to act as your preferred stud.

"Your Attis is good with horses. He's certainly good with Pegasus-psychopomps. He should be able to handle hellhounds. And my dearest Apple-Kore, as you still so sweetly refer to her even though she hasn't ruled much more than her Hell for the last two or three dozen centuries, will be needing a new charioteer come sundown."

"Who has Father tasked you to ill-star?"

"What's this? Concern? How touching! Don't worry about me. Whoever he is, we'll be sharing a bucket of beer together after I show Attis the ropes, as it were. Just make sure he doesn't rise until then, okay?"

The Bull of Mithras must have thought that witty. Sniggering to himself, he left her to return downhill and rejoin Divine Coueranna, beguiling Belialma and the rest of the Mithradites gathered in the cow pasture below. If they'd been expecting a renewal of their legendary animosity, yet another heavyweight tilt between deviant and monstrosity, they had to be disappointed.

Nonetheless, as if he'd just won a pugilist tournament, Bouncing Belle tossed Plathon a bathrobe. Uncharacteristically, she was already wearing one herself. As an unusual mark of respect they must have gone in to see Mithras minimally covered.

========

"I wonder if the robes have 'His' and 'Hers' stitched onto their backs," came a female's voice out of the ether.

"Bull's right about the beer," came a male's voice. "They brew an especially fine pilsner in these parts."

"He drew Chaos, didn't he?" Pyrame asked either ether.

========

"Only because I insisted on Order," the male's air-voice replied chillily. "The braggart's been boasting he can best me."

"The Masochist only said that to provoke you," the female's air-voice countered, more haughtily than heatedly. "Father wants me, he always has, but he must know by now I'm a woman beholden to no man. I'll no more submit to him, in the way he wants me to, than I would either to you or to Grandfather.

"That must also be why he assigned Gravedigger Byron's Beast. Sinistral Lust doesn't do much in the way of azuras anymore so he's setting himself up to take the Nergalids' place planting and reaping Fecundity, who doesn't do much of anything except pup the useless things."

"Sounds like a complete mismatch to me," said Pyrame. "There's only one grave Planter will dig if he takes on Savage Storm and that's his own."

Hate-Sedon, Utopian Illuminaries of Weir long ago identified and named three Nergalids: Zuvem, Vetala and Yama. *'Zuvem planted them, Vetala grew them and Yama harvested them'* was another originally Lazareme-coined aphorism; one that applied specifically to them. Farmers were big on Zuvem, Plathon's brood brother, because his power focus was a Brainrock spade. Toothy Vetala, as a twelfth-born by far the youngest of the three, had as hers a moon-sickle.

Miners worshipped Yama, a so-called *'Earthling'* born only one litter of three below Zuvem and Plathon, not just because his Tvasitar Talisman resembled a scythe. They venerated him, considered him their Underlord, because his was actually a pick-axe. As such, the Nergalid Reaper was one of the many Devil Deaths Attis made a succession of careers, lives and legends outwrestling.

The two Silverclouds were the only members of the Unmoving One's firstborn set of triplets that remained. The third one never made it to the Whole Earth. Once Rumour of Lazareme, before his disappearance around the time of the Crimson Conspiracy's endgame, told them her perhaps apocryphal story – how she bolted from Sedon's authority and became a highest-level angel whilst the Sedonshem was delayed in the Celestial Sphere for multiple thousands of Earth-years – bygone Illuminaries decided to name her Serathrone Hallow.

Rufous Rudra, Byron's Beast or Savage Storm, was the lone male of the three. Old-time Illuminaries had the other Silvercloud, his sister-wife, as Umashakti. Her attribute was gravity, but she doubled as Byron's Moon. With good reason, firstborns only considered other firstborns their equals. Indeed, if not for the fact they couldn't disobey them, firstborns would regard themselves superior to their fathers.

"Still," Pyrame reconsidered, "If you think about their major adherents, the Nergalids' azuras animating Dead Things and thereby rendering them zombies, versus the Beast's were-creatures, it does make a degree of sense. You shouldn't reckon it a surprise them agreeing to take on Byron's Beast or Everyman's Chaos, though. Planter and the Bull's brother was Satanwyck's first Prime Sinistral, Domdaniel Pride."

"Hubris and humus do tend to go hand-in-hand," agreed the air's female voice.

"So," continued Pyrame conversationally, visibly talking to no one except her prone, personally drugged, unconscious lover's body "I imagine Lust opted for APM All-Eyes or Lazareme's sex slave, the one Illuminaries have as Hetaera. Either/or, they'll probably try to out-fuck each other. Who'd you go for, Virgin: Byron's Moon or Everyman's Balance?"

"Neither. I took Sedona Spellbinder, as Illuminaries styled her."

"A second-born? That doesn't seem proper. Surely she's beneath you."

"It's poetic. Spellbinder's smoke and I'm fire. Concord got Harmony and if Discord were still around she'd have drawn Gravity. As it is, that'll fall to one of Mithras's moon-goddesses. He has a few pantheons. That means he has a few moons. With the exception of Fecundity, maybe he intends to sic them all on her. It's moot anyhow. So, shall we go in to see Father?"

"You'd accompany me?"

"Sedon's Whore?" came back the male of the two voices. "We'd be honoured."

"Your Attis?"

"He'll be fine, Virgin. A little bird will watch over him."

========

"A little Gynosphinx, don't you mean?" countered Tantal Thanatos, Lathakra's King Cold, as he materialized as if out of the air itself.

========

Fully 12-feet tall, he was a blue-skinned, icicle-bearded, approaching impossibly immense, humanoid iceberg. Lathakra was Sedon's Horn, the tip of which tapered about as far north as one could go on the Hidden Headworld without having to tie on bone-skates. Its Snowman furriers must have slaughtered a whole herd of reindeer in order to clothe him.

The Thanatoid's Tvasitar Talisman was a double-headed war-axe or twibil known as a Labrys. Pyrame was familiar with identically named and similar-looking objects from the roughly five centuries she, as Lady Tanith, ruled the devic third of mainly matriarchal Crete alongside the Moloch Sedon, he as Lord Rhadamanthys.

Phaistos, on the Libyan Sea side of Crete, became their home beyond the Dome after the Dual Entities, and the male's *'illuminated'* Xuthrodite followers, destroyed their twin splendours of Sodom and Gomorrah circa the Year of the Dome 2000. They did so, at the start of Helios's Attis-eventful seventh lifetime, by packing their similarly time-tumbling asteroid, Trans-Time Trigon, or something like it, with horribly dirty explosives they called Atomics then ploughing it into SAG from their base on Mnemosyne's moon.

"You haven't any spare pills in that bottomless bag the Medusa left you, have you? I'm thirsty and a vat of beer would go down well right now."

"When aren't you?" teased Mithras's Virgin, as she too materialized out of the Weird, the dark-grey matter of between-space, the Universal Substance of Samsara.

At almost 10 feet, Methandra didn't quite match Tantal's enormity. Nonetheless, she was as proportionately massive as her beer-guzzling brood brother. As was her wont, she was masked and clad in varying shades of red, mauve and purple. Her homeland was Mythland, the jewel of Sedon's Crown. Possibly, if not overly likely, its Athenan dressmakers made her voluminous garments from a colony of fire-resistant, fairy salamanders.

As was also her wont, as soon as she made an appearance she went silent: went mute rather than moot, as fays might say. To be seen with someone, Pyrame appreciated of the Virgin, was one thing. To be seen talking with anyone, even with one of her two brood brothers – one of whom had been a star in the night's sky since the disaster of the Crimson Conspiracy – let alone their grandfather's most frequent partner, the maternal half-preserver of the material Sed-Sphere, was quite another.

Star Domdaniel may have been the devic epitome of pride, but Methandra's most notable attribute, besides size and heat, had to be a snooty affectation of supremacy.

Unexamined, the Pauper Priestess left the Lazaremist Anthea's bottomless bag where it lay, next to her prone Attis. Flanked by Thrygragos Varuna Mithras's last two acknowledged firstborn, she began to make her way down the slippery slope of All – still camouflaged as an ordinary hillock on an early winter's day – toward their fellow Mithradites.

Cold trudged. Heat flickered. Pyrame stepped gingerly, in constant danger of sluicing between them. Giant and giantess propped her up. As embarrassing as the slipping and sliding was, needing their assistance to not end up with her lovely butt a slinky sled was worse. Divine Coueranna smirked as they passed her on the way to the next hillock and their father's now resplendent pavilion.

The Bull and Lady Lust, both moderately if not particularly modestly robed, stood beside her. Heat and Cold glared at them. Plathon and Belialma bowed, effectively genuflected, with their eyes averted. Concord nodded, eyes locked on them. The two Thanatoids simultaneously sparked their third eyes. Myrionymous Kore got her knees dirty. Pyrame was very happy.

Pigs enjoyed wallowing in the mire even more than bulls did. You roasted a pig suckling on an apple. Pork was best served with applesauce. Muck suited Apple Goddesses.

========

Inter-spatially, safely back on Mithras's non-All mound and standing invisibly beside the Masochist, the Smiling Fiend had to quell gales of glee lest Domitian detect him.

'I see' as IC, as in intercourse: Pyrame got kudos for best crack. It was a toss-up as to which event provided the best bit of physical comedy: her slipping and sliding downhill until the Thanatoids propped her up between them or them forcing Kore-Concord, nine months pregnant and evidently about to burst with birth, to her knees.

Devils were funny folks.

========

Smiler chanced a glance at the Attis, asp-bit asleep as he was over on the All-mound. If any of the re-embodied devils had wanted to kill him, again, they wouldn't dare try now. The undeniably talented Mother of All Mandroids, no doubt at Pyrame's unspoken command, had improvised a further feat of ocular legerdemain. It caused a comparatively minuscule, but highly visible version of a winged, breasts-protrusive, Ginny the Gynosphinx to manifest itself on the boulder-bump of its hillock-hump.

Like a vulture on a desert cactus it perched overtop the golden-brown deviant. The She-Sphinx actually looked not so much a buzzard waiting for its next meal to expire as an eagle, or a Godbadian garuda, waiting for its baby eaglets to awake, whereupon it'd feed them with whoever ventured too near to them.

Devils were rightly wary of the Machine Master Moulder – as some referred to it when it was manufacturing monsters for the likes of the Bull and the Apple Goddesses. They were just as wary of it when it was manufacturing Mandroid guard-bodies for the female, and therefore amphibious, Lemurian Frog Folk of Akadan, the Hidden Headworld's southern, interior ocean. Even Father Sedon stayed away from the semi-sentient, partially Brainstone or Stoprock construct.

Smiler wasn't quite as concerned. It may proclaim itself *'the All Invincible'* but he realized it came its closest to invincibility, as well as indestructibility, when it was on, not just of, Incain. He wasn't foolish enough to attempt to figure out why that was – the Dual Entities were as essentially unknowable as the ineffable Godstuff that granted them their near-godlike abilities only to offset them with their all-too-mortal fallibilities.

Had he been on the Prison Beach, All would have detected then eaten him. That was a certainty. He also suspected a sizable, if between-space insubstantial, chunk of it was still on Incain. Pyrame wouldn't want to risk losing it in the volatility of this afternoon's potential Theomachy by bringing all of All up here.

Something else he understood was how Pyrame commanded it to do her desires. The sanity-saving misgivings of the two-in-one demon-devil he professed to so admire aside, he could mimic her authority.

Whatever else it was, All was so dense it had to have bricks for brains.

========

The Gynosphinx ate devils, but she could chew them half-up and spit them out just as readily. She could also hunt, which was probably why the lion-headed Masochist was nervously fluttering all four of his wings, readying himself for a quick getaway. Thus far no one had come forward to volunteer for pre-mastication. Then someone did, though he wasn't necessarily a devil. He therefore did so as not only devils could – he materialized out of the Weird.

Smiler recognized him immediately. He'd joined the brown-skinned newcomer barely an hour ago, if that. Playing his primary power focus – a set of panpipes, as Sedon's corrupted priestess did recall – he was one of a number of instrumental accompanists backing up an impromptu band of roving storytellers, gypsy dancers and Songstress Sirens in a domed, otherwise keg-shaped booze-tent.

He did that sort of thing regularly, in whatever form he chose to take. It forestalled boredom. Plus, he enjoyed being a musician almost as much as he enjoyed being a fiend. He'd done the same thing, with many of the same folks, last night in the very same place: just beyond the kept-separate encampments of Attis's two Mithrant legions, Lathakra's Fire Kings, Mythland's Intuits and the lad's own Rajput warriors out of Ophir-Moorset.

That wasn't the first time he'd performed there with him, and most of the others, either. Once he'd twigged whom many of the young ones had as a common father he couldn't resist playing the fiend and getting them to play together. Kanin City's Master of Weir, Helena Somata, had been pissing him off for decades and deserved being pissed off in return.

Over the multiple millennia of his existence Smiler developed and refined many diverse abilities. Some, most especial his ability never to be remembered unless he was there and chose to be both seen and remembered, were unique unto himself. Others he shared, at the minimum, with the three Great Gods and their firstborns.

Notable among these, he could detect who possessed whom as easily as he could tell who was a devil masquerading as a non-devil. In that regard, no matter what guise he or they took on, another thing he couldn't resist doing, as fiend and musician both, was performing, gratis, for the five other surviving firstborns, their two fathers and the Thanatoids, his two remaining, second-born siblings.

Of course, at least in terms of today's anticipated payback, last night's performance hadn't been altogether gratis. Eyefire was coercive, but nothing was a coercive as his panpipe playing. If Thrygragon was to be successful, he had to guarantee their complicity and he had.

Bodiless Byron occupied the fat guy in a wide-wheeled pushchair. Smokey Sedona, in her latest shell, a nurse of some sort, shoved it and him into the booze-tent alongside her fellow highborn Byronics. These numbered the two firstborn Silverclouds, Chimaera Glimmenmare, APM, and the rest of that Great God's second and third born Nucleoids, they either in their latest shells or in their shells' likenesses.

Lackland Lazareme, Thrygragos Everyman, entered as a tall, almost elfin, blueskinned, golden-haired faerie fart. Quite the coterie accompanied him. Significantly, the lone non-devil with them was the remarkably recurring fauna, Pusan Wanderlust, Attis's similarly deviated half-daughter by just as goatish Amal-Althea, Lazareme's polyamorous as well as polyandrous, female healer.

As per usual when she was in the vicinity, an approaching irresistible urge to experiment with not only your own reproductive organs overrode the inhibitions of nearly everyone there. Before long Abe Chaos was in Steg-mode while his brother Unity, Lord Order, instead of the Rajput-type he'd been appearing as lately, was in satyr-mode.

Pusan's presence affected Smiler as much as anyone. However, even if the unsettling sensualist hadn't been around he wouldn't have wanted to rein in his impulses. Incomparable Balance, the solitary female Unity – whom unimaginative Illuminaries had as Datong Harmonia – looked like herself, albeit minus the third eye and in leathers and furs rather than glowingly golden chain mail. That is to say she looked to be Miracle Memory, the Mnemosyne Machine humanized. For most of the ensuing evening he performed for her exclusively.

He may never have played so well but it was hardly the first time he'd been rewarded that well. Since firstborns regarded other firstborns as equals, he allowed her alone to recognize him for whom he was, her grandfather's firstborn by the Trigregos Sisters. She did, hence the rest of last night's wondrous non-rest.

Why couldn't Pyrame Silverstar do the same? Did she really believe she was only Sedon's whore? Was he really Sedon's Stooge?

========

Rajputs were from Ophir-Moorset, which lay on the eastern or occipital side of the Aural Sea, Sedon's Ear. They weren't supposed to drink but this one, being a Tethys, was a notorious drunkard. Somewhere in his early to mid twenties, he had readable tee-tee tails stuck, with their own bodily paste, onto his largely hairless pate.

Across his back he'd strapped a battered, multi-stringed lute. Highly significantly, this morning, and all the other times he'd played with him previously, it had been an ordinary, albeit well-used instrument. Now, though, it glowed with the telltale luminescence of Brainrock-Gypsium.

Smiler knew what that meant. It was coated by, or recently transformed into, a devic power focus whose new owner, the newcomer, hadn't got around to dimming as yet. Obviously the lutanist should never have drunk so much of the Fire Kings' firewater last night. Obviously as well, something just as fatal must have happened to his father since the last time he'd seen him.

The dinky Gynosphinx glared at the revivified Rajput. Smiler far-heard it say, in typical All-fashion: "Go away, Jordan Tethys, or All eat you."

"Don't get your feathers in a snot, She-Sphinx. I just want to see if the Attis left any beer behind in that bottomless bag of his." He bent down, opened and looked inside it, whereupon he instantly turned into stone.

What a distressing development! What an unmitigated disaster! How could there be two of them? No, it suddenly occurred to the fiend, there weren't two. There were four of them and the Medusa had been too proud to prove it when the time came for the Hundred to reclaim their proper power foci. Now that was worth smiling about!

Then something even more disturbing happened. Attis's onetime Cap of Invisibility formed around this latest Tethys-incarnation's petrified skull, Attis's mirrored shield turned him from stone into just that, a glassine mirror, at which point a curved blade ejected from Attis's sword shattered it, him, the already again late lutanist.

Smiler hated touching, let alone going too near, the six Great Godly Glories, the Thrygragos and Trigregos Talismans. That was why he'd wanted Pyrame to check on the bottomless bag's contents: to make sure they were still there, not to see if the Unnameable's head was in it. He knew it wouldn't be because he and he alone knew where and what it actually was.

The triple talismans times two had been the Attis's aces in the hole since his very first lifetime. Smiler had known all along they could be used to kill devils, but this was the first time he'd witnessed what both Pyrame and Attis himself had warned him about, albeit without remembering they'd warned him about anything. Somehow they'd seemingly learned to think for themselves.

So why had they turned on the latest 30-Year Man? 30-Minute Man? What could 30-Beers' quill do that they feared? More pertinently, since he'd only witnessed the female three dispose of young Tethys; did the male three remain inside Flowery Anthea's kibisis? If they didn't, if Mithras kept them, what did he intend to do with them?

He had a number of thoughts about that. And if he had them, then likely so did his brother in Thrygragos Sedon. He also had a single thought about what he was going to have to do about it. Using Pyrame-Lilith's daemonic mind-print, the fiend shot All that thought.

========

The ground grumbled; even Mithras's resplendent Tholos reverberated with yet another quake. Horrified, the ever-observant Masochist took flight. Many of the re-embodied devils in the by now well-trampled cow pasture landed on their butts: those that had butts and not just top and bottom bits.

Those steadier on their feet, like Sinistral Lust and the Bull, though his were hooves, or levitating above it like Divine Coueranna, didn't have to worry about muddy behinds. Instead, they gaped or gasped in awestruck amazement as the entire hillock opposite the barrow mound upon which Mithras conjured his then ordinary tent transmogrified. Most of them had no idea they'd been that close to a devil-eater. If either Apple-Kore or Plathon did, they nevertheless looked as shocked as everyone else.

The She-Sphinx gained shape, grew colossal and spread her enormous wings. Mouth open, she inhumed Attis whole. Then she flew off between-space not just to await recall. At Smiler's command, she didn't just take Attis with her either. She took the bottomless bag, whatever else it contained, and the three accursed objects that had just done for Jordan Junior, the most recent in a long line of Legendarian deviants, whose remains she left behind.

Better her contacting them than him, Smiler reckoned.

========

Poor Ravi, reckoned the Rajput's unsighted half-brother equally between-space.
****

THEO 9:

MITHRADITE MOMENTS
========

Someone screamed.

Until that moment Kore-Concord only had muddied knees. Now she fell flat out onto her back in the mire. Almost involuntarily spreading her legs, she began shaking with uncontrollable paroxysms. Evidently Taurus Chrysaor Attis – the moments ago vanquished, then vanished deviant – was about to become a deviant daddy once again.

Divine Coueranna was bang on her time as usual.

========

On the Inner Earth of Sedon's Head, as indeed they were throughout most of the Outer Earth, the two solstices were considered Midsummer or Midwinter, whereas the two equinoxes were simply designated midseason. During the first half of the spring season she'd be a maiden, Kore-Iris or Kore-Eos, one who was often blonde and blue-eyed, but who was invariably desirable, teasingly good-humoured and scantily attired.

She'd wed, become Kore-Maris or Kore-Connublis, within a month to six weeks after that equinox – on Apple Isle her marriage was celebrated on Mithrada Moon Day – and by mid-autumn she'd be Queen Harvest, Kore-Khosa, Kore-Bethulah or Kore-Ceres, the Cereal Goddess. Accordingly she'd wear yellow garments to offset the rosiness of her complexion and the tawniness of her hair. By then, as was also traditional, she'd show herself many months pregnant, the promise of youth become fruition.

After the harvest, her hair would change to black and her belly would finish swelling. Her birth-giving, that of Kore-Isis or Kore-Claris, would take place on or about the winter solstice. That done, and she was doing it now, her hair would go grey then white, whereupon she would complete her final transformation of the year.

As Kore-Hel or Kore-Hecate, she would wither and not so much die as disappear, hiding herself away in Mt Maenalus, at the volcanic core, the beating, ever overheating heart of her Apple Isle homeland. Myrionymous Kore, Divine Coueranna as antique Illuminaries' named her, wouldn't re-emerge until early spring rolled around again and she began to repeat the cycle.

That Apple-Kore went through the same progression annually. She did so even when the Korants' Corn Queen for a Day hadn't conceived on Suffering Sapienda, the night of her defloration by the Mithrants' chosen Attis, as possessed by Mithras himself. Yet, regardless of whether she had conceived, the next day, Fools' Day or Black Lazam, the Mithrant Brotherhood and the Korant Sisterhood got together to scourge then crucify, on an apple tree, her designated Attis of the night before. By then, though, the Masochist, Djinn Domitian, was both occupying and in effect insulating him against true death.

Some Attis surrogates and Corn Queens for a Day matured to become, respectively, the Mithrants' Taurus, or Boss Bull, and the Korants' Miracle Maenad, their High Priestess or Boss Cow. The Korants' current Miracle Maenad was one of the latter, but the most recent Chrysaor Attis had been Taurus for 20 of his 35 years.

He hadn't had to endure Black Lazam because the wound in his side, a leftover from his relatively early-on succession as Adonis, made him instantly recognizable. However, whenever he got the urge, as he had last spring, he personally performed the requisite defloration duties.

Since despised Father Mithras was always inside Attis or his surrogates, she had been leaving that aspect of Ap Isle's Rites of Spring to her brood sister, Kore-Concupiscence, for the last 300-plus years. She still dealt with the birthing business, though. She'd even dealt with it for the more than 2,000 years during which her successor in Mithras's affections – their other triplet sister, Attis's hated half-mother, Kore-Eris, Strife-Discord, Marut Kanin or just plain Marutia – was around to handle the pre-pregnancy process.

Indeed, with the lone exception of the standard nine months that third Apple-Kore was simultaneously humanizing the Mnemosyne Machine whilst carrying the Attis, she couldn't abide possessing pregnant women. For that reason the mystique of Marutia included the perhaps not so far-fetched notion she bled rather than bore her azuras.

No wonder it remained axiomatic amongst Korants that Strife and Motherhood didn't mix. At least they didn't mix until the sons of Korants moved into dormitories at age five in order to become the brothers of Mithrants.

========

Her screaming snapped back to the immediacy of the moment those Mithradites still aghast at a devil-eater's emergence, from the consequently resolved-unto-non-existence hillock beside them, and All's subsequent departure into the Weird. Some of the more faint-hearted of her brothers, more so than her sisters, promptly went off to examine the hacked apart body the She-Sphinx left behind.

As they did so, Kore-Concord wafted out of the young woman – Meroudys was her given name. Gaining solidity, she proceeded to midwife her former shell. The crowd of Mithradite Master Devas who stayed behind encircled her like a living privacy curtain until her Korant priestesses arrived via between-space to erect a birthing tent.

From his airborne vantage the Masochist observed what was happening. Having bonded with him on last spring's Black Lazam, he knew whom the girl's husband had been and sort of still was: Jotan Tethys. He also knew the sad fate that befell him while the actual Attis was in their mutual father's Tholos divesting himself of his purloined goods and glories. Sangazur-reanimated or not, it was a damn shame really.

As a surrogate Attis and therefore as the winner of a paternalia, as well as the son of a highflying Hellion Valkyrie, the young Mithrant was a double disgrace. However, while he may have made for a terrible skirmisher, Jot was a tremendous hornpipe player. Musicians appreciated other musicians and Domitian was a top class instrumentalist himself.

He would be. As Mithras's messenger and herald, his power focus was a fanfare trumpet. He was so good with it he could and often did play it out of both ends. Only last night, in a more down-to-earth Tholos, a booze-tent, he and Jot performed one ovation-rewarded duet after another. He demonstrated his nethermost prowess a number of times while there, which only added to the ego-bolstering applause factor.

In human guise the entire time, he'd at first done so at the urging of the band's panpipe player, a leering sybarite called, appropriately to Domitian's mind, Bad Rhad. He did so a half dozen times later on at the insistence of a drunken pseudo-elf wearing a cloak made out of what he reckoned were the feathers of a Sedon-proscribed ravendeer, ergo the roustabout had to be a libertarian Lazaremist.

Bad Rhad departed with the drunkard's presumed date – why was it bad boys had all the good luck? Sometime after that the night ended memorably when Jot's half-sister, Saudi the Steg Sari, took exception to the bereft pseudo-elf attempting to pluck her naked whilst ostensibly dancing with her. In the fighting that followed a much bigger male Steg bashed the bilged bastard with a torn-off tabletop then carted him away on it.

A tatterdemalion on tattered wings, he flapped off to inform last spring's Attis that, even though he was technically dead and howsoever-resurrected, his Moon Day wife was about to present him with a newborn baby. It may not be his but Jotan and Meroudys did profess to be in love, so it was the least he could do.

At heart the Masochist was a sentimental softie. Besides, he and Jot had been underneath the table when the male of the two Saurians used its top as peacemaker. Comrades in cowardice should always stick together.

========

Along with Tantal Thanatos, one of the few Devil Deaths her Attis never outwrestled, Pyrame Silverstar left their joint father's pavilion between-space. At the same time Tantal's snobbish, immediate sister and very nearly constant companion, except in bed, took herself similarly elsewhere.

The Virgin didn't approve of much – wine, red of course, was about her only in-dulgence – but she expressly didn't approve of beer-guzzling buffoonery. Her brood broth-er couldn't wait any longer to pop a proper pill, a pilsner.

========

As it happened, Tantal knew of an excellent booze-tent to go for pills. Accom-panied by Methandra and a very few other, highborn Mithradites – primarily because, due to too many successions of the Attis, there were very few highborn Mithradites left – he'd been there the night before.

The gathering of top level Master Devas, what amounted to the aristocracy of all three tribes, had been organized by the Mithradites' major ally in securing what their father always denied them, namely their own inviolable protectorates. That would be Pyrame's pal Datong Harmonia. She was the much-cherished Unity of Balance, yes, but also, as she'd decreed herself, that of Panharmonium.

Culminating as it did with Abe Chaos, the Unity of same, whacking his father alongside the old ear-hole with a tabletop, from Tantal's eyewitness report it turned out to be quite the eventful get-together. In a way Pyrame was sorry she'd missed it. All was proving intransigent, though, and Attis still hadn't convinced his father – his half-father, rather – that a thousand azuras amounted to too high a price to pay for her to release Mithras's Hundred.

The booze-tent's brew master was a black woman, which may or may not indi-cate she had a Utopian heritage. It was irrelevant anyhow. Outside their Weirdoms, Hate-Sedon Utopians generally denied their heritage so vigorously some of them would go so far as to publicly worship devils. While the truly dangerous Utopians, their Tri-nondev Warriors Elite, would never descend to such depths, they rarely ventured far beyond the cyclopean stonework of their city-states either.

Even when they did, unless they were openly hunting devils – an exceeding-ly unwise thing to do on a Hidden Headworld where devils were regarded as gods – they virtually never ventured forth with eye-staves visibly to hand. You hunted dev-ils, the devils' fanatical adherents hunted you. And there were multiple hundreds of thousands more of them than there were Utopians, let alone Trinondevs, on the In-ner Earth of Sedon's Head.

Lathakra's King Cold proclaimed no fear of eye-staves. He would – and it wasn't all bravado. With the exception of other firstborns and, occasionally, their Thrygra-gos Fathers, not much bothered firstborns. Still, rumours abounded of Trinondevs, schooled by war witches like nearby Kanin City's Master of Weir, who could mask their looks in glamours and materialize eyeorbs with a thought.

So it was, after stopping in the Fire Kings' base camp in order to acquire more suitable clothing for the giant, the two devils entered the tent incognito: human-eyed, human-headed and, for Tantal, human-sized. Pyrame knew herself immune to Tri-nondev prison pods. Nonetheless, if only because it was a chilly midwinter's day and her goose bumps might attract too much in the way of ganders, she wore an ordinary woollen sweater she'd taken out of the Thanatoid's duffle.

Despite the doped condition she'd consigned him to for the next little while, she wasn't worried about the Attis. The Gynosphinx would look after him and the bottomless bag she'd left behind with them. Some one or some ones did go for him, or it, All would eat him, her or them. To fay-say some – fay-think it, more accurately – that made it their fate to be ate.

Although she wasn't much on beer herself, like Methandra of Mythland, the jewel of Sedon's Crown – where many of the Virgin's worshipful Intuits still dwelt even though she mostly resided on Lathakra, Sedon's Horn – Pyrame did enjoy the occasional glass of wine. Her preference was silvery white rather than red or rosé.

The tent's brew master – Mrs Tethys, she recalled, one of quite a number – not only had white wine, the product of Plantagenet vintners in the southwest corner of Sedon's Cheek, just north of Sedon's Moustache, she also had glasses. And, knowing who or what she might have to unleash within a matter of hours, if not minutes, Pyrame felt she could do with some fortification.

They were still there an hour later. Since he wore the same semblance he'd worn the night before, Mrs Tethys recognized him. As a result, while no one fawned over them, they were treated courteously and served expeditiously. There may only be two of them, but brawlers of Tantal's calibre earned a degree of deference.

Some of last night's musicians were playing, sirens were singing, terpsichoreans were dancing, she was getting tipsy and Tantal was rapidly draining the last vat of pilsner the brew master had stashed. She'd just realized that most of the entertainers looked related – she was pretty sure whom they were related to as well – and was about to point that out to her drinking buddy when faraway trumpets blared.

King Cold burped. Then, oblivious to their pretence of being human, he materialized his Brainrock Labrys. Brazenly brandishing it, he cut himself to his Lathakran regulars, be they Fire Kings, Intuits, Snowmen or all three. Sombre quietude quickly replaced gay frivolity.

Calmly Pyrame drained her glass. She could do that too; take herself through the Weird instantaneously. She had a number of power foci trophies of her own, didn't she? She was about to do just that when a reptilian staggered into the booze-tent. He was around five feet tall, had tee-tee tails glued to his bald pate – Lizarados didn't have hair or skin as such, they had plates or scales – and a knife stuck into his back.

No, it wasn't a knife. It was a Brainrock quill. "Jordy?" she haled him. The Lizarado saw her, managed a nod. "What the fuck happened to you?" she demanded as he stumbled over to her table.

Pain-wracked to the point of monomania, the native of Sedon's Sweat Glands – which lay in the lower side-section of Sedon's Forehead – did not answer her right away. Instead he slumped into a chair across from her, yanked the quill out of his back and began using it to draw discernible shapes on the linen tablecloth. Tablecloths were another nice feature of the brew master's booze-tent. And who said Brainrock ink couldn't be diluted with blood and still work? Nobody.

"This morning's me?" he sputtered, clearly not long for his newest go at this world of theirs. "Ask them." Obligingly Pyrame two-eyeballed those with them in the booze-tent. To a two, one set per person, their eyeballs averted hers, finding focus elsewhere.

She was hardly the only one who recognized the newcomer as a Tethys incarnation. That much was at once observable. From the looks of her, the older Lizarado over there, leaning against the bar and speaking in hushed tones to its proprietor – a definite Mrs Tethys, she'd by now confirmed – might have been this one's mother. They were exchanging nervous glances with each other even as they were surreptitiously shooting them at her and this latest Jordy.

Although Cold's abrupt method of leaving had probably done it for her already, she broke cover, revealed her third eye and let her head on its neck do a 360, a stunt that always wowed non-devils. Glasses, mugs, tabletops, walls, the floor and the ceiling suddenly became even more fascinating for the boozehounds in the tent's attentions. Leaving didn't, though. It wasn't even an option.

Sedon's Whore or not, Pyrame was more of a Mithradite than anything else. She was so good at coercion she didn't need to even minutely spark her devic eyeball to ensure compliance with her desired steadfastness. Punishment outstanding, punishment paid. Satisfied, smiling her best silver smile, she returned her attention to the Lizarado.

"I'm asking you."

"Jealous wives, one of whom was an oak tree. This me? A sentient Stegosaur the day's first me, this one's dad, saw here this morning took exception to my son playing an alligator didgeridoo – she probably figured it was a relative – and tail-tallied a harsh one on him. At the time I was doing the limbless limbo; that is to say I was as bodiless as I was mindlessly waiting in Limbo for my next eligible offspring to start dying.

"Once this boy's body did, mindfully as well as bodily, I revived him, as this me. As soon as my quill did its between-space boomerang bit seconds later, I splotched out my splotch-pad and was in the process of drawing myself to you when the Steg came back for seconds.

"She grabbed the quill out of my hand and, when I politely asked for it back, she stabbed me with it. Fortunately all my kids are born with enough Brainrock in their bloodstream I was able to dot myself here before she could do for me again. Unfortunately I didn't have enough time to splotch back in my splotch-pad, so this will have to do."

Stegs were dinosaurian anthropoids. Male Saurs referred to themselves as Saur Tsars. Being female, the Steg Lizarado-Tethys encountered would have been a Saur Tsarina. Lizarados were much smaller, though still man-like lizards. Both worshipped brood brothers from Mithras's Seventh: the former Klizarod Rex, he of the Floodlands, and the latter the Emperor Chameleon, he of the Lake Lands.

Their other immediate sibling was Pteraterror, a pterodactyl popular with the demons of Satanwyck, if only because her leathery wings were distinctly demonic. She was among those cathonitized in the aftermath of the Crimson Corona, a third of the way through the 41st Century of the Dome.

As the Pauper Priestess knew, before she became a star in the night's sky Pteraterror performed much the same function Harmony did as the female third of the firstborn Unities of Lazareme. She was the buffer between Klizarod and Chameleon. Like Chaos and Order, the reptilian brothers hated each other. So did their subjects.

"Now it's my turn. What the fuck's going on, Pyrame? More to the pen-prickly point, what the fuck are these things? A lifetime ago, which is to say about an hour ago, I drew my now most recently previous self to the Attis. He was out like a candlewick at noon outdoors on a windy day. All was watching over him and told me to get lost or she'd eat me.

"I made the mistake of opening his bag and looking for a beer. All I really remember after that is spotting these three trinkets, then spotting a severed gorgon's head spotting me, three eyes open. Between them they turned me to stone then proceeded to dice and slice me into bits and bites all by their lonesome."

She recognized the thrice-cursed Godly Glories right away. Had he not been so distraught from enduring one death immediately after another, Tethys should have too – though he'd probably never seen them reduced to knickknack size before.

She was about to remind him they were replicas of Queen Gomorrah's regalia that Tvasitar Smithmonger ill advisedly dedicated to the devils' second generational mothers, the Trigregos Sisters, when the tablecloth burst into flames. Then the Lizarado-Tethys did as well. Fuelled by various alcohols, the entire booze-tent followed fiery suit.

It wasn't her doing but she felt confident it served Tethys's bastards and bitches right. She left them scrambling for safety.

========

"It's a boy," proclaimed Divine Coueranna, as she clipped off his umbilical cord and raised him for all there in the hastily thrown-up birthing tent to see.

========

Childbirth being time-consuming, among other things, most of the devils who'd been with them had wandered off. Kore-Concord's immediate sister and fellow Apple Goddess, who did for the day's Corn Queen on Suffering Sapienda, de-inhibition-wise, what Djinn Domitian did for the Attis, insulation-wise, on Black Lazam, had hung around, however.

"What shall we name him?" enthused Bouncing Belle.

"He's a quarter yours, Lust," said her brood sister. "You decide. Here, take him."

"Don't be disgusting, Kore. Give it to them." They were Kore-Concord's human attendants. For the most part tiptop witches, they'd come through the Weird on specially ensorcelled *'stepping stones'* largely composed of Brainrock-Gypsium.

Every Headworld sisterhood had their own version of the things. Their life-loving, but not necessarily soldier-loving, rivals in the Antediluvian Sisterhood of Flowery Anthea called their teleportive gems Anthean Agates. Hecate-Hellions, an even older, pro-daemon, anti-devil, Mother Earth worshipping sect, called theirs hellstones. Saurian Saris had theirs as glitz, as in glittery bits. Just as fittingly Korants called their witch-stones Corn Kernels.

Miracle Maenad, an elderly woman who bore the honorific their Boss Cows always took, accepted the infant from her goddess of just about everything. She motioned to her fellow priestesses to lift the exhausted, barely conscious new mother and carry her, Meroudys Tethys, on her cot, between-space to the safety of their encampment beyond that of the Mithrant legions.

As they were doing so, Mithras's lion-headed Heliodromus, having returned from his self-imposed mission, entered the tent. "I'm sorry, sisters," the Masochist half-apologized, sounding truly regretful. "But his fellow Mithrants killed the baby's official father, Jotan Tethys, not so very long ago. I brought his hornpipe. His Swan Mother stuck a Sang into him, but neither he nor she want it anymore on account of Hell's Halls having better quality instruments."

"It seems there's a mini-epidemic of that going on," said Plathon, as he too entered the birthing tent. "The fool on the hill – what was a hill – had tee-tee tails glued to his skull. He also had a beat-up old lute, a satchel full of drawings and a beer gut. There's no glowing quill but everything else points to him being a Legendarian."

"Sounds like the Whore's covering her ass as usual," said Kore of the Many Names. She was aware that Pyrame and Harmonia had suckered Tethys into selectively 'reading' to Mithras as a lead-up to Thrygragon. "Where'd she go, by the way? And where are the Thanatoids?"

"No idea," said Bouncing Belle. "They went into father's tent and never came out the same way."

"Anyhow," Plathon continued, "What with All showing up then showing off, and what with you deciding to give birth in a cow pasture, none of us saw what happened over there."

"I did," Domitian contributed. "I was standing outside father's tent when All manifested itself. I already knew it was there. Attis did as well, I think, though why Sedon's priestess put him down I couldn't possibly begin to speculate. What are you keeping from me? Put better, what are you keeping from Father Mithras?"

"How could we keep anything from Father Mithras?" countered Sinistral Lust.

"Precisely," Plathon snarled. His bident was gleaming so brightly the Masochist felt himself in imminent danger of the Bull skewering him with it. For once, he wasn't looking forward to the sensation.

"But you're probably right about Sedon's Whore, Kore. All took the Attis and that kibisis of his away with it between-space and I for one don't fancy a jaunt to Incain in order to retrieve either/or. Neither should any of you, especially any of you who've never been imprisoned there."

That, the Masochist realized, was directed at him in particular. What was going on? Apprehending the tension developing in the birthing tent, Miracle Maenad interrupted the devils. He further realized she would never have dared do so if Kore-Concord hadn't just prompted her to do it telepathically.

"In my teens, long before I attained my current position as my Lady's High Priestess, I too married a potential Quill Tethys. He was like Jotan in that he'd tricked his way into winning a paternalia. My fellow Korants expected me to marry him anyways. And I did, on a Mithrada Moon Day more than 50 years ago. We even named our son Jordan. Are you saying our boy's as dead as my husband?"

"He must be," consoled the Masochist, who recalled how her husband, a former shell of his, died. The current Miracle Maenad killed him, what must be close to 30 years ago by now, once her Jordy of a son was struck down by a cuckold and almost expired from his wounds.

"Otherwise the Rajput prince who just got turned to stone, then a mirror, then got shattered, with a curved blade, minus a hilt, wouldn't have had a glowing lute strapped to his back when he looked inside the bottomless bag."

"Turned to stone?" Lady Lust exclaimed incredulously. "A sword, a mirror? Are you trying to tell us the Pauper, who wasn't even there, somehow managed to trigger the Unnameable's head and two of the three Trigregos Talismans just to get rid of a Tethys?" She was another one in on the Panharmonium Accord.

"That doesn't sound like Sedon's Whore covering her pretty brown ass so much as Grandfather Sedon covering his big hairy red one. He must be planning a Sedon-play and doesn't want any yappy blabbermouths like a Jordy around to malign him afterwards. What have you and the Thanatoids got us into, sister?"

Satanwyck's Prime Sinistral, Sedon's viceroy when it came to demons, demanded this last three-eyeballing the other remaining Apple Goddess. As she did, she imparted to Plathon a private worry: Could Divine Coueranna, Kore-Concord, be Marut Kanin, Kore-Discord?

The Bull shared many of the same concerns his charming – and amply charmed – preferred bed-bouncer had just psychically expressed.

========

For tens of thousands of Earth-years – some claimed it could have been as many as 200 thousand Earth-years – the Sedonshem wound its way throughout the heavens searching for a haven for devakind. Many were found, colonized and, one way or another, abandoned over the course of its approaching never-ending journey.

During that astonishing quantity of both time and expanse, only Sedon and the Thrygragos Brothers were consistently solid personages. They sustained their substantiality by holding onto all the other Master Devas as yet still in existence, Plathon amongst them.

For female companionship, the four often split hundreds of women, female devils the lot of them, out of themselves. These fused into howsoever temporarily tangible individuals. Although they lacked names until Illuminaries gave some to them many multiple millennia later, most agreed that Sedon's darling, his main squeeze, became Pyrame Silverstar, whilst Thrygragos Byron had Serathrone Hallow, and Thrygragos Lazareme had Harmonia.

For his part, Thrygragos Varuna Mithras had Kore. Enjoying variety, he allowed a whole host of different devils, all of them his daughters, to dominate her. Consequently she developed as many personalities as she eventually came to have names. However, after the Whole Earth, the Genesea, and Sedon raising the Cathonic Zone out of his own essence in order to enclose his eventual Head, Mithras unquestionably settled on Kore-Concord as his primary companion.

Such remained the situation for much of the roughly 2,000-year, so-called Age of Taurus. All that changed circa 2000 Year of the Dome, by which time virtually every remaining devil had gained daemonic bodies and power foci of their own. Not long thereafter it became apparent the Dual Entities, sometime during Heliosophos's seventh lifetime, had time-tumbled back into devakind's linear timeline.

As per normal they proceeded to thoroughly muck things up. Somehow or other Helios got hold of Mithras while Mnemosyne got hold of Strife-Marutia – eventually aka Marut Kanin, Kore-Eris or Kore-Discord – and used her to humanize herself. That left a correspondingly jilted Kore-Concord, aka Divine Coueranna amongst many another name, on the outside looking spitefully to the inside of her former bedroom atop Ap Isle's Mithradium.

Throughout what became the Age of Aries, she spent most of her time doing everything she could to get even with Mithras and her backstabbing brood sister. Plathon was among those who suspected Concord, who'd been boss-cowing him around for the majority of that same sheepish era, re-subsumed her third triplet either before or shortly after the Crimson Conspiracy so dismally backfired. Had Strife-Marutia finally reasserted herself decades more than three centuries afterwards?

Regardless, the Moloch Sedon was hardly the only one who could and did play insidious games. Panharmonium Accord or no Panharmonium Accord, he and Lady Lust had made plans of their own – ones that would sideline Mithras, Kore and the Attis hopefully forevermore – and he was not prepared to tolerate anyone else, even his grandfather, interfering with them.

True, no one but Sedon ever won a Sedonplay. Nonetheless, there had to be a way he could he turn this one to their advantage. The question was how?

========

"Whoever he was," Plathon deliberately deflected, attempting to get everyone in the know back on track, as well as the Masochist off it, "And however it was done, some one or some thing chopped him up right royally. It looks like he was put through a sausage grinder. Unless it's for dinner, not even the Nergalids' zombies can make any use of him so Gravedigger's burying his remains. He enjoys that sort of thing."

"Be that as it may, your bull-ship, I'd say we know what to name junior here," did say Miracle Maenad, without a token cringe at the Bull's description of what had befallen the Rajput prince.

Her distant as well as distaff predecessors – orgiastic Bacchants, maenad madwomen and maypole hysterics whose heyday came during the era of the Outer Earth's Goddess Culture – had regularly slaughtered their male, onetime loved ones in order to fertilize Mother Earth. While that was ancient history, to this day Korants honoured their past with the Masochist-permitted pantomime of Black Lazam. They thus deserved their unsavoury reputation for being human sausage grinders.

Morally, if perhaps not quite so brutally, she'd done far worse. Some time, perhaps mere seconds before the deviant's then newest incarnation met his gruesome comeuppance, his earlier self, her presumed son, must have met a similarly terminal fate. She'd slain his presumed father, her husband, in order to preserve their son, the fruit of her loins, for potentially 30 additional years. Another Mrs Tethys, a Rajput daughter-in-law she never knew she had, might well have done the same thing.

In a way, therefore, there was nothing to either mourn or regret. The Rajput boy never made it anywhere near 30 years – he might not have made it anywhere near 30 minutes – but if his mother had killed her Jordy, then the Rajput boy's demise was both fitting and probably to be expected.

She couldn't hold herself altogether blameless, though. She'd unfortunately told more than just the two Stegs who came to see her a few months back on Ap Isle – lately altogether-eaten mother and mercantile-minded daughter – about her firstborn son's deviancy. More recently she'd told Helena Somata about it too; as a top-notch Anthean Nightingale, nearby Kanin City's Master of Weir was very well connected.

For a life-loving Ant, nowadays Miracle Maenad's counterpart as the Mother Superior of the Superior Sisterhood, she was also a notoriously vindictive so-and-so. Forty odd years ago, well within Miracle's memory, Helena slew her own daughter in order to get to an actual Attis, not a surrogate Attis like her husband had been a decade or so earlier.

She, like probably a majority of her Korant sisters of a certain age at that time, married and unmarried, rather fancied that Attis. However, once they discovered, after his death, that he'd been born Helena's grandson, it was the new Master they almost universally started to admire. As someone like the Bull might say, Helena had bellies of eggs for a nightingale.

If only to spread the misery around, Helena likely told any number of other Mrs Tethyses whom they'd inadvertently married. That being the case, there could be a bloody competition amongst her Jordy's ex-wives or conceptive partners to ensure their offspring, Miracle's effective grandchildren, benefited as much as hers did from having a Tethys for a father.

Which was all the more reason to ensure this particular baby was well looked after; which in turn meant he was brought up properly by her Sisterhood in order to become a Mithrant brother. A minimum of 20 years from now he could be a very valuable commodity. So long as no one thought to sink the deviant's soul first, it went without saying.

"Take the instruments along with his Corn Queen mom, sisters," she instructed her underlings. "Our latest Jordan is obviously going to grow up to become a musician. I wonder which one he'll take a liking to, the lute or the hornpipe?"

"I predict neither," said Belialma-Belle, with a twinkle in all three of her eyes. "For all his fiddling around, every Jordy I've ever known, which is most of them, makes his livings telling tales. A liar like that should only ever play a lyre."

========

Still humanoid-headed, silver-haired and with her third eye once again suppressed, Pyrame used her thresher's flail to whisk herself to where she'd left All and Attis.

Cautiously she didn't bring herself all the way through the Weird. It was just as well she didn't. Not only was hillock-All gone, the two remaining Apple Goddesses, the Bull, two of the three Nergalids – the two who'd never been imprisoned on Incain – and the intentionally, but to her mind unnecessarily grotesque spider goddess were where the She-Sphinx and the Taurus should have been.

To echo Lizarado-Tethys: What the fuck was going on?

========

Bygone Illuminaries had Fecundity and the Medusa's twelfth-born brood sister as Kala Tal. Pyrame would have been tempted to name her Arachne, after one of Tralalorn's more fabled playmates. Trala, whom fays had as Lost Lorna, was as short-tempered and free with fecal faeriedust back then as she was now. Consequently, when that Arachne proved a better weaver than she did the Demon Child turned her into a spider.

Due to the fact that Kala chose to have four arms like Kali, the Hindu goddess of natural more so than wanton destruction, much later-on Illuminaries had gone that route instead. To Pyrame's mind the name only made sense in so far as the number of arms, not their placement.

Paintings and statuary representing the Hindu Kali had her with four arms in the same place the Medusa had her four arms, attached to her shoulders and off the sides of her chest. By contrast Kala Tal – the Forbidden Forest of Tal, her principal haunt, was Sedon's Moustache – regularly presented herself with two of her arms growing out of what passed for her forehead as if they were antennae. The rest of her form of the moment wasn't quite right either.

Oh, she had four jointed legs, making for eight appendages in total, which was at least moderately arthropod-like. Moreover, as was also sort of proper, her legs did depend from a chitin-crusted, horizontal abdomen. Somewhat centaur-like, however, the balance of her body was mammalian. If they weren't so hairy her humanoid breasts might even be considered shapely. Her face, though, unless you were a fellow spider, was only vaguely feminine.

In some respects it was no wonder creatures of nightmare had been known to run from Kala Tal on sight, in fright, as fays would say. Of course creatures of nightmare – and you could see scabrous scads of them without having to be dreaming almost wherever you went on Sedon's Head – just as often ran from their own reflection.

The Masochist, Mithras's faultlessly loyal jinni or angel, was once again standing watch outside their mutual father's splendid Tholos. Perhaps significantly he was now flanked by the Great God's just as loyal, yet far more intrinsically powerful torch-bearers, Spring and Autumn – Tammuz and Osiraq as Illuminaries had them, but whom the Legendarian said were known as Cautes and Cautopates in the iconography of Roman Mithraism.

Zuvem Nergalis, Gravedigger, was finishing off what he did best, filling a grave. Perhaps the wine she'd been drinking had left her addled, but Pyrame instantly dreaded the worst. She feared the Medusa jumped the whistle, killed her Attis and then had the Nergalid bury his corpse where it lay.

It was an irrational fear. She'd not only left the She-Sphinx, who ate devils, perched very visible guard over him, Plathon and the self-declared murderess-to-be-tonight promised them Attis was safe for the time being. And devic oaths were inviolable.

Perhaps emboldened by proximity to Mithras's Tholos and the three watchmen, she panicked anyway, stepped altogether out of the Weird. Wait a micro-minute, she flashed as she did so, too late to reverse course. Irrationality: that was one of the arachnid devil's talents. She drove people, and not just people, to non-lunar lunacy.

As one might expect, Spidery Kala had an even more predictable talent. Pyrame got a gullet full of it as soon as she came wholly into the open. Then she got the rest of the web. It stuck her to a different boulder than the one she and Attis had been sitting on just before the Medusa came a-calling, retrieved bottomless bag in hand. This boulder wasn't a bump on All's head. It was an actual boulder, one that must have always been in the cow pasture.

"Where's your Attis?" Kala demanded. "What games are you and he and All playing at, pauper? We had a deal."

"Um," said Gravedigger, who was as black as any pureblood Utopian male. "Webbing in the chops does tend to have a gagging effect."

"Not a problem," said Nergal Vetala.

As repulsive, not to mention adhesive, as Kala was, as stupefying as the three gorgons were at the height of their petrifying potency, Vetala was stunning to behold. Long, raven-black tresses; a mouth packed with sharp, pearly white teeth; ruby red lips; a slightly greenish tinge to her otherwise creamy white skin; she concealed, barely, her pedestal-perfect body in a burgundy gown slit down the front to her navel, down the back to her butt-cleavage and split along either leg from thigh to ankles.

Decidedly Mithras's highest born moon goddess was in Seductress, as opposed to Fecundity, mode today. That confirmed that, since she would only become fertile again come the New Moon, the moon had to be waning. Unfortunately, as the wine had also made Pyrame temporarily neglect to recollect, when she wasn't pregnant, which she tended to be as many as 13 times a solar year, as the moon waxed unto fullness, Vetala was prone to what might be charitably termed lunar lunacy.

"Here, let me help you, Whore." Materializing her Brainrock moon-sickle, Vetala made short work of her brood sister's webbing. She also made short work of Pyrame's neck. Hoisting her severed head up by her silver hair, she tore the gagging web out of her mouth. "That's much better. Now answer my sister!"

"You've got a lot of nerve, Nergalid," sputtered Pyrame's gore-dripping head. "How dare you, of all devils, call me a whore? Besides, I've no idea where any of them went and I can't lie any more than any of you can."

"That's no lie," agreed the male Nergalid there, with a wink. Gravedigger was being facile, genuinely gallant or, most likely, a bit of both. If he was verbally coming to her defence, the other Nergalid, Underlord Yama, freshly freed, must have already demanded dibs on Vetala for tonight and he was making a play for her in lieu.

Other than digging graves, there was nothing Zuvem Nergalis liked better than planting his seed. It would hardly be the first time they spent a night together. Pyrame often got lonely when the Moloch Sedon was upstairs, being the mighty Eye-Mouth in the sky, and Chrysaor Attis was off conquering, or re-conquering, some other part of the Head for Papa Mithras.

"Fork her body, Bull," sneered Divine Coueranna, the fork being his two-tined bident, "And bring it along. Without All, Attis and the Unnameable's head, there's only one way out of this mess and that's to trade her to Grandfather for his intervention on our behalf. Any one of us goes up against a top dog Byronic or Lazaremist and it won't be just Sedon's Whore our hellhounds will be having for table scraps."

"You're out of your mind, Kore," said Pyrame, knowing full well the Apple Goddess was prone to both kinds of madness: anger and sheer craziness. "Give me a few seconds to pull myself together and I'll tell you Plan B."

"Tell me now."

"Kanin City. Its Master Helena and I go way back. Or have you forgotten how we've managed to come this far?"

"You'd deal with Trinondevs?" hissed the spider goddess.

"I'm the only devil who can," Pyrame's head reminded her.

========

Strictly speaking, he supposed, George Masterson rode a hippo-hind inter-spatially.

========

It was a natural born cross between a Pegasus-stallion and a ravendeer-hind. Both were immature when sexual congress occurred so it was probably sterile, which was why his masterly mother sometimes called it a mutated Mole mule. Although it was a planned hybrid born on the outskirts of Sedon's Mole, its sterility, albeit as yet unascertained due to youth and the current dearth of an opposite sex, made it a flop as a mutation.

It wasn't much of a mule in that its darkly reddish, more black than brown, skin-covering was more feathery than furry while its head was more corvine than equine. It came closer to a hippogriff, the cross between a Pegasus and a Garuda Phoenix, in that it was bodily pony-like as well as pony-sized and had griffon-like wings. They were stunted, though.

It also had the talarial wings of a fully-grown ravendeer, but they barely flapped. Beyond the Weird it couldn't even fly. Ungainly and uncomfortable to ride, it nevertheless performed brilliantly as a psychopomp. It was stubborn as a mule, however. That was partly why he called it Hinny the Hippy.

As for why he thought of it as female – other than the between-the-back-legs obvious, that is – until Ute Tethys came along Georgie was a disappointment when it came to fulfilling his Tethys-inherited procreative imperative. Consequently he considered her his platonic girlfriend.

Besides, Hinny sounded like a girl's name.

========

The Steg rode a Terror Donna.

========

"Saudi?"

"Don't take this personally, Georgie Boy," the Steg shouted as she spurred her psycho-pterosaur against George Masterson and Hinny the Hippy. "I'm not killing you because I don't like you. I'm killing you for deviant daddy's quill."

Even though he was most of a decade too young to be one, he wore the indigo robe and turban of a Trinondev Warrior of Weir. A Sari witch, Saudi was mostly naked. The extruding plates of her backbone were festooned with grim reminders of past meals, among the least grisly of which were chopped-off tee-tee tails.

Her Terror Donna was a much more traditional form of psychopomp than his hippo-hind in that she'd concentrated her soul-self into an otherwise standard, albeit dead or dying, vessel, a pterodactyl in this case. They both being saurian, the Saur Tsarina and her Terror Donna were colossal compared to George Masterson and Hinny the Hippy.

They tilted between-space. Saudi didn't have an eye-stave.

========

"You, brother, what idiocies are you planning to do with the Male Three?"

"Ah, there you are, worm. Do it: Grovel!"

The Smiling Fiend did as bade, fell onto his knees and prostrated himself. He had no choice in the matter. Devils couldn't disobey their fathers and this wasn't his brother in Thrygragos Sedon.

It was the Moloch Sedon himself!

****

THEO 10:

PEREGRINATING PYRAME

========

"Just so we're clear on one thing," *boomed the Devil,* **"Varuna was Zeus, the Great God reduced to infancy by Tralalorn.**

========

"To frustrate me, more so than anything else, the other adult Perpetual Presence hid him in a cave on the Outer Earth Island of Crete.

"She did so right under your oversized nose, dirt bag. I didn't find him again until he'd grown back to manhood; whereupon he returned the favour I did him just before the Demon Child devolved him. He unmanned me.

"So, yes, Varuna was Uranus. But you, fiend, you're my asshole!"

"Your audacity knows no bounds, does it, brother? Father Sedon will hand me your head on a platter for sure now. I won't even have to supply the chain let alone the chainsaw."

"Castration hurts, 'D' for Daemonicus, but not as much as this is going to hurt you.

"Worm? Better make that snake in the grass. And what does one do with a snake in the grass? Exactly what Alorus Ptah reputedly did to you after he captured your Demon Queen in Andy the Androsphinx: One crushes its head beneath one's feet then one squishes it into the ground until it expires."

He trod on something. Too late, he smelled it. It was stuck to the underside of his sandal. Who dared leave that there? Probably the cheeky Pauper Priestess, the very same Perpetual Presence who hid Uranus as the baby Zeus on Crete more than two millennia earlier. And why was he suddenly thinking about that pathetic as well as painful pile of antique crap today of all days?

No matter. It was his birthday. His brothers had a present for him, namely the rest of the Hidden Continent of Sedon's Head. It was time to collect it.

========

At what must have been a psychically silent signal, Mithras's Masochist blasted his trumpet anew.

========

Simultaneously his two torch-bearing epitomes of the equinoctial seasons, Spring and Autumn, burst into towering pillars of whooshing, pulsating flames. Between them, growing titanic, Thrygragos Varuna Mithras rent his resplendent tent asunder.

Except he didn't look at all like the third Great God as he'd appeared either earlier in the day or at any other time in the previous multi-millennia. Presumably that was because he was actually the Moloch Sedon.

"Come along, children. Best we're about our business. You can leave my precious priestess behind. She's already performed her role in this Theomachy."

Responsively, not that she dared do anything else since Master Devas no more disobeyed their collective grandfather than they could disobey their fathers, Nergal Vetala tossed Pyrame's severed head onto her still oozing body. Without any visible needles, the Pauper Priestess immediately knit herself back together again.

Looming high above them, already taller than the torchbearers' blazing, pyrotechnic displays of themselves, Sedon appeared in his commonest form, as the Dual Entities' Devil Incarnate. Two-horned, red-skinned, bare-chested, hairy, though balding on top of his knobbly head, with a forked goatee and a long, tightly braided ponytail, he might have passed for an oversized, cloven-hoofed satyr, Pan himself perhaps, except for a few anomalies.

Although Pan was often depicted with a tail ending in a triangular shard of bone, he was seldom shown with a third eye or sharpened teeth. Neither did Pan ever have one arm, his right, cut off just below the elbow. He never carried a four-tined pitchfork in his consequently solitary hand either. As well, Pan usually foreswore the torn fur flaps covering Sedon's genitalia in favour of a thicket of fur similar to that of the Bull of Mithras.

For someone who rarely felt the need to appear other than human-sized, the mighty Moloch no longer in the sky seemed strangely satisfied with Vetala's swift compliance. He did not seem quite so pleased with Pyrame's hurried restoration of herself, however.

"As for you, my lovely, silver-haired lady. Be sure you're more presentable come our return. I may be in the mood to make some new Sed-sons by then and there's a particularly fetching, not to mention virginal, Swan Maiden in the Valkyries' camp. She looks kind of like you so I've had my eye-mouth watering over her from up top for a while now.

"Her name's Ute. Ask the Legendarian about her when you see him again. I think she's his daughter from a few life-times ago this morning."

As grateful as she was to be back in one piece, Pyrame was much happier to be so summarily dismissed. She whisked herself back into the Weird. She didn't go off to be instantly obedient, though. Finding Ute Tethys could wait until later on this afternoon. If this madness were allowed to continue until then, locating a fledgling Valkyrie, a Swan Maiden in all senses of the word, would be dead easy. She'd be harvesting heroes slain on the frontline.

If it didn't, and the full measure of the Panharmonium Accord could be realized before evening, then there'd be no need to look for her, would there? Dark Sedon prematurely coming to ground was too good an opportunity to squander.

Sometimes the fates could be kind. Much more satisfying was when your own machinations, properly conceived and put into play, rewarded you kindly.

========

Saudi wasn't quite dead. Then she wasn't quite Saudi anymore.

Jordan Tethys hated coming back as a woman, of any species. As bad as that was, he especially hated coming back without his Brainrock quill. In truth, that virtually never happened. He searched the Sari witch's memories. It hadn't happened this time either.

Next question was: How was he going to retrieve it? An answer was looking at him dolefully. Now all he had to do was learn how to ride a Terror Donna.

========

Brutal battles had been fought in and around the Gregarian Fields, Sedon's Mole, many times in the past. Some were naval engagements. Self-evidently that was prior to the powers-that-were on Old Eden declaring the entire archipelago that became Sedon's Head, after it drained, Pacifica, the Places of Peace.

In other words, that was when the Mole was part of a solitary island, one of thousands, in the then shallow sea of what was now the Outer Earth's effectively bottomless and mostly landless North Pacific Ocean.

Many more times, both before and after devils fell out of the sky, the Gregarian Fields hosted games and generally peaceful congregations. Athletic competitions still regularly held here by the Cheeks' heterogeneous Marutians inspired the analogous, if not precisely identical, contests Hellenic Greeks conducted for hundreds of years at Olympia on the Outer Earth's Peloponnesian peninsula. Indeed, the Fields had been the site of comings together since civilization emerged on the then Whole Earth late in its last Ice Age.

Leaving its vulturous perch on the Moon, 669 years before the raising of the Dome and more than half a century after the death of Alorus Ptah, the Sedonshem landed near here. To be precise, it landed on the Fields' southeast outskirts, in the midst of Kanin City. At the time the megalithic metropolis was teeming with long ago liberated, but nonetheless tormented descendants of Old Eden's gruesome experimentations into the limits of life, the extension of sentience and the practicality of achieving self-aware immortality.

To be far more precise, amongst many another it landed on top of Droch Nor, the seventh patriarch of humanity's golden-apple-eating rainbow class. He, the Biblical Enoch and great-grandfather of Number Ten, Xuthros Hor, the Biblical Noah, was the only Golden Age patriarch who did not live to a very ripe old age. The poor sot was only 365 when the Sedonshem squashed him unto so much speedily blood-sodden sod.

Sometime after the Moloch Sedon trapped them beneath the Cathonic Dome, that is to say within a couple of decades of their arrival on the Whole Earth, space-faring Utopians of Weir took over Kanin City. The devil-detesting extraterrestrials who'd chased the Sedonshem across the heavens on their generational ships for multiple ten-thousands of light years thereupon turned it, with its even then justifiably world renowned, cyclopean masonry, into one of their many Headworld Weirdoms.

In the order of 35 centuries later, Illuminaries returning from the Outer Earth derived from Kanin City the surname they applied to Thrygragos Mithras's primary mate, the mother of the vast majority of his azuras and, as a result, Sedon's Cheek Lands' most widely celebrated devil-goddess.

For about 1500 years before then, ever since Kore-Concord first dubbed her Kore-Discord, devils had been addressing Marut Kanin as Strife. Which, given the metropolis's turbulent, not just antediluvian history was all too tragically appreciable. It was almost as if Concord had cursed the land as well as the immediate brood sister.

As far as anyone recollected or recorded, the devic Strife, also Kore-Eris or plain Marutia – the designation they gave the entirety of Sedon's Cheek – never entered the Weirdom once Illuminaries gave that Apple-Kore its Edenite name. The fact of the matter was, whatever name she went by, or anyone called her, she'd likely avoided the city-state since the day it became a Utopian stronghold. Indeed, with the extraordinary exception of Harmonia, the Unity of Panharmonium, a week ago, most devils still shunned it.

True once, due to its infusive alien majority over the centuries intermingling with Marutian locals, devils and azuras could nowadays easily possess non-pureblood Utopians living there. True twice, that made the city and its close vicinity not so much an impregnable stronghold anymore. True thrice, most of its technology from both the First and Second Weir Worlds was useless these days.

However, numerous Trinondev Warriors Elite resided in Kanin and all of them had eye-staves. When opened and properly directed, by means of the superior willpower of a thoroughly trained and Hate-Sedon-motivated Trinondev, the eyeorbs atop their eye-staves acted akin to mini-Alls. They could capture and hold onto Master Devas and their azura offspring indefinitely.

Except, that is, for a solitary demon-devil!

========

"Silverstar?"

"Happy non-birthday, Hel," Pyrame greeted Kanin's Master of Weir as she fully stepped out of between-space into her dayroom.

"Got a kink in your neck?" Helena Somata asked her entirely unexpected guest. "Your head looks a little off kilter."

The Pauper Priestess performed some suitably chiropractic adjustments. Her host winced at the clicks, crackles and groans she made snapping her skull as into place as it should be. "That better?"

"Much. To what do I owe the displeasure of your, um, presence?"

"Grandfather's here, in the Fields."

========

Pureblood Utopian females were as comparably white-as-daylight as pureblood Utopian males were black-as-midnight. Ambulatory alabaster was an accurate, if pejorative, description of them. Master Helena wasn't a pureblood. She could show shock in more than just her eyes or the tone of her voice. She looked and sounded stunned nigh unto hyperventilation.

"Thrygragos Mithras is so desperate he called down your grandfather to help him humble the Devil's other sons?"

"Either that or Sedon is so bored he came over from Cabalarkon unbidden."

"Then call out the She-Sphinx. I'll summon my Trinondevs as backup. Celestial God Above Us All, Pyrame, we've done it without the Dual Entities."

"Sorry to say, Master, something's happened to All and to my Attis and to his bottomless bag. And I've no idea what."

"The bag had Demogorgon's head inside it?"

"It had the Unnameable's head inside it, amongst dozens of other leftover talismans. At least it better have. The Medusa certainly isn't wearing it overtop her own anymore."

Now the Master looked positively dreadful. If she could go any whiter, she would have already. "No worries," she blustered assertively, if apprehensively. "My Trinondevs can handle Dark Sedon."

"Like the Trinondevs in Cabalarkon handle him every year around this time?"

========

Most purebloods lived in the Whole Earth's first Weirdom, that of Cabalarkon. On a map of the Head its location was Sedon's Devic Eye-Land. Geographically its capital, or pupil, also called Cabalarkon, was on the coast of Fearsome Fobbiat, the Headworld's western ocean, only a few hundred miles sundown-side of Grand Elysium.

The Moloch Sedon regarded Cabalarkon – who preferred Cabby in order to distinguish himself from both the city and the Weirdom – as his father. He did so because, in the Male Entity's fifth lifetime, Helios plucked out one of Cabby's two eyes and had the Mnemosyne Machine fashion it into the genetic grid they used to engender the Devil.

The Entities, along with Trans-Time Trigon, having been forcibly moved onto Helios's sixth lifetime shortly after his 'birth', Sedon and one-eyed Cabby subsequently used the same genetic grid in order to bring about the Six Great Gods and Goddesses. As playful providence would have it, when he was altogether ambulatory-alive Cabby the Daddy was a scientocrat whose specialty was genetics.

Today the consequently Undying Utopian lay sealed in a stone sarcophagus filled with life-preserving, but animation-suspending, Cathonic Fluid, distilled Brainrock, beneath that megalithic city's Citadel of the Thinkers. Dark Star Sedon annually visited him around this time of year. Sometimes Silver Star Pyrame did too. If you pricked a thumb or slashed a wrist and dripped enough blood into Cabby's tub, he'd sit up and talk to you.

One time, with 'son' Sedon standing right there beside her, Pyrame dribbled in too much of her own daemonic blood. Cabby not only sat up, he grabbed her and tried to pull her into the fluid-filled sarcophagus with him. Sedon stopped him. Then he slammed shut its lid, resealed it and told Pyrame never to do that again.

Being the Devil, Sedon tolerated, even encouraged, all kinds of perversions. Yet for some reason he drew the line at mostly dead daddies diddling devic daughters-in-law in front of him.

========

Helena huffed: "Cabalarkon's Trinondevs haven't the mental wherewithal to handle their own washing, let alone enough sense to control their own bedwetting. They're inbred imbeciles so terrified of polluting the Blood Pure they screw their own brothers. And vice versa."

"So do we devils. I screw my own grandfather a few times every human generation."

"So? Even if all you can get out of them are your next-to-useless azuras, you devils have daemonic bodies. That means the near-universal laws of genetics don't apply. Plus, your deviants aren't entirely useless, are they? And you can possess anyone not wearing agatine eyes ensorcelled against it."

"Except purebloods."

"So long as any are left, which won't be for much longer if they keep going the way they are up there. They rely on Mandroid automatons programmed thousands of years ago, when they knew what they were doing – them and the disgraced Sarpedon underclass – to do everything that needs doing."

For the first half of the Headworld's Third Millennium Pyrame, commonly as Lady Tanith, was the lone, perpetually present co-regent of the devic third of Etocretan Crete. The Sarpedon dynasty ruled the Utopian third of it throughout most of the same period. That was why the few extant mosaics or shards of pottery urns from the era depicted dark-skinned men and white-skinned women.

Because the Sarpedons coexisted with devils, as well as Minoan humans in their third of the Island, once their descendants began returning to the Inner Earth, starting around the midpoint of the Head's Fourth Millennium, Cabalarkon's purebloods disenfranchised them.

Their Warriors Elite had been using the coercive qualities of their eyeorbs to keep the so-called Sarpedon underclass successfully enslaved ever since. Machines salvaged from their grounded generational ships generated the same edible slop they always did, but fresh food wouldn't be possible without them and even idiots of Weir enjoyed the occasional naturally grown raspberry.

"I agree. They're contemptible cretins. Unlike yours, though, the replication devices your ancestors brought from the second Weirworld still produce proper eyeorbs. And the eye-staves they power, unless it's the other way around, are so very useful, aren't they?"

"No more so than ours," Helena disputed. "Eye-staves are only as good as the warriors wielding them and Kanin's Trinondevs are special. Impure we may be, but we've the will and we still have the way. Abolishing the Devil is the be-all and end-all of our existence."

"Watch it, Master. Be-alls and end-alls can bite both ways."

"We'll have to see about that. Georgie, if you're out there, get in here!"

When in doubt, start ordering folks about, Pyrame thought but didn't say. Even if they are phantoms, she mentally amended when no one responded to the Master's cry. What she did say was: "That's another thing I'm sorry to say. Your Jordy's already bit the big one. From the sounds of things, an awfully angry Acorn Ant did for him a few hours ago."

"I was calling for my son, Pyrame, not Jordy. I'm hoping there's still a difference."

The Pauper Priestess performed a mental reboot. "Right, your son's a Georgie, not a Jordy. Sorry, I'd forgotten. I gather you know your Georgie's a Jordy."

"A potential Jordy, don't you mean?"

"So you're hoping."

Helena took that as a justifiable, if figurative, slap in the face. "Celestial God above us all," she ardently exclaimed, "You devils really are infuriating."

"That's why folks like you think we thrive in hellfire."

"Pyramid does mean the middle of the fire."

"So I'm told."

"All right, have it your own way: So I'm hoping. Georgie's a proper black George as well. And before you say anything else, smart aleck, Utopian women are supposed to have black boys and white girls."

"Constantine wasn't black."

"Him I had beyond the Dome. Besides, I'm an Ant Nightingale. We cast illusions like sinners cast stones."

"You weren't an Ant Nightingale then. Truth told you were still only an ant-novitiate; not even close to being an Astarte let alone a full-fledged Ant. How could you be otherwise? Constance didn't come around until years later."

"Have it own way again. Somehow or other, you in me and Sedon in Chlorus combined to squeeze a white boy out of me. Hope you had a good laugh about it."

"Can't recall if we did or we didn't, to be honest. We've been squeezing out Sedsons for almost as long as there's been a Sed-Sphere. Georgie isn't 20, is he?"

"He's a few years older than that, Pyrame. As to what an old lady like me is doing with a son so comparatively young, even Utopians with mixed blood age a lot slower than regular humans. We also live a lot longer. That's why I came back to the Head in the late Twenties. Constantine's advisors did not approve of someone who was supposed to be 80 acting as spry and energetic as someone who wasn't much more than 40, if that."

"Georgie does sounds a little like Jordy."

"Look, I'd heard of the Legendarian long before I married my second husband. You don't get to become an Ant Nightingale, or a High Illuminary of Weir for that matter, by being an ignorant witch. Plus, I always realized my Jordan Tethys was a drunken carouser and inveterate wanderer at heart, the same as the legendary 30-Year Man. And maybe that's why I couldn't bring myself to name Georgie after Jordy.

"Anyhow, call it blind love if you want, but I just assumed my Jordan Tethys was only named after that Jordan Tethys. Why would I think differently? Jordan's a name common to thousands of Tethys families throughout Marutia, Ap Isle and the Forehead regions. I didn't discover until a week ago they were, or were now, one and the same; that he was or had become an incarnation of the actual Legendarian."

"Chicken or eggs stuff that, Helena. It's irrelevant. The point is, when you did discover it, you decided to sic a deadly dryad on him."

"Among others, and that includes a vengeful Valkyrie equipped with crystal skulls. I've also trained some of my Trinondevs to use invisible gargoyles to mask their eye-staves when they're out and about in the Mole or the Cheeks, though I'm by no means convinced eyeorbs can sink deviant souls."

"Neither am I," Pyrame admitted. She was convinced Trinondev eyeorbs didn't work on her, however. How could they? The Mnemosyne Machine made them and, when Machine-Memory was contemporaneous, she usually chose Pyrame to humanize her.

The Female Entity liked nothing better than being Miracle Memory. No matter how miraculous they were, computers – even the computerized insides of Trans-

Time Trigon, the always tri-peaked, always Gypsium-imbued, sometimes island, some-times asteroid or other landform that accompanied the Dual Entities' to wherever and whenever they time-tumbled – couldn't interact in the manner Memory preferred to interact with whomever was twiddling her keyboard, namely sexually.

"Why would you want to?"

"Holy Matrimony is a sacred sacrament, pauper. Constantius Chlorus had the courtesy to divorce me before he married Theodora. My Jordy didn't bother with any suchlike niceties. Maybe a decade after our Georgie came along he just walked out the door, if not the city gates as such, and never came back.

"Plus, as I only just learned, he wilfully practised polygamy. Me, I don't know what's worse: the degradation of divorce, the embarrassment of being ditched for some-one younger and lustier, or flagrantly trivializing what's supposed to be a lifelong com-mitment. I'm thinking the last. Even you devils don't do that, do you?"

"Actually, most of us don't dare make lifelong commitments. I certainly don't, not even to the Moloch Sedon. Nor he to me, truth told. We don't dare because we don't just have long lives. We have endless lives. We make an oath; we're genetically incapable of breaking it. Whatever else you think us, we're not stupid enough to do something we can't undo."

"No, you're evil. Pure evil!"

"Like I just said, Master: You're welcome to think us anything. Just bear in mind, unlike any other sentient species I've ever come across – and, believe me, I've come across many more sentient, or even partially sentient, species than your extraterres-trial ancestors could have – we don't dare kill lesser beings either, not even in anger. We do, Sedon'll ill-star us instantly."

"Antheans only kill as a very last resort, Pyrame. Even if you can't recall much about my family or me – my families, on either side of the Dome – because you've had so many families you can't recall ever affecting, you can't deny recalling that. Un-less you are stupid, it goes without saying."

"Which you've just said I am – as well as evil, whatever that means." Helena didn't rise to that bait. She was looking at her definition.

"Even then," she did retort, "Many Ants would rather die themselves than de-prive someone else of their life. But, in Sylvia's defence, from what I've also recent-ly learned – from his likely mother, the current Miracle Maenad – my Jordy was al-ready dead or dying when she got the Legendarian's soul into him. A conscious soul that transmigrates to his descendants, one after another, that's the essence of his devi-ancy, isn't it? The gist of his gift – his curse, put better."

"Not to each and every one of his descendants," Pyrame quibbled. "He makes it his main mission to have many offspring. And they tend to make a point of having many more of their own. As a result, the vast majority of his descendants never get him. But you're close enough. And *'gist of his gift'* is a fay-worthy turn of phrase. Ex-cept, it's more like the gist of one of his gifts. Jordy's stacks of knacks, to quote him directly."

"He always did say he was a poet and he knew it."

"And now he's wreaking poetic justice."

"From the sounds of your *sounds of things*, so he is," acknowledged Helena. "Ironic, isn't it? Sylvia Tethys acquitted herself adequately, if distastefully, as a deadly dryad, but she's a piss-poor Acorn Ant. She should have sunk his soul; taken him out endgame big time, to use your terminology. She didn't and look what it's got us?"

"Open season on Tethyses," Pyrame understood. "A cluster of them might have died awhile ago when a Lizarado-Tethys perhaps intentionally set a booze-tent on fire."

"News flash: a bundle of them could have died, if they were firewood. They weren't; they had legs and, from what the tents' brew master far-spoke to me a few minutes ago, they all got out, singed but breathing.

"There is this loose-lidded Steg out there, though. Her name's Saudi. She's the one who first found out my beastly beloved of all those years ago became a Legendarian. She's a Jordy too, potentially, but she only wants his quill; figures she can sell it up in the Floods, or over on Ap Isle, and get rich quick."

"News flash? Loose-lidded? Beastly beloved? You've been talking to the Mnemosyne Machine, haven't you? Who's humanizing her?"

"From what I understand, only devils can humanize her. I've only spoken to one of your sort lately and that's Datong Harmonia. And she's only supposed to look like Memory, not be her. If the Entities are back, she'd pick you to humanize her, wouldn't she? She does that so she can get to the Moloch Sedon the moment Heliosophos decides to make his move. At least that's what everything I've read or heard about her indicates."

Pyrame cogitated rapidly. It felt to her almost as if she was processing information the same way Machine-Machine did, automatically. Except, she further felt, her synapses were snapping the way they did when they were just her synapses. Ergo, she didn't have Mnemosyne and Mnemosyne didn't have her. That didn't mean they weren't back, of course, just that if they were they weren't acting as they usually did.

"I don't get it. Helios decides to make his move; he'd employ Trans-Time Trigon, meaning he'd employ its innards, the Mnemosyne Machine. What with Grandfather Sedon already physically down here in the Mole, what time would be better than right now to make his move? So why withdraw both All and his Attis, if he did? And why does it fall to us to do their job?"

"Maybe they aren't back. Maybe it's a Sedonplay aimed at drawing us out of Kanin, in our cosmicars, then destroying what little there is left of our aerial arsenal."

"Can't be. Even for Sedon it's too convoluted. No one who's signed onto Harmony's Panharmonium Accord is threatening him, not immediately anyhow. We're happy to leave him upstairs, preserving Cathonia, so long as he leaves down here to us, minus Mithras. You're just being paranoid, the same as you're afraid the Steg's after your Georgie."

"Don't tell me I'm being paranoid. She already tried to kill Hopi's Yeast. If Pusan Wanderlust hadn't been around she'd have succeeded too. Saudi rides a psychopomp, a Terror Donna of her own extrasensory extension. She's met Georgie so chances are she can get to him through the Weird.

"Even if she can't get to him that way, she's a Sari witch. She can get about on witch-stones. Like an idiot, I gave agates to him and his musician friends, along with their moms, so they can get hold of me should the Legendarian ever show up."

"Where is he?"

"Don't know, do I? Which only goes to prove I'm not paranoid. I was, I wouldn't have taught him how to mask an eye-stave with an invisible gargoyle and let him loose in the Mole, would I? I'm his mother, but I don't hide him under my skirt."

"You're not paranoid then why are you wasting so much time? Grandfather Sedon's out there, in the Mole. You want your crack at him, you better get cracking."

Never trust a devil, Helena commended to herself. Still … "Georgie, you hear me? Get your hind-end in here; just your hind-end, not your hindy-pomp."

"Hindy-pomp?"

"A hinny's a hybrid of a stallion and a she-ass, Pyrame. I might call her a Mole mule sometimes, but Georgie's hindy-pomp is actually a cross between a Pegasus-pony and an immature raven-doe, a ravendeer-hind. It doesn't look like much, but it is a psychopomp and, pending the acquisition of a compatible unicorn, that's a start."

"Unicorns are extinct," Pyrame pointed out.

"Unicorns are extinct in here," the Master confirmed. "At least they are as far as we can ascertain. But faeries have an uncanny flair for finding functional Tholoi or other sorts of rifts in the Dome. And, being earthborn, they hate devils like you as much as we Utopians do. They come back with one, we'll soon see if Georgie's hindy-pomp can reproduce. What would you call it, by the way?"

"A hi-bird?" Pyrame chortled.

Devils had a sense of humour. For supposed immortals they also had a strong sense of self-preservation. She caught herself mid-laugh. It'd just dawned on her what the Master and Kanin City's Hate-Sedon scientocrats were trying to recreate.

========

As his last recorded act as patriarch Xuthros Hor caused the Genesea 600 years after his birth. At the time he, numerically the tenth patriarch of Golden Age Humankind, rode a mono-horned ravendeer. Named, altogether unimaginatively, Raven's Head, the first of her kind allegedly came into being when a pair of mutated ravens, presumed daemons belonging to Number Six, Jaro Dan, combined with Oriartes Ma's unicorn, a presumed faerie.

Ma, Hor's father and therefore Number Nine, acquired his unicorn at the moment of the death of Number Four, Kemem Seb, in 421 Pre-Dome. No doubt as significantly, the first mono-horned ravendeer somehow melded together at the moment of Number Five's death, by devil, in 366 PD, some 66 years before Hor succeeded to the patriarchy at the traditional age of 300.

The devil that killed Number Five, Mahurus Zir, was none other than Great Byron. Not at all allegedly, that Thrygragos became Bodiless Byron almost immediately thereafter. A Great God's non-daemonic body from the neck down was hardly everything the composite creature, which Hor claimed as his own, could atomize. Daemonic bodies were equally vulnerable to being roasted beyond reclamation on the fiery spit of her unicorn horn.

Hor's Raven's Head was so exceptionally long-lived because she thrived on golden apples. She could also exorcise Master Devas then in possession of sentient shells by her mere presence. Of course that was mostly due to the fact that, the moment she was in the vicinity, devils fled for shells much farther away.

Her abilities transferred to her descendants, all of who also thrived on golden apples, via ordinary ravendeer, which were definitely products of Eden's scandalous experiments with living beings. Circa 2500 YD, about the same time Pyrame ceased being Lady Tanith on the Outer Earth, Sinistral Pride and his mostly demonic allies attempted to overrun the Inner Earth.

Their cavalry rode mono-horned ravendeers, bucks and does or hinds, into battle. Devils foolish enough to get in their way soon discovered to their detriment an unexpected facet to their, by then, both feared and fabled talents for atomization and exorcism. Mono-horned ravendeers could cathonitize Master Devas.

Pride called himself Lucifer. Much later on Illuminaries named him Domdaniel. Not surprisingly with a name like that, the devic Lucifer inevitably had a fall from grace of his own. Actually, Pyrame recalled, his fall was more of a hoist. He fell off his personal Raven's Head, whereupon she speared him on the end of her horn and hoisted him into the air. He thereby became a deliberately kept dim star in the night's sky, thus far forevermore.

His rebellious fourth-born son out of the way, Mithras proceeded to have a series of Attis's successions, together with his legionnaires, ruthlessly hunt down and exterminate every mono-horned ravendeer in existence anywhere on the Headworld. With the support of every devil left, they succeeded as well. As for ordinary raven bucks and raven hinds, Abe Chaos preserved enough ravendeer to breed and hunt himself on the Cattail Peninsula just because, being Chaos, he felt like it.

Now Helena Somata was seeking to facilitate the baleful beasties' return.

========

Datong Harmonia, the Unity of Balance as well as Panharmonium, chewed on the last chunk of beef sausage she'd had for breakfast, even if it was more like brunch. Unholy Abaddon, the Unity of Chaos, had found a full jar of beer and was chugging it. Lord Yajur, the Unity of Order, helped their mutual father, Thrygragos Everyman, on with his ravendeer cloak.

"You better be right about this," Lazareme said to his firstborn daughter.

"Hey, when have I ever misled you?" she responded, swallowing the sausage.

"Devils are veracious," he all but recited. "We always speak the truth."

"That too," she agreed.

========

"You spouted, mother?" wondered the young man as he, eye-stave in hand, eye-orb atop it closed, finally walked into his mother's sitting room in response to her repeated shouts.

"Do I look like a whale, Georgie?"

"Perhaps a beluga on a starvation diet," he responded good-humouredly.

"So you're Master Helena's Black Jordy," said Pyrame Silverstar.

"That's Black Georgie Masterson to you, devil."

"Devil? Is this not the Weirdom of Kanin City? How could I be a devil?"

"Your slip's showing," he observed sarcastically.

Somewhat podgy, he looked somewhere in his early to mid twenties. Although he wasn't black as midnight, he did have black skin. Which, despite his Illuminary as well as masterly mother's entirely unsolicited elucidation of a few minutes ago, struck Pyrame as strange. While purebloods were undeniably either black or white, unless they were striped like a zebra, this morning's Jordan Tethys, the boy's presumed father, wasn't any more black than Helena once Augusta.

Wine or no wine, that business about Constantine Caesar being conceived and born on the Outer Earth, so he didn't necessarily have to be black, didn't ring true to her. She supposed there were any number of other explanations for the seeming discrepancy. Maybe she and Sedon had indeed combined to overrule Utopian genetics. Or maybe only children like Georgie, who had been born within the walls of a Weirdom, who had at least one Utopian parent, and who'd been brought up eating the slop churned out by their remnant, originally extraterrestrial gadgetry, were either black or white.

Now was hardly the time to try and figure out anything as alien to her mind as hybrid heredity. It boggled her brain, caused her head to ring, wrongly. It also caused it to ache, badly. Was she experiencing warning signals or a premature hangover? The brew master hadn't poisoned her drinks, had she? Not that, if she had, that couldn't be rectified with not much more than a thought. Devils didn't have to be physicians in order to heal themselves. Or maybe she hadn't reset her skull properly.

Unless you disposed of a devil's daemonic body, preferably by immolation, then buried its severed head a minimum of a thousand miles away from where you chopped it off, decapitation was no way to get rid of a Master Deva. Imprisonment or cathonitization were the only reliable methods to do that. Nevertheless, she'd have to insist Attis bring her a moon-sickle as his next tribute to her unmatched wonderfulness. With Nergal Vetala's head attached to it, naturally.

"It is not. It can't be. It's a sheath, not a slip."

"He's referring to your third eye, Pyrame," Helena Somata advised her with a smirk. "You popped it open when you were mimicking a chiropractor."

"Oh, sorry." Silverstar suppressed it. She really did need to lay off the booze.

"Not that there's any excuse for you," George Masterson sneered smugly, "But don't be. I recognized you right away. And it wasn't just because of your third eye or silvery hair. You're fabulously famous, have been for damn near forever.

"There are mosaics, frescos and murals of you or someone who looks just like you going back thousands of years scattered throughout the palace. I've seen them featuring you with two or three eyes. There are even some with you having a triangular head and a solitary eyeball on each of its three upper sides."

"So there are," she acknowledged, not at all wistfully.

Kanin City's Palace was antediluvian. Masters had been adding onto it not so much since its day one as the first day Utopians took it over, post Deluge. Although when it came to devils they were usually less real than imagined, the artists they hired to decorate its walls and ceilings – some of which were in extensions of its great hall now underground – often took inspiration from their exploits.

She'd posed for more than a few of them, and not just as herself either. Artists prized shape-shifters. They came cheap compared to having to hire dozens of different models for dozens of different designs done over more than three dozen different centuries.

"So don't be so modest. You're topnotch among bad blotches, as my pan-piping pal Bad Rhad used to say before mom made me toss him out of Kanin. No other devil, not even Sedon Himself, dares come to Weirdoms such as ours, full of able-minded Trinondevs and armed with eye-staves, prison pods atop them, because you're the only devil who made them. Half-made them anyhow."

"One-third made them," the two-thing corrected him, internally noting the name. It reminded her of Rhadamanthys, the name Dark Sedon took when they co-ruled the devic third of Crete thousands of years ago. "Elementary school demonology that. Machine-Memory becomes a three-thing, Miracle Memory, when devils humanize her. I gather you're not much of an Illuminary."

"Not exactly," said the young man, continuing to grin disconcertingly. "I'm a born reporter, though; play a mean recorder to boot, or at least dance to. And I've always wanted to meet the famously female Perpetual Presence. Not as much as I've always wanted to help extirpate the infamously male Perpetual Presence, it goes without saying."

"You're about to get the chance."

"Sedon's down here?" For a moment, Masterson ceased smiling.

"In the Mole," said Helena, who didn't.

"Fantastic! I'll call out our Trinondevs. I just hope we've enough Godstuff left to fuel our cosmicars between-space. You couldn't help us out with that, could you, Mistress Silverstar?"

"I'm not humanizing the Memory Entity right this minute, Georgie. Truth told I don't even think she, or he, has tumbled back into our time stream."

"It's up to us," said his mother, rearranging her smirk into a look of grim determination.

"As it should be," said her son, beaming naughtily again. The boy was irrepressible.

Virtually every potential incarnation of Jordan Tethys was a reporter, a recorder and a taleteller. However, it was a rare Jordan Tethys who fancied himself a warrior, let alone a Warrior of Weir. Even if she was immune to Trinondev prison pods, Weir's Warriors Elite were not only equipped to dispose of devils for the duration. They were also bred to do whatever they could to take them out.

That in mind, Pyrame asked to see his reporter's recorder. He produced it out of the right sleeve of his galabia or djellaba, as Outer Earth's North Africans referred to similar sorts of indigo robes. She asked to hold it. He handed it to her. It didn't glow when she mentally tried to activate it so she figured it couldn't be a Brainrock anything.

She could be off base, as Memory might say. Every devic power focus was as dimmable as it was transmutable. If only because he was one of a very few recurring deviants, an eminently killable fellow like Jordan Tethys would have learned many lifetimes ago how to dim it from a distance.

Devic power foci were valuable objects and not just for collectors. You didn't need to be a devil or a deviant to use one and there were plenty of cutthroats out there who took the telltale glow they gave off as an open invitation to murder then steal, in that order. There were also plenty of devils that didn't mind having a backup talisman.

Still, even if a Tethys-deviant – were he a Jordan, a Georgie or a Georgina – had learned to prevent her activating it, he would never use it against her. They were friends and Jordy's personality, not theirs, took over his dying or newly dead, only to recover miraculously, children and grandchildren. That was why she further assumed Masterson hadn't been recently deceased, or even on death's precipice, as was the usual case with potential Tethys types just before their father or grandfather incarnated inside them.

Then again Master Helena, a first-rate Nightingale, a highest level, life-loving Ant if ever there was one, was supposed to be another of her friends. Rather, she was supposed to be Harmony's friend as well as that of the other two firstborn females who'd helped organize Harmony's latest version of the witches' Panharmonium Project: Methandra Thanatos and Umashakti Silvercloud.

Too bad Helena had gone monotheistic on them prior to Constantine, his full-sister Constance and, decades later, his half-brother, Black Jordy, being born. A far too young, severely overconfident Warrior of Weir and a credulous, devil-despising Master of it: No, she couldn't trust either of them. She was about to hand him back his recorder when he proved her correct.

"This is what you're looking for," Masterson said, grinning again. He'd reached into the left sleeve and withdrawn his father's Brainrock quill.

"You killed someone?" realized Pyrame, feigning serenity.

"Thought-ballooned her with this," he said of his ever-so-useful eye-stave. "Then I bounced her to within an inch of her life. It was no more than she intended to do to me, though she'd have probably tried to do something having to do with her backbone rather than an eyeorb. You should have seen the disks on that dino. As soon as the quill started to appear I snatched it and beetled back here on Hinny."

"Her?" Come to think of it, why shouldn't she be serene as a bean, calm as a clam or tranquil as a mandrill? What could he do to her?

"My half-sister, Saudi the Steg Sari. There are plenty of them around, half-brothers too. I've met a beautiful bouquet of them recently. Mother tells me father was a deviant who did a lot more than sticking his nose in where it didn't belong. Apparently he's spent most of the last 30 years, or howsoever long he's been around this time, sticking his dick in where it didn't belong."

"I'd have said deviant dick," did say Pyrame. "I didn't even know Saurs and Lizarados and dryads and suchlike were species compatible with humans."

"Sooth said," sooth-said Helena, "Neither did I; not until Georgie brought a gaggle of the dastard's goslings home to perform at my birthday party a week back. Maybe you should make a note of it."

"Want to use this, Cooked Goose?" queried Masterson, provocatively as well as flippantly to Pyrame's ears. As excusable as enthusiasm was in young mortals, his brashness was beginning to get on her nerves. He reached into the pocket of his indigo robe and pulled out what could have passed for an oversized notebook.

"After I whacked Saudi and beetled back here on Hinny, I couldn't get it to work so I shook it a couple of times and this just sort of plopped out. Masterly mom's witches can store stuff off their witch-stones or in their bottomless bags, so I reckoned dastardly daddy had it stored in his quill."

"That's his splotch-pad," gasped Pyrame, reaching out for it. "Let me have it."

Lizarado-Tethys said he hadn't had time to splotch it back into his quill before the Steg stabbed him with it. This Saudi must have picked the pad up before she went in quest of Georgie and once Jordy started coming back inside her the two, pen and pad, must have reunited.

"Well, if you insist." He flipped forward a few pages. "Maybe you should look at this first, though."

Every potential Tethys had a number of recognizable traits. Some were quirky; some were even admirable. Besides cocksureness, a capacity for drinking unhealthy quantities of beer, cracking wise, musicianship and collecting tales to tell, as well as tee-tee tails to read aloud if they could, all were fairly accomplished artists. The page he showed her, without giving it to her, featured a signed, black and white sketch of three of her trophy power foci in some sort of cloth pouch.

Clearly his father prepared and retained sketches of the commonest Tvasitar-trinkets she kept about herself as one of the fallback methods he used to find her. Jordy's drawings filled in backgrounds by themselves. Once signed and dotted, the Tethys-deviant could thereupon go wherever the background revealed. It was a stupendous ability; one of many his quill granted him.

Fortunately, what he couldn't do was draw anyone away from where they were without first securing his or her permission. Unlike Helena he wasn't the resentful sort but, if he were, and if he could do that, interrupted coitus would get him killed more often than over-drinking or jealous wives and/or husbands already did.

Masterson looked expectantly at his masterly mother. "Since devils can't lie and we now know she isn't humanizing Machine-Memory, can I finally say it?"

"If you must," Helena allowed, with a triumphant smile of her own. They'd planned this a while ago, Pyrame realized too late.

"Your asp is mine!"

========

Taurus Chrysaor Attis regained consciousness, wearily. He opened both his eyes and looked up, warily. Astride her three-headed chimera, the devil child, the demon child, Tralalorn to devils and Lost Lorna to faeries, looked down at him, wryly.

"Diddle the piddle, daddy," she challenged him, "What's up with the pup?"
Why was there a miniature She-Sphinx parrot-perched on her shoulder?
****

THEO 11:

THEOMACHY AS THEOMEDY

========

With deviant daddy's Brainrock quill, George Masterson dotted the signature at the bottom of the sketch he'd quickly altered in his masterly mother's antechamber once he entered it, from out of between-space, atop Hinny the Hippy.

She'd already mind-to-mind spoken to him via their eye-staves as to whom she was entertaining. However, she didn't realize what he had and, despite her briefing him on it after confirming her Jordy was that Jordy a week ago, he'd never had it such that he could try to make it work.

He had now.

========

Something happened to the already gore-splotched sweater the silver-haired devil borrowed from King Cold of Lathakra. In addition to woolly, it got holey. Three of her trophy power foci – the uraeus, threshers' flail and crooked rod – tore through it into the cloth pouch Georgie had already sketched out: the pocket of his indigo djellaba.

Panicking genuinely this time, Pyrame Silverstar whirled on Helena Somata. The long-lived, albeit only by human standards, yet nonetheless non-pureblood Utopian had already done her witch-thing. She'd materialized her Master's Mace in one hand. The non-gargoyle cloud she manifested atop her miniature eye-stave rendered it reminiscent of a puffy lollipop. It evidently doubled as a sprinkler because out of it sprayed some kind of clear liquid that soaked Pyrame to the skin.

"What's that splat, Hel? It sort of stung."

"Holy Water!" the Master trumpeted with an Ant-anserine, not to mention un-dignified, Mother Gooselike honk. "I've been saving it for Harmonia, in case she ever tried to humiliate me in my own Weirdom again, but it should do for you too."

During the decades she'd spent beyond the Dome as Helena eventually Augusta, Kanin's Master of Weir had become a Celestial convert: worse, a monotheistic zealot. Pyrame knew that. Rapidly regaining her composure, she also appreciated how filthy she must be. Finding humour in the most trying of circumstances, she couldn't pre-vent herself smirking almost as much as Master and Masterson were already.

"You've got to be joking." Grandfather Sedon had made a crack about her di-shevelled looks and Tantal Thanatos would be miffed about the sweater. She hoped it wouldn't shrink before she took it to a seamstress for cleansing and repairs. "Thanks for the shower, though. I needed it."

She reopened her third eye. Devic eyefire could burn anything, including stupid grins off stupid faces. Abruptly she was encased in a brain-bulb or mind-globe, what Masterson called a thought-balloon: a bubble-like, but solid, all-encompassing, tele-kinetic projection emitting from the cocky boy's eye-stave, the orb atop it still closed. She let loose anyhow.

Eyefire did burn anything. She screamed reflexively as it backfired off the insides of the brain-bulb. Abruptly it was her turn to do a booze-tent and Lizarado-Tethys. She hoped the sweater wasn't one of Tantal's favourites because about the only use a seamstress would be now would be to weave her a replacement, preferably one made out of flame-retarding wool or sheared salamander.

The Master, like every other Ant Nightingale – and most tiptop witches of any sisterhood – being ensorcelled against it with at least one, so-called '*agatine eye*', Pyrame sought to possess Georgie. It was only then she realized somebody already had him; hence perhaps all the fay-saying they'd been engaged in howsoever inadvertently.

No matter. Whatever de-brained demon's body she occupied, that didn't mean she was de-brained herself. It occurred to her devil's brain that demons weren't just shape-shifters. They were state-shifters as well. Thus, with very nearly the speed of thought, she didn't need a shower any longer so much as she was one.

Georgie gaped at the Pyrame-puddle she'd made of herself within the thought-balloon he projected about her. Then he began to laugh so loudly he literally bifurcat-ed, split in two, dissolving the telekinetic enclosure he'd cast about her as he did so. One remained him, blackish in blue with two eyes; the other was pinkish in black-ness with three eyes.

Her spirit being self as much sensing as well as seeing him, Pyrame re-formed her daemonic body. Backfiring eyefire snuffed due to drenching, she once again stood in the Master's dayroom wearing her thus cleansed, breasts-baring sheath. She may be immune to the imprisoning aspects of Trinondev eye-staves, but their orbs operat-ed on willpower. Evidently one devil's willpower was greater than the combined will-power of a non-pureblood Master and her deviant son.

"Where've you been, Judge?"

"*Getting rubbed out, among things.*" He responded as he materialized a pan-pipe to match Georgie's recorder.

Both could play. For Helena, dancing became the only option to dying.

========

"This sucks," snorted the Bull of Mithras, he of the many forms, who was some-thing of a teat-man.

========

Somewhere in the gently rolling hills, idyllic woodlands and pleasant pastures that were the Gregarian Fields, comparatively ragtag hordes of Byronics and Lazaremists were advancing on Mithrant and Mithradite positions. Having heard the sounds of many more fanfare trumpets echoing that of Djinn Domitian, Mithras's tattered an-gel, the two, thoroughly well-drilled legions Attis gathered in the Mole were already on the go, albeit without their inexplicably absent Taurus to command them.

So too, doubling their numbers, were the human, semi-human and absolutely non-human armies brought here by the likes of Klizarod Rex, the Emperor Chamele-on, Dandset Typhon, Geld Neargon and the two Thanatoids, Heat and Cold, Meth-andra and Tantal. Interspersed amongst them were the sometimes man-eating, but properly disciplined, demonic shape-shifters out of Belialma's Satanwyck, the sham-bling zombies reanimated by the Nergalids' northland azuras and the Glorious Dead of Valhalla.

Jotan Tethys, bugling on his high quality, albeit not exactly new hornpipe, marched as a member of the band at the head of these last. For the most part – he be-ing a somewhat inglorious exception – they were the corpses of men and women, of any species, that Valkyries like mother Volsanga and, scheduled to make her debut to-day, sister Ute judged to have fallen heroically on northern battlefields over the course of recent centuries. To a one, symbiotic Sangazurs animated them.

Almost exclusively sired by Mars Bellona, the Apocalyptic of War, Sangs had numerous mothers. War's serial infidelities spoke to why Drought, his first and high-est born mate, caused herself to become fallow rather than rewarding him with more of her azuras. Although she'd spent most of the last 2,000 years imprisoned within All of Incain, a remarkable number, perhaps even a preponderance of them, called mom the Medusa who now styled herself Mater Matare, Mother Murder, the Apoc-alyptic of Death.

Near Valhalla, which lay far to the northwest of the Gregarian Fields, were the Elysian Fields, the so-called Laughing Lands of the Exalted Dead. At their centre stood Grand Elysium. There, in the midst of the Inner Earth's Sedonic as opposed to Celes-tial City, rose Pyrame's ideal pyramid, the one that dwarfed the Outer Earth's Great Pyramid of Giza. For virtually all of the Headworld's existence, Great Gods and Mas-ter Devas alike visited Grand Elysium not so much to pray to the Moloch Sedon as to speak with him personally.

Priestly plagues of all three tribes nevertheless insisted their everlasting souls, and indeed the souls of all those who followed their *'do as I say'* tenets, attained their afterlife reward as the Elysian Fields' Exalted Dead. Intrepid pilgrims who made it that far rarely returned with verification of that assertion. Equally so, they rarely returned with a lack thereof. The fact of the matter was they rarely returned at all.

Devils were happy to keep suchlike questing peregrinations mostly one way. They considered the crest of the Headlands their private playground. Be they ambulatory Dead Things, daemonic horrors or altogether alive leftovers from tortuous experiments performed by immortality-seeking, pre-Flood, pre Golden Age, Edenites – the likes of winged, cannibalistic Angelycs, ant-like Myrmidons, Saur Tsars and Lizarados – natives of Sedon's Crown were almost as pleased the Laughing Lands remained largely human-free.

Both resultantly and howsoever reluctantly, most sentient southern species, especially sentient humanoid species, resolved it best to leave the northlands to northlanders. About the only folks who weren't happy with that conclusion were certain rich and overfed epicures whose much-prized chefs were thereby deprived of some of their choicest ingredients.

The collective multitude of armed warriors loyal to Mithradite Master Devas numbered in excess of 20 thousand. Scouts and spies in their midst signalled the oncoming forces of Byron and Lazareme counted at least that many. They had plenty of exotics with them as well.

Reputedly the Diamantes of the Crystal Mountain Range, who therefore followed Lord Order, had impervious hide. The Metal Men of the Cattail Peninsula, Sedon's Ponytail, who would be Chaos loyalists, did as well. They weren't even partially flesh and blood. Neither were they partially Mandroid, which was just as well since Mandroids, like be-brained and improperly disciplined demons, munched devils.

Fire-breathing dragons could handle them. There wasn't much fire-breathing dragons couldn't handle. Unfortunately, while there were a variety of related creatures on the Head, by far its biggest, brightest and most hellacious dragons adhered to Byronics. Their devil gods were Sedona Spellbinder, a second-born whose most noticeable aspect was smoke, and Yati, a fourth-born whose preferred likeness, as might be expected, was a fire-breathing dragon.

Both sides – so long as one believed Byronics and Lazaremists could make up one side long enough to fight a battle in unison – had killer witches. Appropriately Miss Myth Methandra's were called Athenans. The single breasted Amazons of Gravity, Umashakti Silvercloud, Byron's Moon, generally rode male centaurs, and not just into combat. The were-creatures of the other Silvercloud, Rufous Rudra, Savage Storm, Byron's Beast and last remaining firstborn, would eat anything, though they considered demons a delicacy. They didn't need a full moon to come out and frolic either.

Both sides had berserkers. But Chaos would bring Barrings, who didn't have to put on bearskins in order to go berserk. They already were anthropomorphic bears. Both sides had psychopomps. But the hollow-boned, avian-human garudas of Djerrid Ruin, Byron's Green Man, had a normal intelligence, whereas the Valkyries' swans were birdbrains and the Sari witches' Terror Donnas, besides being dead, were snakeheads with brains the size of peas.

The oversized Vultyrie ridden by Apocalyptic archers and the just as alive pterodactyls ridden by Klizarod's Saur Tsars and Tsarinas made for an acceptable, if eminently killable, air force. However, Chrysaor Attis's Pegasus was hardly one of a kind and, like garudas, every one of ever-changing Chimaera's winged horses could get about between-space.

So too could hippogriffs, who were exclusively Byronic, and mature ravendeers, who belonged to Chaos and therefore to his father, Thrygragos Everyman. While a great many creatures of nightmare came into existence due to long-cathonitized Dream, firstborn Phantast, and were thus Mithradites, faeries, fickle as they were, tended to be Lazaremist extremists. Like properly conditioned Mandroids and their chthonic cousins, Sinistral Lust's more wilful demons, faeries could both shift shapes and weren't averse to nibbling on devils.

Both sides also had an abundance of just that, devil-gods. Only Mithras had more of them, a lot more now that the She-Sphinx had released a further hundred. That was supposed to be the one major advantage he had over his two fellow Thrygragos Brothers. Of the 500 Master Devas scholarly demonologists calculated survived the Great Flood, or Genesea, and made it to the eventual Head, fully half were Mithradites.

It was too bad they had more experience fighting Attis's successions, their legionnaires, and each other than they did fighting Byronics or Lazaremists. It was just as too bad, for one specific Great God of Civil Society, that they had no intention of fighting anyone. Or so they'd pre-agreed amongst themselves until Grandfather Sedon, not Father Mithras, popped downstairs to lead them to consequently inevitable victory.

They didn't march, though. They took themselves through the Weird to the vanguard of those who did march. Appearances must be maintained.

========

"Suck it does," agreed Divine Coueranna, Kore-Concord, Kore of the Many Names and Multiple Personalities. The Korants' goddess of just about everything appeared in no condition to give the Bull any refreshing suckles should he so request. Barefoot and levitating she was already in appallingly withered, wintry greyness mode.

"How could we have been so gullible?" whimpered Bouncing Belle, Satanwyck's current Prime Sinistral.

Unless Kore-Coitus stuck, thus far in her near-endless existence beguiling Belialma's only Kore-name was Concupiscence. Although like almost everyone else alongside her she was prepared to add Kore-Judas to her list of alter egos, she had not come here to play Belting Beltis.

She'd already pelted pal Baal in the cow pasture's muck.

========

"You're enjoying this far too much, Judge. The Master's a murderous, even maleficent megalomaniac, but she's still a mortal."

"Am I, Queen of Courts? Why shouldn't I? Why shouldn't you, too? Here, have a bongo-brain. See if you can keep time with us."

The Smiling Fiend ripped the Gypsium chain off from around his neck and tossed it to her; skinless, hollowed-out and shrunken skull still attached. The fabulously female Perpetual Presence caught it easily but, in the process, Smiler missed a beat or two. His erstwhile, moments ago vacated shell George Masterson didn't.

The boy – and, being well short of 30, he was a boy by Trinondev standards; a seconds-only foetus by both devic and daemonic standards – kept the tempo going. The fiend, once again tooting on his panpipes, picked it up like the practised professional he purported to be. He smiled the more as Pyrame Silverstar proved she too had rhythm.

Helena Somata, once Augusta, might dance herself into terpsichorean oblivion before they were finished. It wouldn't count as a killing if she did, though. Kanin's Master of Weir would never have worshipped devils anyhow.

Besides, the real Moloch Sedon would be up north, in his Devic Eye-Land, the Weirdom of Cabalarkon, visiting his thought-father around about now anyway. Which, Smiler appreciated, was something else that devilishly clever brother of his would have counted on in his preparatory calculations. Sometimes Mithras didn't so much mean myth as it meant math.

The three male objects? That was a masterstroke. The Mask of Byron allowed Smiler's brood brother to look like anyone facially; Lazareme's Cloak of Many Colours allowed him to appear to be anyone physically; and his own Cross or Crutch could be a pitchfork as easily as it could be a javelin.

That wasn't the whole of what they granted Mithras either. Truth told as well, Truth, Light and Justice getting hold of them might make all the difference in this wretched excuse for a world for Smiler – Untruth, Darkness and Injustice, as some would have him. It might yet force him to risk a masterstroke of his own.

Once his wherewithal arrived, that is.

========

The Byronhead, bodiless and hairless, spherical with facial features like the man in the moon, as huge as Mithras – unless he was Sedon – ballooned over the horizon in the distance. In a halo of light, a tiny dwarf star to Unmoving Byron's comparative red giant, Thrygragos Lazareme orbited bug-like about lunar-him.

It wasn't that the former was any mightier than the latter. In fact – in legend, make that – the Lackland Libertine saw the first Weir Star years before Byron, Mithras or any of the three Great Goddesses existed. It was just that Lazareme wasn't big on self-aggrandizement.

Unless he was bagging one of his daughters, it went without demonstrating.

========

He was called Thrygragos Everyman because he seemed humanoid to a human, saurian to a Saur, ophidian to an Ophidian, androgynous to an Androgyny, and so it went. For their part, many devils saw him as today, as a bright blur vaguely in their own chosen shape. The one commonality of his seeming was members of every species – save for pureblood Utopians, who despised devakind – perceived him as the faultless embodiment of his, her or its own genus.

In that, Lazareme was in some respects proof of the theorem that in every individual there resides the spark of godhood. Put another way, if God, as he'd heard, was made in the image and likeness of whomever or whatever, he had an innate as well as, to quote him at his acerbic best, God-given aptitude for unthinkingly making sure he looked the part.

He was called Lackland because he claimed no land as altogether his own. Neither did Mithras. He left the claiming, and retaining, of most of the Upper Head to Chrysaor Attis and his legionnaires, who did both in his name. At best Mithradite Master Devas were local deities of smallish fiefdoms.

Something similar held for Thrygragos Byron. The difference was he claimed, as exclusively his own, much of the Lower Head. That included the entirety of Godbad, the Penile Peninsula, most of the landforms within the Head's Interior Ocean of Akadan, and regions of the Cattail touching its southernmost coastline.

The Subcontinent of Aka Godbad consisted of Sedon's Mouth, Lower Jaw and Goatee. The Penile Peninsula consisted of Iraxas and Krachla, which together made up Sedon's Mutton Chop. The Cattail, most of which amounted to Chaos's preserve, was Sedon's tightly braided Ponytail. Akadan didn't just have islands. Being warm and consequently hospitable, especially for water-breathers, it also had subsurface realms, which Byron claimed as well.

Byronic Master Devas were little more than territorial ambassadors the Great God their Father shuffled about should their popularity ever threaten to eclipse his own. Even if it didn't, he sometimes shuffled them about just because it was his right to do so. Third generational Master Devas were as genetically incapable of disobeying their fathers as they were of lying or violating their sworn oaths.

As for their mothers, that was most of the reason why their Father Sedon abandoned them on the Second Weirworld when he formed the Sedonshem an approaching impossibly long time ago now. The Trigregos Sisters, whose Entities-given names and titles were Demeter the Body, Sapiendev the Mind and Devaura the Soul, were unacceptably disputatious.

Lazareme was called the Libertine because he was an absolutist when it came to liberty. It certainly wasn't because he was immoral or licentious. To be either you first had to believe there was any need for morals, let alone licences. In the same sense, he wasn't lawless. Mortals didn't need laws any more than gods, even if they were devils, did.

Every mortal was born knowing the difference between right and wrong. Negatively put, it was as simple as the Indic or Ophirant concept of ahimsa: *'Do no harm!'* Put more positively, if prosaically, it was the Golden Rule – and not the one that read: *'Those with the gold make the rules'*. The one that read: *'Do unto others as you would have others do unto you!'*

If someone did, or even threatened to do unto you what they thought they could get away with, well, wasn't that what we gods were there for? You want worship; you earn worship. *'We dare not kill,'* his more simplistic offspring would nevertheless counter occasionally. *'We do, Grandfather will cathonitize us.'*

'You don't have to kill,' he'd yawn, and then patiently reply. *'Nor should you punish them too closely to the proximity of their death,'* he'd invariably add. *'The trick is to demonstrate, once in awhile, who's the real boss. Remember, rashes beat lashes any day of week. Mind you, swarms of locusts or storms of frogs aren't necessarily bad things to have in reserve. Locusts and frogs have to eat too.'*

'*But,*' they'd object, quite presciently given that was why he was here today, above the Gregarian Fields, flitting like a gnat-nincompoop around his full-mooning sibling in Sedon's Byronhead: '*What about when the gods themselves are the ones causing or threatening to cause harm to you, not just to your adherents?*'

'*Well,*' he'd respond, '*that's why devils were born with something besides knowledge of the Golden Rule. That's why you minor immortals in particular have fathers.*'

Then he saw him – his own just that: angrily red and arrogantly colossal, a veritable tree of a pitchfork in paw, striding at the Mithradites' vanguard.

The Lackland Libertine couldn't believe his three eyes. He might have blinked. Bodiless Byron saw him too, though he definitely didn't blink any of his three eyes. He was called the Unmoving One not because he couldn't transport himself physically either inside or outside the Weird. He was called thus because none of his man-in-the-moon facial features ever moved.

"Oh, oh," the younger psychically imparted to the elder in his distinctive voice.

"Isn't that cheating?" the latter queried the former.

========

Thrygragos Lazareme came to the Gregarian Fields with no more intention of fighting Varuna Mithras than Mithras's Master Devas, Harmony assured him, did of fighting anyone. His firstborn daughter had everything arranged, didn't she? She even had a name for what they were going to start accomplishing today.

It was not Thrygragon. That was how Mithras had named the day, though the way they had it figured Mithras was the Great God who'd be gone, gone, gone by the end of it. Her alternative was, not surprisingly, Panharmonium.

He was here to show solidarity with her. Her immediate brothers were here because, if one came and the other didn't, she might begin to favour the one who had come, which would never do. The Great God Everyman's Unities could only maintain unity because Harmony bound her brothers, albeit figuratively and with herself ever between them, as much as she bound him to her, the pride of his loins.

Although no one ever called her Lazareme's Virgin, because he didn't have any virgins left, no one ever called her Lazareme's Whore either. While he did have a whore – Illuminaries named her Hetaera – that wasn't why they never called her that. Harmony didn't appreciate putdowns. Plus, she was as ruthless as he was with all his children when it came to ordering about her younger brothers and sisters. Which is to say that her reputation for ruthlessness rendered her ever having to exhibit it virtually unheard of.

The three main, male devils in her ever-ongoing existence, her second generational father and two brood brothers, enjoyed the company of her younger sisters far more than she did. Other than the other two firstborns, Byron's Gravity and Mithras's Heat, the only female devil she got along with, let alone treated with a degree of equability, was Pyrame Silverstar.

Which was yet another reason not just Lazaremists never dared to annoy Harmony. The Unity's sheer, raw might was such she could, and would, feed any third generational devil who pissed her sufficiently off to Pyrame's pal on Incain. What's more, she'd done so, and would do so again, as happily as the Attis had any devil he'd pulped and disarmed, in either order, for almost as long as most devils had been independently solid individuals.

As for the main, non-devilish male in her earlier-on existence, that would be the celebrated Cadmus, he who in legend brought the Headworld's alphabet to Greece. A prince of Phoenician Sidon, which may have been named after the Moloch Sedon, his sister's name was Europa whereas their father was Sidon's King Agenor. Many a tall-tale was told about the three of them.

For one, in the form of a white bull Olympian Zeus – likely Varuna Mithras – kidnapped Europa and swam her across the Middle Sea to his birthplace, the mountainous island of Crete, meaning strength. There, on by far the largest landform in what was now commonly called the Roman and/or Mediterranean Sea, she reputedly became its first altogether human queen.

Via Zeus, she also became the mother of its three deviant as well as dynastic kings. These were, nominally, Minos, Sarpedon and Rhadamanthys. Reality wasn't so cut and dried, but an entire continent was named after Europa Agenorid. By contrast the best brother Cadmus could do was found Grecian Thebes. Thereafter, with Harmonia's inestimable assistance, he conspired to sire their even more famous, ultimately Dionysian dynasty.

In myths regarding he and her, all the gods of Olympus – to a man, woman or child, in the case of Eros – attended their wedding. Among the gifts mythologists similarly had her receiving were a robe made by Arachne from gold she'd spun herself, much to heady Athena's infuriation, and a necklace, also golden, made by Hephaistos, their smithy.

Mythologists were mistaken.

========

"Kill him, Chaos."
"I can't, dad. That's granddad."
"Exactly. He's my father. I'm yours. Do as I say!"
"Leave him to me," thundered Lord Order.
"We'll do it together," boomed Harmony, typically and just as vociferously.

========

Datong Harmonia already had the necklace, a golden torc. She'd had it for 500 years before she encountered eventual King Cadmus. It was how she first attained, then sustained, independent solidity. Plus, it was made by Anvil, Tvasitar Smithmonger, the devils' artificer, their Prometheus more so than their Hephaistos. As such it was her power focus. As well, Arachne, who wasn't Kala Tal, had nothing to with her robe. Neither did Methandra, Mithras's Virgin.

Dark-haired, butterscotch-skinned Harmonia extruded it herself out of her torc. And, while her robe was golden, it was composed not of gold thread but of interlinked Brainrock chains. Hence derived the double notion her Tvasitar Talisman amounted to the Chains of Justice and that her power manifested itself in the form of chain lightning.

Although she took seriously her role as Lazareme's Balance, and although the lightning she emitted did come off the fittingly broken chains she visibly sported manacled to her wrists, the whole notion of Chains of Justice was wrong, wrong, wrong. She no more approved of chaining up prisoners than she did of slavery, another absolute no-no for Lazaremists no matter how far gone they were in the way of extremism. Furthermore, even though her killing Cadmus was justified, she strenuously objected to the whole concept of capital punishment.

She was all in favour of the term Scales of Justice, however. She wouldn't have minded if Tvasitar, in his anvil-headed wisdom, had crafted them for her instead of the much lower born Byronic Zodiacal, Libra No-Eyes, as bygone Illuminaries styled her. He hadn't, so she fashioned her own scales of justice, a pair of them, and wore them as earrings.

She wouldn't have objected if he'd crafted the ostrich feather Egyptian Maat was often depicted using as a counterbalance either. He gave that, in the form of a clipped quill, to her younger brother, Rumour of Lazareme. Still, being as idiosyncratic as any Lazaremist, she sometimes attired herself with scales-like plates as bust-cups depending from her torc by their chains.

Today was one of those days.

========

"Do it then," concurred their father. "Unless of course you've a better idea, Harmony."

As it happened she did. She showed them. Her two firstborn brothers emitted earsplitting hoots. So did Unmoving Byron, albeit without moving his man-in-the-moon lips. He imparted mirth instead. Lazareme controlled his long enough to recommend a strategic adjustment.

"Our Father who art a Sedon does not wear a Brainrock bustier, Harmony."

"This better?"

========

Divine Coueranna floated barefoot, but monstrous Plathon and the other remaining Apple Goddess, along with somewhere in the vicinity of 200 of their siblings via the Trigregos Sisters, strode in the frontlines of Mithras's forces. An appearance proving deceiving, at their head, maybe 30 feet tall, evidently wasn't their grandfather. Not unless he was one of a set of quadruplets, since three identical Sedons were plodding their direction in front of the forces of Byron and Lazareme.

Quadruplets? Suddenly there were quintuplets and two of them were on their side. The newest one carried a double-headed war-axe, a twibil, aka a Labrys. King Cold was drunk. The Virgin wasn't. Make that a set of sextuplets, with three on their side.

Then it was four, the newest Sedon had a pitchfork just like the Devil as well as the Demon King, albeit one with two tines rather than four. Call it a bident. He also had four horns instead of the usual stubby pair. His tail was distinctly bullish instead of satanic and he avoided the goatee, which would have been too goatish to be bullish. His skin was red, though, and the fur covering his nether regions, fore and aft, might have been an article of clothing rather than bullish bushiness.

The Byronics weren't to be left out. Neither was the balance of the Lazaremists. Finally the rest of the Mithradites got into the spirit of the shenanigans. Some didn't bother hiding their gender with fur, a bush or even a token seeming. Hell's Belle, as was her wont, was the Devil as an entirely female voluptuary. Virtually all of them opted for the red skin. Chaos, on the other side, was only too happy to materialize his version of a pitchfork, albeit as a trident. Soon two veritable forests of Sedonic looka-likes were tromping toward each other.

Theomachy meant combat amongst the gods. And maybe that's how it'd go, eventually. However, the way it was shaping up had the makings of a divine comedy, a '*Theomedy*' perhaps. All it really needed to become a full-fledged farce was for someone to fart. The first Sedon, still the biggest and purely hellish Devil of the lot, must have sensed it because, at his signal, the Sedon with a fanfare trumpet butt-blasted a big, smelly, brimstone tart of one.

Everyone halted. Some sniffed the air. Most felt uncomfortable, a few had the concomitant decency to revert to their regular forms. No one laughed, not out loud, not in the great outdoors of the Gregarian Fields.

========

Someone chortled inter-spatially. It wasn't Smiler. It was Saudi-Jordy. Chortling hurt. He hurt, unless she hurt. He hated coming back female.

========

Maybe they both hurt. Someone certainly hurt. It had to be both of them. They shared crushed vertebrae, at least one broken leg and a smashed skull. Being killed definitely hurt, but being flung, any number of times already, from a flying pterodactyl was a very hurtful way of learning how to ride one.

One thing about having a Brainrock quill is you could draw yourself healthy and happy, if not always altogether hurt-free. So long as you had a Brainrock quill, and the splotch-pad that went with it, it went without saying. He shared the Sari witch's memories. Once again he read them. Jordan Q Tethys wasn't big on raw food either.

Another pissed off woman who thought marriage meant monogamy, only this one happens to be a tiptop Nightingale, one in contact with the superiors of just about every Witch Sisterhood on the Head, as well as a High Illuminary and a Master of Weir. That explained that then. Holy Matrimony was a sacred sacrament and this morning's Tethys had only been its first sacrificial oaf.

He-she-they spurred his-her-their already toilet-trained, but at last relatively docile, Terror Donna between-space. It was past time to dump back.

========

Maybe his brothers didn't want to give him a present for his feast day. Maybe he had to give them one instead. He'd named it Thrygragon. He'd make it Thrygragon.

========

Virtually every iconic depiction nominally of Thrygragos Mithras found on either side of the Cathonic Dome was actually of his ever-dying, but thus far ever-revivifying, deviant of a son. Often these representations showed a youth wearing a Phrygian cap slaying a bull while various other critters gnawed at the beast's undersides.

A Phrygian cap was a close fitting, brimless head covering made from a soft fabric with its crown loosely folded over forward. Perhaps peculiarly, given that Attis was best remembered as the Universal Soldier, Roman freedmen wore the same sort of headpiece. Only they called it a Liberty Cap. Although slavery was not tolerated throughout most of the Head due to the need for devic adulation to be given freely, his brothers definitely needed liberating from their lives.

The Sedon-form not having had the desired result – complete submission to him on the part of every devil in the Mole – Mithras wanted no part of such a comparatively unimpressive semblance. He re-devil-devised himself munificently, no smaller, still man-mountain-sized, yet as if in all his former glory. Bipolar disorder, ha! He was a Sky God without borders.

Dispensing with affected reddishness, he manifested himself as having golden-brown skin, the same as his mortal, yet immortally recurrent son. It was so tawny there was an element of the feline to it. There was unquestionably something solar to his sunlight beard and sunbeam hair. He seemed a leonine Sun King – and not just of beasts, of everyone, including Thrygragos Everyman. He wasn't done yet either, not by any measure.

Many a Mithras depicted on the ceilings of Mithraic Cave Temples, including the one Bishop Damasus usurped on Rome's Vatican Hill not so long ago, had him wearing a stylized star-cape, the Milky Way itself thereby rendered. That aspect of Attis's image the Great God didn't mind, though he had a much more personally appropriate manner of showing off his far-fabled stellar qualities.

Every ancient astronomer on the Outer Earth – from sub-Sahara Africa and Arabia, to the Mediterranean, the Levant and Europe, to India to Tibet to China, and across the oceans to the continents betwixt and between, what the Dual Entities referred to as the Americas – knew the Planet Saturn, as the Romans had it, after him, had rings orbiting it. Thrygragos Varuna Mithras had been an ancient astronaut. He had seen them firsthand, aboard the Sedonshem after it entered the Earth's planetary system in excess of five thousand years ago.

It, the Sedonshem, with not even close to every devil who ever existed on it, as part of it, settled on the moon. There it remained, those on the moon absorbing starlight for nourishment, for many solar years. Meanwhile, down below, the expeditionary party led by Thrygragos Lazareme checked out the suitability of the planet's population for devic colonization.

There was a good reason for Sedon's reticence to go any farther. It had to do with why the Sedonshem no longer contained even close to every devil who ever existed. Sure enough, the completeness of that rationale had preceded the Sedonshem to Earth.

The Male Entity, Heliosophos, Helios called Sophos the Wise, was already on its surface. He may even have been born there, though probably not in the lifetime he was then currently living. Even with the Sedonshem up top, poised like a cosmic tomcat ready to pounce on an unsuspecting, golden-apple-eating dodo, Lazareme did not deem it safe for it to come down until over half a century after Anti-Patriarch Cain did an Abel on Helios as Alorus Ptah.

Mithras had heard Cain finished off his father in revenge for the Dual Entities refusing to release his birthmother, Primeval Lilith, from within the Androsphinx. He hadn't been there, though, so he couldn't say for sure. He'd never forgotten the sight of Saturn's rings, however, so he could say for sure they deserved emulation.

Accordingly, he haloed his head, as Uranus-Varuna often had, in an approximation of Saturn's rings. He also did away with Sedon's stubby horns and went back to having his horns akin to a crescent moon. His brows were central to its crescent. His third eye shone out of the centre of said crescent's horniness.

He glanced at Beltis-Belialma, Sinistral Lust. She was still adopting the glamour of a red-skinned, Sedonic voluptuary. She often did that anyhow. Her power focus was the Ruby Red Apple of Concupiscence. He winked at her. Then he gave himself a nose job. The nostrils he made for himself might pass for his scrotum. He arrowed the bridge upwards, phallus-pointing to his third eye as if it was a vaginal orifice.

Bouncing Belle winked back at him encouragingly. Which was when he realized he was standing in front of her, and everyone else, including his Virgin and Fecundity, stark naked. The temptation was irresistible. It was almost as much fun as when he, after he first manifested himself as his father outside his pavilion, told the Pauper Priestess she should make herself more presentable; that he might be back to help her make more Sed-sons come nightfall.

That fledgling Valkyrie was no Judge Druj lie. The Legendarian had shown him a full-colour picture he'd drawn of her – Ute Tethys was his daughter – a few years earlier and thus barely blooming. Mithras had mentioned her existence to his father, during one of their infrequent get-togethers in Grand Elysium, and Sed said he'd keep her in mind. The Devil loved women with natural, silky silver hair.

Who was Judge Druj? Who cared?

By definition Sun Gods were always hot stuff, even hotter than his Virgin. There were as many or more fertility gods as there were fertility goddesses. In case they missed the import of his nose job, he gave himself an Attis-like tunic in that it was seemingly made from the impervious hide of an enchanted elephant, although Attis's was really the power focus of Byron's Elephantine. He next rendered its trunk bodily much lower down and unambiguously penile.

All the Mithradite Sedons, none quicker than his Virgin, recoiled reductively away from his latest improvised improvement. Someone in front of him snickered. It was his reputedly eldest brother, the insufferable Thrygragos Everyman.

"You done demonstrating how frosty it is out here yet?" Lazareme broadcast, for all in the Mole to hear. "Leave the chilling to King Cold and let's get on with the killing."

Mariamne Dawnstar, Flowery Anthea's brood sister, the fairest of his second-born spawn by the three long lost sisters and his version of Venus, was venerated by chthonic or earthborn faeries. She must have taught him to fay-say. If she did, it would have been before Attis confiscated her power focus, a peasant's handheld, multi-spiked Morgenstern or morning star, and incarcerated her within All.

"Precisely my thoughts," Mithras boomed back as far heard as Lazareme had boomed forth. "Shall I warm things up for you, brother?"

His Cross of Mithras was as transmutable as any devic power focus. As often as not Attis carried it in the form of a slender, yet sturdy, metallic javelin pointed at either end. Mithras could do much better than that. He willed his satanic pitchfork to become his commonest symbol, emblem or labarum: the letter '*X*' with a perpendicular line through it and turned over at the top such that it resembled the letter '*P*'.

The sabres Taurus Chrysaor Attis and most of his officers armed themselves with closely resembled this version of his monogram. The '*D*' tops of the '*P*' on their sabres were the grips, the '*X*' part the guards, and the remaining '*I*' part the blades. Usually their sabres also featured a spherical knob or pommel-like bauble on the uppermost extremity of their '*D*' grips. Invariably this otherwise strictly ornamental attachment was scored with another '*X*': the solar-cross used by his loyal legionnaires on both sides of the Dome to represent Mithras as Sol Invictus.

A Circled-X was probably the oldest sign for a deity on the Whole Earth. Variations of it approached limitless. Initially, as it still did in the bulk of lands beyond the Dome, it stood for the sun's disc. Out there's extraordinarily enduring Xuthrodite Brotherhood had also appropriated it as the symbol of their inspirational namesake, Xuthros Hor. Contrarily, certain ill-informed sub-sects of Outer Earth faiths believed it was the mark Celestial God placed in the middle of Anti-Patriarch Cain's forehead after he murdered his half-brother Abel.

Some had it as the All-Seeing Eye; others as the Evil Eye, both effectively making it the equivalent of a devil's third eye on a stick. Some gave it wings. Some did away with the circle; others did away with the '*X*', made it upright or turned it into the letter '*T*', an unembellished Cross of Mithras. The Swastika used by Outer Earth Hindus, as well as Dandset Typhon's Rajput fighters and Ophirant pacifists in here, was yet another variation of the same venerable motif.

The Egyptian Ankh, the Key of Life held by the likes of Kore-Isis or Maat-Harmony in so many Pharaonic portrayals of them had the circle as an egg-like ovule atop a Tau Cross. The Great God preferred this variant. He shook it into that likeness, albeit with an '*X*' in the centre of the ovule.

He still wasn't satisfied. He shook it again, transformed it the more. The shaft sharpened to a point at the bottom end only. The crossbars became the golden wings of an eagle or a griffon or a garuda. The '*X*' in the ovule ignited and began to spin about on a two-dimensional, frontal axis, a sun-fan on a stick with wings. He made it rotate on a three-dimensional axis, as the sun itself did. Finally happy, Mithras became his own standard bearer.

Alone he trod toward his two thought-brothers, their devic children and their forces, occupied as the majority must have been by their children, azuras adherent to Byronic and Lazaremist Master Devas.

"Oh, look, Brother Moon-Face," Lazareme transmitted as volubly and as mockingly as he had moments earlier. "Brother Boykin has his crutch back. Are you shaking in your boots yet?"

"I don't have boots," Bodiless Byron psychically shot back, though those in the vicinity nonetheless clearly comprehended him.

"Aren't you even sweating then?"

"No!"

"Soon you shall be, both of you," Mithras bellowed. "Sweating Blood – but not that of your followers! Worshipful mortals shedding blood is not just wasteful, brothers. It is pointless. Send me your champions. I shall dispatch them, one by one or batch by batch. Your choice!"

========

Chaos couldn't abide choices.

****

THEO 12:

KRONOS QUAKE

========

Definite-she, the Terror Donna, got them only so far. She lurched forward, flinging Saudi-Jordy out of the Weird and the rest of the way into Helena Somata's dayroom. Stegosaur backbone plates would have grated a dog's breakfast, or a Saur Tsarina's lunch, out of Kanin City's Master of Weir had she not already protected herself with an impervious brain-bulb.

Once-Augusta, Constantine Caesar's mother of record, mentally conjured it off her Master's Mace, what had recently doubled as a holy water sprinkler. She was exhausted, though. Likely she'd never dance again. She was still alive, however.

For about a breath!

========

Illuminaries believed the three Unities of Lazareme might once have been revered on the subcontinent of India as its Trimurti. They had definitely dwelt there for a few centuries after gaining independent solidity and Chaos did fit the Siva or Shankar mould in many respects, most notably in the trident department.

Similarly, and not just with his *'vajra'* thunderbolts, Lord Yajur, Order, had many of the qualities attributed to Vishnu the Preserver. The difficulty with such identification was the third member of the Hindu trinity, Brahma the Creator, was as male as the other two whereas Harmony was femininity devil-deified.

Personally Chaos had no problem with Chaos, especially in the sense of infinite potential. Illuminaries rarely took the easy way out, though. Somewhat euro-centrically, they reckoned he could be identified with Apollyon, Apollo as the God of Destruction, as convincingly as Siva-Shankar, Apollo's Hindu equivalent in that regard.

The main problem with that notion was that he wasn't a pretty boy like Byron's Apollo, third born Damon Goldenrod. He liked to look as rough as he lived. Consequently, not much more than 200 years ago they stuck him with Unholy Abaddon, after the Dark Angel of the Abyss, the Bottomless Pit of Apollyon in the Biblical Book of Revelation.

Nominally he was commander-in-chief of the Cattail Irregulars, his contribution to what passed for Lazareme's legions. That is to say, absolute anarchist that he was, his clannish, otherwise disorganized and resolutely disputatious followers went wherever he invited them to go. The only reason they didn't slaughter each other was purely a matter of self-preservation.

Their family-first focus generally meant redeemable exile was the utmost penalty any of them inflicted on each other in terms of castigation. The virtually inbred concept of death before dishonour all but guaranteed they behaved predictably. If Chaos took offence, they took offence, and Chaos took offence at Mithras's notion that crime demands punishment.

As far as he was concerned, punishment required enforcement. You had to force anything on anyone else then you were the criminal. Rabid dogs and plague-carrying vermin, them you killed. Human beings, you only killed them if they threatened to kill you. As for mercy, well, the pitiful fools shouldn't have been trying to kill you, should they have? You didn't start wars but you made damn sure you won them.

Master Devas were headstrong. When, thanks to your de-brained, daemonic bodies, you can shift states as well as shapes, intractability was just one of your many characteristics. Like his fellow devils, from any of the three tribes, he did away with any semblance of being his grandfather. He did retain the red skin, however, mostly because he didn't feel blue or green or, most especially, yellow.

He elongated and then quadrupled the horns fringing his head – eight horns tipped by arrowheads were among Chaos's many symbols. Now dressed in a black silk shirt, matching pants and boots, with his equally dark and tied-back hair stretching to the middle of his back, he thus regained his most familiar appearance: That of a shipwrecked, years' maddened wild man with three feral, as well as fiery, eyeballs and holding Poseidon-Shankar-Triton's trident.

Abaddon was more of a berserker than any Barring. His Tvasitar Talisman only gave the nonetheless fully functional facade of being a trident. It was actually a scabbard. Its central prong was the grip and its outer prongs the guards of his real power focus, the Chaos Blade, the black-bolt opposite of Yajur's Lightning Blade. Both legend and, thus far, reality had it he would never draw his sword completely out its sheathe. To do so would bring true chaos into the cosmos.

The Unholy One, who'd been known to occasionally guzzle buckets of beer with the likes of King Cold, Rudra Silvercloud and even a certain lowly, but legendary, 30-Year deviant, was therefore not so much the Unity of Chaos as the Keeper of Chaos. No devil had ever come close to besting him in combat: to besting either

Abaddon or Yajur, truth told. Yet Chaos and Order hated each other with a passion so irreducibly intense that, if they ever went at each other unrestrained, it'd be bye-bye Hidden Continent.

More so than their Lazareme-lazy father, Harmonia somehow restrained them, prevented them fighting. Since her power focus was a Brainrock torc from which depended chain lightning in the form of both her clothing and her body, from the neck down, maybe that's how she did it: used her chains to restrain them. If so, though, she did it invisibly.

Grandfather Sedon didn't cathonitize her when she executed the Theban King Cadmus – for getting Novadev, as Illuminaries came to name Mithras's epitome of midsummer, so drunk and boisterous he accidentally blew up Strongyne, thereby precipitating the closing stages of the devil goddesses' 500-year long Mediterranean matriarchate. She took that as proof Cadmus was Heliosophos, the Male Entity in his first or second lifetime.

If she hadn't killed him he never would have gone on to help Sedon demolish the first Weirworld's Mother Machine in his third lifetime and co-create Sedon in his fifth. If Helios, Cabalarkon and the Mnemosyne Machine, who was largely based on Weir's original Mother Machine, hadn't engendered him first, then the mighty Moloch couldn't have gone on to do a dot for her parents and, thereafter, they a ditto for her.

Something else persuaded Harmony she was at least as responsible as the Male Entity for every other devil. Whenever any devil, including she herself, humanized Machine-Memory, the Female Entity facially and physically looked exactly like her.

========

Before Chaos or either of the other two Unities could answer the Great God's challenge, from out of the nowhere and the everywhere that is, was and always will be the dark-grey universal constant of Samsara, Mithras pulled on the multi-coloured Cloak of Lazareme. Thus unmistakably accoutered, he ordered them to back off.

Chaos was flummoxed. Despite his attribute, he could not disobey the direct order of his father and Mithras was wearing Lazareme's garb of authority. He looked to the Great God his father for instructions. The Lackland Libertine appeared dumbstruck. Not needing one in order to maintain his solidity, he'd given his talisman to Chrysaor Attis close to 2500 years earlier as proof against the malfeasance of Coueranna and Plathon.

Lazareme shook his head. Abaddon, his immediate sister, brother, and every other once-released or never-imprisoned Lazaremist extremist, obediently retreated well behind their father and his other brother.

"Come to my side, sons and daughters of Thrygragos Everyman," Mithras encouraged them, with practised confidence. "Come to my side, brother."

Little-Star Lazareme flickered alarmingly, but continued to hover about the full-mooning Byronhead. Finally Bodiless Byron did begin to perspire. A dense, acrid mist sweated out of the Unmoving One's skin. It smelled positively foul, albeit not of gassy fog or fecal faeriedust so much as terror.

The two remaining firstborn, Rudra and Umashakti Silvercloud, followed by the six Primary and Secondary Nucleoids – Vayu Maelstrom, Chimaera Glimmenmare, Sedona Spellbinder, Damon Goldenrod, Aphropsyche Morningstar and Nevair Neverknight – squelched wetly out of their father's Byronhead prior to re-solidifying themselves. Or, in the case of Sedona, who was mostly smoky particulates in a female shape, semi-solidifying herself.

As he had done with the Cloak of Lazareme, Varuna Mithras covered his Saturnian face with the double-horned, boar-tusked Mask of Byron – also given to that Great God by Tvasitar, and him to Attis, when the Universal Soldier was in his initial lifetime. Just as he had with the Lazaremists he insisted they forsake their father.

"Join me!" he bid them, more forcefully than he had the Lazaremists.

His tone was cadenced purposefully. Lazaremists didn't take orders very well, not even from their own father. By contrast Byronics generally acted like sycophantic toads. As he'd observed over the millennia, the reason for that was their father conditioned them to act precisely that way. He did so by the paternal expedient of always treating them as 100% dependent children never allowed to grow up except externally.

"By the power vested in me by Father Sedon, I wear Great Byron's talisman. You are mine to command!" Mist re-formed around the eight remaining, highest born Byronic Master Devas. Their father's man-in-the-moon head re-absorbed them, much as a dried up sponge did bathwater, but remained otherwise motionless.

Still a man-mountain, Mithras surveyed the two opposing armies behind and in front of him. He'd been waiting for this moment for what seemed like untold multiple millennia mostly because it had been untold multiple millennia. Would they actually obey him if he appeared as himself and not as Father Sedon?

"Attack, my children! Attack, my legions!"

The tension was almost palpable. Yet no one, not one in 40 thousand, on either side, moved more than a twitch or a shudder. Beneath the Mask of Byron, Mithras ground his teeth audibly. It was better this way, he resolved internally. A supreme being ought to prove he was a supreme being.

He drove the javelin tip of his power focus, his Cross or Crutch, the emblazoned, winged sun, into the earth. The resultant rumbling rivalled anything that must have been heard 2,000 years ago when Strongyne blew its heart into the sky.

Time may not march for any man. At least once though, on the Hidden Continent of Sedon's Head, on Mithramas Day, the 25th of Tantalar in the Year of the Dome 4376, the day Mithras himself had already declared would go down in history as Thrygragon, time did march for one devil. It marched backwards. Then, after reversing a quarter again more than 2,000 years in a matter of instants, it stopped.

Not for nothing was he once known on the Outer Earth as Saturn or Kronos, Father Time, he who devours his own children.

========

The Smiling Fiend and the fabulously female Perpetual Presence were with George Masterson in his masterly mother's oft-times rebuilt, personal cosmicar of 40 years. More correctly, Smiler was in George Masterson whereas Pyrame Silverstar appeared to be the

boy's masterly mother. Theirs was at the apex of a flying-V fleet of the mostly prayerfully
maintained contraptions.

Hey-ho, hey-ho, it's off to slay Sedon we go!

========

Utopian cosmicars were practically identical to Edenite vimanas. As such they were yet another reason why Illuminaries – and not just Illuminaries – believed Edenites derived their advanced civilization from wayward Utopians who'd arrived on the Whole Earth towards the tail end of its last Ice Age.

Alien-astronaut Utopians used cosmicars to shuttle between their sometimes asteroid-sized generational ships during the multiple tens of millennia they spent pursuing the Sedonshem throughout the cosmos, from one inhabited planetary system to another. Whilst their mother vessels stayed in orbit, or at a safe distance away from whatever they were investigating, they also used them to explore galactic phenomena or survey atmosphere-occluded surfaces close up.

Vimanas, the Edenite counterpart, were still in use during the Golden Age of Humanity. Number One Patriarch, Alorus Ptah, and his equally long-lived beloved, Trishtar Thrae, would have flown in vimanas. So too would have Number Ten, Xuthros Hor, and his similarly rainbow-class wife, the non-devic Anthea – though probably not after Ragnarok, which occurred some 200 years before Hor called up, as well as called down, the Genesea.

Having lost track of All the Invincible, her Attis and the devic Anthea's kibisis – with the power foci of dozens of still-imprisoned Master Devas inside it; they in addition to what she assumed was the Unnameable's head – the Pauper Priestess had expressed, in no uncertain terms, her concern time was running out on their Plan B option.

As enjoyable as bongo braining was, she demanded the fiend curtail the dancing of Helena Somata to terpsichorean oblivion. As deserving of death as Kanin's Master may have been for her duplicitous dealings with not just her but Harmony and Jordan Tethys, she brooked no dissention in the matter. Should they be so inclined, they could always finish her off after they hastened the closing moments of father-brother Mithras's version of the Fatal Fandango.

He consented. He was done here anyhow.

========

Cosmicars and vimanas were powered by teleportive Brainrock, the Godstuff Edenites had as Gypsium presumably because that was as the Dual Entities had it. What neither Pyrame nor Georgie knew was that they had plenty of fuel. Smiler knew it. But, because Master Helena never got around to telling her son of the arrangements she made with Harmonia a week ago, he didn't know it from Georgie.

He knew it because the pride of Lazareme's loins – and the beneficiary of his – had been more than just physically forthcoming last night. The self-determined Unity of Panharmonium proved positively effusive when, between go-rounds, she detailed how hard she was going to get his brother come tomorrow without going anywhere near him.

Needless to say, he hadn't told the other two any of that. Something else that went without saying, because he chose not to say it, was where exactly the She-Sphinx had taken Attis and his kibisis. He knew it because, once he snapped to an assortment of perilous options Mithras gained by holding onto to the Male Three, he'd used Pyrame's mind-print to send All with them there.

Still, he was never averse to improvising; the more so when he wasn't the one chancing the consequences of improvisation. Trinondev eye-staves were ever so useful in the right, polydactyl hands, even if they had too many joints in the too many pinkish fingers they did have.

His weren't going to be the right hands today, though. Nor were they going to be the left ones, as far as that went. Georgie and his masterly mother wanted to give their Warriors Elite the opportunity to demonstrate their worth against the Moloch Sedon or die trying. He was all in favour of that, especially the latter.

His inclination was not in the slightest bit due to the fact he'd been possessing Masterson ever since he'd taken himself out of Mithras's Tholos, whereupon he stumbled upon Georgie bravely but foolhardily spying on the Praetorium from nearby between-space. Smiler shared their desires because, as per usual with him, he reckoned it was better them than him.

That was why he also hadn't bothered informing the other two that a desperately nervy Brother Mithras was currently masquerading as Father Sedon. Why show his cards, not to mention himself, unnecessarily when there was still a possibility either Plan A or Plan B could work?

Well, maybe not Plan A precisely as Helena, Pyrame, Harmony or any of the other highborn Master Devas had initially conceived of it; with his unremembered encouragement it had to be said. The effect would be the same, though, and that's what would matter. Would, that is, were it not for one thing.

Brother Mithras too often thought the same way he did.

========

'Well,' the Great God reflected, as he surveyed the havoc he had wrought from the vantage of his man-mountain enormity, 'Maybe not the devourer of his children but definitely the devourer of their children, their azuras. The devourers of my grandchildren then: A large percentage of them anyhow.'

He couldn't be more satisfied. Actually, come to think of it, he could. The greatest of the great gods turned to face his fellow Great Gods. He'd caused time to go past tense. Present tense was time to gloat.

========

"You should never have come here, brothers. I was always your better, always Father Sedon's favourite son. Now I have my power focus and wear yours."

Already Thrygragos Byron was having difficulty staying aloft. His Byronhead deflated like a slowly evacuating pig's bladder once filled with helium. As he did so, fizzling all the way, he flip-flopped towards the ground. Little-Star Lazareme followed suit, the halo of light surrounding him blipping less and less luminously.

Even more distressingly – for Thrygragos Everyman, not Thrygragos Varuna Mithras – his most hated sibling abruptly started to wink into and out of sight. A glance behind his brothers told him why. Sun-circled labarum blistering the brighter the more excited he became, his Hugeness could barely prevent himself tunic-trunk-spurting over them in delight.

"So, it's as I thought. Neither of you have left the Head since Father Sedon raised the Dome. Just as his is of ours, your power is wholly reliant on your children and their children's genetically reinforced adulation of you. Beyond the Dome no one has ever heard of you, whereas the mighty Moloch in the sky is reviled throughout both sides of the world as the Devil himself. Deprived of your offspring, via the traitorous Trigregos Sisters, you are fast fading away. Soon you shall be entirely gone.

"Know you this, brothers: Your meagre abilities have always been minuscule compared to mine because I have never needed my children or their children, azuras or deviants, to provide me sustenance. Intelligent beings throughout the cosmos champion light, truth and justice. As a result I am venerated everywhere anyone can go.

"Prostrate yourselves before it is too late. I have mastered Time Quakes to precision. By the time Master Devas return to Sedon's Peak and the Anvil Artificer crafts them new talismans, if he can, you will be beyond retrieval. It's your decision of course. So, shall I watch you vanish or shall I save you?" Neither Great God cared to respond. Which only made Mithras the bolder.

"Swear me an inviolable oath of unending submission and I shall reverse the time quake. Your Master Devas will have their power foci back. They shall return to their former state of godliness and you two shall be resuscitated. Except for a minor change in circumstances – namely that you and all your children, of any description, shall henceforth be beholding to me before you are beholding to Father Sedon – everything will be back to normal. Speak, acquiesce, now!"

Thrygragos Everyman was often perceived as something of a Helios or Mithraic Sun God himself. He smiled beamingly broadly. Always more of a moon unit, Unmoving Byron didn't, couldn't or wouldn't. His three eyes did twinkle as if in amusement. They both disappeared.

'Guess I just watched you vanish,' Mithras muttered to himself.

========

Recall the precise Plan A?

The Smiling Fiend still hoped to hold that in reserve exclusively for use against the real Father Sedon. Now that Pyrame Silverstar had seemingly bit on the thought-first-born females' Panharmonium fantasy hook, line and proverbial stinker, it might even work this time.

Devils didn't need their own power foci to render themselves independently solid individuals. They needed any devil's power focus.

========

George Masterson would have been a willing accompanist regardless of whether he was possessed. However, the rest of Kanin's Warriors Elite – male, female, black, white or any shade in between – stepped much livelier when their consensus Master of a maestro was doing the conducting rather than her ambitious, yet pathetically immature son and second fiddlehead.

Georgie was nowhere near 30. That meant he was technically too young even to be a Trinondev. Besides, it was hardly the first time Pyrame had played at being a Master of Weir. Neither was it the first time she'd taken Helena's place. More than a hundred years earlier, Helena Somata was just a promising Ant novitiate handpicked for the inferior purposes of Panharmonium's breeding pool. She'd managed to become Constantius Chlorus's concubine but hadn't got much further along until Sedon's loyal, but too often taken-for-granted, priestess showed up to work her wiles on him.

Pyrame saw to it they were married such that their Sed-son-to-come, Constantine Caesar, who was born beyond the Dome in 4272 YD, could claim legitimacy. Thereafter she returned outside often enough to poke him and his successors along the slow slog to affirming the, to devils, nonsensical notion of an omnipotent, omniscient, omnipresent, three-in-one, but still somehow solitary God as the Big Boss Blob Above.

As Harmony put to her when she put her up to it: Never underestimate the power of those in authority to set even the most moronic of attitudes. If their credulous subjects could regard Roman emperors as living gods, when so many of them were demonstrably worse than any devil could possibly be, then God as a plop of slop wasn't all that much more farfetched.

No devil-god either wanted or anticipated monotheism to prevail over the long term. That said, led by the Unity of Balance most of the female ones in particular felt propagating the absurdity of an amorphous deity was the most sensible way to break the stranglehold male exclusivists had on ruling virtually everywhere you went on either side of the Sedon Sphere.

When the inevitable day came the Dome collapsed, and devils re-emerged in all their ocular magnificence, monotheism would go the way Mithraism was going on the Outer Earth and soon would in here: into the compost heap of history as strictly his-story.

Panharmonium had as its goal achieving equality for everyone's good. While it would undoubtedly take a few more kicks in the proper pants before it could be brought into reality, it was hardly a fanciful concept. Pyrame had long ago cowed Sedon and much the same could be said about Harmony in terms of her relationship with Lackland Lazareme.

A tweak here and a tweak there, since her father was already Thrygragos Everyman, Harmony could foresee him becoming Thrygragos Everyone, Every Woman included. As for Byron, being bodiless and consequently sexless he wasn't worth bothering about, she'd assured her sisters and female cousins.

Thrygragos Varuna Mithras, though, was incorrigible. The self-proclaimed, but insufferably sanctimonious, Sire of Censorious Civilization, on both sides of the Dome, had to go.

========

Recall the cestus, the Medusa's glowing girdle, Smiler asked himself.

Whatever she was calling herself as of today; Tvasitar Smithmonger didn't make it for her. No, although she was the one who put it to use in order to entice, most notorious-

ly, Sedon himself into her lair, Anvil made it for Flowery Anthea. The Medusa was just a lowborn gorgon, one of three.

Recall Demogorgon's actual head? It was on its way.

========

Machine-manufactured clothing and ornaments, plate armour and metallic weaponry had instantly dissipated everywhere within the epicentre of his Kronos Quake. Like an ever-dilating bull's-eye, Mithras sensed its circumference widening inexorably. Throughout Sedon's Mole well over 2,000 years of military and civilian advancements went where stone-throwing slingshots, spear-chucking atlatls, obsidian blades and tree-branch clubs had gone before them, only in reverse.

Behind where his brothers had been were a small number of seemingly stationary statues. By far the best looking of them was of the unbeatably exquisite, albeit evidently ex-Unity of Balance. His Hugeness couldn't resist. He'd always wanted to do it, to do her. He poked her, what he realized wasn't statuary, with the pointy tip of his javelin-labarum. His tunic-trunk twitched the more as he did so.

It, Harmony's de-brained daemonic body, caved in on itself, as if unto *'dust thou were and dust thou are again'*. Damnation! Gloating wasn't going to be anywhere near as gratifying as he'd imagined it would be. There remained other consolations, however. Too bad there was no one left who could match his majesty. It was lonely at the top.

Even so, even if he had expended the life force of hundreds, make that thousands, of fourth generational Mithradite azuras to effect it; he felt supremely proud of his thrust-backwards. It was a strike accurate to the moment Tvasitar Smithmonger began fashioning for the late Everyman's Harmony her golden torc. And hers was the first power focus he forged after his own anvil and the six Godly Glories he dedicated to the six Great Gods, his simultaneous mothers, the Trigregos Sisters, in absentia.

Mithras as much meant math as it meant myth. Varuna-Uranus becoming Zeus and ruining him, as Kronos-Saturn, was an act of folly. Much smarter would have been them re-fusing and staying Father Time, he with the power to devour everything.

Although he still held his own talisman – his Labarum, Cross or, ha-ha, Crutch – as well as wore that of his two ex-brothers, the Mask of Byron and Lazareme's Cloak of Many Colours, Master Devas no longer had their Tvasitar-trinkets. That left them bereft of godly qualities, though not of individuality nor even of mobility.

Nonetheless, just as he had Lazareme's Unities and a few of Everyman's mostly forgettable lowborn; just as he had the Silverclouds, various Nucleoids and Yati, Byron's Dragon; his Hugeness recognized a number of familiar but abandoned, hence motionless, demonic shapes down below gargantuan-him.

He impressed himself even more by recognizing what many of them were by name: husks left behind by his highest born children. Of course he was in the process of impressing himself, period. An incarnation of Jordan Tethys had better be around to record all of this – either that or some of Rumour's rodent tee-tees.

This was how legends were made. This was real!

========

As they came to within sight of the yet distant battlefield, the perennially retooled cosmicar George Masterson was piloting began to wobble violently. The boy couldn't con-

trol the flying scrap heap. It started to fall apart. Reflexively the two devils, one in another, the other as another, sought to materialize their Tvasitar Talismans and thereby take themselves elsewhere between-space.

They materialized what was already visible. Nothing! Their power foci no longer existed. This might prove painful.

========

There were the de-brained deadheads of his firstborn Thanatoids, Heat and Cold. Over there were those of the two second-born Apple Goddesses, his Bull and the three Nergalids: Gravedigger, Plathon's fellow fourth-born, most satisfyingly. Those now hollow shells there once belonged to Yama Nergal's fellow *'Earthlings'* from his Fifth.

That had been Dandset Typhon's demon and, though he wasn't as sure about this, maybe that husk there had once belonged to Typhon's immediate sibling from his Sixth: Geld Neargon, as Illuminaries had the Neuter. The she-he Deva Dand of Androgynia never could determine his-her sex and thus normally appeared to be both genders concurrently. The husk he couldn't be sure of was that of an immense, noticeably hermaphroditic frog.

His first and highest born had gone the way of his two brothers' first and highest born. Perhaps he should have expected it. They were among the most gifted of his offspring. As no matter how highly born spirit beings without power foci, they would have realized the totality of mercy he'd allocate them after refusing his command to attack their cousins – 100% of nil – and jumped out of their demons into the nearest mortal to them.

That didn't mean any of them would attempt to prolong this combat of the gods of theirs, devils that they were. As his recurring Attis had it, albeit not in the same context, that would be ill advised. Increasingly the odds were against dogged freespirits, of any tribe, lasting independently for much longer.

Their mortal adherents, leaderless and mostly without weapons of their own, were panicking, seeking hoped-for safety as faraway as they could get from the non-battlefield by foot or flight in the case of a few Saurs or Lizarados on their pterodactyls and wyverns, Apocalyptic archers and Sangazur-animated Dead Things on their Vultyrie, and demons on demons. Approaching 40 thousand fleeing fleas – devil-possessed or otherwise – were scattering helter-skelter throughout the Fields. Nobody worships failures.

Especially after his incontestable display of chronological potency, their Theomachy had become a competition of cowards trying to outrun each other. Individually, and inevitably, the chips were stacked to the point of toppling in favour of him singular. No wonder he also spotted demonic dozens upon not yet dispirited dozens more of just as familiar, just as no longer godly shapes blundering toward him.

There had to be close to 200 of them, probably more. Highest born and therefore most personally pleasing were the remnants of his reptilian seventh: Klizarod Rex and the Emperor Chameleon, as Illuminaries had them. Klizarod's demonic body was that of a tyrannosaur type whereas Chameleon's was of a bloated Lizarado.

The entirety of the Eighth, the three Primary Apocalyptics, War, Plague and Disaster, were just behind them. They were hard to miss. Mars Bellona was a spike-haired bonehead with muscles and a beard, Carcinogen the Leper was a pustulous, be-band-aged mummy and Ramazar was as headless as he had been for 2 millennia, ever since he lost it, quite literally, over the Lazaremists' springtime charmer, Flowery Anthea.

With them were their most frequent, early-on mates: Bellona-War's Matare-Medusa, Carcinogen-Plague's Milady Malaise and Ramazar-Disaster's Ran-Flood. The Medusa was still a four-armed, snake-haired gorgon. Contrarily Sickness, as dev-ils had Malaise, looked to be as robust and outdoorsy tanned as any of the Valkyries or Athenan War Witches, both of whom prided themselves on their fitness. As they should – for them athleticism was an occupational requirement.

Diluvia Ran was a pastry-puffy, humanoid rain cloud prone, as one might im-agine, to soppy emotionalism, whereas a fourth female with them, the last third of his Tenth, Famish by name, Famine-Hunger-Pestilence by combined attribute, was a skeletal starveling with washboard ribs and a locust's head.

Not surprisingly, of the Ninth there was only Cathune, Desiccated Drought, she whose power focus, an hourglass, had stood in his Tholos atop Apple Isle's Mi-thradium for hundreds of years and which, knowing she'd need it, he'd thoughtful-ly brought with him to Attis's Praetorium. He'd done so, perhaps, in the additional hope she might purr again – for him alone, needless to say.

Cat was Pyrame's other brood sister, the one besides the Demon Child, Trala-lorn as she'd self-styled herself. Illuminaries called her Cathune, first of all, because she squealed catlike when she made love and, second of all, presumably because Cathune sort of rhymed with sand dune. How she came to acquire the attribute of Drought had everything to do with the fact she'd chosen to become barren.

Not only couldn't she have any more azuras – more like wouldn't – but those she possessed invariably had stillborns. That was why War gravitated to the three Graii and various gorgons, the higher born Medusa in particular. She was almost as fecund as Fecundity. War went through scandalous scads of soldier boys and thus needed scab-rous scores of Sangs to keep them going afterwards.

========

When Sedon divvied up the Whole Earth, shortly after bringing the Sedonshem down from its perch on the moon, more than six and half solar centuries prior to Xu-thros Hor causing the Great Flood, he kept his future Headworld – Pacifica, the Plac-es of Peace – for himself. He assigned not-yet-unmoving Byron what the Golden Age Patriarchs called the Americas and today's Lackland Lazareme exclusive rights to ter-ritory on the other side of his Pacifica, what they called Asia, albeit only as far west as what was now Persia and the Ural mountain range north of the Caspian Sea.

Mithras received what eventually came to be called Europe, Africa and the Asian lands bordering the Middle Sea eastwards up to and including Persia. The demonic shells of what was left of their pantheons, that of the Sub-Sahara and Arabia, the Le-vant, Mesopotamia and Aryan Iran, Scythian Russia, Crete, Greece and Northern Eu-rope – the ones who were his, not that of interloping Byronics or Lazaremists – were staggering toward him.

Many of their top dog, tiptop gods were as highborn as his Teens or Twenties but, after Cat, the highest born stumbling his or her way to him were his torch-bearing

Equinoctials, his epitomes of Spring and Autumn, from his Eleventh, and the spidery grotesquery, Kala Tal, the Medusa and Fecundity's brood sister, from his Twelfth.

As he'd instructed Attis, that meant All kept Magnetism, the third of his Sixth, and a large number of other, albeit very much lower born troublemakers to power itself on Incain. Good! They were bad cess; he hadn't wanted them. They'd proven in the past to be dangerous egoists but, unlike the equally obstinate Thanatoids and Kore of the Many Names and Multiple Personalities, as well as both Pyrame and Tralalorn, they were imprisoned. Let them stay that way.

Painstakingly coming his direction as well were the four other, non-cathonitized Vices: Wrath, Avarice, Envy and Sloth. Two of them, Thordin-Wrath and Mammon-Avarice were Belialma-Lust's predecessors as Satanwyck's Prime Sinistrals. The first, Domdaniel-Pride, became a dull star in the night's sky within half a millennium of attaining individual solidity whilst the seventh, Gluttony, Arisandesam or the Conqueror Worm, had been a member of Phantast-Dream's Crimson Conspiracy a third of the way through the Dome's 41st Century.

Wrath's demonic body was that of a still steaming Lava Lout; Mammon's was of a chubby, jollily leering, self-satisfied greybeard; Envy's of a cupid; and Sloth's vaguely egg-shaped, a chinless Hellblob with stick arms and stick legs. With them were Lust's vizier, Cyclopean Ibal, and her demon-disciplinarian, another Cyclops, Trawl the Taskmaster as antique Illuminaries aptly had him. Ibal was a hairless pinhead whereas Trawl was a skinless ogre.

Among the even lower born lesser lights whose names or designations he actually remembered were the three haggish Graii and the two extant gorgons: the Cockatrice and the Basilisk. The third one, Lamia as Illuminaries had her, was as speculative as his long-missing third-born triplets in that she never did become a solid entity. That hadn't stopped the Artificer crafting her a power focus, however; one that War's Medusa absconded with because she preferred it to her own, a love-inspiring golden girdle or cestus.

It took Attis, as Perseus, quite some doing to retrieve it, Mithras recalled with a chuckle – and an involuntary wince, in memory of his twice re-grown manhood. Prior to Attis decapitating her, she'd caused Father Sedon considerable personal discomfort. Once he regained his mobility, the humiliation of being hardened under her gaze kept the mighty Moloch upstairs, more dully than duly hiding above his own Headworld, for most of the ensuing Olympian Age. As Zeus, the Varuna aspect of his bisolar disorder had never been less hapless and more happy.

Did his sons and daughters really think he'd let them have Lamia's snake-haired head back so effortlessly? They were transparent to him, his third generational children by his sisters, the Trigregos Goddesses. He could read them like the open books they were, greedy sods the lot of them. They never had any intention of standing by him. If his brothers and their highborn offspring failed to take him out, they fully intended to fuse together a replacement Unnameable in order to try to do so themselves.

Andy the Androsphinx and Ginny the Gynosphinx having thoroughly consumed the original during the decades Mithras remained on the moon, as part of the

Sedonshem, long pre-Flood; they planned to use non-existent Lamia's snake-haired head as the focal point for their ersatz conglomeration of a surrogate Unnameable. That was why the ungrateful Medusa, no doubt on hate-filled Kore's instructions, left it in Anthea's bottomless bag.

Well, good luck to them now. No more power foci, no more substitute gorgon's head, and no more chance at becoming the Unnameable. They knew it too, hence so many heading his way. Some were crawling on their hands and knees. Others, even some that did have hands and knees, were more like slithering. Humbled yet be-brained, they remained foolishly expectant of his magnanimity.

He'd let them in, but that didn't mean he'd let them out again. Within minutes 200-plus, now completely deadheaded demons were piled up at his feet. Mithras wasn't just swelling with satisfaction anymore. He was swelling with Master Devas coming unto him, as in into him. Maybe monotheism was the way to go after all.

Then she trotted out of the Weird far below him. Rather, the three-headed thing she was riding trotted out of the Weird. His Hugeness very nearly barfed all over them.

========

"My quill?" Saudi-Jordy demanded.
"Georgie took it with them," Master Helena responded.
"Them?"
"Him and Pyrame and ... "
"And who?"

========

Even if Kanin City's Master of Weir – as well as its symphonic maestro of con-sensus – could remember who else had gone off with Pyrame and her son, it was too late for her to answer. Terror Donnas, soul-self-animated but otherwise dead pterodac-tyls that they were, still had to eat. They also readily got about between-space.

A mind-globe wasn't impervious inter-spatially. At least her mind-globe wasn't impermeable to that direction of a terminal assault. Hel didn't exactly bite the prover-bial big one. She did, however, bodily die big-time, endgame big-time and nowhere near proverbially, when the Terror Donna bit her in half then proceeded to chow down on that half of her. Saudi-Jordy involuntarily vomited.

Humanoid stegosaurs had to eat too, even Stegs with crushed vertebrae, a bro-ken leg and a smashed skull. Omnivores, they weren't ones for cooking. Sari Tsari-na took her ruminative time chewing on the juicy bits of Helena Somata's other half, burped, and then remounted the Donna.

Semi-sated, they recommenced his and her simultaneous – as in circumstances-unified – quest for Rumour's quill.

========

"Tra-la-lo, daddy. Have you seen mommy, tra-la-glee? I've something for her, tra-la Pyrame. And Daddy Taurus said she'd be hereabouts-the-shouts, tra-la try-beer, tee-hee."
Devil-gods were devils and Sedon may well be Satan, but she was pure evil!
****

THEO 13:

MYTHIC DISTORTIONS
========

Year 725 Pre-Dome
The neither impossibly mobile nor impossibly huge granite atrocity with a lion's body and the head of Heliosophos reared on its hind legs in anticipation.
Hind legs weren't all it reared.

========

Romping straight at her apparent male counterpart was a slightly smaller, but be-winged and proportionately equally enormous, she-lion with the head of Miracle Memory. They collided, got cavorting, all rough and tumble, bites and bellows. Pebbles, not fur flew. Between-space, not yet Thrygragos Everyman hugged the presumably partially daemonic Hellion who'd been internally holding his firstborn daughter as a hostage for far too long.

"It is going to work, isn't it?" Lazareme asked two-in-one Hecate, herself a wholly humanoid, top to bottom mirror image of the Female Entity, more optimistically than positively.

"It bloody better," she responded, in his daughter's unmistakable voice. "I'm tired of being stuck in here."

"No more so than I am of you being stuck in there."

He was frustrated. She was frustrated. Andy and Ginny were not frustrated. Lazareme looked to her like Alorus Ptah. Hecate looked to him like Trishtar Thrae. They got oscular. As they embraced even more heatedly, a third eye opened in Hecate's forehead. Wisps of smoke eked out of it.

A third eye opened in Ginny's forehead. Foul-smelling faeriedust emitted from it. Earthly follicles grew out of its skull. They looked blackish. They writhed, corded hair-like but more so twisty snake-like. Its skin looked pinkish. A four-fold passion play ensued.

As hard as the leader of the devic scouting party was at that moment, Andy was much harder. Andy was so hard he was hardened beyond adamantine hardness. Ginny wasn't Ginny. Whoever or whatever she was nonetheless eviscerated him with cut-anything – cut even Mandroids – claws and fangs, inserted its snout into his guts and began to devour his innards along with everything daemonic that they entailed as entrails.

Meantime, Lazareme opened his mouth and began to gasp as he neared orgasm. Climaxing, he involuntarily sucked in the smoke by now fuming out of Hecate's third eye, thereby momentarily reinforcing his already impressive hardness. He screamed. She screamed. Neither screamed in pleasure. She screamed because she combusted spontaneously. He screamed because she'd ignited, him in her, and he was suddenly aflame, physically, not passionately.

The Unnameable screamed. So did Andy, audibly hard no longer. Then Ginny screamed. Too busy playing the fireman and hosing down Hecate, the extraterrestrial devil failed to register the sounds of three, not two, inhuman beings echoing his and her screams. It was too late for the Hellion. In his arms she crumbled unto ash. Lazareme was out, extinguished in all senses of the word.

To his surprise he rolled over in the Saharan sand. He and Hecate must have fallen from between-space during the course of their overheated lovemaking. He looked up just in time to see Ginny the Gynosphinx and Andy the Androsphinx tussling over what was left of the Unnameable, namely its snake-haired head.

It hadn't worked. If anything it had been a trap. The Dual Entities must have somehow discovered what he and Hecate-controlling-Eventual-Harmony, together with his devils and her daemons, were planning. At their command the She-Sphinx had to have been waiting between-space for her demon-devil doppelganger to show up, whereupon both Mandroid monstrosities shared the biggest feasts of their semi-sentient existences.

Who could have betrayed them? Now was hardly the time to worry about that. What could devour daemons and devils could devour putative great gods and firstborns. First and second generational devils had always had a knack for telekinesis. Before the sphinxes spotted him, he mind-over-matter stirred up the desert, particlyzed himself riskily and got away in the ensuing sandstorm. No doubt Lazareme lost more than a few motes of himself in the process.

Indeed, when one of his seventh-born triplets, Rumour of Lazareme, heard about it after his Pyrame-directed liberation from All, on the Prison Beach of Incain circa 2000 YD, the youngster – youngster comparative to a second generational Great God at any rate – coined the word *'scatterbrain'* to describe what must have immediately happened to his father.

Be that as it may, when he finally regained consciousness Lazareme found himself occupying a member of small band of camel-riding Bedouin nomads. They'd evidently travelled to the nearby Giza Plateau from the oasis of On. Which, once it was urbanized many hundreds of years later, was in the area of what the Classical Greeks dubbed Heliopolis, Sun City; one of a few they thus renamed.

Curiosity to satisfy, they'd come to confirm reports of an incredible sighting made there recently. It was true. Above him, above all of them, loomed the He-Sphinx, as stock-still then, more than 700 years pre-Genesea, as it remained today, 4,376 years post-it.

He coughed, coughed some more. Master Devas coughed out of him. Soon the nomads with him had three eyes. Helped by one of them, his firstborn daughter – the Datong Harmonia of the future – in her latest shell, he performed an inventory. Being otherwise bodiless, the only way to identify them was by their personalities.

Most were his, including his other two firstborns, Future Yajur and Future Abaddon. Every one of them were members the exploratory expedition Father Sedon cautiously sent down from the moon to accompany him on his initially speculative search for the Dual Entities. They'd been decimated in reverse. Nine-tenths of their number had been in the Unnameable and those same nine-tenths, to a one, remained unaccounted for.

Someone else was missing: the little shit he'd learned to call Daemonicus. From that day forward Thrygragos Lazareme believed he knew precisely who had betrayed them to the Entities. And maybe he had, though Harmony was hardly the only one to demur.

The Entities were non-linear time-tumblers, these logicians argued. They'd have known, from future dealings with devils, about their ploy with respect to the Unnameable and taken steps to ensure that whatever had transpired, in what to them was the devils' past, transpired in their then present.

Alternatively, if their ploy with the Unnameable had been successful in one linear timeline, the Entities were able to thwart it in another timeline, the one that would thereby become the temporal flow of their present from then onwards. They could do so because they not only knew of it, they knew how to counter it and did.

The lately vanished, in 4376 YD, if not necessarily altogether late, Little Star Lazareme never could wrap his howsoever scattered brain around the concept of time-tumbling. Like every other devil, he was about the here-and-now. Whenever Harmony or anyone else got waxing suchlike philosophic inanities, he wrapped his hands around another mug of beer.

Were he there, one of those logicians would too: one of 30, max, per day.

========

Years of the Dome Pre-4376

30-Beers' innate thirst for reliable information on the Unnameable forever lacked remediation. Potentially, he, she, Saudi the Steg Sari, had something that could quench it.

If she did – he being otherwise occupied being her – he hadn't had time to read it as yet.

========

Tee-tees were a rat-like, possibly chthonic by-product of old Eden's discredited science.

In the centuries prior to their comparatively small continent, or big island, sinking into the Atlantic Ocean – where the flotsam-choked Sargasso Sea has been bedevilling shipping lanes ever since – these Edenites deposited the living, breeding results of their biological experiments on the opposite side of the planet from their homeland. Eden's zoo or dumping grounds were the thousands of islands dotting the then archipelago of Pacifica, the Places of Pieces as the joke went, in what was the North Pacific Ocean of today's Outer Earth.

In addition to having vocal chords, a highly selective memory and the triggering device of pulling their tails, tee-tees were almost as good swimmers as they were stowaways. They rapidly overran Pacifica and thereafter, in boats embarking from the archipelago, spread across much of the rest of the world. That there weren't any left outside came down to one thing: Tee-tees made better eating than storytellers.

Some of them recorded via the nodules of their tails – tails some of their descendants inherited much as humans do the colour of their skin, eyes or hair from their ancestors – the arrival of a devic scouting party on the Whole Earth over 700 years prior to the Great Flood of Genesis. They further recorded how many of the devils accompanying the expedition's leader, Thrygragos Lazareme, fused together with dozens of daemons in order to launch an assault on the nowadays millennia-moribund Androsphinx of Egypt's Giza plateau.

Successive incarnations of Jordan Tethys could read tee-tee tails. Most devils, Utopian Illuminaries, Ant Nightingales, most other tiptop witches and most of the Head's wise men or wizards, for want of a better word, could as well. Despite many puzzling gaps in them, virtually everyone agreed Demogorgon was the name tee-tee tails ascribed to the form the initial Unnameable took.

However, at least as oddly as the gaps in tee-tee tails, Pyrame Silverstar, the first of the captured devils to get out of All, albeit not until very early in the hidden continent's history as Sedon's Head, claimed she'd never heard of any then-contemporaneous Demogorgon. Neither had any of the devils Tethys interviewed that had been there. Half-mother Metis was one of them and she wasn't called Wisdom of Lazareme for naught. For them, the original, fake-Ginny conglomeration remained unnamed and, for that reason, the Unnameable.

'*Demos*' meant people. A collection of individuals, even if they were daemons and devils, qualified as people. '*Gorgos*' meant terrible. The name therefore made etymological sense. Snake-haired or not, almost by definition a conglomerate devil had to have made for a terrible collective.

'*Demo*' also had more than a whiff of demon about it and the three devic gorgons – Euryale, Stheno and, by default, if nothing else, the Medusa – acquired the ability to temporarily turn folks to stone just by looking at them. They did so because Anvil, Tvasitar Smithmonger, made them pullover power foci in the form of snake-haired heads.

Except, he denied he'd made the Medusa one, didn't he? He claimed he'd made the third one for the Lamia nonentity. It was around that point a conspiracy-minded fellow like Jordan Tethys began to detect a whiff of something stinky besides faeriedust, agathodaemons or cacodemons. That stench was of latter day revisionism, or redaction, and he didn't like it.

Along with the three Unities of Lazareme, a number of their siblings, and their father himself, Future Tvasitar was among those on the exploratory expedition who managed to avoid capture by either of the two devil-eating sphinxes. When Tethys asked him how the Androsphinx and the Gynosphinx both became moribund, the Artificer stated they'd made the mistake of looking into call-it-Demogorgon's three eyes.

Although that worked for the Androsphinx, as far as Tethys was concerned it didn't for the Gynosphinx. Nonsense, Tvasitar hedged unconvincingly. It did if the two sphinxes hadn't consumed the entirety of the Unnameable, if they'd only managed to swallow its body. If, say, the She-Sphinx didn't have enough room for its head, or spat it out once she returned to her roost on Incain, someone, anyone – presumably one of the Dual Entities – could have turned it on her.

As for what became of it, that was easy. Alorus Ptah was Heliosophos, the Male Entity in whatever lifetime he was in then, and everyone knows that when Helios dies he tumbles back into the time stream. For reasons having to do with the ineffable Godstuff of Brainrock-Gypsium, Trans-Time Trigon tumbles with him. So does the just as mystifying Mnemosyne Machine, who began making up the walls of Trans-Time Trigon's hollowed-out innards in Helios's third lifetime. The Unnameable's head must have time-tumbled away with them.

Tvasitar admitted he hadn't been there when it happened. He nonetheless figured that was as good an explanation as any. Pyrame Silverstar didn't buy it any more than Tethys did. She'd been there when All shut down on Incain. What's more, she attested she'd been conscious when the She-Sphinx deactivated. She could guarantee All hadn't done so because she looked into the face of any nominal Demogorgon either of the Dual Entities, or anyone else, showed her. In her opinion All had deactivated simply because Machine-Memory flipped a switch in Trans-Time Trigon.

In any event, Tethys put to Tvasitar: That crap about him forging a Medusa-head for this confabulated Lamia was a Jordanian chamber pot full of bilge water, wasn't it? The truth of the matter was Lamia was, for all intents and purposes, a hypothetical devil. If she existed at all she was only one of the thousands of otherwise nameless devils who may or may not have made it to the Whole Earth, but definitely did not survive the Genesea.

Tvasitar stuck to his story. He'd crafted the Medusa-head at the request of her two brood sisters, the Cockatrice and the Basilisk. Self-admittedly, having been among the devils eaten by the two sphinxes, the terrible legacy of the Unnameable inspired them. Plus, the smithy put to him, surely they'd know if their third sister was this Lamia and not, as Tethys also speculated, the Medusa herself. Moreover, Tvasitar insisted the Medusa's power focus was a golden girdle or cestus: a love-inspiring woman's garment akin to that which the mythic Aphrodite wore.

Why couldn't Jordy accept that? Grandfather Sedon deeded Middle Sea regions to Mithras. Its and subsequent traditions often paired Love, as Peace, with War and therefore, implicitly as well as explicitly, with Hate. Recall as well that before Attis, as

Perseus, lopped off her head in Libya, then returned to the Head and deposited her spirit being aspect in All, thus far for eternity, the Medusa bore many of the eighth-born Apocalyptic of War's Sangazurs.

Given Mars Bellona, as Weir's long ago and far-travelled Illuminaries had the bearded, muscle-bound deadhead, was such a relative highborn – and given what she must have looked like after she made off with Lamia's gorgon-head – the Medusa probably needed a love-inspiring cestus to keep War interested in her affections.

Far more significantly to Tvasitar's reckoning, why would the Moloch Sedon abandon his glorious-to-behold, silver-haired partner of 2,000 years on Crete in order to cross the Libyan Sea and hook up with someone wearing a gorgon's head if she didn't have a golden girdle? For the anvil-headed smithy, that was a remarkably perceptive wonderment. For the Legendarian it was one worthy of putting to someone even more wonderful.

"I'd have thought that obvious, son," his devic half-mother, Wisdom of Lazareme, said to Tethys when he posed her Tvasitar's question. "Your bewilderment comes down to the European ethnocentricity of antique Illuminaries. Beyond the Dome they don't use what we call Sed-Speak, but which is more accurately called the Universal Tongue. They use hundreds, make that thousands, if not hundreds of thousands, of different languages and dialects thereof.

"Since we involuntarily understand and speak whatever lingo whomsoever is using whenever we're out there, we still think of them as the same, pre-Flood speech. But the truth of the matter is they only stem from it. That's why your lamentably absent half-father rather crudely declared the lot of them *'Garbled Gargle'*. He was right – but it's unseemly for privileged folks like us to disparage those less cranially capacitated.

"That said, there's no denying we from in here really do have to concentrate in order to distinguish between one tongue or another out there. You wouldn't bother with it, Jordy, because it'd take too much effort, but I'm aptly named. Purely for the sake of wisdom, I'm one of the few who has tried to differentiate them analytically.

"I can therefore tell you, with no fear of contradiction, that in one language beyond the Dome *'Medusa'* means *'sovereign female wisdom'* whilst in Sanskrit it's *'Medha'*, in Egyptian it's *'Met'*, *'Mut'* or *'Maat'*, in Greek it's *'Metis'*, hence Illuminaries coming up with my name even though I'm a Lazaremist, and so on. Implicitly they refer to the same goddess, not distinct devils like Harmony, me or even the Medusa.

"Once you accept that, you should be able to accept that the same deity was also called *'Neith'*, *'Anath'*, *'Athene'* or *'Ath-enna'* in North Africa and *'Athana'* in Minoan Crete. You get where I'm going?" Tethys didn't so she as good as spelt it out for him.

"First of all, recall that at first only the Dual Entities called the middle sea between Europe, Africa, Asia and the Atlantic the Mediterranean. What happened was Illuminaries jumbled up many of the same letters or syllables comprising Medusa, Maat, Athana, and rest. They then came up with Methandra as the name for that goddess. They did so because, to their mind, Hot Stuff, Mithras's Virgin, represented *'sovereign female wisdom'*.

"So, Sedon got the Medusa, yes, but he wasn't after her. Nor was he after Harmony or me, as wise as I may be. He was after Methandra Thanatos."

"And he got a stone-staring gorgon," Tethys finally understood, "Because that's what the Dual Entities set him up to get."

"Ah, but couldn't that be what we've been set up to believe? Don't forget what era we're talking about."

"The mad goddesses' Mediterranean matriarchate, what of it? Are you saying Methandra set him up all by her lonesome?"

"Not necessarily and maybe not all by her lonesome," Metis qualified. "In all likelihood she'd have been in cahoots with Kore-Concord, who, as Cybele or Magna Mater, was perhaps the maddest of the mad goddesses until Harmonia lost Helios and assumed the role of Nemesis."

"Divine Coueranna hated the Attis."

"She hates the Attis," Titanic Metis corrected her half-son, changing his statement to the present tense, "Because he was Strife's half-son and Strife, whom she dubbed Kore-Eris, ergo Kore-Discord, took Mithras away from her at the outset of the Mediterranean matriarchate. There might not have even been a matriarchate if Machine-Memory had possessed Coueranna instead of Marutia during Helios's seventh lifetime."

"From what I've been able to piece together there's no *'might'* about it."

"Don't be so quick to absolve Methandra of anything, Jordy. There's plenty of anecdotal evidence matriarchies originated in Africa long before we gained solidity and, until she bodily moved to Strongyne, her power base was in Libya."

"I gather you're not her biggest fan."

"Look, all I'm saying is it's within the realm of possibility, if not necessarily probability. The next time you go outside to copy parchments in the Alexandrian Library for the benefit of your monomaniacal patron, Thrygragos Mithras, search out material on Medusa. I guarantee you'll discover all sorts of perhaps lesser known but nonetheless intriguing connections between her and Mediterranean Athena.

"For one thing, you'll usually find her starting off as a beautiful young woman whose most notable attribute was long, silken hair *'the colour of golden embers'*."

"Which sounds like the kind of hair Methandra would have, I'll grant you. Except, I've never seen Methandra's hair. She keeps it hidden behind that purple hood and scarlet mask she's always wearing. Have you?"

"No, but it is unquestionably in stark contrast to Pyrame Silverstar's long, silvery hair; at least it is when she bothers to wear hair."

"So? Maybe Sedon grew bored of Pyrame. Two millennia seems a mite much to expect a monogamous relationship to last."

"You would say that, you whose relationships are lucky to last two days."

"Hey, I've a procreative imperative. And so does Sedon."

"One that doesn't require monogamy, does it? Grandfather always wanted Methandra. He still does and he's hardly the only one. You've seen her. How would you describe her mask?"

"Other than the three eyeholes seem set too widely apart, the mouth is kind of skull-like and it's bloody red?"

"Menstrual crimson, also gorgonian-like, wouldn't you say?" He allowed as to how he might, if she insisted. She did, whereupon she added, as if for his further edification: "You do know why Methandra wears a mask and hood, don't you?"

"Because she's ugly as a gorgon?"

"That depends on how you regard death. She fancies herself the same as her two brood brothers, Dream and King Cold, in that she's a Death Goddess. For a mortal to look upon her face, unmasked and unveiled, is to look upon his or her own death. In other words, the stone she'd turn them into is a funerary statue."

"Figuratively speaking," he added, needlessly.

"Don't be too sure about that either. What you can be sure about is the stone the Medusa turned Grandfather Sedon into when he tried to leave her was a gorgon's stone, a literal state of temporary immobility, nothing more. He'd have recovered eventually.

"However, if Pyrame hadn't dispatched Attis, as Perseus, in time to cut off her head and thereafter use it to remobilize Sedon next to immediately, Machine-Memory would have had All eat him. You can take that as a given. It happened, which it still might someday, who knows what would have become of the Inner Earth. That happens, for those of us dwelling beneath the Dome it could well be sink or swim time."

"It sounds like we owe Pyrame and Attis a debt of gratitude."

"Oh, we do that all right. But you missed my point. If the Dual Entities were around then why would Machine-Memory be so slow to finish the job? She'd have had All waiting between-space to inhume Sedon the moment the gorgon turned him to stone."

"There does seem to be a time lapse."

"An explicable one, though. As you know, most of the mad goddesses, particularly in the Mediterranean, were Mithradites. Many of them were also Pyrame's elders. They couldn't have ordered her, as Lady Tanith, to have All at the ready while Grandfather Sedon, as Lord Rhadamanthys, was with her in Phaistos because he'd just overrule them.

"He's stone, they could order her to sic All on him. She can't disobey her elders, male or female, yet she somehow bought enough time to dispatch Attis to rescue him. If Machine-Memory were around Pyrame wouldn't factor into any of this. Ergo, the Dual Entities weren't around and that's why the mad goddesses, Methandra foremost, failed in that version of the Panharmonium Project."

"Hypothetically failed," Tethys cautioned his half-mother. "I'm as conspiracy-minded as you are, but I find it difficult to accept Sedon fell for any of it. Face-dancing shape-shifters or not, he's far and away the mightiest devil there is. He must have been able to tell the difference between Methandra and the Medusa."

"Not if Methandra herself, without the mask, acted as the initial lure."

"Then, when the time came to stone Sedon, she had the Medusa take her place." Tethys shook his head. "Sorry, but I just don't see it. I mean, I can appreciate what you're saying, but do you really think any of it's feasible without the Dual Entities around?"

"I can't confirm it, if that's what you're asking. Pyrame claims Machine-Memory had hold of the Medusa, that the whole sorry episode therefore rests on the Dual Entities' shoulders. Methandra won't talk to me, and if she won't talk to me she won't talk to you, but everyone else I put it to agrees with me. That said, there's usually a kernel of truth in old myths and I'll wager you can't find a single myth regarding Medusa that doesn't interlink her with Olympian Athena."

"The only time I'd bet against Wisdom of Lazareme is when he's dealing the cards and I had the last unopened beer."

Metis ignored that; said instead: "For instance, one legend recounted by your dead pal, Publius Ovidius Naso, in his Metamorphosis, tells how Athena, read Methandra, effectively made the Medusa. To quote him as close to accurately as I can from memory: '*when Medusa was a virgin Foaming Poseidon in Heady Athena's temple raped her. Athena, who saw it happen from behind a slotted curtain, rejected the ocular proof of her own eyes and blamed Medusa for the sacrilegious act.*'

"She thereupon punished Medusa by changing her loveliest feature, her fiery golden hair, into snakes; dreadlocks as the Entities call their African facsimiles."

"Ovid never mentions any dual entities."

"I didn't say he did. He also didn't say Athena lay with Pan or a Pan-like deity but some myths I've heard or read say precisely that. Substitute Poseidon for Pan and recall who likes to look like Pan."

"The Entities' Devil," Tethys acknowledged: "Great-grandfather Sedon."

"The fact that Ovid describes her as '*Heady Athena*' is highly suggestive. So is the fact that virtually every myth I've ever seen has Perseus giving Athena the gorgon's head afterwards and her attaching it to her aegis or armour. Why couldn't she have had it beforehand?

"Then there's the commonality of their supposed Libyan origins in that both are associated with Lake Tritonis. It's even said of the pillars holding up the Athenian Parthenon, her greatest temple outside of Mythland, that they're Athena's men turned to stone. I could go on."

"Please don't bother."

========

Jordan Tethys spent many hours, in many lifetimes, within the Alexandrian Library researching, reading and copying, into his Brainrock quill, thousands of parchments deposited there. In the process he uncovered almost as many myths about Titanic Metis as he did about the Medusa and Mediterranean Athena.

When he asked his devic half-mother about them, especially about the oft-repeated statement that she was Zeus's first wife and Athena's mother, she pooh-poohed that they were just myths. Similarly when, duly blindfolded, he confronted the two other nominal gorgons – whom Attis stuck inside All almost as often as Pyrame let them out again – they told him that, having no name of her own at the time, Demogorgon was the name Lamia adopted when she came to overwhelm the conglomerate devil's collective psyche.

They further asserted the She-Sphinx still held onto their brood sister. Pyrame, though, the lone known devil that could go into and out of the Mandroid Monster

Maker without being imprisoned by her, dismissed that as well. All didn't so much digest devic spirit beings as kept them between-space, in a state of permanent stasis within her.

As for their subtle matter daemonic bodies, they almost invariably transferred to their power foci, which All usually spat up such that Attis or Harmony or whomever could keep them wherever. In other words, eating devils hardly provided her with any sustenance whatsoever. She therefore assured Tethys that All held no entity that might have been either Lamia or Demogorgon inside her.

On top of that, unless it was she, Pyrame, there'd never been a female Mithradite who dominated the Unnameable's collective psyche. As for the theory propounded by antediluvian Hecate-Hellions such as Valhallan Valkyries, that Demogorgon was actually the She-Sphinx's real name, Pyrame couldn't resist reminding anyone who believed suchlike drivel that All herself had always called herself All, as in the all-invincible, and not Demogorgon.

She also correctly pointed out that a lamia was an afterlife revenant of witches who died during childbirth. Their psychopomp-form was that of a hoot owl. Those selfsame Hecate-Hellions, members of the world's oldest, pre-Genesea Witch Sisterhood, considered hoot owl medallions symbols of wisdom. So did Methandra's Intuit worshippers. Devotional Athenans on either side of the Dome did too.

You could say the same thing, not that it was particularly relevant, about many of those living in what the Dual Entities had as the Americas: the vast, continental landmasses Dark Sedon assigned to Byronics shortly after bringing the Sedonshem down from the moon in 669 PD. What was relevant was that an owl was considered the sacred totem of Primeval Lilith, the assuredly non-legendary Demon Queen of the Night. Truth told, Pyrame restated what everyone including Tethys already knew, the name Lamia was interchangeable with Lilith.

Often represented as having an owl or harpy's talons, everyone also knew Primeval Lilith was Alorus Ptah's first wife. By him she was the mother of Cain, he who slew Abel, Ptah's firstborn by Trishtar Thrae, the somehow then humanized Mnemosyne Machine. Anti-Patriarch Cain not only went on to slay his father, he blew himself up, along with thousands of his followers, outside the Gates of Eden circa 660 PD.

Tethys pressed Pyrame as to what reactivated All shortly after the Head became the Head. The answer to that was simplicity in itself, she proudly responded. The Moloch Sedon came to Incain in order to get her out. That shouldn't surprise anyone. They'd spent multiple multi-millennia on the Sedonshem as lovers.

Registering more so than seeing him, the She-Sphinx automatically switched back on and, as the Dual Entities had pre-programmed her to do, promptly sought to eat him. To make room for Sedon, All disgorged her, Pyrame. The Moloch snatched her up and beat a hasty retreat to Grand Elysium, which he was then a-building and where they'd lived happily ever after.

Yeah sure, Tethys rudely snickered: "If the Moloch Sedon was so in love with you why did he leave you inside All for well over 700 years?"

Pyrame didn't like anyone casting aspersions on her lofty stature and thereby seeking to diminish her correspondingly alpine regard for her own self. Devils can't lie. Besides, need she remind Jordy she was the fabulously female Perpetual Presence? Of course not! But, um, wasn't it true she'd been stuck inside All for such a very long time by then? And wasn't it equally true she'd spent most of that time asleep?

That was incontestably true for the rest of the devils who'd been stuck inside the She-Sphinx with her. He knew because he'd interviewed the majority of them and, to a man, a woman or an it of them, they claimed they'd been totally asleep until Pyrame prevailed on All to let them loose. In other words, double-um, unless it was triple-um by then, wasn't it true no one remembered how All deactivated or reactivated?

The obvious person to ask about that was the Moloch Sedon himself, Pyrame huffed.

========

The Tethys-deviant did ask Sedon. So did Mithras. Tethys must have got to her because Pyrame said she did too, in time.

At their pyramidal palace in Grand Elysium Sedon told them, and anyone else daring to inquire, that it was no more any of their damn business how he pulled it off – or why he pushed it on, if it was just a switch – than it was whether Tralalorn was his demon child. Nor was it any of their business, he let drop with a wicked wink, whether Trala's White Dwarf, her perpetually self-kneading, non-Anvil-made power focus, was the compressed placenta and facial-foetal membranes Pyrame expelled as her afterbirth.

Fearlessly, foolishly, or both simultaneously, the Tethys-deviant once, only once, persisted with his line of questioning. Did that mean the Dual Entities had returned for yet another of the Male's many lifetimes so soon after Sedon raised Cathonia out of himself?

Did the Mnemosyne Machine turn All back on and have her release Pyrame such that she could be humanized again? Or did she do it because, without Pyrame out and about to half-mother his Sed-sons, the Whole Earth would be destroyed in a second Great Flood?

Magnanimous host that he was, the sky's mighty Eye-Mouth, howsoever then at least partially in Grand Elysium, allowed that last in particular to be a fascinating proposal. *'Why don't you ask them the next time they're back?'* he suggested pleasantly enough.

Funnily, though not to him, Tethys died in his sleep that night: the night of his last, self-instigated interview with the Moloch Sedon. He supposed he must have been so shaken by the experience he drank more than his 30-beer allotment and expired due to alcohol poisoning.

There was nothing funny about where he woke up inside of, however. It wasn't the first time he'd incarnated as one of his daughters or granddaughters but it was the first time he'd come back while she was giving birth.

Now that was painful.

========

In the dozen or so lifetimes after their interview, the deviant Tethys would have followed Sedon's advice and asked the Dual Entities how All deactivated or reactivated.

He also would have asked them, amongst a nigh-on world-encircling catalogue of other things, if they were around when the Medusa stop-stoned Sedon. He never got the chance to ask them anything. Neither did Pyrame, not that she told him anyhow.

Thrygragos Varuna Mithras never would have asked them. Like the mighty Eye-Mouth usually in the sky, like most other devils as well, he reckoned the first thing you did when you came across the Male Entity was kill him, thereby sending him back into the time stream where he belonged. No one knew when Helios had his earliest lifetime. However, they all knew that if he never had a first, he could never have helped create the Moloch Sedon in his fifth.

To state the obvious, it was all very mysterious. To state the startling, it turned out tee-tees weren't alone when it came to recollecting Demogorgon's name. Adepts in secret societies or enlightened faiths on both sides of the Dome did as well. Yet, due to a superstitious dread that saying it aloud would bring death or disaster to the speaker, his or her family, friends or cronies, they too referred to it as the Unnameable.

Rather, they had.

Earlier this century, the Dome's 44th, during one of her occasional jaunts to the Outer Earth in order to co-conceive small-case sedons, Pyrame discovered that tantalizing tidbit. When she told it to the Tethys-deviant's then-incarnation, he took All's tongue-tug through the Dome and not only verified it; he scanned a copy of the manuscript into his quill and brought it back.

The treatise's writer and publisher was a certain Lactantius. A nearly exact contemporary of Constantine the Great, who became his patron, this Lactantius claimed to be Christian. While that may be, more than likely he was also a renegade Xuthrodite or Horrite, as devils referred to that astonishingly enduring, esoteric brotherhood.

Given the place and date of his birth the previous century, his looks, drinking habits and proclivity for telling tales, he may have as well been a Tethys son or grandson that circumstances conspired to prevent becoming a full-fledged Jordy. At any rate, there it was: Demogorgon's name spelled out for anyone to read.

========

Although he'd bit the proverbial big one more than 40 years earlier, Pyrame didn't know if this Lactantius personally suffered death or disaster as a result of publishing Demogorgon's name. If the Tethys-deviant did, he hadn't mentioned it to Mithras. He had made an impressive study of the Unnameable, however.

And, for a meal or three, and a beer or three times 10 – which Mithras gladly provided during the course of their increasingly frequent, information-sharing sessions over the past few centuries – Tethys recounted various legends that many other traditions, on both sides of the Dome, had of their version of Demogorgon.

Seemingly there were as many euphemisms as there were legends. For example, a number of mythologies had it as the World Serpent. Sumer, the first postdiluvian civilization on the Outer Earth, called it Tiamat, the dragon of chaos. Despite its reputedly snake-like, thusly undeniable phallic shape, in comparatively recent Roman times it assumed a female gender, as *'Dia Mater'*, Goddess Mother. Other names Tethys heard included Anata, Kadru, Kundalini, Leviathan, Ouroboros, Per-Uachet, Quetzal-Kukulcan, and Tohu Bohu.

Chrysanthemum, Golden Flower, the Petaliferous or Many Fingered Thing, had to be the queerest name and quirkiest legend Tethys uncovered during his investigations. Possibly pre-Flood, it was preserved by vegetarian diggers and farming folk of the lower Cattail Peninsula, the Byronic territory bordering the Akadan coastline.

It referred to a formerly all-strangling vine that flowered only once, whereupon it immediately died. However, even in the world of herbivores, death begets life and life begets death. Its seeds, caught up in the wind, fertilized the plant's planet. Their sprouting, in all their diversity, resulted in the propagation of life everywhere.

Tethys found in Chrysanthemum an oddly suggestive, perhaps even serendipitous combination of Chrysaor Attis's first name and that of both Xuthros Hor's and Lazareme's Anthea, the Flowery Anthea of Attis's bottomless bag or kibisis. It twig-triggered another fay-faerie-fanciful, as in whimsical, notion.

When it came right down to it, what was so special about a kibisis anyhow? Plenty of witches had so-called bottomless bags of their own. More than likely Hor's Anthea did as well. Furthermore, even if they didn't have bags or purses or sacks as such, witch-materialists from every sisterhood secreted stuff between-space off their witch-stones.

Devils did too, albeit in their power foci. Hell's Teeth! Devils could secrete their own minds and bodies inside Tvasitar-trinkets. The smithy himself sometimes spent decades as an inanimate obelisk. So why would Tvasitar forge a bottomless bag for a life loving second-born like Lazareme's Anthea? Why not craft something far more grandiosely appropriate for such a highborn? Why not craft her, say, something like a love-inspiring cestus, a golden girdle?

Was that one of the deliberate edits, revisions or redactions he thought he detected when it came to divining the unadulterated veracity of the Unnameable's final minutes, what became of its skull, and whether the Medusa used her own gorgonian head or this dubious Lamia's on Sedon?

Could it have been neither? Was it remotely possible Methandra had accidentally stumbled upon the Unnameable's actual head, what inspired the gorgons' power foci? Had she located it beneath the desert sands of Libya, where she ruled during the early centuries of the matriarchate and where the two sphinxes had devoured everything except said head three thousand years earlier?

After all, half-granddaddy Lazareme hadn't seen them swallow it. He only saw them fighting over it. Them being thus distracted was how he managed to escape before they noticed him.

Had she, Methandra of Mythland, the Jewel of Sedon's Crown, held onto it until she got a chance to turn it on Sedon? Had she stoned him only to have Pyrame, at that time Lady Tanith of Etocretan Phaistos, balk at releasing All from Incain in order to chomp their mutual forbearer and thereby properly finish the job she'd so successfully begun?

That being the case she wouldn't have needed to be a personification of sovereign female wisdom to realize the Moloch Sedon would eventually regain his mobility and start looking for heads on platters as payback. Had she thereupon done as mythology claimed? Had it been her as Mediterranean Athena – her and not Pyrame Silverstar – who equipped and guided Attis, as Perseus, to the Medusa's lair in order to deflect the blame to the gorgon from herself?

Maybe Wisdom of Lazareme was the wisest Master Deva of them all.

========

The Legendarian would have loved to interview the Medusa with respect to what her original power focus had been but, as cautiously sociable as they were with each other, All of Incain didn't allow those she consumed to grant interviews. Neither would either Pyrame or Attis countenance All releasing her long enough for a quick chat in order to satisfy his curiosity. Which of course only made him more suspicious.

Even if the Medusa was a twelfth-born, and not one of the three far lower-born gorgons, she was still Pyrame's junior. That meant Pyrame could have arranged everything herself. She might have done so just to prove to the mighty Moloch in the sky how indispensable she was to the preservation of Cathonia.

Tethys did know where whosoever head it belonged to was, however. Regardless of whether he'd once turned it over to Methandra as Mediterranean Athena, Chrysaor Attis admitted he currently kept it in his bottomless bag.

Thanks to Thrygragos Varuna Mithras, Attis's kibisis had just gone the way of every other Tvasitar Talisman the Great God knew to be in existence save four, one of which was the smithy's own anvil. He'd done so at the cost of an incalculable number of azuras, his and his devils' children by each other, but obliterating Attis's kibisis via his Kronos Quake was vital to the success of Thrygragon.

Azuras, regardless of whom their parents were, were otherwise useless, irrelevant and therefore expendable. The Anvil Artificer's anvil wasn't. At his command Tvasitar Smithmonger, who never left his abode atop Sedon's Peak, could and would craft replacement power foci for Mithras's soon to be newly sworn, third generational devils, the vanguard of his ultimately Whole Earth, devic army.

As for the Thrygragos Talismans, he wasn't done with them quite yet.

========

Year of the Dome 4376

Mithras hadn't been down below when the sphinxes devoured the conglomerate creature, what comprised 90% of the Master Devas who'd joined Thrygragos Lazareme's ill-starred exploratory expedition commingling with an unspecified quantity of the no doubt duplicitous Daemonicus's earthborn daemons. He'd listened attentively to an abbreviated version of Lazareme's account of that first pre-Flood debacle and, in the spirit of give and take, assured Tethys that the head in contention definitely didn't belong to then Demon King Daemonicus.

He knew precisely what had become of the main male daemon's head – that is to say he knew what had become of Daemonicus's head until today. Not that he told this to Tethys but, should push came to shove and it came down to a matter of him or her, he had the same fate in store for Sedon's Demon Child.

As for the other female Perpetual Presence, the only for-sure, third generational devil who could independently function without a Tvasitar-trinket of her own, well, he'd accounted for her as well. Rather again, since all she could throw at him besides defiance was All itself, he'd accounted for the Mandroid Monster Maker just as precisely.

In truth, he'd accounted for every eventuality, even the off-chance Father Sedon might turn against him. He knew how the Dual Entities activated then deactivated the sphinxes. He knew it because he'd had hold of Heliosophos during the latter stages of the Male Entity's seventh lifetime and remembered what he'd read of him then; what Machine-Memory had read from All of Incain and then told him-Helios, put more exactly.

The Giza Sphinx could be reawakened. He was wearing the wherewithal. Rather yet again, he was wearing facsimiles of two of them and carrying the third.

========

He instantly apprehended the little horror wouldn't have come all the way here from Apple Isle just to meekly meld with him as if she were one of his.

She wasn't. He'd been convinced of that for a very long time.

****

THEO 14:

DEMOCHILD

========

Terrible to behold in the boar-tusked, boggle-eyed Mask of Byron, shockingly priapic with his elephantine tunic-trunk bulging beneath Lazareme's cloak of stellar tinctures straight out of the Milky Way, and wielding his ankh-like cross with its sun-circle roaring meltingly hot, Thrygragos Varuna Mithras glared down at the Demon Child.

He hoped to frighten her away. It was a forlorn hope. She may never age beyond six or seven at the most but, with the kind of clout she had, Tralalorn was the frightening one.

========

Sure, he had overweening ego. It was so large that, circa 2000 YD, he self-admittedly split literally into separate, bi-solar entities, Uranus and Kronos. Jointly or disjointedly, a few years, decades or centuries later Varuna and Mithras added a third god, none other than Zeus, to their résumé.

His memory not being what it should be, it probably wasn't the first or the last time they'd done that. There were three-in-one trinities everywhere you looked in the nowadays-archaic Outer Earth. The Persian Magi's VAM Entity, and the Vedic Aditya version of it long before the Magi, was one-as-three of them. There were also female trinities virtually everywhere you looked, in here included. Usually representing the Virgin-Mother-Crone triad, his Apple Goddesses were only his highest born female threesome.

They'd had many lively discussions, the deviant Tethys and the Great God of Justice, Truth and Light, on the face of it back to being singular throughout them.

They concurred on a number of issues, though the brilliance of beer wasn't one of them. Mithras was so depressingly saturnine he never drank anything more concocted than honeyed water.

When he wasn't bedding Myrionymous Kore, or temporary embodiments of one of her myriad personalities, he was sitting on the moon as part of the Sedonshem twiddling his thumbs in 725 YD. He therefore could have no firsthand knowledge of who had helped set Andy and Ginny up to make munchies of so many Master Devas then-constituting the devic contribution to the Demogorgon-abomination.

However, unlike Tethys, who believed his first incarnation didn't come about until the Dome's 41ˢᵗ Century, the Great God was down here when other variations of the Demogorgon legend developed. Not lost on either of them was that, of those primitive quasi-civilizations, most dreamed up their folklore prior to Tvasitar supposedly forging for the Lamia nonentity the Medusa-head.

Neither was it lost on them that its prototype appeared on the pre-Flood Whole Earth during the early years of the Seventh Patriarchy of Golden Age Humankind, that of Droch Nor. What made that interesting, perhaps even highly significant, was that Number Six, Jaro Dan – a name Tethys couldn't help but note contained the makings of Jordan, albeit with a surplus 'a' – was the Odin of Ragnarok.

He outlived his son, Number Seven, by a considerable margin. He also outlived his predecessors, though not Nor's successors: Amemp Tut, Oriartes Ma and Xuthros Hor. Like Eight, Nine and Ten, Number Six had been there on the day in 366 PD that his father, Number Five, Mahurus Zir, fell victim to fallen angel devils, extraterrestrial invaders of the planet.

Five dabbled in arcane arts. In the oxygen-starved high plain of the Andean mountain range, where he'd established his home base, Power Point Tiahuanaco, he was showing them a three-eyed oddity he'd captured in an amber-like trap when the Byronics attacked.

Jaro Dan very nearly went down himself, never to rise anew, during the course of what amounted to a rescue mission; the same revelatory foray that cost Thrygragos Byron his body. As a result of what they saw and experienced firsthand at Tiahuanaco, the retired patriarch retroactively blamed devils for the unnatural deaths of his son as well as Patriarchs One through Four and Anti-Patriarch Cain.

He might have been wrong about Alorus Ptah but – even though, as a golden-apple-eating member of the Golden Age's rainbow class, he couldn't be possessed – the Anti-Patriarch might have been under devic influence when he poisoned his own father. In a manner of speaking, Dan was wrong about Cain's death too.

He was certainly right about Numbers Two through Four, though. The Mithradite Illuminaries named Nergal Vetala claimed credit for Two, Pseth Ra, whereas Eventual Yati, Byron's Dragon, notched Three, Enolon Su. Sedon himself was largely responsible for the death of Four, Kemem Seb, and of course it was the Sedonshem landing that did for Seven, Droch Nor.

Cain committed suicide, something not even the strongest devil could cause by means of possession alone. He did so by blowing himself up at the Gates of Eden.

He was hardly the only one exterminated that day. Thousands of his followers were beside him when he triggered the atomic heart of his golden calf.

A chain reaction emanating from the explosion just as thoroughly wiped out Enoch City, which he'd founded, nestled at the foot of three suspiciously Trigon-like pinnacles in the Arabian Peninsula, after Adam-Ptah disinherited him for slaying Abel and he countered by establishing his anti-patriarchy.

Nonetheless, as Mithras recalled because he'd been there when his father ordered that particular Sedonplay, Future Plathon, in the form of Cain's Apis Bull, suckered him into crafting the calf in the first place. Furthermore, the devic personalities Illuminaries came to name Marut Kanin, Aphropsyche Morningstar and Mariamne Dawnstar were in possession of Cain's three young, non-rainbow-class wives – whose names were, curiously, Cybele, Eden and Mnemosyne – so they probably had something to do with the calf as well.

Rightly or wrongly, Number Six vowed to prevent devils butchering him the same as he reckoned they had his son and predecessors. In what amounted to one of the most tragic ironies of Earth's pre-Genesea era, his determination not to duplicate their ignoble demises resulted in Number Ten, Xuthros Hor, sentencing him to death.

Jaro Dan's crime was so egregious even Hor's life-loving Anthea couldn't bring herself to argue against his execution. Six was meticulously massacring the planet's millions of non-golden-apple-eating, sentient beings with technology sourced from the same place, pre-Golden Age Eden, as that which Anti-Patriarch Cain used to construct his golden calf and thereby destroy Enoch City and the Gates of Eden.

Both vindictively and unconscionably, he was deploying the first arguable civilization on the Whole Earth's hidden arsenal of weapons of mass destruction against them simply because they were vulnerable to devic possession.

At the time of his hanging, in 234 PD, amongst Dan's most effective, anti-devil allies were Mother Earth worshipping Hecate-Hellions and the daemons whose descendants were now largely confined to Belialma's Satanwyck. Leading the latter was none other than that selfsame Daemonicus Thrygragos Lazareme believed had betrayed him to the Dual Entities almost 500 years earlier.

The Moloch Sedon celebrated Six's too mercifully brief date with the gallows – and, with it, the final act of Ragnarok – by cutting off the thusly labelled, ever-treacherous Demon King's head. He thereupon disposed of it in the frequently erupting volcano of what he thereafter-dubbed Sedon's Peak.

Varuna Mithras and his two, second generational brothers witnessed him melting away Daemonicus's head. Immediately subsequently, they had the honour of presenting their father with the symbols of the daemons' kingship: a crown, a robe and a sceptre.

Prior to being so rudely decapitated, Daemonicus had confessed, under irresistible duress, that Alorus Ptah activated then deactivated Andy the Androsphinx hundreds of years earlier using them. Similarly, and at roughly the same time, Trishtar Thrae used symbols of the daemons' queenship, a different crown, a mirrored shield and a curved blade, to activate and deactivate Ginny the Gynosphinx.

The original six were destroyed circa 2000 YD when the Dual Entities, during Helios's seventh lifetime, attempted to assassinate Sedon, as King Sodom, and Pyrame, as Queen Gomorrah, by asteroid. Unless, as some alleged, it was an until-then left-in-orbit, generational ship abandoned by Utopians from the second Weirworld, said asteroid was nothing more nor less than Trans-Time Trigon loaded with the same filthy atomics Cain used to construct the heart of his golden calf.

Not wanting anything to do with them, Mithras had intentionally left the Tvasitar-crafted facsimiles of the Female Three in Attis's Time-Quake-obliterated kibisis alongside what might or might not have been the Unnameable's head. He now wore or wielded facsimiles of the Male Three, the Thrygragos Talismans. In both cases, obliterated and wear/wielding, he couldn't envision a better situation.

Actually, all things considered, he could. What would be far more preferable was not seeing her and her malodorous mount crowding his feet right this very minute. Still, if she didn't go back to Ap Isle damn soon, what he wielded he could use to obliterate her right this very next minute!

========

He concentrated almightily; internally rotated the sun-circle atop his labarum the more. There, he had it: an interspatial portal to the Brainrock Lake still bubbling within the caldera of Sedon's Peak.

Gods, God or the Devil Above, he was utterly without equal! Why don't you come down, or come over from Grand Elysium, and congratulate me, daddy? Just wait a little while longer, okay? Until I decide what to do with your miserable little horror!

========

Even if he hadn't seen her arrive, due to the ridiculous singsong rhymes she was always making up he'd have known it was Tralalorn the moment she spoke. Unless she was the Pauper's earthborn daughter by the Moloch Sedon, she was Pyrame's other brood sister, the one besides Desiccated Drought. She certainly had Sedon's reddish skin and pair of stunted horns. Today she also sported zebra-striped, black-and-white hair as well as three different coloured eyeballs: one blue, one brown and one yellow.

Father Sedon had long, long ago made it known his immortal daughter, without admitting she was his immortal daughter, was as indispensable as his mortal Sed-sons were when it came to maintaining Cathonia. That made Trala as untouchable and as much of a perpetual presence as Sedon and his Whore, Pyrame Silverstar, whom she called mommy. Of course she called almost every woman mommy and many men, including himself, daddy.

Like any six or seven year old, male or female, devil or otherwise, she was undeniably endearing. She was also disgustingly powerful. The source of that power came from her power focus. It predated Tvasitar Talismans by somewhere in the order of not quite 2,000 years. Orb-like, devils called it the White Dwarf. They often called her that as well.

There were those who claimed it wasn't of this earth; that it was an actual white dwarf, a chunk of cosmic debris, a meteorite or something similar. That didn't explain the faces perpetually forming then deforming as it self-kneaded in and upon itself.

Not much could explain those. Truth told about the only thing that explained them was Tralalorn willed them thus.

Sedon teased it was her afterbirth, but no one took him seriously. What he considered facetious, Mithras considered crass. About the only devil that shared his uncivilized sense of humour was his most hated brother, Thrygragos Everyman. Mithras took that as proof they were more Dionysian than Apollonian and, hence, deserving of the doom he was beginning to bring about for them both today.

She called it her Powder Puff. The powder it puffed was faeriedust, which smelled so much like fecal material many assumed that that's what it was. Whatever else it may be, faeriedust was definitely of the earth, as in Mother Earth. Faeries, like demons, were chthonic critters entirely inimical to Cathonic – skyborn – devils like he and his sometimes-unkind kind. Her powder-puff-stuff had once reduced Varuna-Uranus to the infant who eventually grew into Olympian Zeus and thereafter unmanned him.

Sedon had had her do that then and Mithras couldn't help worrying if he or Pyrame had ordered her to do unto him that double discourtesy a third time. Devic daughters could no more disobey their mothers than they could their fathers. They just obeyed their fathers first.

In case she was Sedon's, and not his, he either vanished or subsumed both Byron's mask and the tunic-trunk. He now looked down on her as he'd looked out at his two brothers after abandoning the guise of their father, as a resplendent celestial, the three-eyed, 30-foot tall, living embodiment of Sol Invictus.

"Oh," she giggled, simultaneously seemingly unimpressed and a tad disappointed. "Tra-la the doggie-dough. And here's the queer, I was just about to ask if I could ride-the-slide it. Want to play ball instead, tra-la the All?"

"All?"

"She-Sphinx stinks. Besides the slides, Daddy Taurus said no. All might eat me. More is the pity and less is the shitty. So I Chimera-Keres rode here, tra-la that's clear. She stinks too the boo. That's why I call her Stygian Stynx."

The Styx was the molten Brainrock-flow separating this side's innards of Mt Maenalus from the between-space orchard of Kore's Hell, where reputedly still grew trees bearing golden apples. Korant and eventually Mithrant youngsters called it the Stynx because it stank, like the brimstone magma it was, and Trala's best gal-pals were Korant girls never forever her age.

The Demon Child was sitting on the back of this Stygian Stynx. Visually it wasn't a three-headed Cereberant identical to the ones Divine Coueranna, Plathon as her charioteer, employed to pull her wheeled cauldron to the Mole. Beyond the Dome, when they served as ferocious as well as fiercely loyal pets for Kore-Concord in her aspect of Cybele, Magna Mater – arguably the greatest Great Mother of the Goddess Culture's matriarchate – suchlike chthonic canines were known as Keres Hellhounds.

On Apple Isle, Sedon's Human Eye-Land, where he ruled from atop his Mithradium mastaba on the summit of Theopolis Hill, Cereberants were seldom seen away from Mt Maenalus. Stynx – a never-ending succession of Stynxes, put better –

went wherever Tralalorn went and, mindful of Sedon's affection for the little horror, Mithras gave her free rein to go wherever she wanted to go so long as she stayed away from his Mithradium.

The reason for that was, except for the three heads, Stynx appeared to be a chimera in the sense that, in Outer Earth Latin, 'chimaera' meant she-goat. To this day, even though it had been Varuna, his nocturnal yet nonetheless bi-solar alter ego, sucking it in as the baby Zeus, the mere sniff of goat's milk made him nauseous. A Great God vomiting off the balcony of his palatial domicile, especially overtop his prayerful adherents down below, whenever Trala and Stynx were in the vicinity was neither stately nor conducive to his devotees coming back to repeat their devotions.

Trala's initial chimera had been one of Cruel Plathon's more notable forms: a fire-breathing creature of nightmare with a serpent's tail, a goat's body and a she-lion's head. That she could breathe fire had everything to do with the fact the Bull made the mistake of consuming Trala's White Dwarf, thus annoying the Demon Child so much so she changed him into her pet goat from the inside out.

Attis as Bellerophon-Chrysaor killed Chimera during the devil goddesses' Mediterranean matriarchate, but Trala was as fond of her pet goats as she was of her equally fragile human playmates. That Stygian Stynx had three goatish heads attached to a she-goatish body, complete with milk-secreting dugs, suggested Trala used her Powder Puff power focus to faeriedust-transform an ordinary hellhound bitch into her latest replacement beastie.

Her referring to Stynx as a Keres-Chimera tended to confirm that theory. But, not that hellhounds, of either sex, would be considered ordinary anywhere on the Head except Apple Isle, there was no denying Stynx's stench was far more sickeningly capric than canine.

Mithras had only reversed time until just after the Anvil Artificer made his and his two now vanished brothers' Godly Glories, their Thrygragos Talismans. That explained why her White Dwarf hadn't ceased to exist. It being so pre-Tvasitar old also probably explained why she hadn't lost her solidity. Naturally, if she had been born on the planet, if not necessarily of the planet, she may never have been a spirit being anyhow.

As for how she got here, regardless of whether Stynx started out as a Keres, the chimera was observably a psychopomp. As for why Trala had come here, the implications of two statements she'd made finally registered. She'd something for Mommy Pyrame and Daddy Taurus wouldn't let her play ball with All because All might eat her. Had everyone, even his own mortal, yet thus far ever-recurring son, turned against him?

If she was a demon, she should be easy to immolate. Contrary to an impression prevalent on the Outer Earth that they thrived in hellfire, most demons were highly flammable. Yet, if she was the Moloch's daughter, and Sedon realized what he was about to do to her, he'd be the one burnt unto ash by its blowback for attempting something so inexcusably sacrilegious. There wasn't much the mighty Eye-Mouth in the sky couldn't do and taking remote-control-command of a devil's power focus was one of the most minor of his abilities.

Still, if indeed everyone had turned against him, if perhaps his father was attempting to seize Thrygragon and make it a Sedonplay from a discreet distance, maybe his brothers hadn't vanished unto nothingness as he'd thought. Maybe Sedon forewarned them she was on her way. Or maybe, independent of Sedon, they'd been expecting her impending arrival all along and didn't want to be here when she finally showed up.

No, he'd come too far to back down now that he was so close to total victory. Sedon be damned in fact as well as fable! He had to show him he was afraid of nothing, that he was worthy of becoming top god beneath the Dome. He had to cremate her irredeemably.

Then providence provided and someone sought to do it for him.

========

The cosmicars blazed out of between-space, blasting him with fireball projectiles. They didn't just blast him of course. They blasted everything near him. That included the de-brained, daemonic husks his devils abandoned at his feet when they merged with him, Trala's Stygian Stynx, and the Demon Child herself.

Those that didn't just crash and burn, that is.

========

Even so, while the Trinondevs in the ones that did crash and burn weren't daemonic, fire-resistant salamanders like his Virgin's generously proportioned body or voluminous clothing must have been made out of, their eye-staves were ever so useful. Protected by self-generated mind-globes they levitated out of the wreckage completely unharmed. They continued to come at him either on the ground, by foot, or in the air, by strength of mind augmented by their extraterrestrial gadgetry.

The cosmicars that hadn't crashed and burned couldn't have been pieced together again and again with replacement parts made locally in the last roughly 2500 years. They kept whizzing at and past him; their pilots, gunners or bombardiers futilely strafing or dropping their ineffective loads as close to him as they dared. Mithras hoped their Master was with them. Her, Helena Augusta, Sedon wouldn't mind him killing. The Moloch hated it when Ant Nightingales turned his Sed-sons against him.

Willpower activated eyeorbs, yes, but they worked best in heavily populated areas. As a rule, unfocused brainwaves charged them. In that respect they were reminiscent of thunderstones Utopians placed atop obelisks in order to collect and thereafter distribute solar and stellar radiance along their Weirdoms' impressive energy grids.

Focused brainwaves were even better, though not just for Trinondevs. Right now there were tens of thousands leaderless soldiers and their hangers-on scattering throughout Sedon's Mole. Some were azura-depleted. Many had given up trying to run away. Of them, almost as many were already on their bellies, desperately directing prayers his way for their deliverance.

As was his right Mithras absorbed their every entreaty, even the stray ones. He'd earned their adulation and wouldn't disappoint. But they had to earn his sufferance also.

He'd been intending to send Attis and his Mithrant legionnaires against Kanin City and its recalcitrant Trinondevs anyhow, after they finished mowing down the ragtag leftovers of his two brothers' armies. Ancestors of the Weirdom's Warriors Elite had been a thorn in his foot almost from the day he was born – or at least since the day he'd acquired a foot – during the tail-end time-space of the first Weir System. He might as well take care of them now as later. Besides, he'd been wondering what to do with his brothers' excess grandchildren, their azuras.

Fanatics, the Trinondevs in the few still airborne cosmicars were unrelenting. Nonetheless, about the only consequence their unabated incendiary barrage had on the conflict was to keep their grounded fellows from advancing any farther and to toast anyone who did. Their Illuminaries – and, being an Ant Nightingale, Helena Somata had to be their Highest Illuminary as well as their Master – would have instructed Kanin's Warriors Elite that devils had highly combustible, daemonic bodies.

He didn't ignite. He wouldn't ignite, and not just because the Mask of Byron and Lazareme's Cloak of Many Colours protected him. Mithras had been solid for many, many multi-millennia pre-Earth. Like his Great God brothers he gained solidity by hardening perhaps millions of protozoan Master Devas within himself.

On the Sedonshem, the same held true for Pyrame or Vetala or whomever as company for Sedon; Kore-Concord for him; long gone Serathrone Hallow for a then be-bodied, and therefore not at all unmoving, Thrygragos Byron; and, presumably, Harmony for Thrygragos Lazareme.

Howsoever incongruously, third generational devils only became bodily vulnerable to flames once they discovered they could independently solidify themselves within the bodies of Brainrock de-brained demons. And that didn't happen until Tvasitar came across mounds of the things somehow accumulated on Sedon's Peak in the aftermath of the destruction of Sodom and Gomorrah beyond the Dome. Plainly not coincidentally, that was also shortly after he learned how to make devils their own power foci.

In their zealousness, Kanin's airborne Warriors Elite didn't care who else they fried. He could afford to do no less.

========

The Devil or not the Devil, the real Moloch Sedon may or may not have finished visiting Cabby the Daddy in Cabalarkon City by now. The infamously male Perpetual Presence may or may not be waiting in their Grand Elysium pyramid for the famously female Perpetual Presence to show up occupying the fetching fledgling, Ute Tethys.

For her part, the silver-haired, still teenage Swan Maiden was preparing for her first real ride as a Valkyrie. As for her mother, Volsanga née Nibelung, she was AWOL in hopes of atonement.

========

George Masterson may have had something that could quench the Tethys-deviant's innate thirst for reliable information on the Unnameable. However, if he had, he would never have strewn it and its ilk along his non-extruded backbone or nonexistent, piton-fletched tail. Nor would he have stuck them to his already balding pate.

He would have left it attached to one of the living tee-tees he raised in a terrarium back home in Kanin City. Either that or he would have detached then reattached it, by its own ichor, to a Tantalus display case he kept there. What he also had, having as yet inexplicably escaped her cosmicar before it went the way of half-sister Constance's 40 odd years earlier, was no idea as to what had become of his masterly mother.

Helena Somata had been there when it started falling apart. Something whooshed into it through the Weird just as he thought they were going to crash and burn. That same something had inhumed him and her. Moments later, once they were safely on the ground, that something puked out just him, along with his eye-stave and what looked to be a single-sacked saddlebag of some sort. It then took off back between-space again, whereupon Hinny the Hippy came through it.

Hinny might be ugly as stink, but the hippo-hind was faithful. She was also really good at tracking him through the Weird – which was also a word not just his mother sometimes used to describe the otherwise damn near unheard of kind of mind-bond he shared with the hotchpotch beastie.

Clutching his eye-stave and, on a whim, grabbing the nearly weightless saddle-bag, he jumped onto her back and contemplated his next move. Suddenly, it, contemplation, wasn't an option. First his tummy rumbled upwards then his bowels did a ditto downwards. In short order he owed Hinny an as yet unexpressed apology.

He stank worse than she ever did. In truth, they both did.

========

Characteristic patience at last rewarded his Hugeness.

========

Helena Somata, or whoever was transmitting them their orders, must have finally apprehended the senselessness of trying to obliterate him with flames. At whoever's command, Trinondevs began ejecting from their cosmicars. It wasn't because they were about to crash and burn either. If their reckless, but not entirely unanticipated, assault on his person was to have any chance of success whatsoever it was a frankly overdue grasp at the, for them, last straw of tendentious triumph.

Step 1: The Trinondevs' eye-staves projected gargoyle-like gliders or shielding parachutes to prevent their plummeting to their deaths. Step 2: Preparatory to attempting to shred and thereafter suck his magnificent mass into the eyeorbs or prison pods atop their eye-staves, Kanin's Warriors Elite had to first open them.

Mithras had been waiting for just that moment. "Azuras away!" he bellowed.

Thousands of surplus azuras came out of not just him but out of those of the Mithrant legionnaires who still had them inside them. They came out of the lefto-vers of Byron and Lazareme's armies as well. In the absence of their parents and two grandfathers what else could they do except obey him, ever the greatest, not to mention last remaining, Great God?

The azuras tore out of their shells, leaving most of their thus vacated, former hosts barking mad. As if moths to light they slurped into the open eyeorbs, filling them, their prison pods, to the point of bursting. And when they did burst, many of the airborne Trinondevs did indeed plummet to their deaths. Those that didn't have enough sense to close their orbs and finish coming to ground, that is. Remarkable devices, eye-staves!

Unfortunately, the staves' still lamentably far too numerous, surviving warri-
or-wielders proved themselves just as remarkably sensible males and females. Seeing
him standing there unwavering in the distance, a primordial sky-god unfazed by fire
– what's more, evidently basking in it – they turned tail and ran.

Dictatorial monomaniac that he'd often been accused of being, his Hugeness
had to stifle the urge to laugh maniacally. It wouldn't be dignified. It also wouldn't be
dignified if he had to trod after them, stomping them one by one into the dirt like
he'd done the 'D for Daemonicus' pest only a couple of hours ago.

Attis used to brag about how disciplined his forces were compared to any other
organized or disorganized army on the Inner Earth. Leaderless or not, azura-deprived
or otherwise, they were about to get their opportunity to validate his bluster. Mithras hesitated momentarily, mulling the degree of face he'd sacrifice if he had to order
them to go after, sweep up and slaughter the fleeing Trinondevs.

It'd be much better if a Leo or higher-ranking Mithrant issued the command to
wipe out the Utopians. It was too bad, if not exactly tragic, that as yet no one seemed
inclined to step to the forefront. At that instant, as if to prove the righteousness of his
cause, external circumstances intervened once again.

"Legionnaires, to me!" someone else bellowed. It was his legionnaires' Taurus.
About time too: Where had the boy been? Then he realized what Attis was riding
through the air. It wasn't his Pegasus. It was All of Incain.

Except … what was the She-Sphinx doing with a tetrahedral head? Sedon's
Whore was inside it answered that. And Attis wasn't riding the Mandroid monstrosity so much as hanging on for dear life. Having no talismans left to cosset him, what
other choice did he have?

Next question was: Had she taken over All in order to attack him because he'd
just immolated hers and Sedon's precious Demon Child? He had the answer to that
right away as well. All, Pyrame plainly in control of it, veered away from him and
began chasing down the fancifully once thought victorious, but now inevitably vanquished, Trinondev transgressors.

So, yes, she had come to avenge Trala's incineration, but she somehow must have
realized he hadn't been responsible for it. Weir's Warriors had crisped her, not him, and
being Sedon's darling, probably she alone, of all the never-cathonitized third generational devils, could get away with punishing them for it properly, as in terminally.

In every way imaginable, Thrygragon was turning out to be his best day ever.

========

The day was done before it had really begun.

========

Ungodly spires of what might have been hellfire licked at him like the terrible
tongues of wanton lovers. The Moloch Sedon didn't look anything like how his masterly mother described the Devil Satan, however. On the contrary, with his appalling
immensity, blindingly luminous hair and beard, instantly recognizable halo, and the
mantle of the heavens above draped about him, George Masterson reckoned he more
closely resembled her notion of God Himself.

With Chrysaor Attis desperately clinging to the unbelievably airborne sphinx's stone-like neck and unambiguously four-sided, triangular head, there was no mistaking who had hold of All. Through no fault of his own, her talismans were as gone as the Legendarian's Brainrock quill. Nonetheless, after what he and Mama Helena put her through back in Kanin City, the Pauper Priestess had every right to be pissed – and a she-sphinx probably pissed corrosive acid.

Eye-staves, the prison pods atop them open or closed, had so many uses. Like witches with their witch-stones, and devils just because they were devils, Trinondevs could far-speak via them. Recovered from his brief bout of upwards and downwards, gastric insurgence – and even though he had no inherent authority to do so – in the unaccountable absence of his masterly mother Georgie took it upon himself to usurp her communicative command.

Trusting they'd recognize and respond to his voice, as they would do to hers, he used his eye-stave to order any Trinondevs not yet in the air to think butts up. He next ordered those in the cosmicars yet aloft to fly butts backwards and pluck their levitating fellows out of the sky like they'd trained to do so many times in the past.

There wasn't much of Kanin City's originally extraterrestrial weapons systems left functional but, if the Mithrant legionnaires were as intent as they appeared to be on slaughtering them, they'd stand a better chance of surviving in their Weirdom than out here in the open Mole. Then again, could anything stop a maddened devil-goddess, with or without the Devil's dispensation to maim and murder disbelieving Utopians, in control of a rampaging she-sphinx?

A better question might have been: What could he do to dodge becoming a psycho-pterosaur's dessert? The answer was zilch.

========

Saudi the Steg Sari and her deceased but always voracious Terror Donna ripped through the Weird. The Donna promptly swallowed he and Hinny the Hippy whole.

========

Georgie didn't have time to dodge anything. He was, however, already holding onto a lifesaving countermeasure. Reflexively hugging his legs around Hinny's belly, he encased them both in an externally impenetrable, brain and eye-stave generated mind-globe with the speed of thought. Unbeknownst to him, he and his hippo-hind thus avoided the fate that befell his mother, monsters-masticating minutes ago.

Realizing immediately she should have left her Donna between-space, the same as she had just before it came through the Weird into her brain-ball and bit Helena Somata in twain, the psychopathic Saur Tsarina furiously pounded on his thought-balloon. Equally infuriated, and without even a residue of its saurian sentience left, her psycho-pterosaur clamped its teeth onto and into it. Squeezing them inexorably together, it sought to break open Georgie's ego-egg as if it was an ordinary egg.

The hippo-hind screeched in appreciable alarm. It was an unnerving sound, more high-pitched squawk than whinny. He knew the crunch was coming. Desperation does wonders for willpower. So does years of Trinondev training, even for someone still well shy of his 30th birthday. Prayer power, especially when it isn't all self-generated and therefore strictly self-serving, never hindered anyone either.

George Masterson found the mental wherewithal to swell his mind-globe. Solidifying it the more, he forcibly widened the Terror Donna's jaws beyond even their expansive limits. A welcome crack greeted his psychical exertions. His half-sister didn't let up, though. Other than breath-briefly, neither did her pterodactyl.

It wouldn't, he realized too late. The only thing keeping it going was Saudi's soul-self. Snapping its jaw didn't do anything to harm Saudi's soul-self. Nor, no matter how subsumed it might be by deviant daddy's internal presence, and Jordy's by and large strongly held scruples against physically harming anyone, did it do anything to frustrate her single-minded resolve to regain the Legendarian's now gone quill.

The same way Saudi and her Donna just had – off the witch-stone his mother always made him wear – an Ophidian came to his rescue in the nick of dick-time. Why did she facially look so much like Mama Helena?

========

"Muddle the puddle, daddy, that unkind of hurt the squirt."

========

His Hugeness looked down, way down. Obviously as oblivious as she was immune to the blistering carnage going on all around them, Tralalorn still sat on her somehow just as unaffected three-headed Keres-Chimera. The little horror was speaking to what looked akin to a humanoid groundswell: the physical manifestation of a man's head and torso, yet nonetheless as muddily black as the night's sky without any stars in it.

Raised, perceptibly segmented humps of its slithery root system palpitated decreasingly backwards, toward where Mithras had first spotted Attis, atop Pyrame-All, coming at him out of the nowhere that was the everywhere of Samsara. If it had come from that direction, it must have diverged from them according to plan. That meant their pursuit of the Trinondevs was a feint.

Everyone was against him after all. This was going to be fun.

Suddenly the groundswell-humanoid's shape wasn't there anymore. Neither was a significant something else.

'She'd something for Mommy Pyrame and Daddy Taurus wouldn't let her play ball with All because All might eat her.' That wasn't the real reason. The real reason was All might eat it. What she had for Mommy Pyrame, who was ever so conveniently off with Daddy Taurus false-routing Kanin's Warriors Elite, had to be the White Dwarf, her Powder Puff power focus.

Maybe he should have played ball with her after all.

========

They had such interesting appendages, did Ophidians. This one must have been part scorpion, a super-scorpion at that. Its penile tail injected into his half-sister extraordinarily fast-acting venom. Saudi-Jordy died again.

Something skull-like and crystalline detonated at her feet. The Sari Tsarina instantly revived. With a reflexive swipe of her spiked, stegosaur tail, she swatted her assailant hard enough to return the favour. The scorpioid Ophidian recovered just as instantly, with no need for an exploding crystal skull.

========

Jordan *'Quill'* Tethys hated incarnating inside a woman for a number of what he felt very legitimate reasons. Primary amongst them was men didn't have to go through such a time-consuming process in order to propagate. Five minutes, if that, would do it. In a manner of speaking that was true for women as well. But they still had to endure the discomfort of the next nine months, otherwise their yearning and subsequent squirming would have been in vaginal-vain, to fay-say some.

Giving birth hurt almost as much as getting killed did. Added to that, in his considerable experience most women gave birth more often than they got killed. If he wanted to keep himself going lifetime after lifetime, which he did, whenever he was incarnated inside a daughter or granddaughter he had to make sure he gave birth as often as she could. Non-Korant girls with Tethys for a maiden name often changed it before they gained the reputation as a trollop and, thereafter, as a serial baby-popper.

He wasn't too happy about incarnating inside an Ophidian either. They had interesting appendages due to the fact they were often both sexes simultaneously. What he really wasn't happy about, though, was his quill hadn't come to him when he came back inside the Ophidian.

What had the Utopian bastards done with it?

========

"Get the fuck out of here, Georgie!"

========

Uncharacteristic cursing aside, there was no mistaking his mother's voice. Now he didn't need to know why the Ophidian looked so much like her. He'd forgotten – not that there'd been any reason for him to remember it until right then – that Saris were hardly the only witches, let alone the only sentient beings, who had soul-selves.

What he'd also forgotten was that witches didn't need to be bodily alive for their soul-selves to keep functioning. Instead of daydreaming when he was attending classes taught by Illuminaries, he really should have been paying more attention. He didn't need to be told twice, though. Hinny might now be as smelly as she was faithful, but she was also slow as stink outside the Weird.

Without another thought, he spurred her between-space.

========

That wasn't his voice, not even close. Whose then?

========

Saudi's first killer – George Masterson he'd realized too late to do anything more than just that, realize his identity – disappeared. With him went his pet psycho, Hinny the Hippy, whom Tethys had also encountered, and chose not to pet, outside of Hopi's booze-tent just prior to his first and most painful, in the sense of most shocking, death today. That only fleetingly fazed Saudi's Terror Donna, though.

There was nothing foul about fowl. Psycho-pterodactyl gulped down psycho-swan the moment it, Volsanga Tethys astride its dorsum, came out of the Weird. Volsanga's pomp had thus sung its last swansong. Talk about bloody; its plumage would never be described as radiantly white again. It was just as well that, as near as he could make out anyhow, none of its feathers were his Brainrock quill. He'd hate to have to dive down a Donna's throat after it.

The Valkyrie remained impressively supple for her advanced age. She tumbled expertly off her doomed psychopomp-swan, regained her feet and sprinted toward Ophidian Tethys. She had something in each of her hands: a hellstone and a crystal skull. Saudi the Steg Sari lumbered ponderously after her.

That wasn't right. His presence coming into his children or grandchildren at the moment of their death or near death was what forestalled it. He couldn't prevent their bodies dying what amounted to a second time when he she or it was killed, though. He she it, the now Ophidian Tethys, was part-scorpion. Its backend-bite should have been instantly lethal. It should have stung him right out of her and it had. Yet, fractured, pulped, and now stung unto what should have been a lasting death, Saudi was already up and on the move again.

"Two and two together, Jordy," he involuntarily thought to himself. "Valkyries hold onto symbiotic Sangazurs in crystal skulls." Except, he hadn't exactly thought it to himself, had he? He especially hadn't thought it to himself in a woman's voice.

Someone was in the Ophidian with him!

========

He knew he was seriously losing it. Without devilish daddy's quill he supposed it was to be expected. Besides, in nearly 400 years of dying and coming back he had never, ever, died and come back on the same day. Today, well, he'd already lost track of how many times he'd died and come back.

Nevertheless, how could someone else be inside the Ophidian with him? Even if his offspring or their offspring's personality lingered – as they often did and had in the exceedingly upsetting case of the viperously virulent Saur Tsarina – his should be dominant. He was no symbiotic Sang. He was an Alpha Male.

"And I'm an Alpha Female," he thought to himself, once again not in his voice. "Plus, I was here first." He had her voice now. He still didn't have the how, however. Nor would he get it. Not right away anyhow.

"Do it, Volsanga," Ophidian Tethys loudly shouted in a female's voice. "And don't fuck up this time!"

Maybe she was distracted by the scrunching sounds Saudi's Terror Donna continued to make as it finished crunching her psycho-swan. More than likely she was moving too fast to do it right. She wasn't going to hang around long enough to get whacked her own endgame big-time. As good a Valkyrie as she was, she wasn't such a tiptop Hellion.

Toss it, drop a hellstone and get away between-space before Saudi got her. Those were both her thoughts and deeds. Whatever the excuse, Volsanga very definitely fucked up. Tethys wasn't there to hear his internal, female voice screech: "You idiot! Him, not me!"

========

Incinerate the little horror. Incinerate her powder puff power focus. Make it puff with smoke, not with excremental faeriedust. Make it cook, overcook, thoroughly burn it unto inedible crud. Why waste eyefire when you've a scorching bright, sun-circled labarum linked to Sedon's Peak?

    It belched infernal.

****

THEO 15:

FOODCHAIN OF FOOLS
========

For purposes primarily of self-security, the Pauper Priestess stayed inside misnamed Ginny the Gynosphinx. Safely therein, the Head's perpetually adult, female presence far-heard the perpetually childish, female presence shriek into their consequentially conjoined skull.

Maternal instincts thereupon took over.
========

Taurus Chrysaor Attis was in no position to do anything to prevent the She-Sphinx bucking to a halt and flipping him forward off her back. Fortunately, though airborne at the time, she hadn't been too far off the ground. Groggy as he still was, he landed professionally, rolled, and was on his feet in time to see All of Incain racing off into a veritable firestorm. For the first time it registered she had a tetrahedral head.

Also for the first time, at least for the first time since after he kissed the Medusa, he felt close to lucid. Whatever Pyrame Silverstar injected into him earlier in the day via her suddenly seemingly alive, cobra uraeus, it had to have been more than just a mild soporific. He'd been operating borderline mindlessly since recovering from its knockout effects so it was likely a will-sapping witch-toxin of some sort. Why Pyrame would resort to a potion instead of coercive eyefire, well, the haze hadn't cleared enough to let him think altogether straight yet.

Nonetheless, it was a familiar feeling. He experienced something similar, as if waking up in the midst of sleepwalking, every time he realized he was Chrysaor Attis. For some reason this didn't feel quite like that, though. He touched his chest then he touched his forehead. Correction, this didn't feel anything like that for a minimum of seven reasons.

He had a thought and it was there, around his neck, his bloodstone tiara, the Crimson Corona. He clenched the fingers of his left hand together and suddenly held the Susasword. He raised his right forearm and grinned as the Amateramirror appeared strapped to it. He had a number of additional thoughts, four of them, then he had them a few more times. The result was the same. Zilch! There were no discernible results.

His skin was golden-brown and the gash in his side was weeping again, but he was still next to naked, in a torn tunic and sandals alone. He'd lost Pyrame's ordinary woollen cloak somewhere and couldn't think Lazareme's shape-shifting Cloak of Many Colours back about himself. His face was skin, just skin. Where was the Mask of Byron, what allowed him to look like anyone he damn well pleased? Where was his javelin, what could be anything he wanted it to be? Where was his kibisis, with all it contained?

Now it was coming back to him. He'd regained a dopey approximation of consciousness on Apple Isle, Sedon's Human Eye-Isle. All must have carried him there whilst he was still out of it. He had the bottomless bag, but he was acting like one of Trawl the cyclopean Taskmaster's mainly manly marionettes, something that had happened to him too often in the past.

The Demon Child was there, on her three-headed chimera, which was how he knew it was Ap Isle since she seldom left it. A miniature version of the She-Sphinx was perched on her shoulder like a pet parrot. Tralalorn called him daddy, she always did. She wanted him to play ball with her. All squawked in protest. She didn't want him to play ball with either her or her chimera. She wanted him to deliver Mistress Pyrame's message to Trala.

"Deliver the mistress's message," All said to him, "Or All eat them," meaning the Demon Child and her faeriedust-transformed Keres hellhound. He delivered Pyrame's message, whatever it was. Then All ate him instead. "Mistress needs help. All help mistress."

It was back between-space for the both of them. All emerged ... where? Somewhere he'd died before? Couldn't be. All ate ... whom? Could it have been a black man and a white woman? Could be. He was losing it again. Maybe he'd landed harder than he'd reckoned.

All squeezed him out of her back. He was riding her when the She-Sphinx reemerged from the Weird. All threw someone up, a male Utopian. She threw up a couple of other things as well. His kibisis was one of them. That explained one-fourth of the mystery of the missing talismans. The other was an eye-stave. So it wasn't any ordinary Utopian. It was a Trinondev, a member of Weir's Warrior Elite. He was getting there.

They'd looked like he should have known them. He had. It was only somewhere like where he'd died before, inside a cosmicar. The other one he'd seen was

Kanin City's formidable Master, Helena Somata. Pyrame must have been occupying her. The apparent Trinondev was too young to be an actual Trinondev. He was her boy, though. Georgie was his name. His father's name was Jordan Tethys. Helena insisted he wasn't that Jordan Tethys. That must have been when All got all tetrahedral-headed on him.

Hold on! It couldn't have been Kanin's Master in the cosmicar. It had to have been just Pyrame, masquerading as her, otherwise the She-Sphinx would have thrown up Hel too. Not everything was coming back to him. It would. It always did, shortly after he'd had a fencing lesson, he recalled, even if it was just with a fencepost.

He'd had a bath or a dip in a stream. He'd look into a mirror or his reflection in the stream. He'd notice his balls had dropped. He'd notice, for the first time, he had a weeping wound in his side. He'd notice, usually also for the first time, he had golden-brown skin. He'd have a curved sword in his hand. P-shaped, it was a skinny falchion with a 'D' for its grip and an X-shape for its guard. He'd have a bloodstone necklace or an identical, ruby-red diadem around his forehead.

He'd step forward, into the mirror or the stream, only to discover he was elsewhere. Or else a Pegasus would gallop out of the Weird to retrieve him. One way or another he'd soon find himself wherever lay his kibisis, with all its talismanic goodies, his gains of gloriously single combat, still inside it. More often than not it was in the tomb of his predecessor's corpse.

His predecessor's corpse would be accoutered with the Thrygragos Talismans. He'd accouter himself with the Male Three, to go along with the Female Three, the mirror having reattached itself to his arm like a shield. He wouldn't recall he was Chrysaor Attis again. He'd have succeeded the previous Chrysaor Attis. He would be himself again.

Where was he? Sedon's Mole, he realized with a start. A firestorm, what's with a damn firestorm? The Utopians caused it, ably abetted by his half-father – not his Helios half-father, his Mithras half-father. Oh, no, he realized with even more of a start. He couldn't possibly know that any more than he could know where he was, not with such assuredness. What he'd long feared had at last come to pass. Without the Male Three to balance them, the Female Three were doing his thinking for him. Yep!

He reached for his whistle to summon Peg. Wait, right, he'd tossed away his kibisis, Whistler's whistle with it, back in devic daddy's Tholos tent. The Medusa had returned it, the bottomless bag. She told them, Pyrame and him, she'd given herself a Latin-sounding name that meant Mother Murder. Then he'd kissed her because her nonetheless gorgon-looking head wasn't glowing the way it had been when he cut it off her a couple of thousand years ago.

Maybe it was still in it, or on it, Whistler's whistle. No, he'd forgotten already. He didn't have it anymore, his kibisis. He didn't need a Brainrock whistle in order to whistle. He had lips, teeth and a tongue. He whistled. Zip, 100% of nil! It must be time to run. Run into a firestorm? If needs be – his half-father might need help.

He made to run. He ran straight into nothingness. Solid nothingness!

========

George Masterson knew he must look a fright.

========

He'd lost his turban somewhere. His just as indigo-dyed garment was rent nigh unto shreds and spattered with his own shit and sick. His face and thus exposed skin had to be covered with unsightly scrapes and the grossest of gouges. Although he could feel, in his last remaining pocket, his ever-so-ordinary recorder – as opposed to deviant daddy's ever-so-valuable Gypsium quill – he further knew he wouldn't be making it with any of the lovely ladies in his masterly mother's court anytime soon.

That was for sure. So was that he was young and would rapidly heal. He was alive and, he felt confident, so was she, his masterly mother, in a manner of speaking anyhow.

========

As psychotic and psychopomp gorged themselves on her physicality, Helena Somata sent out a psychic scream to Volsanga née Nibelung Tethys: "Jordy's in Saudi, Hellion. They're going to go after my Georgie. He's in my cosmicar but he's wearing an agate. That means Saudi can get to him as easily as we can.

"The Steg needs killing again and no snakehead can resist an Ant Nightingale. So here's what you'll do, here's what I'll do and, after all that, Jordy's all yours!"

========

Outer Earth annals went silent on Helena for many years after Constantius Chlorus divorced her, in 4289, in order to marry Theodora, the stepdaughter of Maximianus Herculius, Imperial Rome's Western Emperor at the time. The best the Tethys-deviant could find out about her when he left the Inner Earth to look for Lactantius's treatise was that she'd gone into a nunnery until son Constantine rehabilitated her circa 4306.

Constantine didn't declare her Augusta until 4324 and it wasn't until a couple of years later, just before her recorded death, that she acquired her perhaps spurious reputation as the discoverer of the True Cross of the Crucifixion. Nowhere could he find any reference to the fact Constantius Chlorus had impregnated her again prior to their separation. More than likely he never realized he had.

Even if he did he probably never got the opportunity to see their daughter because she was born and subsequently raised in the *'nunnery'* Helena supposedly went into after Chlorus ditched her. It wasn't a nunnery as such. It was an Anthean Shelter on the Inner Earth. Helena named her Constance presumably because Chlorus had proven far from constant.

Every Ant spent a minimum of 14 years being trained in their Shelters: seven as a girl, a novitiate, and seven as a mother, an Astarte. Only after graduation, as it were, could an Astarte legitimately consider herself an Anthean witch. Helena spent a lot longer than 14 years learning her craft, which was how she became such a tiptop Ant Nightingale. While most high-level witches, in most sisterhoods, learned how to utilize their soul-selves to energize psychopomps, they generally learned to do much more than just that with them.

One of their commonest tricks was trance sending, astral travelling or, as they sometimes glibly put it, going for a psychic walkabout. Nonetheless, only a very few could do what Kanin City's Master of Weir did when she bodily and, in a way, oppositely bit the big one. She transferred the essence of her being into her killer, Saudi's Terror Donna, as it chomped her corporeal self in half.

Maternal instincts thereupon took over. She didn't need to be a mind reader to realize Saudi would go after her son. She also didn't need a body to access Saudi's witch-stones, her glitz. As is, she could easily in effect step to Georgie as quickly as she could to, say, Volsanga's Jotan, Ute or Gordon, Hopi's Yeast, Sylvia's Woody and indeed all the perfidious polygamist's left living offspring she'd met, in retrospect not all that fortuitously, a week earlier at her 128th birthday party.

But what good would that do? Both Jordy and Saudi were obsessed with getting hold of Rumour's Brainrock quill. Even though they were acting two as one, their conflicting personalities were clearly still clashing for control of the psychotic Saur Tsarina's material being. Insinuating her soul-self between them, and thereby making it a three way psychic struggle, didn't strike her as a winning strategy. Saudi's soul-self, which was almost as strong as hers, was animating her Donna and Helena already sensed she couldn't overpower it.

Soul-sinks were obviously part of the solution. In preparation for this afternoon's anticipated bloodbath, the Valkyrie – whose eldest son became a member of Valhalla's marching band a few hours ago and whose only daughter was in love with Helena's last surviving son – would have stocked up a surfeit of crystal skull soul-sinks. But, as near as Helena could be sure of anyhow, they only worked when a soul was in transition. Ergo she had to find a way to get Jordy's soul-self on the move again.

An Ophidian scorpion would do the trick and she knew just the one, another of the degenerate Legendarian's once lovingly devoted wives, his thereupon callously discarded dishrags. The real trick was getting them in the same place, and at the same time, as swiftly as yesterday. More realistically, and far more importantly, she had to get them together before her Georgie became second course to his mother's first course.

That was something else Volsanga, with her psycho-swan, could facilitate.

========

Gypsies, minstrels or gleemen – thespians, jugglers, puppeteers, poets, raconteurs, fortunetellers, instrumentalists, singers, dancers and suchlike performers – came by the Weirdom regularly. They put on everything from impromptu street theatre to full-blown pageants in order to earn their meals, their drinks and, for those that didn't bring their own tents or caravans with them, their lodgings.

Georgie often pulled out his recorder and played with the musicians amongst them late into the night. Since he gambolled rather than gambled, for the most part this suited Helena fine. Occasionally, however, some of the more rootless wanderers turned out to be entirely unsavoury characters. One in particular, a hairless, ever-grinning, pinkish-skinned sybarite from Apple Isle, so alarmed Helena she forbade Georgie seeing him anymore.

But Bad Rhad, as she referred to him, might well have been a misguided angel, of the non-fallen variety, compared to the Steg. A reptilian Sari from the Flood Lands, Saudi wasn't just a cold-blooded witch. She was a cold-hearted killer.

At first Helena felt sorry for her. For one thing, the young Saur Tsarina was the only member of the company Georgie brought to Kanin City, in order to perform at her party, without a mother in tow. As she discovered, once they got to talking, and the Steg got to single-handedly polishing off the sumptuous spread Helena's culinary specialists laid on, Saudi's mother had been munched, unseasoned, by a pterodactyl that, courtesy of selfsame Saudi, didn't live long enough to finish her as its last meal.

Given her saurian size, the Steg was definitely not a delicate tap-dancer. Her contribution to the ensemble was mainly as a foot-stomping, tail-thumping, rabble-rousing, get-the-people-moving enthusiast. She had a strong sense of rhythm, however. Very little of Saudi wasn't strong, including her odour. Her mother only partially devoured, Saudi had pounded the pterodactyl unto a Terror Donna prior to, as was traditional amongst Saurs, chowing down on the rest of mom herself.

Although she'd been forced to kill her own daughter 40 years earlier to get at the Attis's then succession, being at heart a life-loving Ant Nightingale Helena wasn't sure she approved of the pounding unto Donna-Dom Come. She did approve of the Valkyrie Volsanga's proposal to put an end to the deviant polygamist's prospects for ruining the lives of any more women, however.

So did Durga, the now no doubt doubly dead lutanist's mother, she whose kingly sire was named after a Mithradite Death God, Underlord Yama Nergal. Getting into the spirit of the enterprise, the Rajput Princess passionately lobbied to do unto Jordy what Kore-Coueranna had so often done to Chrysaor Attis in the distant past. She still had her father's recipe for roasted pee-nuts, as she unappetizingly put it.

Like most Mithrant praetors or adjudicators in neighbouring territories, Helena drew the line at mutilation. However, she agreed to put, in order, arrest, detention, an unbiased trial, a humanely executed sentence and duly sinking his soul onto Jordy's dance card.

The last two were very much unlike Mithrant judges, whose devic overlords, for fear of losing potential worshippers, forbade them imposing capital punishment, or even enslavement, upon those they found guilty of anything. They were very much unlike Utopians as well but Jordy's deviancy was so unique, and his crimes so despicable, needs be exceptions had to be made.

Although none of them knew where he'd got to, his alcoholic addiction to Hopi's pilsners would bring him to her booze-tent's doorstep sooner than later. It was simply a shame the young Steg, the middle-aged Valkyrie and the centenarian Master were the only witches at her party. Very much inopportunely that meant far-speaking might prove a problem if the Tethys-deviant didn't show up before the various encampments over in the Mole broke up at the conclusion of Thrygragon, howsoever it ended.

Helena offered to assign Warriors of Weir to the women and their Tethys-offspring. However, Trinondevs being considered unwelcome interlopers throughout most of the devil-worshipping Head, that idea was nixed. As a compromise she supplied them with Anthean Agates such that, after some cursory training, they could keep in touch with her. As an ancillary benefit, as soon as she far-heard he was with whomever, wherever, she could step between-space and, Master's Mace in hand, nail the pernicious philanderer in a thought-balloon.

Cursory was a curse. Their compromise had a fatal flaw.

========

That morning Sylvia, the deadly dryad, skipped everything except the execution aspect of Tethys's sentencing. The virtually simultaneous, and therefore twice-over tragic, demise of the Valkyrie's hornpipe-playing son precluded sinking his soul in the dryad's acorn of a nut-ball.

Only minutes after Jotan's 'resurrection', Helena was long-distance castigating Volsanga via witch-stone for wasting a crystal skull. "Soul-sinks work both ways. You should have taken out Jordy before you sank the Sang in Jot."

"I was getting to that, Master," the Valkyrie snapped right back at her. "You've got to break an egg to make an omelette and I had to re-kill him before I could crack the egg-skull on his egg-noggin. Yet another Tethys-bastard must have died at almost the same time because his spirit already wasn't around anymore."

"Another one? Goddamn Jordy to hellfire everlasting! His deviant blood must have some kind of cross-body trigger to it. He dies, his next-in-line must start dying."

As she knew from subsequent communication with Hopi, the Lizarado Mrs Tethys – not that they were officially married – and Durga, that wasn't true. Or, if it was, that wasn't all of it.

On the surface of it, his fellow Mithrants beat Volsanga's Jotan to death with his own hornpipe for, having just lost his bellicose azura to the She-Sphinx, seeking to flee the battlefield before it became blood-soaked. As for the next Tethys to die, Hopi's Yeast, Saudi knocked him down only to have Pusan Wanderlust help raise him up again. The Lizarado Tethys's distraught mother told Helena that Saudi was also responsible for initially killing the alligator-didgeridoo player, whereas her very own Georgie accounted for Saudi's first, by then inexcusably overdue payback.

As for Durga's son, in whichever order he died Ravi couldn't be considered next in line in terms of predestination so much as overindulgence. The multi-stringed lutanist had partied too heartily, with the Fire Kings' over-proof firewater as fuel, the night before. It just took until the next day for it to prove lethal. Tethys-deviants should always stick to beer.

Whatever the prince's failings as a Rajput teetotaller, neither his failings nor Saudi's tail flailing could be blamed for his second death. Durga had reported her son's first one, and his corpse's ensuing disappearance, just prior to Pyrame's appearance in her dayroom. That made it about the same time Saudi would have been going after Georgie in the vicinity of the Mithrants' Praetorium.

Which suggested Saudi didn't know boo about either of Ravi's deaths. Of course he could have been a victim of body snatchers. Still, no matter how he died the second time, assuming he had, Saudi bashing Yeast in his mother's booze-tent should have instantly alerted Helena as to the appropriately poetic defect in their very much non-Antlike pursuit of retribution in the name of jilted womanhood.

Tagging the dastard's bastards polluting Sedon's Mole with witch-stones would have made perfect sense except for one thing. Anthean Agates were for all intents and purposes identical to a Hellion's hellstones, a Korant's kernels, an Afrite's Love Beads or a Sari's glittery bits, their glitz. Any decently trained witch could get about on any other witch's witch-stones and, as Helena now very much regretted, one witch probably never had any intention of using them just for far-speaking.

Although the Steg admitted stomping the pterosaur she now rode to death after it killed her Sari of a mother, Helena had severely misjudged Saudi's resultant psychoses. Blinded by her own sense of betrayal, she'd also forgotten – or neglected to remember – that, when it came to Sari witches, there was very little debate about which was a more determinant factor in how they developed: nature or nurture. Hellions, Amazons and Athenans were killer witches, too, but Saris would eat their fellow sentient beings just because they were hungry.

On top of all of the above, Helena had learned that Saudi and her vengeance-seeking mother, prior to her death, knew from the Korants' current Miracle Maenad that Miracle's son might have been Saudi's sperm-father. Furthermore, if so, that made him an incarnation of the legendary 30-Year Man.

Both already recognized the value of a devil's power focus and, purely by nature, Saurs had absolutely no reservations when it came to fratricide. Upon enforced reflection, Yeast's brutal brush with death indicated Saudi's sense of sibling appreciation extended only to which one would make the better aperitif.

So, yes, Helena had proven herself as much a fool as any of the pureblood Utopians she'd so disparaged to Pyrame Silverstar mere minutes back; as any of the inbred imbeciles living up north in the Weirdom of Cabalarkon, Sedon's Devic Eye-Land. She should have far-spoken to everyone she'd given an agate to and ordered them to dispose of it right away.

She hadn't, though, and for her it wasn't a question of living with the consequences anymore. Seconds ago, it was a question of dealing with them as best she could without a body. Now, it wasn't a question of doing much of anything except manfully striving to remain at least semi-conscious. She was losing that fight too. The void beckoned.

Fuck-ups do tend to beget fuck-ups. The Ophidian Mrs Tethys she had in mind couldn't get about the Weird without assistance and Helena had tagged her daughter the same as she had too many others. Volsanga must have figured any scorpioid snakehead would do and brought the Tethys-brat, not her mom, here because the former was the closest. Either that or, no matter what their age, Ophidians all looked the same to her.

At least, she mentally consoled herself, now it'll be up to the Valkyrie to break the news of her daughter's demise to her mother. Helena figured that, if Volsanga were smart, she'd find a way to send Saudi to break the news. With a Sang animating her the Steg would be hard to dispose of, but Ophidians were known for feeding in packs.

Add in her Terror Donna and they could invite an entire village to the feast.

========

Georgie didn't need to be paying attention in classes taught by Illuminaries, nor any elderly Trinondev, to learn how to traverse the Weird from place to specific place.

========

He'd been riding Hinny long enough to understand that visualizing then going there was how you did it by psychopomp. With the only maybe exception of Rumour's Tvasitar-trinket, that was probably how you did it via any other power focus,
witch stepping-stone or anything else you cared to think of as well.

Spurring her between-space – especially when you were still mostly concentrating on maintaining the brain-ball you'd thought out of your eye-stave in order
to protectively encase her and you against a Terror Donna – may not have been the
wisest way to go. It did kind of leave the onus of destination on your dumb-as-they-
come psycho.

Given the involuntary rebellion of his belly, in both directions, Hinny was now
as smelly as she was ugly. But she shouldn't have been so stupid. It wasn't that she'd
brought them out in the middle of a raging forest fire that concerned him. It was that
she'd brought them out in the middle of a raging forest fire in front of the Attis. Worse,
she'd thereupon butted him onto his golden-brown behind.

The last time they'd come across Mithras's Universal Soldier he'd wanted to ham-
burger Hinny unto horsemeat. Which was awfully rude considering she already was
half a Pegasus-pony, half of Attis's own Peg of a pony, now a fully-grown stallion. Evidently she was that stupid, though. Now he'd have to kill him.

In that respect it'd be like son, like mother, wouldn't it?

========

Something came out of the Weird. It wasn't his Pegasus. It was his Peg's hinny. That's what knocked him down. Someone was riding the hippo-hind. It was All's
puke. He recognized him right away. They'd met, been properly introduced by the
boy's mother, Helena Somata, the oft-times tiresome, long reigning Master of the
Weirdom of nearby Kanin City.

As if tit-for-tat killing him 40 years ago wasn't enough, Helena ruthlessly played
on whatever vestigial guilt he might have that she had to victimize her beloved Constance in order to get at him, the Attis who'd begun life as her grandson Christian.
She'd managed to prevail upon him to stud out his Pegasus, when he was still a Peg-
pony, to the hippo-hind's mother, an equally immature ravendeer she'd brought over
from the Cattail's Whiplash Range.

Once he saw the results – a feathered, crow-headed, but otherwise hinny-like
ungulate, one with diminutive wings that didn't flap sprouting out of its back and
similarly stunted wings on both sides of its upper hooves – he wanted to put the poor
beast out of its misery. Georgie, who'd formed a baffling affection for the sad-sack
freak, refused to hear it. Even though she called the bond they'd forged 'weird', to use
her word, Hel naturally took her son's side.

When Attis insisted, she banished him from Kanin, which was an improvement
on assassinating him. Then, hardly for the first time, she cut off the tribute she'd been
paying the Mithrant Brotherhood to guarantee his legions kept giving their Weirdom
a wide berth. They'd parted as enemies the last time they'd met, months ago now, and
the airless mind-globe Georgie had just enclosed him inside of indicated nothing had
changed. Plus, the aspiring Trinondev had his until then missing kibisis.

None of this could be an accident. Trinondevs were born and bred to hate devils. Ostensibly – circa 2000 YD, not long before he was born – the daemonic minions of devil-hating Hellions duped Tvasitar Smithmonger into dedicating the Female Three to the Trigregos Sisters. The second generational Great Goddesses' devic offspring were born and bred to obey their fathers rather than them, so they hated devils too.

Having somehow got hold of his bottomless bag, with all his remaining spoils inside it – for the most part, he expected since Mithras's Hundred had re-solidified before Pyrame asp-bit him asleep, devic talismans he'd taken off Byronics and Laza-remists – Hel's lad was trying to usurp his control over the Female Three.

Once Georgie had them he'd use them against Mithras, wouldn't he? Thinking for himself again, now that he had everything figured out to his crude satisfaction, Attis reckoned he couldn't allow that.

He further supposed he'd have to kill him.

========

Jordan Tethys wasn't there to hear his internal, female voice scream: "You idiot! Him, not me!" Neither was he there when the crystal skull re-formed, Master Helena Somata's soul-self trapped inside it. He was an Acorn Ant, one Wooden Tethys by name. Unques-tionably unfortunately his quill hadn't come back to him this time either.

Maybe it would the next time. He wouldn't have to wait long to find out. His dry-ad daughter had burst into flame. So had most of the nearby Mole.

========

Symbiotic Sangazur-possessed, her decidedly nasty disposition thereby incon-testably restored, Steg Saudi had smacked him, her or just plain Ophidian-Tethys slain again. She kicked the body. It didn't move. She wouldn't have time to eat it. This part of Sedon's Cheek was burning and it wasn't from embarrassment.

George Masterson might have Rumour's quill. Thanks to that eye-stave of his he'd twice managed to prevent her and the Donna killing him. He'd be on guard against her now but there were loads of agate-tagged Tethys-bastards left to smash. Smash enough of them and Rumour's quill would reappear, of that she felt confident.

During the Middle Sea matriarchate of ages long gone, the three Furious Sis-ters – Alecto, Megaera and Tisiphone, as not just Illuminaries had them – served their much higher born Mithradite sisters as avengers of crimes against women left other-wise unpunished. Saudi reckoned she'd redefined herself as a one-woman Steg Fury.

The Sang having beaten him to it, meaning he couldn't get back into her, wip-ing out any trace of the Jordan Tethys deviant had become her fortune to fulfill.

========

"I doubt you can hear me, Jordy, but I've been expecting you. So has Woody. Other-wise we wouldn't have grown up in the middle of a firestorm. Do you know what else we can do with our acorns? Let me put it this way: Even if you don't know much of anything anymore, consider yourself well and truly soul sunk!"

========

After their meeting with the Korants' High Priestess, Miracle Maenad, but be-fore the pterosaur that was now her daughter's Terror Donna bit her deceased, Saudi's mother squatted her down and spoke of her father, the legendary 30-Year Man. As a result of their tête-à-tête Saudi knew there was no point going after either Ute or Glee Tethys, Volsanga's teenagers, because the Tethys-deviant couldn't come back in any of his children or grandchildren until they'd turned a minimum of 20.

That peculiarity of her father's deviancy actually benefited Saudi, in terms of knowing who to smash next, for the simple reason that there weren't too many Tethys bastards over 20 left in the Mole. As luck would have it the first one she went to was already firewood. Rather, Woody had been firewood. Now she was mostly charcoal. Sylvia, the deadly dryad, who'd proven far more fire-resistant, loomed over her remains in full quercine mode. Oddly, she seemed elated.

Saudi found it difficult talking to an oak tree. What Sylvia said to her was even harder to stomach. All the more so since even Stegs didn't eat oaks.

========

Belching infernal done, Thrygragos Varuna Mithras waited for the resultant steam and smoke to clear. Finally he could smile again, though not as broadly as he might like. Her Keres Chimera was a thoroughly crispy critter, but the Demon Child yet twitched.

Her ball, her White Dwarf, lay there beside her, as always reeking and roiling as it flashed faces. That was the main reason he couldn't bring himself to smile as broadly as he'd like. Every one of its outwards-then-back-inwards, self-kneading features seemed to be smiling the smile he denied himself.

========

Instinctive alarm bells suddenly ringing alerted his Hugeness just in time. He looked out, way out. The still tetrahedral-headed She-Sphinx was racing through the firestorm he and the Trinondevs combined to cause. Better and better! Thanks in large measure to his many information-sharing sessions with the deviant Legendarian, he'd prepared for every eventuality. Once again his labarum burped volcanic, Brainrock volcanic, Sedon's Peak volcanic!

Sedon's Peak had been erupting since long before the Moloch named it in the aftermath of Ragnarok. It had been erupting since long before Old Eden sank into the Atlantic Ocean and its consequently submersed part of the planet resulted in the Sargasso Sea. Brainrock – the ineffable, there lava-liquid-leftover of the Big Bang's Godhead – bubbled in the Peak's caldera non-stop. Almost as miraculously, aka Gypsium-Godstuff replenished itself when it erupted.

Stopstone – Solidium, as the Dual Entities had it – was Brainrock's neutralizing agent. Stopstone was Mother Earth's excretion: the oily, chthonic crud that made up demons, faeries, nearly all of All's Mandroid monstrosities, and much of All itself/herself. Chthonic creatures were Nature's response to extraterrestrial devils. Truth told, as Helena's soul-self said to Jordy's soul-self inside Ophidian-Tethys, they were here first.

What worked one way worked the other. Having more of one usually determined which one won and Sedon's Peak held way more Brainrock than even All did Stopstone.

========

If you didn't have to, never trust Gypsium, especially not when you're in the air.

========

The Attis had learned that the hard, hurtful way. It'd turn on you like a weasel with a snake's fangs. The gods cursed Godstuff had a mind of its own. Today, though, he had no choice except to trust it.

One slash of the Susasword and he was out of George Masterson's suffocating mind-globe. Another slash and he'd sliced the ambitious boy's eye-stave in two. A third slash he would have cleaved cleanly through both Georgie and his hindy-pomp. Instead, using the mirrored shield strapped to his right arm like a punishment-paddle for naughty boys, he swatted Masterson off his hinny and onto his hind-end. Then he grabbed his kibisis.

Maybe he did feel a twinge of remorse about what happened to Hel's Constance and her Attis of a Christian once they went off to the wars. Or maybe it was more a matter of a Universal Soldier not wanting to sully his reputation by dicing a disarmed youth. It could be the Taurus had a devic half-father to save. It could equally be he had a devic half-father to slay. Mostly it was his resolve to start doing his own thinking again.

Holding what Georgie mistook for a solitary saddlebag in his right hand, he thereupon slashed a gash in the air itself and leapt through it.

========

His Hugeness obliterated tetrahedral-headed All.

========

Thrygragos Varuna Mithras hoped he'd roasted her out of existence, Sedon's Whore along with Ginny the Gynosphinx, but he doubted it. One day can contain only so many good things. Intent upon doing to her what Kronos always did to his children, he bent to pick up the Demon Child's twitching remains. With a couple of hundred extra devils and a few thousand excess azuras to nourish, he was having a snack attack.

Holding his labarum in his left hand he reached for her with his right. The right arm of God the now Singular, Ever Triumphant, promptly fell off. Truth, Light and Justice hadn't expected that. He recoiled. He supposed he should be shrieking in immortal agony, but he felt fine. Better than fine, he felt brilliant. He nevertheless shook reflexively. It was no wonder Mithras felt fine. His right arm was still attached. He shook it again just to be sure. He was brilliant.

An illusion? Some ignorant, now invisible, tetrahedral-headed, famously female Perpetual Presence's last gasp attempt to salvage her brood sister, unless Tralalorn was her daughter, and thereby attempt to wreck his big day? He didn't see how it could be the Whore, but someone was definitely playing silly buggers.

Somewhere in the back of his mind he knew who it was, who it had to be. He just couldn't put his mental finger on a name or a face quite yet. The letter 'D', scratched into a tabletop at an angle of 90 degrees clockwise, with pronounced horns and grinning ever-so-gleefully, lodged briefly in the front of this mind. It dislodged just as suddenly.

His faux arm rooted, fingers first, in the slag he'd made of his sons and daughters' de-brained demonic bodies. They became its legs. Two, the thumb and pinkie, were its back legs. The middle three fingers were its front legs. The palm was its underbelly. The back of the hand was its back. Crane or giraffe like, from the wrist up the rest of the Whole Earth's newest Demogorgon grew out of the Great God's apparently dropped-off arm, grew as enormous as the disbelieving Great God.

Its demonic skin was simultaneously leathern and speckled scaly, akin to both a multi-hued elephant's trunk and the celebrated world serpent itself. The shoulder ball at the upper end of its humerus was orb-like, analogous to a closed flower bud. It bloomed. Its petals were finger-like, worm-like and cilia-like all at the same time. Rounded pinhead nodules were at their tips. The ovule in their centre developed a solitary, pinkish face with three eyes.

It was smiling.

========

"Hello, brother. I hope you're well-fed because I'm famished."
Mithras's snack attack had just become a sneak attack.
****

THEO 16:

THE OUTSTRETCHED GRASPING FINGERS

========

Eyefire interspersed with fecal faeriedust erupted from its head. Faeriedust-interspersed eyefire reflected straight back at the Daemonicus-Demogorgon.

========

The abomination started to harden, petrify, just as both Mandroid sphinxes might have done more than 700 years Pre-Dome, though probably not due to the same cause. Thrygragos Varuna Mithras had pulled off of a variation of the Attis-Perseus myth: the one wherein Medusa looks into his mirrored shield and her own reflection turns her to stone before Perseus lops off her head.

"Mask of Byron, you afterbirth asshole!" the by now thoroughly stressed Great God roared, his mental finger having belatedly identified the arm-thing's animus from their two brief encounters that morning. "I want it to have mirrored eyeballs, it has mirrored eyeballs. You burn too!"

Thunk! Thunk! Clumps of thunks! More, many more! A multiplicity of thunks!

Mithras suddenly started having trouble concentrating on his labarum. Its rotating sun disk sputtered sparks, no longer disgorging Brainrock magma. Pain, that's what disrupted his attentiveness. Pain assaulted him. At least he assumed it was pain. Great Gods weren't known for suffering pain. Great Gods weren't known for suffering, period. Whatever it was, he didn't like it.

The rounded pinheads at the tips of the Daemonicus-Demogorgon's vermicular petals gained faces. Through the one-way lenses of the Mask's three eyeholes his

Hugeness recognized every one of the heads just as they began blazing eyefire not interspersed with faeriedust at him. Not all were reminiscent of his highest born, the ones who hadn't come into him. His brothers' highest born were represented too. They'd gone into the Chrysanthemum concretion, not him.

Did they realize they each had bands of crimson gemstones circled around their foreheads? Could they do anything about it if they did?

There was something else about the pain sensation, could be it was its cause. His Hugeness wasn't just being pinhead-scorched. He'd been pin-cushioned. Hundreds of curved Brainrock blades were sticking into him, up and down his 30-foot immensity. Samarandin acupuncture needles, stinging nettles, thorns, porcupine quills, he'd seen them all. These didn't look like any of them. They did, however, look the same.

He realized what they were: the Susasword's blade many times multiplied and ejected into him, multiplied many times anew and ejected the more, also into him. That was where all the Brainrock had gone. Somehow the Trigregos Talismans had commandeered his Gypsium-Godstuff; made it their own. Only his brothers' talismans protected him. Did that mean his brothers were protecting him? If so, where were they? And why?

Parsing hastily, he deduced his time quake destroying the power focus of Lazareme's Anthea did not destroy the Trigregos Talismans inside it, which no one except the Attis dared touch because not just devils found them both spiritually and corporeally corruptive. They were moderately older than the Thrygragos Talismans after all. Unless, that is, Attis's kibisis wasn't a devic power focus; unless it was, as the Legendarian sometimes speculated, just an ordinary bottomless bag, possibly even one belonging to Xuthros Hor's Anthea originally.

Or, and this struck Mithras as more likely, the traitor Attis realized he was no match for his father now that he'd given up the Thrygragos Talismans. Consequently, with Sedon's Whore, Pyrame Silverstar, in All of Incain attending to interspatial transportation, he fled the Praetorium, taking whomever's bag and all it contained, including Demogorgon's head, to temporary refuge on Apple Isle. There, knowing the Moloch Sedon had declared her untouchable; he passed on the latter to Tralalorn and sent her back here to find Daemonicus in order for the chthonic excretion to make its play.

Since Ap Isle – at maybe a thousand miles from the Mole, maybe more – was probably beyond the range of his Kronos Quake, Attis only had to wait until its effect was dissipating outwards. Once he'd determined that, with far-sight granted to him by the invidious Corona, he'd returned, as if into the calm eye of a hurricane, his remaining goods and glories intact.

If Tralalorn, All, Pyrame, Daemonicus and everything else failed, which they had, he'd strike himself, which he just had. Rather, which they just had, they being the Trigregos Talismans.

========

"You don't know anything about dryads, do you?" Sylvia Tethys said to Saudi Tethys.

"I know you're fucking faeries. And I know female faeries, dryads being an exception, rarely conceive because their children suck the life out of them when they breastfeed."

"Then you know that's why we entice mortals to our knolls, so they can have our children. But, do you know what happens when we sprinkle the ashes of a dead faerie over a live non-faerie?"

"You live anew. You're telling me Woody will stilt-dance again?"

"That I am. Want a shower?"

========

Irrelevant, stop this mind-mincing insanity instantly! Ongoing trauma impaired even until-then impeccable judgement deleteriously. Idle conjecture counter-produced pitiless doom. Reflective, Apollonian reasoning required time and even he, in his aspect of Saturn-Kronos, didn't have that luxury. Reflexive, Dionysian decisiveness's what's demanded. Without it, Thrygragon was becoming precariously close to gone, gone him.

He could feel himself diminishing. Soon he'd shrink to a size whereby he could be fully reflected within the Amateramirror. Then he'd be in it. Then it would shatter into so many shards he could never be pieced together again. No way, any of it; no way, any of you! Sedon curse you all to the Celestials' Hell and, if he's behind it, which he had to be, then Sedon be cursed as well.

Attis had to be somewhere nearby. The thrice-cursed Godly Glories had turned him, his lone mortal, self-succeeding son, against him. Didn't the pinheads realize they'd turn against them as well? Given half a chance, were they as obstinately self-preservative as he was? There was only one way to find out.

Desperate thoughts breed dangerous measures. He expelled devils. He expelled unused azuras. Not content to allow its effects continue to dissipate uselessly over space, let alone over time, and thereafter see what happened, he consciously reversed his Kronos Quake. Weakening as he was by the millisecond, his strength of mind might not have been up to reversing anything. However, returning them their freewill did wonders for the devils inside him.

The incinerated slag at Mithras's feet did not fill out. Instead, because there was so much Brainrock vapour in the air, collapsed masses of Sinistral Lust's accordingly de-brained demons did fill out. In effect they were re-brained, albeit with vastly superior devic rather than demonic intelligence. Familiar, easily-identifiable shapes belonging to many of those who'd merged with him began to re-form all over the scorched, still smouldering and, in some places, notably the closest woods, still burning battlefield.

Inspired by their junior siblings and cousins, those who'd voluntarily taken themselves inside the Daemonicus-Demogorgon, instead of him, speedily followed suit. Abandoned by its composite rats, the petrified enormity of the abominable arm-thing cracked and crumbled. Chunks of it fell off. Some of it struck him. Almost in relief Mithras allowed himself a frivolous whimsy. Maybe he should shake his labarum into an umbrella.

Beguiling Belialma – Lady Lust, Kore-Concupiscence, or Coitus, and Satanwyck's reigning Prime Sinistral – she and her fellow devils, from all three tribes, re-embodied themselves. That didn't automatically render them devil-gods again. Hell's Belle's thus reconstituted chthonic crud could only provide them with a superficial recovery from their ordeal. Without power foci their reformative wonderfulness was worthless. Stopstone wasn't Brainrock.

The Trigregos Talismans weren't done with them yet either. The highest born, the ones who'd come out of the Many Fingered Thing, had Crimson Coronas on their foreheads or around their necks. The rest, the ones who came out of him, had Susasword blades sticking out of them. They were poisoning them just as assuredly as they'd been poisoning him.

The Godstuff the Dual Entities called Gypsium had often been described as not so much unknown as unknowable. About the best that could be said for their future was far too many devils had re-embodied to reflect in the Amateramirror, wherever Attis had it hidden. Fortunately, for devakind, ineffability did not bring about infallibility.

The incomparable Harmony took the lead. She grabbed hold of the diadem choking her. Perhaps to her shock, but no doubt to her delight, she mindfully transformed it into her golden torc, her power focus. As dot does, her immediate brood brothers, Chaos and Order, did ditto. So did the other four firstborns, Byron's Silverclouds and his own Thanatoids. The result was the same as well. They willed their Tvasitar Talismans completely restored.

There were certain laws even Lazaremist Master Devas had to obey and one of them had to do with the conservation of matter. Brainrock and Stopstone were mutable; so was their commingled form, Brainstone or Stoprock. Much of their mass could contort unrecognizably or mesh imperceptibly, and indeed impalpably, between-space. But they couldn't be destroyed as such.

Form might disintegrate, but what composed it would still be around in one state or another: heat, radiation, vapour, et cetera. Evidently, given enough devic willpower, what once composed something could recompose it.

Almost as quick on the uptake, the dozens upon dozens who'd come out of him skewered, gripped the blades piercing them and, presto, they too regained their power foci. Together, the again wholly godlike devils did what Mithras hoped they would. They attacked Demogorgon in unison. He left them to it. He'd spotted his deviant son, the Universal Soldier, the golden-brown warrior, emerging from a slash in the air between-space not far away.

Wearing only the sandals and tunic he'd had on when he left his Tholos-shaped pavilion such a short, but eventfully long time ago, Attis nevertheless was armed and, in a peculiarly detached, possibly demented manner, appeared ready to rumble. He even had his kibisis slung over his right shoulder. Since he looked too glassy eyed to have willed anything reintegrated, its presence essentially confirmed the notion Mithras had had that his Kronos Quake never affected it.

Presumably everything his Hundred hadn't claimed remained inside it. The Female Three were all that really mattered, though. Attis had the Crimson Corona about his head. Attis had the Amateramirror attached to his right arm. Attis wielded the Susasword. To the last Great God there was no question he looked so dazed on his feet because the malefic, male-hating ghosts of the Trigregos Sisters had entranced him, possibly irrevocably.

Mithras still held his labarum, cross or, ha-ha, crutch. He still wore the Mask of Byron and Lazareme's Cloak of Many Colours. "You want a Theomachy, sisters?" he challenged his son as if he was challenging them. "You got a Theomachy!"

Thrygragon was just getting going.

========

"I'm not alive," Saudi Tethys said to Sylvia Tethys. "I'm Sangazur-animated."

"Are you? Hmm. You know anything about Acorn Ants?"

"They're Druidess witches from Lazareme's Land of Daybreak. You're no witch."

"Ah, but I am. Rather, faeries don't need training to become witches. We're natural born tricksters. And our acorns aren't just stepping-stones. They double as soul sinks. I've Jordy, Saudi. I soul-sank him. He can't get out unless I release him."

Stegs didn't eat oak trees but they could smash them unto toothpicks with their pi-ton-fletched tails. They could smash open their acorns as well.

========

Compelled by the Crimson Corona, Taurus Chrysaor Attis raised the Susasword and rushed his devic half-father. Masked and cloaked in his thought-brothers' talismans, Thrygragos Varuna Mithras repelled him almost effortlessly, as a wall would a ball.

Awkwardly crablike, albeit belly upwards and backwards, instead of belly down-wards and sideways, Attis scuttled along the mucky ground away from the devil he called his father. Because he kept the Amateramirror upraised as best he could in or-der to shield himself, and because he wouldn't let go of the Susasword, he could only use his feet and left elbow to propel himself. As a result his kibisis slipped off his right shoulder. It was the least of his worries.

Ten feet away, his kibisis between them, he sprang up and assumed a defensive position. He prominently rested the Susasword against the edge of his mirrored shield, pointing invitingly forward, a shish awaiting a kebab. With the Corona ringing his head, he hunched behind them offering as minute a target as he could.

"Any more bright ideas?" he muttered to himself.

The answer was a no-brainer. Rather, it was partially brainier in that it required a consolidated measure of willpower. Diminished as he was, Mithras loomed large-ly before him; too largely to be altogether reflected in the Amateramirror's surface. Nonetheless, it could still capture partial reflections.

Unfortunately all it captured was part of an illusion; an illusion that spoke.

========

Cobwebs clogging the old brainpan, little frilly stars jittering in front of the eyeballs, and the addition of more bruises than he could shake a broken eye-stave at, these too would pass. George Masterson spat blood and, after some exploratory fingering, yanked out his upper two front teeth. These he pocketed, hoping they'd stay pocketed. Some of Kanin's sci-entocrats practised dentistry.

He felt especially happy his recorder hadn't speared his kidney. Only his mother could transcend death. The impact of his landing back and butt-first in the no matter how soft and squishy mire had snapped it in half. In lieu of standing up, lest the cutesy stars developed cutting edges, he pulled it out of his lone non-torn pocket. Both halves were glowing.

"How odd is that, Hinny?" he asked his hippo-hind.

Even more happily, she just looked at him dumbly. Had she not been at a loss for words, as always, that would have been truly odd.

========

With reintegrated power foci transformed, where necessary, and suitably sharpened, they hacked at the arm-thing mercilessly. They roasted the Daemonicus-Demogorgon with burn-anything eyefire. So much Brainrock, so much devic energy, funnelled into the abomination its petaliferous head blew off its arm-crane as if a fireworks cannonade from the hollowed-out tube of a bamboo rocket launcher.

Preoccupied with what was in front of him – his deviant son armed and bedevilled by the Trigregos Talismans as he was – Mithras wasn't paying attention to what was going on behind him. He heard it, though. Even between-space it was hard not to hear such a thunderous ka-boom.

He briefly entertained the notion of moving his third eye to the back of his skull, which some devils did when they were feeling playful, but immediately dismissed that as daft. His own survival was at stake. Frivolity could wait. Besides, it would have taken too much time to get it right. He chanced a glance instead.

It was too bad it hadn't taken them longer to dispose of the latest Demogorgon. Not a problem. He'd won Thrygragon. His brothers were gone, gone, gone. Regardless of any lingering reticence on their part, third generational Master Devas from all three tribes would be swearing eternal obeisance to him momentarily. He wasn't going to let any one or any things, especially not this pup, thwart him now.

He cremated Sedon's Demon Child, Tralalorn. He melted her chimera unto a candelabrum. He obliterated the Gynosphinx, Pyrame Silverstar inside it, from the Head's facial blotch of Sedon's Mole. He froze the Many Fingered Thing for final filleting. From firsthand experience with the Cousins 2,500 years earlier, as well as from stories told to him ad nauseam by 30-Beers and any number of successions of the Attis himself, he reckoned he knew everything the Female Three could do.

His illusionary self was there visibly, endlessly replenishing itself just because it pleased him to rub figurative salt into the once devoted deviant's wounds before he had to inflict any fatally. His non-illusionary self was there too, invisibly within the nowhere that was the everywhere of Samsara, the Universal Substance. His voice could have come from anywhere. He made it sound like it came from right there, 10 feet in front of the Attis. It wasn't, but it was as if it was coming from him, alternately blipping brighter then duller much as Lazareme had before he blipped entirely out of sight.

He thereby made it a tantalizing target for any backstabbers who might have designs on his henotheistic, top god destiny, especially his Virgin or her Tantal. He made illusions, but he wasn't under any. He trusted they weren't either. Their reprieve required relinquishment of their right to recidivism. In only ticks of time, a second Kronos Quake could follow the first so fast that, if it could affect biological beings, which it couldn't, newborns would revert to the unborn.

"Enough, I say. Those ungodly things have driven you as mad or madder than any of the mad goddesses that so plagued you so long ago. Yet, even with them on, you're no match for me. Show me what you're made of, tear them off, throw them away and surrender. I've no desire to slay my only recurring child. But Father Sedon won't ill-star me if I have to kill you once and forevermore. Any Attis has always been fair game for any devil."

Flummoxed, Attis didn't know what to do. To say he was of two minds belied the fact only one was his – the other one, no matter how improbably, belonged to three at least outwardly inanimate objects, the Trigregos Talismans.

Then, between them, another absolutely inert and until then unthinking object, his kibisis, vanished. What now?

========

Ute Tethys was young, but she wasn't that young. And, even if she was in love with her own half-brother, George Masterson, she wasn't particularly stupid either. Although she only rode a psychopomp-cygnet, she was a Swan Maiden in all senses of the term.

========

Behind her, onto her cygnet's back, Mama Volsanga came out of the Weird off the hellstone she made Ute wear. The Hellion Valkyrie had got away from the Steg Sari. She'd fucked up, though. She knew it too. Helena Somata's soul-self was trapped in a re-formed crystal skull. She had to go back and retrieve it. Before she did that, she reckoned she should at least try to find an appropriate receptacle into which she could sink Helena's bodiless and thus homeless soul-self.

Valkyries weren't supposed to be slayers. They were supposed to be Choosers of the Slain. As potent as Ant Nightingales were in life, she didn't think their soul-selves could reanimate a corpse. Moreover, as appealing as it was, it would be an iniquity to seek to thrust Helena's into a certain Steg, or her Terror Donna, even if she could.

Inspired by the example set by Ute's father, she figured someone not quite slain might fit the bill. A young and pretty Utopian hybrid from over in Kanin City, one who just happened to be suffering from irreversible brain damage, would be ideal. For Helena it'd be familiar territory if nothing else.

You want to cause a potentially coma-inducing head injury on someone like that, you drop something hard and blunt onto her head. You want to do that, you begin by interrupting your daughter's first ride as a Valkyrie. Next you look for, and pick up, something hard and blunt like, say, the burnt branch of a fallen oak tree.

"There's one over there, Ute!"

========

The Amateramirror failed to take him in, not in any substantive way anyhow.

========

Unable to think of anything else to do, Attis continued to retreat backwards, slowly but warily. He never took his eyes off Mithras, or what passed for Mithras. That didn't mean he didn't register those beyond his half-father. In all his successions he'd never seen so many devils clustered in one place before.

It was too bad Rumour of Lazareme wasn't one of them. Rumour used to say a single picture was worth a thousand words – whereupon, between gulps of beer, he'd proceed to churn out thousands of words. However, when it came to portraiture no one came close to matching his excellence, not even his deviant half-son, Jordan Tethys.

The devils behind his father had done mutilating Demogorgon, if that's what the arm-thing had been, and were watching their confrontation. If there was anything left of the abomination, Attis couldn't see it. Neither could he see any sign of the Demon Child, not her corpse anyhow.

There was a shape that did look vaguely like her chimera, albeit as if had been made of wax and was now patiently waiting for wicks to be applied to its three now nearly unidentifiable goat's heads. Plus, he'd seen All of Incain obliterated, Pyrame's tetrahedral head with it. The rest of his legionnaires having scattered hither and yon, in tow with the Byronic and Lazaremist lackeys who followed their devil-gods northwards or westwards, he knew he couldn't expect help from anyone except himself.

Too many of the recently reconstituted devils hated him for inflicting past humiliations and subsequent centuries stuck inside the Gynosphinx with no way out. Likewise, so long as he wore the Thrygragos Talismans even the rebellious firstborn, and the highest born after them, of any tribe, wouldn't risk offending Mithras, let alone daring to challenge him.

Worse than that, since he'd had all six of the Great Godly Glories almost as long as they'd existed, the Male Three had proven superior to the Female Three not so much time and time again as the first time, when the Cousins had the latter, and, thus far, this time. So, yes, he could try to flee between-space but, with their power foci restored, the devils would harry him until he had no choice other than to turn and fight.

He wouldn't stand a chance against any of the first or higher born, should they deign to come after him. But, without all six talismans, some of the lesser lights might be able to kill him and that would never do. As another option he could fight to the death, here and now. He'd done that before, but always in the service of Thrygragos Varuna Mithras, never against him.

Did he come back solely because Mithras was immortal? Would he come back if Mithras was dead? Might it not be better if he slashed himself away, to fight anew another day? Would the Trigregos Talismans let him slash himself away?

Devils couldn't lie. Devic daddy Mithras was giving him an opportunity to surrender. He wished he could, even if it meant grovelling, licking dirt, for a while. He sensed the Trigregos Talismans were disinclined to let him get abject. If All of Incain could be obliterated, then they could as well: with the same Gypsium-Godstuff and out of the same place from whence they'd come, Sed-Peak's lava lake.

Since he probably couldn't kill a Great God, especially not a Great God who'd once been Kronos, Father Time, Chrysaor Attis opted to kill some time instead, if only for practise. "You admit it then," he bluffed. "You said I am your only recurring son. You never fathered the devils who think themselves Mithras Spawn."

"How dare you play absurd word games with me! You may not be altogether mortal, but you can be killed. And when you are, you do die. That you can succeed yourself is a token of your deviancy alone. My children by the Trigregos Sisters are not so much immortal as they are, as yet, ever undying. But I could and would kill them if I had to and you are no different.

"I command you: Remove the so-called Cousins' thrice-cursed Godly Glories this instant!"

Not so unusually Attis felt no compunction to obey. In rapid-fire retrospect, it occurred to him he never had. He generally went along with Mithras's instructions because that's what dutiful sons were supposed to do. Besides again, Mithras rarely issued ill-thought or out-and-out irrational *'suggestions'*.

This minute, though, he felt only indignation at the be-masked and craven devil's arrogance, at his sheer presumptuousness. If he were worthy of obedience, let alone of worship, he wouldn't be cowering between-space casting yappy illusions. In a flash of clarity, one in all probability inspired by the fact he was wearing the Crimson Corona, he thereby attained a profound realization.

"Not a chance! I don't have to do anything you say because you weren't possessing Helios when he inseminated Mnemosyne-Marutia. He possessed you. Strife-Discord, Kore-Eris, Marut Kanin, call her what you want to call her; she wasn't humanizing my mother because she wanted to. She was humanizing her because Machine-Memory was possessing her, not the other way around."

"That is an insufferable inference. Even the lowliest of lowborn devils cannot be possessed and I am a Great God. You do not have to do anything I say because I am not a weakling like my brothers. I can and will enforce my orders with or without you or your legions around to do it for me. It's endgame, Attis. Throw those things away or breathe your last!"

"Then come along, part-father. I have withstood death before. Have you?"

"You have never been killed by me before, boy. I alone gave you life. I alone can take it away from you."

Behind his father he could see Cruel Plathon, the Bull of Mithras, his killer as frequently as he was the Bull's killer, if not more often. To one side of him stood Hell's Belle, Kore-Coitus as Pyrame dubbed Belialma of Satanwyck. On his other side levitated Divine Coueranna, Kore-Concord or Kore-Castrator, his castrator.

They were grinning. So were that bearded bonehead Bellona, catty and caterwauling Cathune – Pyrame and Tralalorn's brood sister, Desiccated Drought – and the rest of the male and female Apocalyptics. No one was grinning more broadly than the snake-haired Medusa.

She held something up. So that's where his kibisis had gone. She may or may not have had the power to spirit it away telekinetically but, having re-formed her golden girdle, she could easily have slipped into between-space herself and hauled it away invisibly. Howsoever she pulled it off, there was no denying she was such a clever gorgon.

========

Dampness lingering in the woods and open fields from last night's frost and sprinkling of snow combined to squelch the already dying out forest fire and concomitant firestorm. A remnant, acrid pall of smoke hung in the wintry air.

========

The Daemonicus-Demogorgon's shoulder ball of a cannonball-head crashing into the muck, not more than 20 feet away from them, so jolted George Masterson he ceased his one way dialogue with his hippo-hind. When he, no longer altogether Georgie, bodily regained Georgie's feet, the non-pureblood Utopian's snapped-in-half recorder, both halves of it until then glowing inexplicably, glowed both explicably and rejoined.

It did not do so as a playable, as in musical, recorder per se. No matter how appropriately that might have been, neither did it do so as a panpipe. Additionally, someone at once childish and devilish was sitting on Hinny the Hippy: "Oh, there you are, daddy. Want to play ball with me, tra-la tra-glee?"

"In a moment, Lorna love. First I have to remember how Daddy Rumour's quill works. Right, that's it. You splotch out his splotch pad ..."

========

Mithras raged out of between-space.

========

Raising his labarum into the air, he simultaneously shook and twirled it. The result was a two-handed long-sword. Hefting it in one, and shouting in deliberate, Dionysian fury, the Great God charged at his deviant son. Attis crossed his hands and, with the Susasword and the Amateramirror, blocked his part-father's slashing blow. He was barely rocked at all.

It being lighter and easier to handle than the much longer sword, he extracted Susal's from their clench and thrust it at Mithras's midsection. It couldn't penetrate the Cloak of Lazareme, deflecting harmlessly to one side. The Great God one-hand-shoved him backwards.

Too experienced to succumb to frenzy, the Universal Soldier pranced away, skilfully not slipping. He opened his stance, spreading his arms apart as if begging attack. Smartly calming down, Mithras didn't take the bait. Instead, inspired by what the Susasword did to him moments ago, he pointed his transmutable weapon at Attis and then ejected its blade as if a dart from a blowgun.

Attis reacted such that it went into, but not through, the Amateramirror and vanished. Mithras wrapped the star-cape around his head and vanished as well.

Two, three times, each time in a different place, Mithras came out of between-space, his long-sword fully bladed again. The Crimson Corona encapsulated Attis in a scarlet aura, heightened his already impressive reflexes and augmented his practised, near impregnability. Two, three times, with the Corona's assistance, Attis anticipated Mithras's reappearance. By aura, sword or mirror he rebuffed howsoever the Great God chose to come at him.

"Over here, Chrysaor honeysuckle." He knew that voice. It wasn't Mithras's. It was the Medusa's.

Honeysuckle, his golden-brown buttocks! She was one four-armed honey overdue for sucking into his Amateramirror.

========

"Mom," Ute protested, in exasperation. "I've a job to do, a quota to keep. It's my first ride. Down there, that's my first corpse."

"That's no hero. That's a demon, a harpy. There's nothing heroic about harpies."

"It is not. It's only got an owl's talons."

"Oh, very well. Go down and gather it up if you must. But then we really have to go find ourselves a young and pretty Utopian to brain with Sylvia."

========

Seconds earlier, dozens upon devilish dozens of Master Devas, from all three tribes, had been standing around watching the two irreconcilable combatants go at each other. This second, yet again, suddenly reared Demogorgon. Even without All around, mostly melted-down Stopstone-Solidium-sludge – the equivalent of chthonic candle-wax spread over the remarkably only moderately bloody battlefield – thus proved itself, in its own way, ever so useful when it came to shaping horrors.

Daemonic-Demogorgon wasn't a snake-like vine with a many-fingered, petaliferous head this time. It was more of a long-bodied weasel with its appendages truncated. It nonetheless coiled above and behind where Attis was waiting for Mithras to come out of the Weird again.

The Corona must have sensed it, sensed all those devils and daemonic *'stuff'* making it up. Forewarned by the Medusa, Chrysaor Attis had already closed his eyes anyhow. He whirled; making sure the surface of the Amateramirror was directed at this latest of a long line of similar abominations. It reflected a good percentage of the gargantuan atrocity, but it was far too large for the mirror to reflect and thereby take in all of it.

The more the mirrored shield did take in, the hotter it grew. It was scorching his arm. His only other choice being to become irreversibly one-armed, he yanked off the mirror and dropped it onto the ground. As the behemoth bent to devour him, the Universal Soldier did the unthinkable to the Unnameable. He leapt onto its snout, slashed through its two non-devic eyes, and then drove the Susasword into its third eye.

The mother of all mammalian serpents thrashed about frantically. The Attis held fast the curved blade. More devils, males and more females, Byron and Lazareme Spawn together with more Mithradites, proceeded to funnel inexorably into the already Conglomerate Devil. Unable to hold onto it any longer, Attis let go of the sword and hurtled himself as far away from the writhing weasel-thing as he could.

As usual he landed catlike, on his feet, and rolled, whereupon he did the only thing he could think of doing. He thought Crinsom's Crown around the leviathan's head. Finally something very good happened to the very bad. Leaving its head behind, face fortuitously down, the corona still wrapped around it, the until-then most current abomination blew into its constituent aspects. Individual Master Devas once again began to solidify in its vicinity. As they did so every last one of them collapsed, as if in exhaustion.

Then Attis went down, hamstrung from behind before he could will the three Sacred Objects returned to him. He spun onto his back. Mithras, still garbed in Lazareme's Star-Cape, stood over top him. No fool he, the Mask of Byron retained mirrored eyeballs. His labarum remained a long-sword, its blade dripping his son's blood.

"You really should learn to listen to your father, boy."

========

"You devic dung heap, you've got to dot it!"

========

The Smiling Fiend, cloaked in darkness with only his pinkish hands – they with too many fingers and too many knuckles per finger – and his pinkish, three-eyed face visible, didn't recognize the voice. It didn't come from Tralalorn.

"Daddy!" That scream, it definitely did come from Tralalorn. He took a fatally fleeting look.

An enormous, unmistakably psychopomp pterosaur had just had the Demon Child and Hinny the Hippy for a late lunch. There was someone else there, riding it. Her he recognized, the saurian witch who'd made up the entirety of the impromptu troupe's rhythm section this morning in Hopi Tethys's booze-tent. Hers was the contemptuous voice he'd just heard.

In the Tsarina's paw was the business end of Georgie's Attis-halved eye-stave, its prison pod open. Being otherwise occupied splotching out another drawing; the polydactyl devil didn't have time to muster sufficiently prophylactic willpower against being sucked wholly out of Georgie – devilish and/or daemonic mind or spirit, subtle matter body, his collection of power foci, the severed bongo-brain of his brood brother's head, the works, everything that made him Smiler – and into the Trinondev eyeorb.

Even if the Harmony Unity left before dawn broke, he'd have been better off staying in Bad Rhad's bed. That wasn't the worst thing, though. No, the worst thing was nobody would ever remember how he'd masterminded Mithras's murder.

========

Lunch for the Terror Donna did not go down well. Quite the contrary, it went up: in a powder puff of flaky, feces-reeking faeriedust.

========

As the Donna devolved distortedly, into an oversized, goat-headed butterfly, Tralalorn and Hinny the Hippy, both of whom were naturally gifted when it came to reflexively accessing the Weird in an emergency, emerged from it unaffected. The hippo-hind returned the favour. It swallowed the feebly fluttering psycho-pterosaur. The Donna stayed down. Ergo, Hinny must have been hungrier. Either that or her tummy was partially between-space, the same as the twin sphinxes digestive tracts supposedly were in 725 YD – and as they remained today.

Tralalorn wasn't happy. She loved her chimeras, even when they didn't look or smell like a Stynx. Neither was Saudi the Steg Sari. Not only had the Sangazur-animated Saur Tsarina grown to rely on her psycho, she'd been formulating as yet vague plans to repatriate her soul-self. She could; she reckoned she'd thereby supplant the Sang and, despite dying twice today already, become wholly herself again. If she pulled that off, it would be a stunt for the ages.

Saudi aimed the eyeorb at the Demon Child riding the hippo-hind. She didn't realize they had a capacity of only one devil per prison pod. Or, if she did, she didn't remember she'd already used it once. Even if it hadn't been filled, it might not have worked on Trala anyways.

As it was, the only appreciable effect it had on the little horror was to enrage her positively incandescent. She tossed her yet-again-face-kneading White Dwarf at the Saur Sari. Smartly, Saudi didn't catch it. It went off anyhow, powder-showering its transformative faeriedust all over her olfactory-offensively.

Before it re-formed in one hand, not quite so powerfully puffed up, Trala had herself a dino-dolly in the other hand.

========

George Masterson had already developed a different third eye. His skin went from black to blue. His scarcity of dark hair got both fulsome and sun-blond. Out of the Grey that was the Universal Substance of Samsara, a black cloak made of ravendeer feathers akin to Hinny the Hippy's hide draped overtop Georgie's indigo robe.

He played ball with them. Only, after willing Trala, her dino-dolly, Hinny and the halved eye-stave, prison pod atop it closed, inside it, he Great-God-rendered said White Dwarf the collective ball. With another thought and a gesture he telekinetically tossed the lot high into the sky. He didn't care where or in what condition they landed, just so long as they didn't bother him anymore. He was feeling artistic, as well as theocidal, and didn't lack for inspiration.

The Tethys-deviant had made scads of sketches of Chrysaor Attis and his regalia, particularly his kibisis and the six Great Godly Glories. He splotched in three of them, splotched out a blank sheet, splotched them onto it, had a quick look round his immediate surroundings, drew in the background as if they were here, and dotted the drawing. He was immune to fire. Then he set to work on another one.

Like he had his devic half-father, he'd taught Jordy everything he knew.

========

Attis anxiously thought the Trigregos Talismans back to him. They were responding just in time. They rematerialized, only to burst into flames and dematerialize. Attis was in even greater pain. They had burnt him all the more before they vanished.

The last time he'd had a day this bad he'd ended up being long-distance-shredded by Helena Somata, the secretly proclaimed and therefore legitimate Master of the Weirdom of Kanin City. Today could be worse. Today might yet see the conclusion of his successions.

Then again it might not. One should never say 'never'.

========

Behind the Mask of Byron, Thrygragos Mithras was unreadable. Then he was eminently readable. He was as naked as he was stupefied. The Mask was gone, the Cloak of Many Colours was gone, even his labarum was gone. He gawped in complete disbelief.

In a blink of any one of his three eyes, crinkly raven-haired, butterscotch-skinned Datong Harmonia, the Unity of Panharmonium, protectively straddled his hamstrung half-son. Unless they formed her body beautiful, she wore form-hugging golden chains. She had her golden torc around her neck, broken golden chains extending off golden manacles about her wrists, and golden scales-of-balance earrings where they should be, depending from her golden earlobes.

She smiled her golden smile. She really was stunning when she smiled.

Talk about stunning; the snake-haired head in her hand smiled too. Thrygragos Varuna Mithras gaped straight into the gorgonian head's three opened, not-ruined-enough eyeballs. Instantly and howsoever temporarily – regardless of whether the Anvil Artificer intended it for the hypothetical Lamia nonentity or whether it was the Medusa's actual power focus – he turned to stone.

Not one for tempting temporality, Unholy Abaddon, the Keeper of Chaos, appeared beside his brood sister. He rammed the central prong of his Brainrock trident into the third eye of the Whole Earth's sanctimonious, but now powerlessly petrified, self-proclaimed Sire of Civilization. With a wrench he cracked the granite-block that was Mithras's head off his neck.

Creakily the Great God's remarkably not completely stop-stoned body stretched out his hands, fingers groping for it. Grinning evilly, if not precisely fiendishly, Abe Chaos held his uncle's head, spiked on his trident, purposely tantalizingly out of his reach. The first thunderbolt came from the Lightning Blade of their immediate brother, Lord Yajur, the Unity of Order. Harmonia contributed chain lightning of her own.

Readjusting their power foci accordingly, their fellow Lazaremists joined in the demolition derby. Byronics and Mithradites were just as complicit, none more so than Byron's Silverclouds and Mithras's firstborn, Heat and Cold. The collective pulverization of Justice, Light and Truth thus underway, the three Unities let them vent.

They, along with every single devil amongst them, including their now All-freed siblings and the similarly released Byronics, collected a chunk of the Great God Mithras as a keepsake.

========

"*Time comes,*" *Harmonia broadcast volubly, for all there willing to hear, and imparted telepathically, for the wilfully deaf among them such as Mithras's ever-loyal torchbearers and herald to heed,* "*And pebbles becomes flesh instead of raw, devic energy; bury them deep. Whatever you do, don't feed them to birds. They might migrate to the same place.*"

Phrasing aside, she wasn't trying to be funny. Nevertheless, many laughed out loud, as much in relief as triumph. Her dumping out Attis's bottomless bag was even more appreciated.

****

THEO 17:

AFTERMATH'S PRELUDE

========

*Sometimes Mithras, like Methandra, meant 'myth'. Sometimes Mithras meant
'friend'. Sometimes Mithras meant 'math'. Thrygragos Varuna Mithras himself had named
Mithramas 4376 'Thrygragon' as in gone, gone, gone his Thrygragos Brothers.*

*In some respects he was only out by one 'gone' by the end of it. Unfortunately for him,
he wasn't the one thought-brother not gone.*

========

The Unmoving One's Byronhead reappeared above them. A humanoid female's
naked, smoky shape fumed out of its third eye.

"**That will do!**" commanded Sedona Spellbinder, in her father's voice. "**You
Byronics, do as I say! We're away home. You others, you may have inviolate protectorates so long as your subjects allow you to retain them. You may never visit
us. You do, your stars shall shine out of the night's sky forevermore!**"

Abandoning their thousands of frenzied fighters to fend for themselves, the devic members of one entire tribe were shortly no longer in Sedon's Mole. As the Byronics vanished into the Weird, hundreds of Mithradite eyeballs, some of them only
solitarily cyclopean, focused on the contrarily-gifted Thanatoids.

The be-masked giantess, who refused to speak to lesser beings, whispered to her
moderately more gigantic brood brother, who not only would but did. "The Mithradium," boomed King Cold, heeding her, "Atop Theopolis Hill on Apple Isle in one
hour's time as Drought's hourglass records it. Bring maps.

"Oh, and bring beer. I do my best thinking when I'm drinking. Go!"

Most went. Some stayed behind. The various Apocalyptics – Drought herself, War, Disaster, Flood, Hunger, Sickness, Plague and Mother Murder – were eight of them. The last and possibly least of them simultaneously glowered angrily, acquisitively and accusingly at Harmonia.

Unperturbed, the female Unity finished re-stuffing the bottomless bag she'd taken off the Medusa before she recovered from the Mithrants' Taurus unthinkingly doing away with the day's second Demogorgon, at the cost of his own hamstringing. She did so with a notable number of as yet unspoken for power foci.

Harmony had already wrapped an obscuring hood possibly akin to a demonic Ghast – a Hankering Hankie, as they were sometimes known – over whoever's snake-haired head. Thus safely bagged, and with the extremity of one side-set of her Brain-rock chains contacting it as if an octopus's tentacle, the petrifying power focus lay on the ground beside her.

Stuffing done, she locked eyes with the arguably twelfth-born Mithradite. Smiling her golden smile tauntingly, she slipped the gorgonian head into the kibisis along with the rest of the leftover talismans. Then she vanished it, Attis's repacked bottomless bag, presumably into her own power focus. The Apocalyptics went away.

Now only five Mithradites remained behind. Like the Unities and their Lazaremist siblings, they were waiting for the appearance of one deity in particular. Brother Byron gone bye-bye, with his spawn; most members of the third tribe just as gone; that deity didn't disappoint. Although everyone perceived him differently – some as a fertility god, some as a solar or stellar divinity, some as human, some as inhuman, and some as not much of anything of any significance – everyone could agree on one thing.

Thrygragos Everyman was picking his teeth with Rumour's onetime power focus.

========

"That how you did it?" Harmonia queried of Little-Star Lazareme.

========

The admitted Unity of Panharmonium wasn't referring to any poorly plucked – and thereafter howsoever sloppily knitted together – ravendeer's feathery cloak, what her second generational father had been wearing since that morning. She was referring to the Brainrock quill nearly 400 years latterly belonging to the deviant Legendarian.

"Hadn't you better preface that with *'Thank you, dad'*, Harmony?"

"Thank you, dad."

"Why'd you take so long to act?" Lord Yajur wanted to know. Order wasn't one who enjoyed being ordered to do anything. He got an appropriate response.

"Let's just say there were complications. And, before you can say *'Thank you, dad'*, let me add I already can't recall all of them."

Yajur got the intimation. "Thank you, dad."

"What do you want done with this?" interrupted his immediate brother, Unholy Abaddon, referring to the grotesquery skewered on the innermost tine of his trident, what in reality was the hilt of Chaos's black blade.

Since a habitually disputatious fellow like Abe wasn't about to thank him for anything, and since Lazareme wasn't about to thank him for not unleashing the Chaos Blade, the Great God of Absolute Freedom gave him a straight answer. As straight an answer as he ever gave anyone anyhow: "I think I'll keep it. I could do with an extra pillow."

"For a pillow fight with them?" Yajur cracked, deliberately double-meaningfully.

He inclined his lightning blade in the direction of the five remaining Mithradites: the two colossal Thanatoids, who were now their indisputable, top-dog gods; the two Panharmonium-complicit Apple Goddesses; and a bipedal bull with a bident. They were standing nearby – four of five on the ground, one in the air – as if they were dukes and duchesses edgily waiting to be summoned such that they could supplicate their newly crowned king.

"A head to hold over their heads?" Lazareme interpreted the crack correctly. "I trust that won't be necessary. Not right away, anyhow."

He accorded the five a token glance. Along with the already absent Gravedigger, they were the highest born Mithradites left on the Hidden Headworld. He'd have to receive them eventually, he realized. The sooner he did the quicker he could be rid of them. Nonetheless, it pleased him to make them cool their heels awhile longer. They'd earned his inattention. Under half an hour ago he'd been their sworn enemy, one of two, excluding their own father.

The delay further afforded him an opportunity to answer Yajur's earlier enquiry. As fine a musician as Djinn Domitian or any of his offspring, he had nothing against tooting his own horn. "But, to get back to what you first wanted to know: Don't ask me how, but Brother Moon-Face figured out what Brother Boykin was up to and had himself a brainstorm.

"The hegemonic head-case from up here – as opposed to the hegemonic fathead from down south – had used his crutch to think himself a pipeline through the Weird to the lava-lake filled with molten Brainrock on Sedon's Peak. He'd done so for the express purpose of using it against Big Mama Monster Maker and, as you should be aware, Attis had beat up on more than just Mithradites over the centuries.

"A bundle of them, including virtually the entirety of his Zodiac, were Byronics. So he asked me to hold off until Mithras baked the misbegotten Mandroid back to Incain. Since stacks of your stupider sibs were still stuck inside of All as well, I agreed. Sure enough, as soon as Mithras vaporized the She-Sphinx they not only freed themselves, a few of them even started re-embodying themselves with Belle's barbecued demons.

"Of course about all the good that did them was to invite more fireballs aimed in their direction from the Utopians still flying cosmicars. Their Tvasitar-trinkets had been in Attis's kibisis and we reckoned Mithras destroyed it, along with everything inside it, in his Kronos Quake – a masterstroke if there ever was one, by the begrudging way. At any rate, we further reckoned we'd have to hide out until the dust settled, as it were, before taking them to the Peak and hope Anvil could forge them replacements.

"Then Attis showed up obviously under the influence of the thrice-cursed Sisters' terrible talismans. More importantly to my mind, he had his kibisis slung over his shoulder. One thing led to another and the first Unnameable's head blew off after you and the rest of the highborn turned on it. I watched where it went, which was in the same direction All and Attis came from, spotted yet another ruckus going on over there, and that's when things got complicated

"The wannabe Raven's Head that Harmony once told me about was back there with its master, my deviant grandson's Utopian get. Amazingly, he was holding onto our Rumour's quill. I say amazingly because, as near as I could tell when I took him over, the lad had never been banged up even remotely close to incurably. Seeing them, I had a brainstorm of my own.

"As for the rest of it, that can wait until I've a beer or 30, in honour of the evidently dearly departed. And by that I mean Jordan Tethys, not thingy there. At least his head might prove useful. My Angela escaped All and she likes her own pillow, if you get my meaning."

Harmony certainly did. She looked gorgeous even when scowling.

========

Two long missing Lazaremists, the Great God's male and female healers, were patiently attending to Taurus Chrysaor Attis.

========

Euro-centric Illuminaries had the female of the two healers as Amal-Althea. Everyone called her Goat because she was hircine, capric or just plain goatish. Her brood siblings being Lazareme's jinni – his primary Heliodromus, messenger, angel or Angela – and faeries-supped Rumour, she'd always made her demon into the form a female satyr or faun, a fauna as she had it, because Daybreak's fauns worshipped her.

They had the male of the two as Azkeecyoos, after the Greeks' Asclepius. Devils called him Surgeon in part because he dressed as if ready to operate, in a floor-length gown, hygienic gloves, hairnet, mask and apron, and in part because his power focus was a scalpel. Lazareme called him Sturgeon not so much because he resembled a fish out of water, which he sort of did, but because he thought it was funny.

Tvasitar Smithmonger, the Anvil Artificer, who never left Sedon's Peak, was one of his third-born brood brothers. The other was Dand Tariqartha, the Lackland Libertine's Persian or Earth Magician, who'd also come out of the Gynosphinx when Mithras caused his labarum to erupt Brainrock volcanically and thereby excise her from the Mole. He stood among the rest of the returned Lazaremists watching the healers dutifully applying their craft: their Gypsium needles, Godstuff threads, Brainrock balms and, most especial, their devic touch.

The Attis had taken on, and taken out, Sturgeon the Surgeon because he kept on healing Kore-Castrator's bully. It didn't help. Attis removed Dand Tariqartha from action because, as an Earth Magician – the same as Pyrame Silverstar and, to a far lesser degree, the fays' favourite, Mariamne Dawnstar, Lazareme's Venus and sovereign presence in the easternmost occipital region of Daybreak – he held an unchallengeable lordship over Mandroids.

He did so after realizing that, even though Azkeecyoos wasn't around to heal him anymore, Cruel Plathon kept coming back inside All's Mandroid monstrosities. It still didn't help. No matter what either did, one or the other kept coming back to re-kill one or the other. The only thing that ended their brutal, 500-year murder-go-round was the collapse of the mad goddesses' matriarchate, which occurred while Attis was between successions.

He'd taken Amal-Althea out simply because devil daddy Mithras didn't approve of her, principally due to her lactic stench. She was the goat who looked after Mithras when he was the baby Zeus. Unless she was the goat who looked after Varuna when he was the baby Zeus, that is. Bi-solar deities were almost as confounding as dual entities.

Fate twists. Sometimes it twists beneficially. Unlike the rest of the long-missing Byronics and Lazaremists, the Goat did not need to reclaim her power focus from Attis's bottomless bag. She hadn't had to because it, a shepherd's pedum or crooked staff, wasn't in it. Once he took it off her, the Attis's then-succession gave it to his full daughter, her half-daughter, one Pusan Wanderlust, aka the Traveller or the Trailblazer, among other names.

Yet another recurring deviant, Yajur could attest she'd been in the Mole last night doing what fauns did best. As Yeast Tethys would happily as well as healthily volunteer if asked, she'd stayed behind in order to witness Thrygragon. In fact, right this minute the three-eyed fauna treating the Attis may well be his daughter's latest succession acting as her devic half-mother's shell. If so then in all likelihood it had fallen to Pusan, rather than Amal-Althea, to re-form more than recreate the crooked staff out of returning Brainrock.

Attis should be grateful anyone was willing to help him. Healers were like that, though. While welcomed, their creed required them to do what they did without expectation of either gratitude or compensation. Generally speaking they also didn't bear grudges. In that, of those watching them at work, they were probably alone.

Any Attis was fair game. It really wasn't appropriate to save him once he'd lost it, today's game.

========

Healers had patients as well as patience. Divine Coueranna, she of the many names and multiple personalities, had neither.

========

Always barefoot, but now in grey crone of winter mode, with a robe to match, she may or may not appreciate the unselfishness of healers. She didn't appreciate much and she surely bore grudges. Tired of waiting for them to finish congratulating each other, she air-strode up to the Unities and their father. Bident in paw, the Bull of Mithras trudged at her heels whilst Sinistral Lust brought up the trio's rear, no doubt admiring the Bull's rear-end as she did so. Their bathrobes were now silken rather than towelling.

"I can't condone your splendour, Lackland," Kore-Coueranna announced with nary a nod nor a hello

Chaos and Order were spoiling for fights. The latter hadn't re-sheathed his Lightning Blade since zapping Mithras, whereas the former didn't need to unsheathe anything to devastate anyone. Harmony didn't approve of fighting. She especially didn't approve of them fighting anybody. They started fighting they'd likely end up fighting each other and that might spell the end of everything, of everything Head-worldly wise anyways.

She was about to speak up when Lazareme raised a quietening hand. "And why might that be? Do I remind you of your father?"

"No, you remind me of your father and we have been fooled once today already with such a seeming."

"So you have," he agreed. The Great God of libertinism and/or libertarianism, more so than liberty within commonsensical limits, had no idea whether Myrionymous Kore beheld him as an incorporeal eye-mouth or as the Devil Himself. Either way her assertion didn't surprise him. Although he only ill-understood his goofy godliness gift, as Thrygragos Everyman he probably should remind Mithradites of their grandfather.

No doubt with considerable input from that undying Utopian, Cabby the Daddy, who'd trained as a geneticist many multiple-tens of millennia earlier in the First Weir System, the Moloch Sedon intentionally engineered devils skewed paternally. Their father being gone, gone, gone, Sedon becoming their default god made sense.

"And who do I remind you of, Harmony?"

"Yourself naturally. Sky-blue skin, sea-green eyes and sun-blond hair."

"And you, Order?"

"Much the same," said Yajur. "Except with bark-brown skin and sparking hair."

"In other words, I remind you of yourself. Chaos?"

"A bottle of beer wearing a jacket."

Lazareme laughed. "Then all is as it should be. I'm not one for any of my unlamented brother's henotheistic hogwash, Concord. If I remind you of your ungodly grandfather you have my permission to venerate him, and him alone, from now on. Just don't expect me or mine to come to Ap Isle and sort you and yours out any time in the foreseeable future. Especially don't expect any of us to sort anything out in your favour."

"Just as well. I'm not about to start venerating you. Come, Bull, our dogcart awaits us."

The Bull hesitated. "Your wheeled cauldron and your hellhounds await you, Kore. I would first have words with the Libertine and his most memorable daughter."

As Divine Coueranna huffed groundlessly away, Harmonia eyed once-Baal and once-Beltis curiously. "Memorable daughter?"

"I see the Libertine as you see the Libertine, Harmony," he said.

"So do I," said Bouncing Belle. "Which is exceedingly strange since, before Father Mithras went the way of a trophy head, I always perceived you as I did earlier today, as a blurry little daystar in the shape of a half-assed human."

"Mind telling me which buttock you pinched?" said Lazareme, matching her sarcasm. "I'll see what I can do about growing it back."

"You know exactly what I mean, smarty pants."

He did. Chaos's crack about him looking like a bottle of beer aside, most of his father-fixated nieces and nephews, as well as more than a few of his own unruly off-spring by the Three Sisters, saw him that way. He didn't mind being seen as not much more than a species-specific sparkle of unimportant godhood. Truth told he didn't think much of them either.

"So as a result of the clouds lifting from your concupiscent cataracts," he put to her, wrapping his tongue around some fay-saying, which was something he was prone to anyway, "You imagine we've the Dual Entities."

"Either that or they have you," Satanwyck's nominal Prime Sinistral quibbled, continuing to ignore his derisiveness.

"Well, we don't," asserted Harmonia. "And devils can't lie."

"Which all but proves they have you, doesn't it?" one devil-goddess challenged the other, her senior in terms of birth if not parentage. "The Dual Entities can and do lie, endlessly."

"There has to be another explanation," the Unity of Panharmonium retorted defensively.

"Of course there does," her father offered, uncharacteristically scrambling for a rational, as in Apollonian, riposte. "And there's nothing suspicious about it. Brother Boykin's the Great God gone as a result of Thrygragon and, not that he has any, you just heard Brother Moon-Face wash his hands of any of its other consequences. In effect, this has just become my age and self-determination is as much my way as it is that of Heliosophos, is it not?"

Harmony either followed her father's logic or faked it convincingly. "Meaning Lust and the Bull just became godless."

"Not godless, Harmony," Lazareme countered, as if lecturing a walrus of an igno-ramus, to quote Tralalorn: "Truly godly!" Her constantly querulous frowning may not damper her incomparably fine looks but it was tampering with his excellent mood.

"And, at the risk of my mouth running off ridiculously, which would make it damn difficult to catch without a stein of ale, by that I mean good golly godly. You do unto others bad golliwog godly, that's what others will do unto you back in spades or clubs or diamonds, though probably not hearts – heartlessness, maybe. You only have to look at what we've just done to thingy there as proof of that."

"I thought this was all about Panharmonium." Harmony sounded hurt.

"Its start, youngster, but it's only its start. The Age of Panharmonium may well follow mine but, in the meantime, I'm thinking Age of Lazareme has a nice ring to it."

In his view what his daughter failed to grasp was, if he suddenly allowed their long put-upon brothers and sisters the same license to do whatever they wanted that he'd just implicitly given to Lady Lust and the Bull, post Thrygragon wouldn't become his Age. Nor would it become that of Panharmonium. It would become un-manageable chaos, small case.

There had to be a transitional period during which he could act as the Mithradites' kindly uncle, albeit with the fallback of them, through his Unities if necessary, obeying him without question. What with him already appearing to two highborn devils as the male of the two universally-recognized cosmic principals, he might as well seize the day Mithras decreed Thrygragon and make it Everyman onwards and upwards rather than every man for himself.

Why was thingy smiling?

"Bravo," Lord Order clapped, sparking palm against lightning blade.

"I still say you look like a bottle of beer," Abe Chaos reiterated.

"Then, regardless of who has whom, if either," the Bull picked up, "Since the needs of our subjects are always foremost in our minds, there's no need to petition your indulgence before we do anything."

"Hey, feel free to crave away," Lazareme qualified carefully.

"Kore needs a new charioteer," Plathon obliged him. "I volunteer the Attis."

"Hadn't you best take that up with her?" said Yajur. "She is your elder."

"No more so than I am, Sparky," said Belialma of Satanwyck. "Now that Mithras is no more, the Mithradium needs new occupants and Apple Isle will always need an Apple Goddess."

"I smell a battle brewing," said Chaos.

"What is it with you Lazaremists anyway?" asked the beguiling beauty, as teasingly as ever. "You, your father, your deviants, something's always brewing with you lot and it's mostly beer."

"I don't drink," said Yajur.

"You wouldn't," smirked the Bull. "It'd make you too disorderly."

"And Order's why I drink," said Chaos cheerfully, waggling head on a stick.

"Look, Lust," Harmonia offered, "If you and the Bull want me to negotiate with Concord, or any other Mithradite Master Deva for that matter, as to how best to divide control of Apple Isle, I'll do it. If you're so desperate for a new address, maybe she'd swap you Satanwyck."

"We've already talked," the Sinistral said. "Apple-Kore won't abandon her worshipful Korants. Besides, she already has her hell there. Let her keep it. As for Satanwyck, Avarice and Wrath are back. Let them split it. Our vizier, Ibal, is the real ruler there anyway and Trawl loves being our chief disciplinarian. So none of that will change.

"What will change is our situation. So you're bang on as usual, Harmony. I'm as bored with Sedon's demons as I am with having to bestow my favours on those two trouser snakes in order to keep them keeping them in line."

The Great God and his Unities were aware that Viceroy Ibal and Trawl the Taskmaster pretty much ran Satanwyck on her behalf. Both being Cyclopes only partially explained her nickname for them, however. They were unimaginative dickheads. Evidently, she was fed up with their ever-increasing demands for her attentions.

With a polyamorous attribute like hers, Belialma was too undomesticated to embrace any semblance of even shared monogamy. Nonetheless, in historical terms the Bull, as Baal, and she, as Beltis, came as close as she ever came to consistently coupling as if in a matrimonial relationship. Indeed, discounting her occasional, sometimes azura-bearing dalliances with the likes of Varuna Mithras, King Cold, Gravedigger and many others, notably the Moloch Sedon, Plathon probably remained her main squeeze.

What they left as yet unsaid was whether or not, her 2500-years-hated father no longer a player in any momentous manner, Divine Coueranna would be taking over, from beguiling Belialma, the role of occupying the Korant Sisterhood's Queen for a Day on Suffering Sapienda. Thrygragos Mithras certainly wouldn't be occupying the Mithrant Brotherhood's chosen Attis anymore and, in that respect anyhow, Plathon clearly had intentions of taking over from his father on much more than an annual basis.

Devils were mind readers.

"No more so than I am being at Kore's beck and call," Plathon provided. "Time's passed for the Attis. Mithrants deserve a real Taurus, as in a proper bull, leading them."

"Kore promises she won't make trouble if we don't threaten what's already hers," Hell's current belle greased the pot. "Even if she does, I'm sure the two Thanatoids can straighten her out. The fact of the matter is, Everyman, though they're far more arbitrarily inclined than you and yours are, so long as they're around, I doubt we Mithradites will ever need you, nor anyone else, to act as mediators or enforcement officers.

"They have a falling out or turn on us together, well, rest assured you and your three firstborn will be the first we call upon. I doubt it'll ever come to that, though. Never forget Heat's as supportive of your Panharmonium Project as both Apple-Kore and I are, Harmony. Handing the Attis over to my sister is small potatoes to pay for our goodwill."

"And a smaller price to pay for my freedom," Plathon pointed out. "She's wanted him for approaching forever and we Master Devas are bound by our oaths."

"Then there's Suffering Sapienda," verbally stroked Lady Lust. "Kore's positively Divine Coueranna in the springtime and it's traditional on Ap Isle for a Great God to occupy the brotherhood's chosen Attis. Once a year she, by herself, would be light years better than any beanbag bed full of virgins."

"It'd be our tribute due to you, Everyman," Plathon plied. "Just tell your healers to back off once they're done de-holing him and we'll be on our way."

"She'll just cut off his balls and crucify him," sneered Lazareme. "I'd rather he didn't come back again, Bull."

"Don't worry, Lackland. Neither Kore – neither Kores – nor I have any intention of killing him. He dies; it'll be of natural causes or suicide. He does; maybe the Masochist or Mithras's torchbearers can take his place. They're out of work as of today and, no matter how highborn they may be, they're still our juniors."

"Attis proves immortal," Hell's Belle chimed in, as if on prearranged cue, "Well, he tossed away dozens of Tvasitar-trinkets in father's tent and, since no one claimed it, I picked out just the dog collar for him."

"Very well," Thrygragos Lazareme decided, as much to get them to shut up as anything else. "He's yours."

Even though he prized self-autonomy above all else, the Great God had no use for the Attis. After him being both Universal Soldier and Mithras's designated champion for nearly 2500 years, he could envisage no place for the golden-brown warrior in either his Age nor any potential Age of Panharmonium that may yet follow it.

"Just be forewarned I'm not about to tell my healers to do anything against their will. Be just as aware that their oaths don't preclude them fighting to protect him."

"They do," Yajur contributed, "And you choose to fight back with all your highborn might, well, let's just say it's on your heads."

"And I've two unoccupied prongs left," finished Abaddon, as triplets sometimes did when it came to each other's sentences.

"Return the favour and leave us alone," Harmonia put to them dismissively.

They obliged. As they did so, Yajur observed: "Lovely apples on that one, very firm stems in particular."

"I wonder who told them to put 'His' and 'Hers' on their bathrobes?" said his brother.

"Apple-Kore should have had 'Mine' written on her back," said their sister.

========

In a flick, someone else was there before them. Rather, missing for over 2,000 years, ever since Attis cut her feet off at the ankles and put on her winged boots, her feet still inside them as arch supports, she was sort of there before them. Vibrating so disconcertingly speedily, it was nearly impossible for even devil-gods to focus on her: she being Lazareme's preferred Heliodromus, his jinni or devic messenger.

Her father couldn't be more delighted. Brows immediately furrowing once again beatifically, Harmonia wasn't so much so. She was used to having devilish daddy all to herself. "My bed's where it always is, Angela," the Lackland Libertine said to his seventh-born daughter, one of two. "Take it there. I'll be along presently. We've a lot of reacquainting to do and I can always use a quicksilver quickie."

Responsively, not unlike one would a mushroom off a cooling baking fork, the devil Illuminaries had as Irisiel Mercherm pulled Mithras's severed and still hardened head off the tip of Chaos's trident. She thereupon ran off with it blindingly fast. Irisiel wouldn't stop until she reached Little-Star Lazareme's between-space domicile on Tympani, the Isle of the Undying One, a thousand miles from the Gregarian Fields in the Aural Sea, Sedon's Ear, mere minutes later.

Once there she washed and pressed his bed sheets, had a bath of her own, plucked and stuffed Mithras's head full of goose down, just for comfort's sake, and laid herself down, the better to compose herself in anticipation of her father's coming attentions. So speedy was she, all of that took barely a few more minutes.

As it turned out she might as well have composted herself.

========

"Well, well, well," remarked Unholy Abaddon, unable to resist fay-saying after surviving Everyman's 'quicksilver quickie' groaner with his stomach contents in place, "That went well."

"Why don't you be a dick and do a dildo, Abe?" Harmonia snarled, clearly wanting their father alone for perhaps more than just a verbal thrashing. As she could recall without any trouble from her days as Nemesis, her chains made superb flails.

"An excellent suggestion," agreed his brood brother, no more pleasantly than their brood sister had been. "Go off with your pal the Thanatoid and have a cold one on me. Just be sure to tell him he better stop boasting he can take me."

"That seems a sensible plan," Lazareme concurred. "Do it!"

"With bliss, honourable father." Chaos essayed a mocking bow, then added: "Oh, and thank you, dad." He left them. Shortly thereafter both he and Tantal Thanatos vanished. The female Thanatoid, Mithras's Virgin, Heat to her brother's Cold, lingered. The female Unity nudged her father. He took the hint.

"You need some marching orders too, Order?"

"Battle Baby's back," Harmonia noted. "So are a veritable bouquet of sweet smelling lady-slippers you won't have seen for a few centuries, including her two brood sisters. Why don't you go off and re-familiarize yourselves?"

Lord Order didn't need marching orders. He liked tough women and when Battle Babe's triad dwelt alongside the Unities on the Outer Earth's Indian subcontinent, they were worshipped as warrior goddesses by its migratory druidic peoples. As such they had combative personalities and attributes similar to Mars Bellona, the Apocalyptic of War, and the Medusa, War's Whore, nowadays self-proclaimed Mother Murder.

Battle Babe gained her nickname because her power focus was called the Sabre Rattle. That made her the inspirational soul of her threesome, the other two being conflict's wits and its facial frontage. She and her sisters were collectively known as the Morrigu or Morrigan, the same as the Hellions' Mother Superior, the equivalent of the Korants' Miracle Maenad.

A few minutes later Yajur went off with all three of them.

========

In the meantime Methandra, as ever masked and covered in voluminous garments made of varying shades of red, mauve and purple cloth, took the two male Unities leaving their father and brood sister by themselves as her cue. She came up to them.

"Sorry, Hot Stuff," Lazareme greeted her, egocentrically pretending to anticipate her forthcoming appeal wrongly. "I'm a confirmed bachelor."

"Who has the six terrible talismans," she responded, also wrongly and not to him. "They must be destroyed, Harmony, in the name of sanity and in the spirit of Panharmonium."

"She's right, father."

"Who's to say they haven't been already?" he challenged his last non-departed firstborn, just as pointedly ignoring Methandra.

"You, I hope," said Harmonia, giving him her best golden smile. It didn't work.

"Because I can't lie. But, as a freshly proclaimed, not to mention generously proportioned Apple Isle Goddess and her just as generously horny Bull rather rudely put to us moments ago, the Dual Entities can and do lie. Is there anything else, Virgin?"

"The Perpetual Presences," said Methandra, this time, lesson learned, seeming to address Lazareme directly. Then again, when dealing with someone wearing a mask, it was sometimes difficult to tell if she was looking at anyone. "I see no sign of the Pauper Priestess and her Demon Child."

"And I see no sign of a second Great Flood. It might snow, though. Of course that could be your brood brother about to give me a cold shower in ultimate aid of him claiming your cherry first. Devils are really good at witching weather."

"You are an impossible man," exclaimed Methandra, in manifest exasperation.

"Wrong, I'm a considerate god who just happens to hold onto an impossible dream."

"Bah! Grandfather Sedon should be through visiting Great-Grandfather Cabby up in Cabalarkon by now. He's probably in Grand Elysium waiting for the Pauper to show up. I shall inform him directly of what you two forced your brother, my father, to do to her and their child. Sedon shall not be amused. You'll become much brighter shining out of the night's sky."

"Do let us know when you see him."

"Why, so you can drop an asteroid on us?"

"It's a thought," said Lazareme. "Isn't it puff of smoke time yet, Virgin?"

She was gone, in just that.

========

The Attis may or may not have passed out while the two Lazaremist healers tended him.

========

However, he was at least semi-conscious when the multi-horned Bull of Mithras grabbed Azkeecyoos's power focus, mindfully rendered it more akin a hacking hatchet than a precision blade and used it to chop off his right foot at the ankle. Attis's reactive shriek of pain betrayed consciousness. Then he wasn't whatsoever. He'd passed out for sure this time.

Just in case either of the Lazaremists might be tempted to sew it back on, Plathon eyefire-incinerated his foot. He next tossed Surgeon the Sturgeon's scalpel back to him and goaded the goat: "Staunch it, bitch."

Her goat's milk was good for many purposes besides making bi-solar entities barf at its stench. So was her shepherd's crook. Flames weren't all it generated. Amal-Althea staunched it. Lazareme's two healers thereupon took themselves elsewhere in disgust, leaving it to Bouncing Belle to reproach him.

"That wasn't very nice, Bull."

"I guess that's why they call me Cruel Plathon. We wouldn't want him to run away, would we?"

"Can I cut off the other one?"

"I wouldn't have thought a foot's what you'd want to cut off."

"Don't confuse me with my sister. Shall we go?"

Plathon hefted Attis onto one massive shoulder. He bounded across the abandoned battlefield towards Kore's wheeled cauldron, newly emergent from the Weird.

Lady Lust, Belialma-Beltis, was right behind him, admiring his bullish butt all the way. She didn't bound; she bounced. She was called Bouncing Belle for a variety of reasons.

Divine Coueranna, Kore-Concord, was already in her wheeled dogcart. Her tethered, multi-headed Cereberant hellhounds, between-space psychopomps that they were – not that devils needed anything more than their talismans to get about between-space – were raring to go. And go they did, once the Bull threw the Attis into the cauldron and both he and Satanwyck's now ex-Prime Sinistral clambered in after him.

Kore of the Many Names and Multiple Personalities clamped the still-missing Jackal God's dog collar around the deviant's neck. It was hers. One of her many names and multiple personalities was Kore-Anubis.

========

"What was all that crap about the Dual Entities can and do lie?" Harmonia demanded of Lazareme once they were finally by themselves. She intended it as a preface to her verbally lashing him for abandoning the principles of Panharmonium, but he had something far more dramatic in mind as a response.

Reaching into the pocket of his ravendeer coat, he pulled out the tee-tee tail he'd started reading to her that morning as they ate brunch. It was the one he'd plucked off Saudi the Steg Sari's backside the night before while he was drunkenly trying to dance with her. "Here, have a boo. And don't say I didn't warn you."

She didn't, though what she hurriedly scanned of it was truly shocking.

****

THEO 18:

THE MASTER'S REGALIA
========

Kanin City's Master of Weir stepped out of the Weird off the Anthean Agate she fool-ishly insisted her son always carry with him.

========

Squatting there, wild-eyed and shivering in the Gregarian Fields' churned up turf on the outskirts of the still smouldering woods, he looked even more the worse for wear than he had when last she saw him. The sleeves and fringes of his badly tat-tered djellaba appeared burnt, though for some reason he didn't, thank God. None-theless, he also looked bordering on dementia, like one of the pureblood nincompoops up in Cabalarkon's Weirdom whom she so often mocked.

Many questions needed immediate answering. Why was he fingering the bot-tom half of his eye-stave as if it was his recorder? Where had the top half of it gone, including its prison pod? And what were those one, two …six glowing talismans do-ing there? He couldn't have become the Attis's latest succession, could he? One per family was already one too many.

"Hi, mom," said George Masterson, as she helped him to his feet. "Where've you been?"

"Having the experience of an after-lifetime, if you have to know. But I'm okay now. How's the rest of your day been going?"

"Lousy. Saudi and her Terror Donna somehow survived me bashing their brains out. She's after deviant daddy's quill and the way I figure it she thinks killing us off one by one will eventually get it for her. The last one I saw her whack not only looked a little like you, in a snaky sort of way, she had your voice. Any idea why that might be?"

"Unfortunately for me personally, it's not just your half-brothers and sisters she's been killing. She's probably still out there somewhere, maybe even listening to us between-space as we talk. Where's Hinny and what happened to the rest of your eye-stave? We might need it."

"I think Saudi's sorted, mom. But I'm no more sure how than I am about what happened to Hinny or the rest of my eye-stave. Everything's kind of fuzzy. Didn't you bring your mace?"

"What you see is what you get." Other than she'd had something that at least looked like her Master's Mace with her, what he saw was his white-as-daylight mother dressed almost exactly as she'd been on the crashing cosmicar just before All and Attis rescued him; always assuming that had been her and not Sedon's Whore masquerading as her.

"Once we're home, safe and dry, I'll tell you all about it. Pick those things up and grab my hand. I'll have to risk walking us back to Kanin through the Weird."

"Maybe you better. The fellow who saved mine and Hinny's bacon specifically said they were for you; that Attis won't be needing them anymore." He used the bottom half of his somehow slashed-in-two eye-stave to indicate the six Great Godly Glories still laying in the mud and muck of the Mole.

"Fellow?" she queried, replete with even more questions. "You sure it wasn't a devil? That would explain the snapped eye-stave and missing eyeorb. He wouldn't want to hazard you sucking him into it."

"Like I said, everything's still kind of fuzzy. But, if he was, he only had two eyes."

"Devils can suppress their third eyes as readily as they can change their glamours. What did he look like? Say it wasn't your father."

"All I can say for sure is he didn't look like my father looked this morning at Yeast's mother's booze-tent. He had brown eyes, long dark hair and a full beard; wore sandals and a robe, except he had something like Hinny's feathery fur draped over top it as a coat against the cold. His skin was neither black nor particularly white. If I were to guess a race I'd say Semite. Come to think of it, he reminded me most of that fellow depicted in all those mosaics dad made for you before he buggered off."

"Did he indeed? Jordy always had gallons of gall."

Knowing what he now knew about the Legendarian, Georgie could appreciate her train of thought. "I suppose that doesn't mean it couldn't have been dad, does it? He certainly knew how to use dad's quill. That's how he disappeared, I think; used it to draw himself elsewhere.

"But, before he left he definitely said those things were for you. I was hoping Hinny would come back with the rest of my eye-stave – or else one of our still airborne cosmicars would show up looking for me – because I wanted to haul them home without having to touch them. They're dangerous, aren't they?"

Helena was about to confirm that when she had what amounted to an epiphany. Georgie knew exactly whom that fellow in all those mosaics represented. However, as a matter of respect – all the more so since most of the Illuminaries, Trinondevs and scientocrats she allowed instruct him in the ways of Weir didn't share her Outer Earth based convictions – she insisted everyone she influenced, Georgie included, refrain from using his name inappropriately.

Clearly he didn't believe he'd seen whom he must have seen. She did, though. Something came through the Weird. It wasn't Hinny the Hippy yet.

========

Sometime shortly thereafter, Hinny the Hippy did trot out of the woods in the direction of her in effect former owner, George Masterson.

Riding the mishmash beastie, her devolved but nevertheless fidgety prize restrained within her now transparent and consequently no longer self-kneading, powder puff power focus, was the hippo-hind's in effect new owner, Tralalorn.

========

Three others were with him, as was a different specimen of psychopomp. One of them looked like ambulatory alabaster in a star-cape. She was pulling a peculiarly mirrored cruciform over her head depending from an apparent rosary of bloodstone rubies. In her hand she held an approximation of her masterly mace, albeit without an actual eyeorb atop it.

Hinny excitedly vomited a bug as if a hairball in greeting. Had you really good eyes you might think it resembled a pterosaur with its wings flapping and a goat's head. Outfitted in the six Great Godly Glories, already transformed to suit both her position as the Master of Weir and in honour of her unwavering faith in a resurrected messiah, Helena Somata promptly stepped on it, crushing it unto mush.

'Vengeance is mine saith the Lady', she mentally smirked to herself.

Either aware the eyeorb atop the approximation of Helena's masterly mace was a fake, or else blissfully unaware of what a real one might or might not be able to do to her, the Demon Child briefly debated devolving her as she had Saudi the Steg Sari. Instead, she said: "You're not my mommy, tra-la I'm gloomy."

"Ah, but I am, Lorna." Altering the Mask of Byron and Lazareme's Cloak of Many Colours, Kanin City's to-everyone-else still externally white-as-light Master gave the Demon Child an eye-opener. It was of a demon-winged, otherwise physically human, owl-faced, two-eyed female with feet that were a harpy's talons.

That she knew her identity and what to show her, Master Helena didn't put down to the Thrygragos or Trigregos Talismans doing her thinking for her. She didn't believe inanimate objects, even if they were composed of Godstuff, could think for themselves, let alone anyone else. Neither did she believe the *'fellow'* that left them for her was the latest incarnation of the legendary 30-Year Man who'd once been her husband.

That he might have been Thrygragos Lazareme still hadn't occurred to her and even if it had, wouldn't have mattered. Her epiphany of a few moments ago had escalated into a series of dazzling realizations. She recognized a gift from God when she got one. And in Tralalorn she just got another.

The Hidden Headworld had two female perpetual presences to go along with a lone male. At last apprehending that Pyrame Silverstar was just sheen on the daemonic diamond, she now had them both. The Devil would have to come to her in Kanin City if he wanted to maintain the Cathonic Zone. He did, she and her vastly superior Trinondevs, led by her stalwart son and not by any of Cabby the Daddy's imbeciles, would be waiting.

On their home ground, rather than out here in the Mole, they'd soon see if they were worthy of calling themselves True Utopians. Of course they had to get back there first. Once there, though, bring him on!

========

"Tra-la tra-trait, you are, tra-la tra-great."

"That doesn't make any sense," complained Masterson.

"It might, Georgie," said Volsanga, the Hellion Valkyrie who'd accidentally presented Helena with her hellacious under-body, "Depending on what your mom just showed her."

"It certainly rhymes," observed Ute Tethys. Despite this Lorna's three eyes and the rest of her devilishly daemonic appearance, Ute figured they were dealing with a feeorin trickster, a fay-saying faerie fart, which they may well be. Fays had always claimed Tralalorn as one of their own. Lorna did mean *'lost'* after all.

Neither the teenage Swan Maiden, who'd first spotted Helena's new body, nor her mother, who'd been hitching a lift behind her at the time, realized it had just been burnt out of All of Incain. Thinking it the corpse of a possibly heroic harpy – which, for a harpy, wouldn't be a contradiction in terms – Ute swooped down from the sky on her psycho-cygnet, the other psychopomp-specimen there with them.

With her Valkyrie's not so much practised as educated eye, she wanted to determine if it was worthy of walking Hell's Halls for the Glorious Dead, where creatures much stranger than harpies were sometimes seen. Mama Volsanga cracked the crystal skull they'd just collected, the one containing Helena's captured soul-soul, onto the apparent harpy's head experimentally. Next to instantly a Utopian's soul-self – rather than a devic Spirit Being – reanimated it.

Unlike virtually every other, onetime devil's conveyance, it retained some measure of brains. Sure, they were long dormant. But with them came memories and, as soon as she could, Helena vowed to spend time picking them. She had no problem dominating it, however. She was still an alpha female.

"Do you want to come home with us, Lorna?" she gently prodded. The little horror didn't, she'd soon discover if the six Great Godly Glories could kill her.

"Can I keep my dino-dolly, mommy?" she hesitated, in a tone of genuine concern, before committing herself.

An Ant Nightingale as well as an Illuminary, Helena had learned a great deal about Tralalorn over the years of her training. She'd also heard about her from Apple Isle's Miracle Maenad. Except that she never visibly aged, Trala reputedly acted exactly like a petulance-prone little girl would.

Punning dreadfully on her fondness for goatish chimeras, the Korants' High Priestess once told her that you had to treat Trala with kid gloves. Helena therefore further vowed that if she said yes, she'd do her best to mix a modicum of motherly love ladled out with sensibly substantial spoonfuls of sternness. She just hoped that come the inevitable day Hinny turned up with a goat's head Georgie wouldn't get too upset.

"Only if you agree to keep her in that big bauble of yours when you take her out," she allowed in that spirit. Then she added an appreciable proviso: "And only if you first make yourself more fit to be feted. Weirdoms aren't known for welcoming cutesy chthonic children with red skin, a pair of pointy little horns, and three eyes."

"This better, tra-la try blacker?" asked Trala, after face-dancing herself two-eyed and black-skinned like the Master's son, whom she'd plainly decided to adopt as her big brother.

========

It was much better, they all agreed.

****

POST-THEO:

LET IT RAIN

========

Something had happened to Pyrame's demon. Now the mighty Eye-Mouth in the sky wouldn't need her anymore. Oh well, she allowed herself to hope; maybe he'd still want her. Maybe he'd come for her like he had thousands of years ago in the Dome's first decades.

Unless she'd made that up of course!

========

Pyrame Silverstar awoke inside All the manifestly not all-invincible. They were back between-space off the Prison Beach of Incain, on the southernmost coast of Sedon's Head just below the Cattail Peninsula's Whiplash Range.

When it came to the miraculous Solidium very nearly beat Gypsium, especially when they combined in the Weird as Stoprock or Brainstone. Following her shared feast with the He-Sphinx on the pre-Genesea Unnameable, the Dual Entities sank All's roots on the then-island of Incain and that's where they stayed after Machine-Memory shut her down by the simple expedient of removing the original Female Three.

She reactivated trying to put the bite on the Moloch Sedon the day he came looking for not-yet-Pyrame at an unspecified time somewhere in the early decades of the Dome. Thereafter the She-Sphinx never altogether detached herself from said roots, not even during her rare forays beyond the Beach. As the Dual Entities might say, in that annoying future-speak of theirs, that was her story and both Pyrame and All were sticking to it.

As someone also once said, devils were veracious not voracious. They can't lie but if they make up something they henceforth convince themselves to be fact and not fiction, they tell it likewise, as just that, as the unvarnished truth. It wasn't so much a matter of wilful ignorance as wilful deception. Best of all, they'd never remember they made it up in the first place.

Chthonic critters such as Mandroids, demons and faeries could, can and do lie. They might not do it endlessly as Hell's Belle claimed the Dual Entities did but, as the Medusa proved so long ago, only one demon's body could co-engender Sed-sons. It was that of Pyrame's now lost Lily – Primeval Lilith, the Demon Queen of the Night.

Drifting off again, she dreamed of someone else Lily may have co-engendered: Anti-Patriarch Cain, Slayer of Abel. She further dreamed Cain was Adam Kadmon or Heliosophos – Helios called Sophos the Wise, the Male Entity – in his first lifetime. She might have been as right about that as fucking faeries were when they claimed Tralalorn was one of their own.

Then again she might have been just as wrong.

========

When they appeared on the Prison Beach of Incain at sunset that Mithramas Day, 4376 YD, All the not-so-invincible-anymore for once did not say: 'Go away or All eat you'. Instead, the comparatively tiny but still tetrahedral-headed She-Sphinx imparted: "Go away, Dual Entities, or I'll eat you."

========

"Well, well as a hell," said the male of the two, "If it isn't the fabulously female Pauper Priestess. We were afraid you'd been sucked into a Utopian eyeorb up in the Mole."

"Afraid or hoped?" All asked, in Pyrame's voice and with her lucidity.

"Don't be such a hard loser, Pyrame," said Harmonia, sounding like herself, the Unity of Panharmonium. "You're a devil, we're not. Well, I am and so is Helios, except he's the dominant one and I'm just humanizing Memory."

"Mithras?"

"He got stoned."

"Everybody must get stones," chimed in her companion, singing in a nasally sort of voice as if he was imitating someone specific, probably from the future. "Except you of course. You always seem to get left out, don't you: no power focus to call your own, no protectorate to call your home and now no Mithradic nugget to call your stone."

"By the Unnameable?" Pyrame wanted to know, pointedly ignoring the verbally as well as mentally meandering male and his incomprehensible inanities.

"We're still trying to work that out," persisted Lazareme, in his own voice, which happened to be Helios's voice. "Then he got pebbled. I kept his head. To say the least there were some rocky moments."

"When did you find out?"

"You're not suggesting you've always known it, are you? Because I only re-realized it this morning."

"I've a good memory," Pyrame responded, "As in a good memory, lower case. Devils have always been shape shifters. Wherever we went in our journeys throughout the heavens we adjusted our looks to that of the dominant sentient species of wherever we were. Yet whenever we were on the Sedonshem betwixt and between stops, you, Mithras and Great Byron eventually reverted to your original humanoid shapes.

"So did Grandfather Sedon, albeit as a faun, which used to make me think it was as much of a fluke as an uncanny case of wish-fulfillment that he was brought into being looking like the Dual Entities' notion of the Devil Himself. It still does."

"And I always looked like the Male Entity?"

"Understand that there were vast periods of time when the mighty Moloch, in his to me unfathomable wisdom, didn't want me as his bunkmate. Nonetheless, whenever he did – whenever he allowed my personality to come to the forefront, that is to say – and whenever I therefore saw you, yes, you did look like the Male Entity; albeit as if freshly recovered from his latest time-tumble. And by that I mean you looked a lot like the Attis always does once he's succeeded himself, as a kind of Middle Sea pretty boy: fit, tanned and with blond hair.

"The point I'm trying to make is that all that changed once Sedon got me out of All the first time, all those centuries ago. That's when I heard you'd acquired that goofy godliness gift of yours, your words."

"Heard?"

"As I've just heard you, Uncle Everyman," she said, spicing her words with a dash of ridicule, "With whatever passes for my auditory channels as opposed to my ocular ones."

In order to semi-normalize their conversation she adjusted All's head, allowing it to attain a semblance of hers as a silver-haired human beauty. She always sported an appealing face, but her mouth and teeth had never seemed quite so disproportionately sized before.

"All I'm saying it that ever since then I've perceived you the same as Harmony tells me she always does: as a three-eyed, Great Godly version of the born Edenite, Alorus Ptah. You might not eat golden apples anymore but you're forever rejuvenating. Golden Age Humanity's first patriarch – and the father-founder of both its dynasties, that of Cain and that of Pseth Ra – saw you, he'd think he was looking into a mirror of his youth."

"So long as it's not the Amateramirror, I suppose I would too."

"Big duh, that, Kadmon," said Harmonia. "You are he."

"You've certainly his sky-blue skin, sea-green eyes and sun-blond hair," Pyrame carried on. "But you never look like you need a shave. In fact, when it comes right down to it, only the hair's much the same as I saw Lazareme's throughout most of those many multiple-millennia we were together on the Sedonshem.

"Everything else is slightly different, which is probably how it should be. Helios is just a man. Without access to Cathonic Fluid or golden apples he ages normally. His hair greys and thins. Sometimes he lets himself go, puts on weight and grows a beard or cuts off his hair. You never do any of that."

"Maybe young Helios is your god," Harmonia injected, speaking subversively. "You've humanized Machine-Memory often enough in the past, our past, and as

I'm already restarting to appreciate, theirs has always been something of a love-hate relationship."

"I'm agreeing with you, Harmony," said Pyrame, via All. "That also makes it typical of most mortals' relationships to their gods and, believe me, I've been in enough of them to know how strained that gets."

"Not to mention how typical it is of most devils' relationships to their fathers and grandfather," the Unity did mention, as a kind of coda to Pyrame's observations.

"Hey," Helios-Lazareme protested, "I am standing right here beside you."

"So you are," Harmonia concurred, with a golden wink.

Pyrame-All caught Harmony's signal, but wasn't sure how to interpret it. She was sure of one thing, however. "Never forget I was part of the first Unnameable. At least theoretically we came together as the Conglomerate Devil in order to break the daemons' queen and the rest of their hierarchy out of Andy the Androsphinx.

"We did so because you two claimed that, once released, the daemons would become our allies against the golden-apple-eaters, whom we could no more possess than we can pureblood Utopians to this day. But the whole thing was a trap, wasn't it?

"Ginny the Gynosphinx, as we thought of All in those days, was waiting between-space to pounce. Which she did, whereupon Andy and her had themselves a fine feast, didn't they. On us!

"That not so trifling misadventure cost Trala and I over 700 years of mostly mindless captivity. We were the lucky ones, though. It cost everyone else stuck inside of All and Andy the better part of another 2,000 years worth of freedom. But it didn't cost either of you anything, did it? And now I know why.

"Helios, as Ptah, had the Mnemosyne Machine build both the sphinxes, there's no doubt about that. You two would have us believe Machine-Memory was his wife, Trishtar Thrae, the Biblical Eve. Yet there's never been any more proof of that than there is it was Demon King Daemonicus or Hecate the Hellion who betrayed us. We've just taken your word for it."

"You think we set you up," Helios-Lazareme understood.

"Didn't you?" snapped Pyrame-All.

"It fits, Kadmon," said Harmony, addressing Helios by the name Machine-Memory usually did. Although it could have been the given name of his original self, whomever that was, or a variation of it, many believed it referred to the notion of him being Adam-Kadmon, the Male Principal.

"When Lazareme went into Andy the first time, he came out with you, the Ptah version of Heliosophos. Only it was more like the other way around; it had to be. As a member of the rainbow class he couldn't be possessed but he could, and did, possess you – the same as he'd done howsoever many lifetimes earlier or later when he took over Varuna Mithras.

"You've been inseparable ever since. That's why Pyrame sees you as Alorus Ptah. Your godliness gift doesn't affect her the same as everyone else."

"Either that or I am her god," he smiled.

"Don't confuse me with Mithras's Masochist," said Pyrame, melded with All, angrily interrupting their too-carefree exchange. "My god is not my tormentor. I see you the way you are because it turns out that's the way you've been for, what, over 5,000 years. Everyone else sees you the way they want to see you, as a waste of space. I guess that makes me not quite so callous as most of our unkind kind, but there you have it."

"Thanks a bundle of bricks in a bathing suit I'm wearing in a tippy canoe."

"You're more than welcome. And don't try to avoid or deflect any of the blame for what happened to us, Harmony. If you're Memory, then you were just as complicit in betraying us."

"I won't deny that. I will deny I'm that Memory, however."

"Huh?"

"We're akin to puddle-jumpers," Helios-Lazareme provided. "Only instead of jumping over puddles we jump straight into them – our puddles being the time-space continuum."

"I know that. So what?"

"Puddle-jumping isn't the only game we play. Follow the leader's another. I die; Milady Memory and Trans-Time Trigon play follow the leader, right? What doesn't follow is that my dying is the only way to get rid of the Mnemosyne Machine and Trans-Time Trigon."

It had started to rain. Pyrame, though, was more mentally muddled than any muddy puddle welling up around All's unusually pint-sized paws.

"Thrygragos Lazareme claimed Anti-Patriarch Cain got rid of that time's Dual Entities, Ptah and Thrae, by feeding them golden apples he and his wife, their first born daughter – whose name was Awan, meaning Wickedness – had previously poisoned then nevertheless also ingested themselves. Only, ever-so-appropriately for a wicked witch like her, it backfired on them and Awan died too."

"I don't want to sound ironic or anything like that, Pyrame," said Harmonia, sounding ironic, "Especially not after today's events. But, do yourself a favour and look up the words mithridate and mithridatic the next time you come close to a dictionary and can flip its pages with fleshy fingers instead of pebbly paws. They don't just refer to your father."

"I know what they mean. I also know mithridates don't always work. Awan's death is proof of that. Helios dies; he goes back into the time stream taking Machine-Memory with her as the innards of Trans-Time Trigon. They don't leave bodies behind. Awan died and she did leave a body behind. Cain buried her in Enoch City, with all due pomp and circumstance.

"Yet his half-brother, Ptah's third born, Pseth Ra, and his wife, Azura, the Biblical Adam and Eve's fifth born, did a ditto with their parents. How am I doing so far?"

"That was our contribution to Cain's parricides," said Lazareme-Helios. "We hadn't done that, Ra and the rest of his dynasty – all but one of whom, Xuthros Hor, were alive by then – would have realized a lack of corpses didn't track and, maybe, figured out we were about."

"We'd been on the planet less than a year," Harmonia, as if on her own behalf, elaborated. "Although we suspected Utopians preceded us, we weren't sure how much, if anything, the rainbow class dynasties, or the Edenites before them, knew about us devils. We did know Cain didn't know anything about the Dual Entities, though, and he was hardly alone in that."

"How?"

"Because I read him while he slept. And I was hardly the only one. Byronics, Mithradites and more than a few of my younger sisters slipped into his bed inside his bedmates. Like father, like son, Cain had a weakness for women and didn't particularly care if they were allergic to golden apples or not. It seemed prudent."

"And so it was, even Sedon was impressed at your cleverness; not to mention the Dual Entities' idiocy. It wasn't much of a problem either, because both of you could possess Mother Earth worshipping Hellions and they can cast splendours on corpses with their hellstones as easily as they can on living beings. But three bodies and the fact he got sick, too, also allowed Cain to convincingly blame their deaths on members of the non rainbow class. Your chicanery let him get away with murder yet again."

"Which Sedon, through Plathon, turned to our advantage 60 odd years later."

"But now you're telling me you were flat out lying. How is that possible, Harmony?"

"Call me Memory. The Dual Entities can and do lie, Pyrame."

"There is that," she granted her.

"Anyhow," Lazareme-Helios confirmed, used to devils all-but-ignoring him when any of his firstborn were around, "With one rather glaring correction, namely that we had to fake my death, that's our story and we're sticking to it. Oh, and in case you think Memory did all the heavy lifting, let me assure you Trishtar Thrae did know about the Dual Entities. Want to guess how I learned that?"

Pyrame-All finally began to gain a glimmer of comprehension. "Trishtar Thrae was just an ordinary, golden-apple-eating ex-Edenite."

"Who wasn't bad in the sack, as I can now recall," he confirmed, "Especially not for a mortal in her seventh century of life. Ptah's Memory made up the innards of Trans-Time Trigon, yes, and Trishtar knew all about her, yes as well. But that Memory wasn't humanized until Harmony went into Ginny the Gynosphinx and came out with her."

"Believe it or not," Harmonia said, "Machine-Memory initially built the two sphinxes so she and Helios could screw each other."

"Now that I do believe. Those two go crazier and crazier the older they get."

Harmonia picked up the narrative. "Ptah's Memory was wiped out when the Trans-Time Trigon whose innards she made up, and which stood in the Cainites' Enoch City, was destroyed by Anti-Patriarch Cain towards the middle of the following century.

"Every other Heliosophos you've encountered; indeed, every other Heliosophos we've encountered since 726 PD – we being Lazareme and Harmony – doesn't realize Lazareme's the Alorus Ptah Helios because the Mnemosyne Machine vets his memories every time he tumbles through time and decides which ones it's safe for him to keep.

"No surprise there, is there? As you've noted a few times already during our un-scheduled shower together, he's essentially a human being. His brain can only con-tain so many memories without overheating. That's why he gets so insane when he lives too long."

"Until I got hold of Lazareme anyhow. For a god he's awfully sane."

Pyrame refrained from commenting on that. However, having humanized her many times over the course of her very nearly interminable existence, she knew the Mnemosyne Machine did indeed vet his memories before she let him wake up and get on with his latest lifetime. She must vet her own as well, before she allowed her-self to be humanized, because Pyrame had never heard any of this before.

It made about as much sense as anything else having to do with the Dual Enti-ties did, though. "All right, I'll bite," she couldn't resist reiterating, via her proportion-ately too big mouth and teeth. "Which Memory has you now, Harmony?"

"All of them and none of them. I'm the original. Machine-Memory helped Helios and Cabby the Daddy create Sedon in his fifth lifetime so I, meaning her, could be forever."

"Why wait five lifetimes?"

"That the tee-tee tail doesn't say," said Helios-Lazareme.

"All this comes from a tee-tee tail? Well, bugger that!"

Pyrame had warned them to go away. He in particular should have paid atten-tion. All didn't kill and, with certain exceptions, Helios being the most exceptional, devils weren't supposed to kill. All, though, wasn't in her right mind. Pyrame was her right mind. At her command, the silver-haired She-Sphinx grew another mouth be-tween-space underground. Wormlike – more like Demogorgon-like – it erupted on a second neck beneath their feet; whereupon it swallowed the pair of them.

For anyone else within earshot, which probably nobody was, she commenced to audibly scrunching on both.

========

Methandra Thanatos, Heat to her brood brother's Cold, did as she'd threatened to do. She went to Grand Elysium to complain to her thought-grandfather about what the Lazaremist Extremists did to the two female perpetual presences and, by extension, if only potentially, to the whole of his Hidden Headworld.

Dark Sedon was there, abed awaiting Pyrame Silverstar in her latest shell – he'd told Mithras he fancied Ute Tethys sometime back but, as per usual, he'd have been happy with anyone Pyrame chose. The male of the Head's perpetual presences informed Hot Stuff she would do just fine in the meantime.

She left him sheets aflame and passion insatiate. Men, even the God-King of Deva-kind, were all the same.

========

After a thorough chew, a bloody belch and a too large tongue licking conse-quentially gory spittle off too large lips, the silver-haired She-Sphinx regurgitated one of them. "You're right, Harmony, you are the original Memory. All can't munch her maker. She could, you'd already be digested."

"Helios?"

"You never said which one he was. There can't be a Number Five without a Number One, Two, Three or Four. Wasn't that why you winked at me?"

"I guess it must have been. Got to have a Number Five before I can be me."

"Or any of the rest of us can be we."

"Can I at least have my father back?"

"My demon?"

"Mithras melted her out of existence, I imagine."

"And Tralalorn?"

"Like mother, like daughter, dot-ditto."

"Sedon will be pissed."

"It is raining."

"So it is. Tell you what, you find me Trala and my demon. Her name's Lily, by the way. Yes, that Lily, Primeval Lilith. Or at least you find out and tell me what for sure has happened to them. You do that, then I'll give you Lazareme – though why you'd want him back, I wouldn't want to begin to speculate. He's such an inconsequential little god, in all respects. All already isn't finding him very nourishing."

"I'm surprised you'd trust me, Pyrame. Don't Dual Entities always lie?"

"Not until they become Dual Entities, Harmony."

"How about I give you a power focus instead, as a gesture of good faith? I could leave you a few of the things, if you prefer. I've a kibisis full of unclaimed Tvasitar-trinkets. That's why we came to Incain in the first place, you know: To have All tongue-tug us to the Outer Earth so we can return them to those they initially belonged to, assuming we can locate them. It was my idea. I am the Unity of Panharmonium after all – quite literally now."

"And a Memory without a Trans-Time Trigon to call her home." The Pauper Priestess could empathize. "I hope you brought a bumbershoot."

Power foci were transmutable. All's tummy was turbulent. Thrygragos Lazareme was such an inconsequential little god. The She-Sphinx really didn't need the added aggravation of trying to digest him. She burped.

Harmonia gathered him into her chains. Dual Entities did lie. Their oaths meant zip. She was the original Memory. The Mnemosyne Machine built All of Incain. Pyrame was Sedon's Whore. Let her stew in there. Better yet, let the mighty Moloch in the sky come down here and try to get her out of there.

All would find him much more filling.

========

On the second day of the deluge Irisiel Mercherm, as Illuminaries named Lazareme's Heliodromus, his angel or jinni, raced into the Weirdom of Kanin City and didn't stop moving. She did, however, race in place.

========

At the moment Irisiel ventured to enter the Utopian stronghold, its long-lived High Illuminary and Master of Weir was posing for drawings Glee Tethys was preparing for a mosaic she'd commissioned him to make of their about to be marriage-bonded families. Helena Somata spotted her blur and realized she had an unwelcome, if perhaps not entirely unexpected visitor.

"You're taking a terrible risk coming here, devil," Helena told her, after leaving Glee to work alone for the time being.

"So I am, Master. Eldest Sister Harmony proclaims you her friend, so I trust you to act accordingly. I am just a messenger after all and she's charged me with locating the Head's two female Perpetual Presences. Can you help me?"

"I might – when the mood hits me." Pyrame Silverstar and the angel's firstborn sister aside for whatever reasons, Helena's Masterly Mace should be all she'd ever need to deal with Master Devas. She hadn't retrieved it from anyone. She'd just picked it up. Having no use for it herself, Pyrame had left it behind in her dayroom.

Ignorant of any of that, but acutely aware of how long she'd been stuck in All, Harmonia had briefed her seventh-born sister with respect to Helena's ability to all-but-instantly materialize her mace out of between-space. Fast as she was, they reckoned she could zip off before the Master finished producing and opening the prison pod atop it.

Irisiel didn't get to report back to Harmonia that day because, lessons learned, Helena now kept it between-space with its eyeorb already open.

Bring him on, sure, but only after she finished enjoying the company of Georgie and Ute's coming kids. It had been a very long time since she'd had the opportunity to fool around with grandchildren. She was in no hurry for it to end and even non-pureblood Utopians lived very long and very healthy lives.

Demon-occupying Masters of Weir might survive even longer.

Let it pour!

========

Forty days and 40 nights the deluge continued unabated. Harmonia, the Unity of Panharmonium, awoke at dawn of the 41st day. Her father, Thrygragos Lazareme, continued to bodily snore beside her, his head pillowed by the by then thoroughly crushed-comfortable skull of Thrygragos Varuna Mithras.

Leaving him there, she went outside the between-space domicile where they'd lain for a month plus. It was still 4376 YD on the Hidden Continent of Sedon's Head. It wouldn't turn 4377 until the beginning of Surma, the first of day of the four-month-long Lazaremist Ternary. There was still a Cathonic Dome. It was sunny.

All was at it should be. The Moloch Sedon had just been playing with them.

****

FEELING THEOCIDAL:

AUTHOR'S AFTERWORD
========

Next time you're strolling from the *Museo Mural Diego Rivera* to the *Palacio de Bellas Artes* in Mexico City, walk along *Avenida Juarez* rather than through Alameda Park. That way you'll spot a statue on the park's perimeter of a muscular, nearly naked fellow with a cloak-like strip of cloth strategically draped over one arm and one leg. He's depicted wearing a Phrygian cap (without a Brainrock quill stuck into it) and wielding a Roman-style *'gladius'* or straight, stabbing sword. There's also a belt and pouch strapped over his chest.

True, the statue's a bronze monochrome but, especially when you're blessed or cursed with a *phantacea* like mine (that's Greek for imagination), it isn't much of a stretch to see his skin golden-brown, his cloak having many colours, his pouch as a bottomless bag and his blade curved. There's no indication as to whom the statue represents but every other statue in the park is based on Greek and/or Mediterranean mythology so, mostly from the Liberty Cap, I'm thinking it is Phrygian Attis. In other words I'm seeing FEEL THEO's Taurus Chrysaor Attis.

On four separate pedestals outside the *Palacio de Bellas Artes* rear magnificent renditions of Winged Pegasus, presumably with either Perseus or Bellerophon riding them. In **PHANTACEA** terms they'd be, once again, the Attis, this time astride Peg, his unimaginatively named psychopomp.

Go inside the Palace, up the stairs to the third level. Lo, there's David Alfaro Siqueiros's *Nueva democracia* ("New Democracy"), probably the most famous Mexican mural ever done. Me, I don't see Siqueiros's wife, Angelica Arenal de Siqueiros, as the iconic, bare-breasted woman breaking out of chains. I see the whole mural as representing Datong Harmonia, FEEL THEO's self-proclaimed Unity of Panharmonium.

Along the same wall to its left is another triptych: Jorge Gonzalez Camarena's *Humanidad librándose* ("Humanity Liberating Itself"). Who's the woman shown on its right third? Surely – better make that serendipitously – it's Pyrame Silverstar, albeit with a normal head and eyes. She's definitely got Pyrame's silvery hair. As for the crucified fellow smashing apart the wooden cross to which he's been tethered, that has to signify Terrible Tethys from PRE-THEO, doesn't it.

To Humanity's left, occupying the entire west wall of the mezzanine, is Diego Rivera's "Man, Controller of the Universe". Nelson Rockefeller commissioned the original in 1933 for New York City's RCA Building. When Rivera refused to remove the figure of Vladimir Lenin, Rockefeller had the entire mural chiselled off the wall. Needless to say, New York's loss thereafter became Mexico's gain.

On the right third of the Rivera mural, he shows a decapitated statue of a Great God. Below it, note the peasant sitting on its severed head as if a cushion. Who do you suppose the god might be? Opposite it, way across the stairwell on the mezzanine's east wall is *La Katharsis* by José Clemente Orozco. Could that red-skinned voluptuary be beguiling Belialma, Sinistral Lust of Satanwyck? Of course it could (not).

There, on the south wall, in the midst of Siqueiros's "Torment of Cuauhtemoc" (Attacking Eagle), is that a Keres Hellhound? Is the distraught woman dressed in various shades of red Hot Stuff, Methandra Thanatos, minus the mask and 3rd eye? And, on the front-facing balcony outside the Palace's second level, is that statue of the mother of the muses really Mnemosyne, the Sophia to Helios's Sophos? Is that therefore a rendition of the miraculous Female Principal once humanized? Wouldn't want to speculate, would I.

Until now I haven't even mentioned the massive statuary found along the *Paseo de la Reforma*, which runs north and south of Av Juarez. Wilderwitch as *Diana Cazadora* (Huntress) is to the south, near the *Bosque de Chaputec*, whilst an arguable Raven's Head caw-whinnies outside the *Torre El Caballito*, at the Juarez intersection. Between them, at *Insurgentes*, there are a couple of John Sundown types within the *Monumento de Cuauhtemoc* and, closer to *Diana Cazadora*, a Gloriel D'Angelo type atop the *Monumento de la Independencia* in the *'glorieta'* of the same name.

Who'd have thought Mexico City would provide a veritable hotbed of imagery applicable to the **PHANTACEA Mythos**? I'm the obvious answer to that. But, now that you've read **"Feeling Theocidal"**, and are about to embark upon the opening chapter of **"The War of the Apocalyptics"**, which I've included immediately after this missive as a bonus, maybe you're another answer.

But wait! Which is to say: *Whoa!* Wilderwitch, Raven's Head, Blind Sundown, Gloriel D'Angelo: weren't they characters from the six issue **PHANTACEA** comic book series that came out between 1977 and 1980? They were indeed, as were the four Primary Apocalyptics: War, Plague, Disaster and Mother Murder, who you'll have noted also appear in FEEL THEO.

And that's what's coming your way next down the *PHANTACEA* **Mythos** print publication pipeline. **"The War of the Apocalyptics"** is the first book in a series of prose novels not so much based on the comic books as retelling their as yet not-quite-finished storylines.

So how does this jibe with **"Feeling Theocidal"** being Book One in **"The Thrice-Cursed Godly Glories"** Trilogy? Let me put it this way: Book Three in the trilogy is set immediately after War-Pox. Like Book Two in the trilogy, it's already written. The pair just need some more of my undivided attention. Which I'll be giving them after War-Pox is ready to roll off the presses in all its thousands.

You can probably find jpegs of every one of the Mexico City murals or monuments I refer to above online. You can definitely find some of them among the stacks of personal photos I've mounted on my long-running website: *PHANTACEA* **on the Web**. A few have even creapt onto *phantacea.com*, which is solely dedicated to the various *PHANTACEA* **Mythos** print publications.

I invite you to visit both websites next time you're in the mood. My email address is on their navigation bars, if you want to get hold of me. Every so often I've been known to respond to readers' queries.

Jim McPherson
The *PHANTACEA* **Mythos**
(*www.phantacea.com*)
September 2008

THE WAR OF THE APOCALYPTICS
- November 30, 1980 to Maruta 5, 5980 -

Jim McPherson

From the creator of the *PHANTACEA* Mythos comes
Fallen Angel Devils, comes unrelentling Action, comes
the Damnation Brigade, comes ...

The War of the Apocalyptics

Children! It's a Trick, an Illusion. We're Under Attack!

Jim McPherson

A *PHANTACEA* **Mythos** Print Publication
published by James H McPherson
ISBN 978-0-9781342-4-2

WAR-POX 1:

THE DAMNATION BRIGADE

========

The last confrontation in the 17-year Secret War of Supranormals took place on Damnation Isle in the Aleutian Archipelago. The date was December 25, 1955. Advised of what was occurring there, the governments of the United States of America and the Union of Soviet Socialist Republics, in a display of cooperation until then unprecedented in the Cold War, bombarded the Island: the Americans from the air; the Soviets with missiles launched from a nearby submarine.

There were eleven supras on the Island at the time. No bodies were ever found. Nearly twenty-five years later, the launching of the Cosmic Express took place on Sunday, the 30th of November 1980.

DAMNATION ISLE 1: SUNDAY, NOVEMBER 30, 1980

========

"What the hell was that?" someone said.
"Looks like some sort of ship. Think it's a spacecraft?"
"Pretty small for a spacecraft, Airhead. Not that I've seen a spacecraft before."
"Looks more like a mini-sub."
"Submarines do not generally fall out of the sky, Diver."
"Thanks, old man. I was aware of that."

========

Devil Wind, one of Thrygragos Byron's Primary Nucleoids, whirled over the apparently deserted Aleutian Atoll.

Long ago Illuminaries of Weir named him Vayu Maelstrom, though his fellow devils called him by his attribute, which was the whirlwind. And devil he was; albeit not one of the cartoon Christian variety, most of whom were corruptions of the pagan gods and goddesses, the demons and monsters of antiquity.

Vayu was a Master Deva, a member of the virtually immortal, third generation of devazurkind. Master Devas, god-devils, were indeed fallen angels. Which of course made them extraterrestrial. It also made them the pagan gods and goddesses, if not so much so the demons and monsters of antiquity.

Humanoid and male, the skin of his muscular upper body and vaguely Amerindian-looking face was blue. A whirlwind obscured his lower body, holding him aloft. Like most devils he had a third eye just above where his eyebrows would have met if they met, which they did not. A knot of hair jetted out of the top of his otherwise shaven head. It glowed not unlike Gypsium.

Even though he called it Brainrock, Maelstrom was very familiar with the miraculous Godstuff that – after years of research and billions of bullion, most of it supplied by New Century Enterprises – Outer Earthlings finally discovered how to process into a teleportive fuel. The Cosmic Express intended to use Brainrock-Gypsium on its still inexplicably and very much violently aborted, intergalactic mission in order to travel approaching inconceivable distances in otherwise impossibly short periods of time.

Vayu's second generational father and some of his siblings in long-bodiless Byron had invested a great deal of time and effort over the past thirty-five years clandestinely guiding the work performed by NCE's dedicated coterie of, admittedly, merely mortal scientists and technicians, the ones who toiled so diligently on Centauri Island for almost as long. Consequently he hated to see it go for naught. What he hated a lot more was being sent out here on damage control duty.

Not only had the Cosmic Express exploded, it had seemingly been blown up deliberately. Even more disturbingly, early evidence indicated it hadn't so much exploded as been intercepted and, thereby, expertly deflected between-space into the Sedon Sphere, aka Cathonia, the Cathonic Zone or Dome.

Just as remarkably, best guess suggested, some of Vayu's previously ill-starred or cathonitized siblings in Byron and many more of his cousins in either Thrygragos Lazareme or Thrygragos Varuna Mithras – Lazaremists and Mithradites being the other two devazur tribes who shared the same three Great Goddess mothers the Byronics did – had been forewarned of its intentional insertion above the Hidden Headworld.

Insertion attained, they had to have seized more than just the opportunity thus presented. They had to have taken physical possession of its 66 occupants, the Express's so-called cosmicompanions: male and female humans in nearly equal proportions. At that moment its Gypsium fuel must have activated because the Express separated into its constituent vessels, its hub craft, central control vehicle and six cosmicars, all of which instantly teleported beyond the Dome, hither and yon.

In other words, the devils that managed to acquire cosmicompanions, that managed to make them their host shells, in effect broke out of jail. Needless to say, his grandfather, the Moloch Sedon, the procreative All-Father of Devazurkind, whom some Outer Earthlings regarded as the Devil, as Satan Himself, was no happier than Maelstrom was about the situation.

The latter-day Demon King – the sole member of the first generation of devazurkind – felt understandably violated. His devic essence made up the Cathonic Dome, the zone of energy that had kept the Inner Earth separate from the Outer Earth since the Great Flood of Genesis. Plus, it was he who had cathonitized most of the devils in the first place; he who enforced their howsoever many decades, centuries or millennia of confinement within Cathonia.

If he had wanted to release them, then he damn well would have, and he didn't.

As a result, because it was the Age of Byron, as opposed to the Age of Mithras or Lazareme, both of whom had had their day, Dark Sedon decreed it up to the Byronics to recathonitize them. The alternative was to take their place. Granddad hated being so alone in the night's sky.

========

"Cerebrus," imparted a spirit voice, "OMP's not with us anymore."

"Cerebrus," imparted another, "Something's trying to take me over."

"Give into it, Gloriel," thought Cerebrus David Ryne for those remaining to comprehend if not precisely hear. "If I'm right, the horror that's been our existence for the last quarter century may soon be over."

========

Of the ones who got away, the majority were third generational Master Devas. However, a few of them were fourth generational members of the Family Thanatos. There were only ten such beings. Until they came along, starting around six decades earlier, the offspring of Master Devas – by Master Devas, without resorting to occupying any intermediaries – were invariably azuras: spirit beings like their parents had been until about four thousand years ago, hence the devazur race. Not so fourth generation devils. They were as solid as he was and given time to mature, which, it went without saying, they had not been given, were potentially as powerful as he was as well.

Vayu Maelstrom, Devil Wind, knew how King Cold and his Scarlet Empress, Tantal and Methandra Thanatos, were able to have five sets of devic twins. Knew as well that the Medusa, Mother Murder, Mater Matare, the Apocalyptic of Death, was pregnant when she was cathonitized more like thirteen decades earlier; cathonitized along with the three male, Primary Apocalyptics: War, Disease and Disaster. What was done was done, though, and even Thrygragos Mithras once failed to turn back the hands of time for very long. Which was one of the reasons he'd been dead for more than 1600 years.

Maelstrom just hoped none of the Thanatoids, nor any of the cathonitized Apocalyptics, primary or otherwise, had attached themselves to the cosmicompanions whose cosmicar he had pursued mostly through between-space to this weather-beaten, ice-rimed blotch of land in the North Pacific. They would definitely resist his efforts to coerce them back inside, let alone stick them back upstairs. And, assuming they were decathonitized with their Brainrock power foci intact, they were more than capable of putting up quite a fight.

Not that they would win. Decathonitized devils were no match for someone like him. How could they be when they had to occupy human shells just to manifest themselves? Still, he was obliged by Sedonic decree not to kill lesser beings and the only way he could be sure of disposing of decathonitized devils without help would be to kill their human shells. No wonder he hated the air out here.

The apparently deserted Aleutian Atoll was a cold, dreary place shrouded by a sheath of icy fog. Using his third eye the Whirling Deva scanned the land, such as it was, warily. There were no habitations he could see. No life save a few birds, some seals on the rocks, fish in the sea, and shells on the beach. Disturbingly, something started bothering him besides the air out here.

'*This Outer Earth is truly strange,*' Maelstrom muttered to himself. '*Either my senses are addled or this smog is somehow sentient. Not devic though, not entirely. Eight, nine different creatures, human I think, or mostly so, except for one. But how?*' Staying sky-borne, he quickly found the cosmicar crashed against some rocks on the perimeter of the atoll. He could detect no signs of life inside it and there were no bodies strewn about outside it. Nor were there any devils manifest either to his human eyes or to his devic one.

'*False alarm,*' the devil breathed in relief. '*Grandfather Sedon must have made a mistake. The cosmicar got away from him but its occupants didn't. No threat here. Decathonitized devils need a body to possess in order to manifest themselves: a proper body, alive and with intelligence, preferably human. Birds, fish, and seals hardly qualify.*'

Touching ground riskily he entered the empty cosmicar and activated its computer, the likes of which he had played with while visiting his younger siblings when they were working on something probably identical back home a few years ago. He had no problem translating the resultant identification display into the universal tongue: '*November 30, 1980; Cosmicar Four; Cosmicaptain Dmetri Diomad; Cosmicompanions....*'

He switched it off. There was nothing here of any interest either. Suddenly the roof of the cosmicar collapsed from outside. Something was beating on it. Maelstrom scrunched low then whirled back into the air. A massive, multiple-eyed, man-mountain of a devil was pulverizing the car. He recognized the fourth generation Thanatoid doing the damage immediately.

"Turn, Antaeor Thanatos. Turn and face Great Byron's Primary Nucleoid." The Thanatoid was fifteen feet tall. Save for its five eyes, it was composed entirely of animate granite. Without lifting its feet off the ground, the monstrosity rotated slowly towards Maelstrom.

"Air sprite! Little wisp of nothingness! I've waited too long for this."

========

'*A quarter century, Brain Boy?*'

"That thing is a spacecraft, Witch," Cerebrus asserted. *"Only it's from down here, not up there. It's called a cosmicar. Got a computer on it. Computers generate data; data includes dates. I'm good with computers."*

"Christ! Is that who I think it is?"

"Sure looks like it, Sea," came back her twin brother. *"Can't be Peter, though."*

========

Forty-seven years ago, in the month of Antheal, Year of the Dome 5933, Unmoving Byron summoned Devil Wind, together with his fellow Primary Nucleoids, Vayu's brood brother and sister, Chimaera Glimmenmare and Sedona Spellbinder, to Aka Godbad City, the Great God their father's then as now headquarters on the Subcontinent of Aka Godbad.

Headquarters was a bit of a pun since Thrygragos Byron was just an oversized head with no body whatsoever. Due to the fact that neither his eyelids nor his lips moved any longer he was, however, aptly addressed as the Unmoving One.

What he had to say astonished them: **"It seems,"** Byron imparted through smoky Sedona, his usual mouthpiece, **"That there has been born a fourth generation. Not azuras please understand me, true devils!"**

"But that's impossible," the always-particulate Spellbinder protested in her own voice. "Only the six gods and goddesses – Thrygragos, you and your brothers, and Trigregos, your three long lost sisters – can procreate the likes of us. All we can bear, by each other, are azuras, near useless spirit beings, the same as we were before Tvasitar Smithmonger crafted our talismans."

"Even when we possess other sentient beings," added ever-changing Chimaera, Byron's Stallion, though today he had adopted the likeness of a be-armed seahorse instead of a centaur, his most common shape, "All we can beget are mortal deviants, short-lived by our own undying standards."

"Never forget the Attis, deviant son of my late, unloved brother in Sedon, Mitravaruna, and his daughter by Trigregos, whom Illuminaries sometimes called Marut Kanin, or Kore-Eris, but we knew best as Strife or Discord."

"An aberration," contributed Vayu. "A freak, not a devil."

"Yet he had near-devic abilities," Chimaera reminded Maelstrom. "Kept coming back to life and could wield our power foci, not that there's anything special about that. Nonetheless, that means it's at least conceivable. Recall, not even a hundred years ago the Medusa, Mater Matare, became pregnant by the Primary Apocalyptics."

"Murder was pregnant; that much is certain," argued smoky Sedona. "While I grant you the Undying One's smithy crafted her four extra talismans in anticipation of her giving birth to not two or three but four devils simultaneously, that doesn't mean it was by the Apocalyptics. Nor does it necessarily mean her offspring would have been fellow devils."

"We cathonitized her before we could find out," agreed Byron. **"And that's exactly what I propose to do to these ones."**

"Who are their parents?"

"Your old friends, my Stallion: King Cold of Lathakra and his Scarlet Empress, the hothead also of Mythland in the Mystic Mountains. Or as Illuminar-

ies of Weir have them: Tantal and Methandra Thanatos. I trust that makes no difference."

"Of course it doesn't."

"So be it then."

And so it sort of was: sort of because one of them, Summer, was executed by his own King Cold of a father. He'd made the mistake of falling for Pretty Parsis, Devil Wind's seductive sister from a much lower brood of three, and subsequently betraying his parents and fellow siblings to the rest of the enchantress's tribe.

As well, there had long been strong suspicions two of the others got away while Vayu and his fellow components of the Byronic Nucleus were in the process of ill-starring them. Now, almost a half century later, Maelstrom was faced with the task of recathonitizing the ground-bound elemental.

Only this time he was not fused with his father and immediate siblings; this time he was acting alone. Fortunately, so was the Thanatoid.

========

"It is Demon Land out there. I swear it."

"Hey, I'm agreeing with you, 'Lassa. I just said it wasn't our adoptive brother, is all. He died years ago, years and 25 more on top of that now. "

"Does that mean Sedon St Synne's still alive and has his devil ray working again, Davy?"

"How am I supposed to know, Yehudi? As I'm sure you'd be the first to agree, I'm hardly omniscient. I doubt it, though. St Synne would be well over a hundred by now. He couldn't possibly be alive."

"What about Strife or the Conqueror? We often speculated she was St Synne's daughter and Jesus Mandam was as close to a son as he ever came."

"I think not, Johnny. Even your abiding hatred for the Conquering Christ isn't enough to make him live again. As for Strife, who knows?"

"Look at their power, Sundown. Look at how they go at each other."

"Would if I could, Diver."

"Very funny."

"Ask me we're dealing with the real thing here," Cerebrus David Ryne speculated, again for those remaining to psychically comprehend. "No unfortunate victims of the devil ray or miracle key these. If such a thing is possible those two are real devils."

"Is it possible?"

"Has to be, Airealist. Extra eyes kind of give it away, wouldn't you say? Not that it matters. The fact is Demon Land's already called out Obadiah and Gloriel. Pray he has to call out the rest of us before he can best the whirling one."

"Then pray we can best Demon Land."

"As you say, Wilderwitch. Never known you to pray, though."

========

Antaeor swung his huge, rock club at the whirling devil. Maelstrom flew underneath it casually. Too casually! The ground erupted, soil and stone, dirt and rock, shot into him. Swiftly, hardly bruised at all, he twirled higher into the sky.

"You're no Master Deva," Devil Wind mocked his foe. "You're nothing more than a shambling, lowly Earth Thing. I'd have more sport with a fucking faerie or an actual demon. At least some of them can fly. Surrender your talisman and slide back into Cathonia. I have pressing business on the Head."

With a flick of his wrist he unleashed a burst of air that struck Antaeor square on the chest. A few pebbles were dislodged. The Man-Mountain bellowed in laughter. "If that's the best you can do, little birdie, you'd better start singing your swansong."

"I'd rather play yours."

Whirring about the giant like a pestering gnat, he stung Antaeor with eardrum piercing air drills. The Thanatoid swatted at him uselessly. The Nucleoid was just too fast. Beneath the monstrosity's knees, Maelstrom summoned a windblast of hurricane proportions. Antaeor was rocked upwards. With cyclonic fury Maelstrom pressed his advantage, never giving his foe the opportunity to regain balance. Finally, judging the moment right, he conjured a fantastic vortex that uprooted Demon Land and rocketed him into the sky.

Deprived of contact with the ground, he dropped his stalactite club and screamed: "I yield!"

"Too late. I gave you the chance."

========

"Cruel fucker, isn't he, Diver?"
"Cocky, Dervish. Thinks it's over."
"Can't be. Something just took out Raven."

========

The Goliath golem blew as much up as he blew apart. Maelstrom smiled in grim satisfaction. Even though he remained perplexed as to where Demon Land acquired his shell if the cosmicar was as empty as it had seemed to be, his work was done. Then something completely unexpected happened. The stones, pebbles and dust that had been the Thanatoid coalesced into another being entirely. He caught the unconscious female in his arms before she could fall any farther.

Evidently in her early twenties and dressed in a sheer satin gown, she was beautiful by human standards: white skin, two eyes, and remarkably long, remarkably silver-coloured hair. Which was what gave her away. Had to be Castella-Day, didn't it?

Like all the Thanatoids, Antaeor-Earth's oldest sister by a few years was one of a pair of twins. Her counterpart was Ereba-Night, whereas his would have been one of the other three elementals: Air, Fire or Water – the remaining four the Byronics dealt with on Sedon's Peak in '33 being the Four Seasons.

As the epitome of daytime Tvasitar Smithmonger, the devic smithy, crafted silver hair to be her power focus. When she employed her abilities, Vayu recalled from seeing her in action, howsoever briefly, it turned into all the colours of the rainbow.

Maelstrom figured Castella had suppressed her third eye in an effort to fool him. Just to be certain he fully opened his own third eye and bathed her in resultant eyefire; the better to probe her mind. Much to his dismay he quickly discovered she wasn't Castella. Was no devil, fourth generation or otherwise, and did not seem to be a deviant, the offspring of mortals possessed by devils, either. Nor was she possessed, not anymore anyhow. She was an ordinary woman. How came she hither?

"So, Thanatoid, this is whom you possessed." He talked to her gently as he lowered himself to the ground. "Slender pickings, this one. Not much more than a strip of a girl. No wonder you fell so easily." Alighting, he vanished his whirlwind. All he wore was a fur loincloth, hardly enough to provide warmth in this desolate place. The girl, in her skimpy gown, was probably halfway to freezing to death already.

As soon as he touched the ground, two rock hands formed out of the earth, grabbed him by his ankles, and held him fast.

========

"Knew it wasn't over. But Demon Land's weak compared to this Devil Wind. He's coming for me. Hope he needs the rest of you. See you shortly."

"That'll be the day, Johnny."

"Ever the smart-mouth, aren't you, Diver?"

"Couldn't resist, Sea Stuff. Besides, Sundown started it. Unless twenty-five years in whatever this place is made him sighted again."

========

Maelstrom dumped the girl unceremoniously on the frozen turf, caused his arms to form wind spouts, and attempted to drill away the rock hands pinning him to the ground. A stalagmite grew out of the earth, gained arms, legs, a head, body, and seven eyes. Demon Land had survived.

"I may be slow, Nucleoid, but what I lack in speed I make up in cunning. I jettisoned one of my shells, the weakest of those I found here. I knew you'd rescue her and have to bring her down. You see, I remember your vulnerability as well as you remembered mine. As long as I hold your feet to the ground, you can't hurt me. But I can kill you!"

"Unlikely!" Maelstrom gave up on the hands pinning him to the ground and brought his arms together. From them jackhammered bursts of air. Demon Land was blown into smithereens, yet again, but this time the earthen hands held. The monstrosity rose anew; lifted his stalactite club in both brick-body hands to strike off the Nucleoid's head. Maelstrom ducked, twisted at the waist, and delivered a windblast that blew off the Elemental's arms at the elbows. Maelstrom caught the club in a vortex and hurled it into the ocean.

The not so much man as man-shaped mountain barely missed a beat. Suddenly he had four more eyes, bringing his total to eleven. Great slabs of granite formed out of the stumps of his arms. He tried to clamp the slabs together, Devil Wind between them, a Samson between pillars. The Nucleoid spread his arms and resisted.

Had to resist. If a single son of Tantal Thanatos, whom ancient Illuminaries had, quite inspirationally, in part named after the Greek God of Death, could beat him, what chance did the rest of his siblings have? What chance did the Whole Earth have? There were definitely six more Thanatoids who might have been decathonitized. And that wasn't to mention the two who may or may not have got away from the ambush on Sedon's Peak back in '33.

He redoubled his efforts. The slabs pressed closer. He felt like a mosquito; only this mosquito had more than just the sting of a dying bug. This mosquito had tornadoes coming out of its arms.

Antaeor Thanatos had fifteen eyes now. Then, greedily, he densified and possessed two more. The last may have been a mistake. It had powers this one, mind-over-mind powers. It was telling him to give up. Antaeor blocked it off and went for more. Too late he realized what the last two were, whom they were. He couldn't do it. Not his own...

SIBLANGSH!

========

Vayu Maelstrom whirled into the sky. He was not going to get caught like that again. Antaeor Thanatos had already blown up and reformed twice during their battle. Perhaps he would do it again. Probably wouldn't, though. Something had happened to the Earth Elemental; something not entirely Devil Wind's doing.

As the dirt and dust settled, Maelstrom realized the sentient fog shrouding the atoll had dissipated. The Island was no longer deserted either. Ten extraordinary-looking beings stood on the ground. One was a raven-headed horse with talarial wings on both sides of all four of her hooves. She also had what might be some sort of monoceros or unicorn horn that glowed similarly to his topknot telescoping out of her forehead; similarly to the objects two of the others held as well.

No, one wasn't standing. His feet weren't on the ground; he was levitating. It was this one, a hooded man in a monk's coarse raiment, who spoke. Spoke straight into his mind, as well as his ears: "Greetings, Vayu Maelstrom, Devil Wind. I am Cerebrus David Ryne. In honour of both you, devil that you proclaim yourself and devil that you undeniably are, and where we find ourselves, thanks to you wholly ourselves again after a quarter century in Limbo, you may call us the Damnation Brigade!"

========

Maelstrom zoomed higher. Feeling much safer, he opened his third eye and scanned the creatures below. Nothing! They were opaque to him. But he had been able to probe the silver-haired woman's memories with ease earlier. Of course then she was unconscious and alone. Now she was on her feet and with nine others.

Either one or more of them was screening her; either that or, now that she was awake, she was doing it herself. Only the hooded monk had demonstrated any out of the human-ordinary abilities but, where he came from, a floating man was hardly extraordinary. Trinondevs of Weir could levitate, but they had eye-staves. This fellow kept himself aloft by force of will.

"Hear our story, whirling one," offered Cerebrus. "There is no need for us to be enemies."

"Open your minds to me, mortals. I shall decide that."

"Our minds are our property," disallowed the levitating man. "Let us speak with our voices."

That the one called Cerebrus David Ryne could levitate, the whirling god-devil had to admit, if only to himself, was mildly curious; all the more so since it appeared his undeniably psychical talents did not come with any noticeable increase in intelligence. Or could it be he didn't know? No point speculating. Opportunity lost forty-seven years ago would not be lost again.

Had he been on the Head it would be simple. Still, as much as he hated this air, there was nothing else for it. *'Look at them,'* he mentally transmitted such that only their apparent leader could internally hear. *'They're startled by their own good fortune. He, the beautiful Adonis with his cloud-white hair, proud jaw, determined stare …'*

The devil was referring to Airealist, Aires D'Angelo, who wore the same circus outfit he was wearing when he was thrust into Limbo by Saul *'Psycho'* Ryne all those years ago. It consisted of a skin-tight, sky-blue acrobat's outfit, folded-flap leather boots, ostentatious gold belt and an even more ostentatious white cape.

'Who does he think he is – my brother in Byron Damon Goldenrod or, as outsiders once mistakenly called him, Phoebus Apollo? And what of her? What of this obvious twin of his, every bit his watery counterpart? With her sea shells instead of eyebrows, her braided, foam-white hair, her garlands of seaweeds, her jellyfish membrane of a dress, so brazen in her near-nudity. Don't you realize their skin is almost as blue as the sea, as blue as the sky, as blue as mine?'

Do they know who they are or did the Scarlet Empress's spell of expulsion rob them of their memory as well as their third eyes? No matter. For anyone who had been on Sedon's Peak in 5933 the objects they held were proof of their identities. The omega-shaped Aerod and ankh-like Water Wand with its seaweed etchings, their power foci, were all he needed to see. They were Thanatoid twins: the other pair of elementals, Air and Water, the ones who vanished through the Wandering SAG Gap in '33.

Not waiting for a response from the levitating monk, Devil Wind hesitated no longer. Held up by his wind spout, he twisted his hands yet again. Dual tornadoes whirled forth, engulfing Aires and Thalassa D'Angelo, Airealist and Sea Goddess being their self-chosen supra-codenames. Irresistibly, the devil whisked their weapons out of their hands and into his right one.

He rose even higher into the sky, speaking aloud such that all could hear him: "The deed is done. I have your talismans. You're powerless now. You'll discorporate shortly, become spirit beings again, and then it'll be an easy matter to cathonitize you. Relax. Accept your fate. The punishment is painless."

"I have no idea what you're on about," spat Airealist. "But if you think we're powerless without a couple of D'Angelo family heirlooms, you're nuts."

Unexpectedly, as if charged with lightning, the Aerod electrified. Maelstrom yelped more in shock than pain. Rather than just drop them, he managed to hurl both objects into the sea. Thalassa – whose name meant *'Sea'* just as her twin's meant *'Air'* – dove into the near-freezing ocean no doubt in hopes of retrieving them.

Maelstrom, his hand still stinging, whirred downwards after her. Gloriella D'Angelo Dark, the one he had first rescued out of the mess he made of Antaeor Thanatos – the one he mistook for Castella-Day – suddenly hurled herself into the air, flying on Castella-like rainbow hair. And he'd been so sure she was no devil. How could he have been that wrong?

This Gloriel, as he'd already ascertained most called her, reached her arms towards him. Obviously some kind of materialist or, much more distressingly, an etherealist, huge hands made of solid rainbows instantly stretched out for him. Hers – the ability to as good as make ether real – may have been a common enough talent amongst Master Devas, but what was she? A human devil was the best answer he could come up with on such short notice. There would be time enough to figure the real one out later.

His speed allowed him to whip away evasively, before the hands could close on him. She made no move to follow, content to stay near the surface and ward him from the Elemental Twins. "They may not be my favourite folks," she shouted. "But they are my adopted brother and sister. You don't attack family. Not around me."

This was getting to be too much for Maelstrom. Decathonitized devils he had been prepared to handle. That was his duty. But almost being humiliated by a pathetic fourth generation pup who had far more raw power than brain power; tangling with two other Thanatos Spawn, ones who did not even realize their devic heritage; and now facing a fourth one, who seemed entirely human yet could fly on rainbow hair; enough was enough. This wretched air; humans with abilities that rivalled his own; no, he could not do this alone. He had to get back to the Head.

Whirling southwards at great speed, he went into and through between-space, the Weird, the dark-grey universal substance of Samsara. Moments later he emerged above Centauri Island, the launch site of the Cosmic Express, off Maui in the Hawaiian chain of islands. Now things became trickier. He could not afford to be seen. No non-Head-dweller should learn about the link way to the other side.

"I won't tell. Promise."

It was as if a veil had been lifted from his eyes. He was not over Centauri Island. Far from it! He had not gone anywhere.

The hooded monk was floating in front of him. He lowered his cowl. The man was not entirely human either. He had a metal plate wired into his skull instead of hair or scalp. A cyborg, a cybernetic organism, possibly a Mandroid, this Ryne-son – this latter day Golden Age Horrite, he now realized – was smiling cherubically, unhealthily proud of himself.

The throwback had learned the secret of both Centauri Island and Sedon's Head. And he had done it by playing Maelstrom for a fool.

========

Something came out of the sky. It was the horse-thing with a bird's head, the wings of Mercury on the upper parts of its hooves, and a vestigial horn growing out of its head. Had to be a ravendeer, he finally appreciated. Except, it had to be one immediately recognizable as superior to the dwindling herds of the once majestic specie that were still found in the lower Cattail Peninsula.

Riding her was an Irache, a red-skinned warrior whose eyes were covered by a beaded blindfold. He had a spear that glowed not just with Brainrock-Gypsium but also with the power of the setting sun itself. He fired. Devil Wind burned; plummeted downwards.

Toward Damnation Island.

****